Raj and J

Copyrights

Dedication

This book is dedicated to my daughter Elizabeth who encouraged me to complete my novel which has taken twenty-one years to complete.

I would also like to say a special thank you to my best friend who supported me in compiling the novel.

Table of Contents

Chapter One

Sometimes, there is silence… but then, I hear patients complaining, people being carried into the wards, and the footsteps of doctors and nurses as they run around looking after patients. At times, the complaints are funny, and I cannot hold myself from silently laughing as I lie here in bed. However, the only constant noise I can hear is the beeping sound from the machine beside me.

I have been in this hospital bed for just over a month now. The doctors say that I am suffering from a disease that cannot be treated. So, I'm probably more closer to death than life. Or perhaps just the opposite, as they say, "I have a fifty-fifty chance."

I don't know which I would prefer right now, having experienced both extremes in my life. I don't know what either life or death is, but I have enjoyed real happiness in my life, along with some sad times when I thought of ending it all.

If I had questioned my family on the subject of life and death before being diagnosed with this illness, they would have said, "You don't need to know," or "You are too clumsy-headed to understand."

Well, let me tell you that I am not clumsy.

Just because I was a quiet child and I dreamed a lot didn't mean I was clumsy. I would say I was a child with a vision and had a plan for my future. However, my family never understood that.

***

When I was about five years old, I remember my mother asking me what I wanted to become when I grew older. She couldn't have been expecting much, as I was only five years old at that time, but I replied, saying, "I want to become like Karam Singh!"

Karam Singh was a big Indian film star of the 1970s who had a string of blockbuster hits. I already had a vision of a highly successful career. I think it was a great answer for a five-year-old, but unfortunately, my aunt Manjit was sitting in the same room, and she began to laugh.

"You become Karam Singh?" she cried, almost choking, and proceeded to laugh even harder.

I felt hurt, and my eyes filled with water. As I fought back the tears, I blurted out, "Yes!" but stuttered as I spoke.

She said, "Karam Singh is a handsome man. Have you seen your nose? He is a strong man, and you have tears dripping down your face. Listen, you are too clumsy to become an actor, so you do things that clumsy kids do."

I didn't know what to say and felt a bit clumsy. I guess the name has stuck around since then.

***

I open my eyes to see my mother and father sitting on either side of the bed. They are both leaning inward, with their eyes closed. They have been sitting at my bedside ever since I was assigned to this private room. They are catching up on their sleep while leaning on the bed. Tears fall from my eyes to see how they are both suffering because of me.

My mother is such a loving person. She has spent all her life pleasing the family. She believes that her life is intended purely for cooking, washing, ironing, sewing, or looking after a relative's kids while they shop for their own selfish needs. She always believes that God will see to those who do wrong and that we should do everything right with God.

My father is also a very soft character, and he spends a lot of his time giving to those who only take advantage. He is a very successful businessman and is very highly respected in our town. Over the years, he has become a strong brother, son, and uncle, but I never see the same strength when it comes to being a father or husband. Yet he is still a great dad, and I know he loves us a lot. However, he just never takes that extra step like he would do for his sisters, father, and mother. He is solely dedicated to pleasing them for fear that the community will look down on him. Dad wakes up, looks at me, and smiles at me. I try to smile back, but the pain does not allow it. He touches my mum on the arm, and she also wakes up. She smiles and kisses my hand. She looks up at me and then asks my dad, "Do you remember when he was born?"

My father answers that he can remember everything that happened that day from the moment she went into labour.

He begins recounting the events in detail.

While he is talking, I imagine the way it must have happened, as if I am watching a movie in my mind.

Chapter Two

I was born in 1975 in a town called Wolverhampton. My mum was screaming with pain. My two aunties were sitting on either side of her as she sat in the back of my dad's Mercedes en route to the hospital. My grandmother sat in the passenger seat, praying to God for a happy blessing. She tried to calm my mum down, saying, "Don't worry, everything will be fine, just keep breathing."

While she was suggesting my mum to breathe, she was using her inhaler to calm herself down!

My mother screamed, "I can't take the pain."

Dad quickly assured her, "We're almost there now; I'm driving as fast as I can."

My two aunties looked at each other in anguish and screamed out in unison, "Breathe!"

They finally arrived at the hospital. Dad rushed into the hospital and came running out with a wheelchair, in which he took my mother into the building.

My grandmother and aunties were sitting in the waiting area when Dad came rushing out screaming, "It's a boy!"

Behind their fake smiles, my aunties muttered, "We wanted a girl!"

My dad's elder sister congratulated him, while the younger one remarked, "We thought it was going to be a girl."

Grandma calmly responded, "No, God heard my prayer."

Dad gave his sisters a couple of pounds and told them to buy some sweets from the tuck shop for the nurses and themselves.

***

My mother says she hears my aunts and grandma gossiping about someone when they return from the tuck shop. Dad says, "I know what that was about, but I never told you at the time."

"What didn't you tell me?" she asks.

"Well, it was the day Raj was born, and my father and I were celebrating his birth at the local pub. We bought everyone drinks in the pub and had our usual sing-song, with the pub owner taking out his dholki and Baja. We sang the song which an uncle has written. We walked back singing and making a lot of noise."

My mother interrupts, "That is you and your father every weekend after getting drunk."

Dad ignores her and continues retelling the story: "We marched into the house, still making plenty of clamours. I tell my father I am going to the toilet, but I overheard something as I walked towards the kitchen."

"What did you hear?" Mum asks.

"I'll tell you if you let me finish," he retorts.

Observing my parents having a discussion has always been highly amusing! Mum always interrupts when Dad is trying to tell her something.

He continues, "I stood outside the dining room to hear what they were talking about. After all, my elder sister Baljit has stopped over, and she never did that, even on happy occasions. I missed the first part of her speech, but as I walked towards the door, I heard Baljit saying, 'The child is bad luck.' My father said that he would take our son to the temple as soon as he came out of the hospital. 'We will get the priest to pray over him and give the baby a name out of the bible. That should put your stupid minds at rest."

'Mother interrupts again, "I remember what that was. It came out of your sister Manjit's mouth when we argued."

"What was that?" Dad asks.

"That the same day Raj was born, Aunty Nirmal, up the road, died, and that's why they were saying Raj was bad luck. But my son is not bad luck. We have had nothing but good luck since he was born." She says as she grabs my hand and kisses it again.

"I remember the look on your sister's faces when your father returned from the temple with Raj and his name," Mum recalls. "Your mother carries our son into the house and walks through the hallway saying, 'Look at my grandson coming home to his house.' Then your sister Manjit remarks, 'He only arrived into the world yesterday, and you're already handing over our home.'

Their faces drop when your father tells them that our son's name is going to be Raj. I remember you proudly stating how the priest says that this name is given to successful children. It means victor or conqueror. Manjit tries to say that Raj is going to be slow, but not successful, but your father tells them they are only jealous and just scared thinking about who was going to feed them now.

"I also remember when your two sisters were trying to carry out voodoo on him when he was six months old. Do you remember how he fell ill straight after that? His right side used to freeze. I know the doctor says he is suffering from low calcium, but I still say it is what they have done that day. This is why he is in hospital today because your jealous sisters curse my son's life."

My dad says, "Don't worry, God is watching and will heal our son."

I thought my sister and I were the only ones who think that my aunties are evil, but I realise today that my parents have the same view.

***

I remember when I was five years old, my mother had gone to the hospital to give birth to my sister, Shelly. I was left in the care of my aunts and my grandmother.

I still remember how, after getting my clothes dirty, my grandma told Aunty Manjit to bathe me. However, she passed me over to my dad's youngest sister, Kuljit, who was eleven years old. Aunty Kuljit took me into the bathroom, took all my clothes off, put me in the bath, and then decided to fill the bucket with cold water to wash me. It was the winter season, and it was really cold outside, but she threw the jug of freezing cold water over me, and I screamed. She carried on throwing the water and laughed while I shivered. Luckily, my grandad walked into the bathroom soon after. He scolded Aunty Kuljit, telling her that this could give me pneumonia. He wrapped me in a towel, took me into the living room, and sat me in front of the heater while he got me changed.

***

Coming back to the present, my mother is still talking about the bad luck I've had and my aunties, "Do you remember when he was ten years old, he got hit by a car and broke his leg? I believe that was also set up by your sister's cursing."

My mother continues to complain, and Dad keeps on listening.

Chapter Three

I remember when I had that accident. It was not the best time in my life as I had to spend ten weeks in hospital with my broken leg. However, a great time was to follow, for it was the first time I went back to school and I first met Julie.

I was ten years old, and I think the only reason I was looking forward to going back was because I had a crush on my teacher. Mrs. Teresa was a very attractive lady who was always nice to me.

On the first day back, I was very nervous, and I recall saying to my mother, "I don't want to go. I'm scared."

However, Mum had a very gentle way of motivating and encouraging me in scary moments. She said, "If you are scared now, how will you look after me when I grow old? I know you are a very strong boy who can bend a metal bar like a cloth with your hand."

This was a famous line from my favourite actor, Karam Singh, and Mum knew I would get excited after hearing it. Straight away, I got ready to go to school.

It was a three-minute walk away, and as we got to the gates, my mother pecked me on my cheek, leaving her usual lipstick mark, and said, "Go and learn how to become a doctor or lawyer."

I didn't know about doctors or lawyers, but I wanted to learn how to become like Karam Singh, my role model. I smiled and walked over to the playground. Then, the whistle was blown, and I joined the class line.

While waiting outside the classroom, I realised that a lot of my classmates did not want to stand by me. Apparently, I didn't smell very nice! It was quite a while before I figured out it was due to the hair oil my mum had used on me.

I entered the classroom and walked towards my desk, where I usually sat. I grasped my chair to pull it out, only for the boy who sat next to me to say, "Mark sits here now."

I said, "Okay," and walked to the next table.

They were set so that four pupils could sit together. Again, I went to sit on an empty chair, but a guy sitting at that table said, "You can't sit here."

Then I heard a sweet voice saying, "You can sit by me if you like."

I looked up to see a beautiful blonde-haired, blue-eyed girl. She said again, "Come and sit by me."

I just stood staring at her. I didn't know what was happening, but my heart was beating fast, and I could not speak. She asked again, "Are you going to sit down or not?"

Feeling embarrassed, I nodded my head, walked around the table, and sat down.

At this point, Mrs. Teresa walked over to the table and asked, "Have you made a new friend?"

I smiled awkwardly as she introduced the girl to me, "This is Julie. She joined us about seven weeks ago."

Julie stretched her hand out to shake mine, and I nervously complied. Mrs. Teresa continued with the introduction, "This is Raj. Raj was involved in a car accident and broke his leg. He has been away from school for ten weeks. I hope you are better now."

I nodded yes.

"Raj is very shy but always carries a charming smile," she continued.

As Mrs. Teresa walked off, Julie said, "Aaah," then leaned over and kissed me on the cheek.

I don't know what happened to me that day. I felt I could hardly breathe, and my heart was beating fast. The feeling carried on throughout the day. Since then, Julie and I continued to sit together daily. I missed that feeling when I was at home on the weekends. I couldn't wait until it was Monday again, and I hated Fridays. Julie and I met every day, and we became very good friends.

We always carried out class activities and spent all our breaks together. It felt great being with Julie. Sometimes, I would sit and stare at her while she talked to me about whatever.

One day, I felt that Julie and I had made a connection. We were lying on the grass in a park behind our local library, both staring at the sky, when she asked the time. I looked at my watch and noticed it was time to go.

I said, "I'd better go, or I'll get in trouble."

Then she asked, "Can't you stay a little longer?"

As she stared at the sky, it somehow seemed that she was searching for an answer in the clouds. But I didn't need to be asked twice—I never wanted to be without my best friend!

I asked her why she was always staring at the sky. She answered, "My mum is up there."

I got a bit confused and repeated, "Up there?"

"Yes," she said, "My dad's girlfriend told me that my mum died and went to heaven and that heaven is up in the sky."

I asked her if she had ever seen her mum. She said, "No, but I know she is looking down at me."

At the time, I didn't understand as I had never heard about things like this. I looked at my watch again and said, "I'd better go now."

She asked, "Do your parents still think you go to football practice?"

When I answered yes, she asked, "So why don't you go then?"

I told her, "Because I'd rather spend time with you."

She said, "Aaah," and kissed me on the cheek.

Her voice suddenly became difficult to hear as someone else was saying 'Aah' as well. I recognised the voice as one of a person I didn't like.

***

I open my eyes, snap out of my thoughts, and 'Oh no!' I am back in the hospital room, and Aunty Baljit, my father's eldest sister, is looking at me, saying, "Poor kid, but what can he do? It's been destined for him to be this way, and we can't change destiny."

I think, "what a lot of crap!"

My mother gets up and defends me again, insisting, "There is nothing stronger than God, and He will heal my son."

Chapter Four

On one occasion, after getting back from meeting Julie and telling my parents that I was going to football practice, I walked into the living room and found all the family staring at me. Aunty Baljit asked me where I had been. I replied, "Football training."

Then Aunty Kuljit butted in, "Well, Baljit saw you walking with a girl by the library."

At this point, I got scared because I thought I had been caught out, and it might have been the last time I would be able to spend time with Julie after school.

My heart started to beat faster, and I struggled for words and breath. Manjit asked if she was my girlfriend and began teasing and pinching me. I answered, "No! She's a friend, and we were walking back from football practice."

"Girls don't play football," said Baljit, "Kuljit went to the same school as you, and she never played football."

"Well, times have changed," I answered, "And Kuljit wasn't into sports."

"Yes, I was," interrupted Kuljit, "I played netball."

This was true, actually, and she wasn't bad either. But she pushed me, so I pushed her back, and we got into a catfight.

Manjit and Baljit pulled us apart, and Manjit stated how I was always too ready to fight.

"She started it!" I shouted, but Kuljit quickly denied that, and I received a slap across the face from Aunty Baljit. Kuljit then began screaming about how she was going to tell my dad when he got back.

"Tell him what?"

"You always pick on me when he's not around," I cried. "And I'll tell him that we saw you with your girlfriend," she replied.

Luckily, at this point, my mother walked in, pulled me away from Baljit, and demanded, "Why are you always upsetting my son?"

Then Manjit butted in, saying, "She's telling him off because he's got a girlfriend, and she's English."

Mum turned to me and said, "Is this true?"

I answered, "She's just my friend from school."

Mum told my aunties to back off and that if I said she's not his girlfriend, then she's not.

Then Baljit responded by saying, "Well, he better understand right now that we're not going to have any English girl in our family."

Mum got angry now and demanded, "What are you talking about? He's only twelve years old. He doesn't understand these kinds of things."

Manjit told Baljit to leave it, then added, "He's too slow and clumsy to understand anything."

All the children in the family laughed at me, apart from my sister Shelly.

9

Then Grandad walked in looking happy and cheerful, as he always does. He never failed to bring a smile to my face. He said excitedly, "I have good news. We have bought the shop up the road, and we are taking over next week."

He walked over to me, shook my hand, and hugged me.

I loved living at our family shop, so I could always eat sweets, even if though I was always getting told off for eating too many!

Chapter Five

I open my eyes and see the door to my hospital room opening. Uncle Ramdass and Aunty Manjit enter the room. They walk up beside the bed, and Ramdass asks me with a smirk, "How are you?"

As far back as I can remember, this man has never had any sympathy for anyone and is a very spiteful person. Then Manjit asks, "What have the doctors said?"

Mum replies, "He is recovering well and should be discharged in a couple of weeks."

Then my uncle says, "Don't worry, you'll be all right. Then you can start doing those donkey workouts again."

My aunty laughs, "You're always making jokes."

I don't know about jokes, but I know that this guy has picked on me since I was young, causing trouble in my life right up to my late teens. Ramdass was originally from Punjab in India. He was forced to leave his village because he had a habit of teasing the women there. His brother, who lived in the city, took responsibility for him. He was a doctor and a good friend of my grandad's, so as they wanted their friendship to turn into a family relationship, they decided to marry Ramdass to my Aunt Manjit. So, unfortunately, we are related.

***

I remember one time when I was thirteen years old, I was waiting outside my father's shop for him to return from the Cash & Carry.

I used to help my dad unload the van, especially the cases of soft drinks and bags of potatoes.

When Dad pulled up outside the shop, I became excited. He came out of the van and opened the back door. I told him I would take out all the stuff myself. He smiled and said, "Be careful then."

I began to take the stock out. I stacked the soft drink cans one layer after another to about six cases high. I picked these up and carried them into the shop. My dad saw me and said, "Just carry small amounts, or you'll hurt yourself."

I used to get excited about lifting heavy weights, seeing myself as Hercules, about whom there was a movie at the time.

But while I was walking back out to the van, Uncle Ramdass walked in and started to bully me by pulling my hair and pinching my chest. I shouted, "Dad, tell Uncle Ram to leave me alone."

However, on my next trip to the van, I plucked up the courage to pick up seven cases instead of six. I felt a bit nervous at first, but my desire to achieve was greater. I stacked up the cases and carried them into the shop. I felt strong, like the Incredible Hulk. I shouted to my dad, "Check this out! I've carried all seven by myself. See how strong I am."

Dad was concerned that I might drop them and said, "You watch and be careful. You don't want to drop them."

A man named Pardip was standing by the till, holding a can of beer. He turned to my dad, who was busy refilling the cigarette section and said, "Your son has tremendous strength. You should get him joined up in a gym."

Dad replied, "He's only thirteen, and it'll stunt his growth. Anyway, I want him to concentrate on his schoolwork."

However, Pardip continued, "When children participate in a sport, it helps bring discipline, and it also keeps them out of trouble. You know how most kids turn out today. This will keep him away from the wrong crowds."

Dad was getting interested but protested, "I don't even know where I could send him."

"Leave it to me," said Pardip, "I'll take him to see the coach. He held the world title in the seventies. He owns a gym not too far from here. It's close to home, so there's nothing to worry about when it starts getting darker."

"Maybe it is a good idea," said Dad thoughtfully as he remembered how last year, when we were watching the World's Strongest Man on television, I had told my grandfather that I would be the strongest man one day.

"This could just be the beginning," observed Pardip, and they laughed.

As they spoke, Ramdass was eavesdropping and became jealous. As I walked in carrying four cases of drinks, Ramdass approached me and began to put pressure on the top of the drink cases, saying, "Let's see how strong you are."

I told him to stop it. The pressure was hurting my arms, but I took on the challenge. I stared directly into Uncle Rams' eyes. However, the pressure was becoming too much, and I was losing my grip. Then my sister walked in and began to tell Ramdass off: "Let him go, Uncle. Stop picking on him."

After a struggle, I finally dropped the top case. Ramdass laughed and ran out of the shop. Unfortunately, one of the cans burst open and soaked Shelly and me. My father shouted from the background, "Clean up that mess."

12

Chapter Six

Another day, I was sitting and watching 'The Incredible Hulk' on television when my father walked in, sat down next to me, and asked, "Do you want to be that big?"

In excitement, I said, "Yes, Dad, and as strong as him. I'm going to be the British Indian Hulk! I'll be able to lift cars and turn them over and...."

My dad interrupted, told me to calm down, and then asked me the wonderful question, "So, would you like to start weight training?"

I jumped up in excitement and blurted out, "Yes, Dad, please, can I?"

He made my dreams come true when he said, "You can start tomorrow. Uncle Pardip will pick you up and take you to the gym."

I couldn't believe it! I had to ask, "Really, Dad, I can start tomorrow?"

He calmly replied, "Yes, but I want you to be very careful and only do what they tell you to."

I said, "I will, Dad, thanks, Dad, I love you, Dad!"

Scarcely able to believe that my dreams were going to come true, I stared into my bedroom mirror that night and said, "I will be the strongest one day."

I began to make various poses as I stood there and told myself, "I'll show all those who call me fatty!"

I took out the bodybuilding magazine I had kept from the shop and looked at the front cover, which had Sylvester Stallone on it. I said, "Get ready to look like this!"

I lay on my bed and looked up at the ceiling, imagining lifting weights. I could hardly wait to go to the gym, and I couldn't wait to tell my best friend Julie, either.

Julie and I were walking back from school the next day when I told her that my dad would take me to the gym that night. She asked, "What will you do at the gym?"

I told her, "I'm going to start weight training."

Julie laughed and said, "You weight train? You're joking, aren't you? You're too fat!"

I was hurt, and my eyes filled with water. I was getting called fat by ninety per cent of my family, but now Julie as well, who was my best friend. I just said, "I'll show you."

I was now even more determined to prove not just my uncle and aunties wrong but also Julie.

Chapter Seven

It was my first day at the gym. I walked into the room, which was the underground basement of a college building. I was so excited. There was no paint on the walls, the plaster was dropping off, and hot water pipes ran along the sides. I could see other people lifting weights.

Uncle Pardip introduced me to Karam Singh, the gym coach. The fact that my coach's name was the same as my favourite actor only added to my excitement. Uncle Pardip left me with Karam Singh, who talked me through the various exercises and what muscle groups they build and develop. Then it was my turn.

I could feel my heart beating faster, and I felt a bit nervous. I wrapped my fingers around the barbell, forming the grip, and then quickly released it. I did this again, and the guys in the gym began to laugh. The coach asked, "What's wrong?"

I felt too embarrassed to explain what I was feeling and just said, "Nothing, I'm all right."

Then, I wrapped my fingers around the bar again and performed the exercise known as the barbell curl. I put the bar back down to the starting position and felt a tight feeling in my arms. I said, "Wow! That was something! And what's this feeling in my arms?"

The coach told me not to worry and that it was something they had all been through. Behind me, one guy in the gym shouted, "It's the pump!"

I turned to my coach and asked, "Pump?"

He explained that when you perform the barbell curl, the blood in your arms rushes up and down, and the bicep (upper arm muscle) tightens.

I was thinking, "Wow! I want that tightness again!"

I lifted the weight again and looked into the mirror to see my arms growing. I did a double bicep pose, and the guys in the gym laughed, but I didn't care because I could see myself becoming a champion.

The next day, I was tired from my gym workout. I slowly walked towards Julie's house, and as she came out, she asked me, "What's wrong with you?"

"I went to the gym last night and worked out with weights," I said, trying to sound Macho while trying to snap out of the tiredness. "It was weird. I felt this funny feeling in my body."

"Was it like sex?" she asked.

I looked at her, surprised. I didn't have any idea what sex was like, so I just said, "No," to which Julie laughed and took out a notepad.

She flicked through this art pad, and I noticed all these drawings. She opened the page with an image that looked like me on one side. "This is you now, and this will be you if you stick to weight training."

I said Wow, I couldn't believe that she was good at art.

"You drew these?" I asked.

"Yes, I drew these last night," she replied.

"How did you manage to draw me?" I asked.

"I have been drawing from a young age. I am trying to draw an image of my mum. Look!" As she showed me, I couldn't believe she had drawn a picture of me. I looked at the images, and they looked like her.

"These look like you," I said.

"I know." She replied. "I've been told that my mother looked like me, so I've been trying to draw her using my pictures and the information about my mum given to me by family members."

"You are really good," I said.

"Thanks," she responded.

We walked to school, and the only thing I could think about was that she had drawn me.

At the end of school, I couldn't wait to return to the gym. As Julie and I were walking back, she asked why I was in such a hurry.

"I need to get ready to go to the gym," I told her.

I walked her back to her house and then ran home to get ready. After changing, I walked through the shop, and my mother gave me some money to buy a kebab before I started training.

I went to the chip shop, bought my kebab, and was still eating it when I reached the gym. A couple of guys I saw last time stood outside, and I walked over to them to say hello. They asked what I was eating, and when I told them it was a kebab, one of the guys, whose name is Jindi, said, "You shouldn't eat too much before training."

I asked, "So what am I supposed to do then?"

Jindi said, "It's good to eat meat, but not too much before training. Here, let me help you."

I'm not sure what happened here, but I didn't like this guy who had eaten half of my kebab.

We went into the gym and began to train. I don't know why, but I kept hearing Julie's voice saying, "Like sex."

After a good workout, I got home, had a bath, and went to sleep.

The next thing I knew, my mum was trying to wake me up in the morning, asking, "Aren't you going to school?"

I opened my eyes and saw the clock read 8:33 am.

"Oh no!" I cried, "I'm supposed to be at Julie's at 8:30."

"Who is Julie?" My mum asked.

"She's just my friend I walk to school with," I said quickly and got ready so fast, I don't even know if I brushed my teeth.

I ran to Julie's house and found she had already left, so I carried on running. I looked up at the clouds and could see they were changing direction. I thought it was going to rain.

As I ran into school, I thought, "I must find Julie to tell her about my training session last night."

I rushed over to the sports hall, and I noticed a girl and boy kissing at the side of the building. I ran past them and noticed that the girl had a coat the same colour as Julie's. I turned back to find Julie kissing a boy named Barry.

15

I felt my eyes welling up and dashed off to our classroom. However, I couldn't go in. I walked into the toilets and locked myself in the cubicle. I just cried. I walked out after about five minutes to clean myself up. I looked into the mirror and asked, "Why isn't Julie interested in me?"

That was one of the worst days of my life. I felt that I had no energy as if someone had given me a right beating from which I was finding it very hard to recover.

That night, I couldn't sleep. All I could see was Julie and Barry kissing. In anger, I punched the bed and cried myself to sleep.

To make matters worse, when I walked to Julie's house the next morning, I found that she hadn't even waited for me.

Concentration was hard at school, and I avoided Julie, feeling that I must have done something wrong to her.

When it came to home time, I was alone and thought, "This is how it's going to be from now on."

However, somehow, I couldn't accept that.

Walking across the field over the road from our school, I heard someone calling me. It sounded like Julie's voice, which initially brought a wave of excitement. I thought, "Maybe she's finished with Barry."

But then I thought, "Why embarrass myself?" and carried on walking.

However, the voice grew louder and closer until I felt a hand on my shoulder dragging me back. It was Julie.

"What's wrong with you?" she asked. "I've been calling you for ages."

I answered, "Nothing."

Then I saw Barry running after us. He caught up and said, "Are you all right mate? You look like you're coming down with something."

I said, "Nah, just tired from weight training."

I wanted to scare him, letting him know that I was a bodybuilder and that he should keep away from Julie.

"Weight training?" he said, "That's good. My elder brother does weights."

Then Julie added, "I hope you start weight training so I can get my arms around your muscles."

Then, to make things worse, they began to kiss. I felt like punching Barry but wouldn't because it wasn't in my nature. Then they ceased their embrace, and Julie decided to tell me that Barry was her boyfriend.

"Great," I said.

"Are you ok with that?" she asked.

To which I replied, "Why wouldn't I be?"

"Well, you've been my boyfriend for the last few years."

Then I thought to myself, "Well, we never did that."

Barry's laughter interrupted my musing, "Was she your girlfriend?"

As I struggled to think of an answer, Julie hugged me and said, "Raj's been my best friend forever."

16

Before I had a chance to enjoy the feeling of Julie's arms around me, Barry pulled her away and into one of his body hugs, saying triumphantly, "Well, now I'm your best friend."

Then, they began to kiss again.

I had enough.

"I'm off," I muttered, and Julie waved her hand at me without even looking. I felt certain that this was it. I'd lost my best friend. Barry had stepped in, and it was all over. I started running as fast as I could. Being fat wasn't helping, but I just had to let my anger out.

I got back to my father's shops and walked in. Being upset and out of breath, I didn't want to speak to anyone. I looked into the shop and found Uncle Ramdass there.

"Oh no," I thought.

My mother asked what was wrong. I said, "Nothing," in a low voice.

Then my uncle grabbed me around the arms and said, "There is something wrong! He's been up to something—he looks guilty to me!"

I tried to struggle away from him, shouting, "I've done nothing wrong!"

Then he squeezed me in a bear hug and said, "Try and get out of this, you big weightlifter."

I tried hard but failed to break loose, and I burst out crying.

He released me, laughing hysterically, and I rushed out of the shop, up the stairs, and into my room, where I fell onto the bed crying.

After a while, my mother walked in. I was still lying on the bed. She sat beside me and asked if I wanted anything to eat.

I said, "No."

She replied, "So how are you going to get strong? You started weight training, so you must eat to build your strength. Come downstairs; I've made boiled eggs, fish fingers, and beans for you."

"No!" I repeated, "I don't want anything to eat, and I don't want to go to the gym anymore."

"My son's not a quitter," Mum declared, "How are you going to become the world's strongest man? Don't forget what you told your grandfather."

I sat up and began to think carefully about this.

"When you grow older and become the World's Strongest Man," she continued, "You can show your cousins, who are always picking on you, what you've achieved. Now give me a smile."

I did smile now, and as Mum walked out, she once more told me to come downstairs and eat before I went to the gym to become a champion. Thus inspired, I got ready to go.

As I walked to the gym, I thought about what had happened at school today and felt convinced that Julie was out of my life. I went to the gym and found Jindi waiting outside.

"All right, Raj. How're you doing?" he said cheerily, shaking me by the hand. "No kebab today?"

He pulled a disappointed face, and we walked into the building.

We began training under Karam Singh's instruction, but I couldn't put the usual energy in as I kept thinking about what had happened that day. The coach took me to one side and asked me what was wrong, but I insisted it was nothing.

"Has someone been picking on you at school?" he asked.

I didn't know how to explain it. Even though this guy was my coach and had the same name as my favourite actor, he was my dad's age, so I believed the consequence would be the same as if I told my dad.

"Well, I hope it isn't a girl's problem," he added.

I thought, "Oh no, this guy has worked it out. I'm in deep trouble now. He'll take me home and tell my dad, and I'll get a slap round the face."

I don't know where that came from, but I could picture it happening if my dad found out.

Having said that, my dad never smacked me. He probably knew that I got enough from my aunties and cousins.

Karam Singh continued, "I don't like young boys getting involved in relationships with girls in this sport as, firstly, they are too young, and secondly, it distracts them from training. You have to choose one or the other."

"I've only one choice left now, anyway," I thought.

I told him there was no girl and I would workout harder.

I pushed myself to the limit that day, and my coach had a big smile on his face by the end of the session. He came up to me and said, "Well done. You see, if you put your mind to it, you can conquer anything."

I asked what conquer meant, to which he replied, "To achieve or win."

"Excellent," I thought.

He carried on saying that he could see me becoming the UK's strongest very soon. This made me really happy, and suddenly, Julie and Barry hardly seemed to matter anymore.

Walking home from the gym, the only thing I could think about was becoming the UK's strongest man. I imagined myself receiving the trophy and the thrill of being number one.

I walked back into my father's shop in a very good mood. Mum saw me smiling and asked if I was better now.

"Great!" I replied, and picking up a muscle-building magazine, I went up to my room.

I sat on the bed, flicking through the magazine. I told myself how I was going to be just as successful as these bodybuilders one day. Of course, this meant I had to train harder and avoid any distractions. I began to think about Julie and Barry kissing again, then immediately screamed, "No!" and slapped my head a few times.

As I went to school the next day, I kept telling myself that I only had one dream, and that was to become a champion powerlifter. I managed to avoid bumping into Julie - although she was probably too busy with Barry to notice me, anyway.

For the next week, I trained very hard, really pushing myself to the limit. I was doing fairly well at school as well, but my mind was set on becoming a champion.

Then, one day, as I was stacking the fridge with cans of coke, helping my parents with the stocktake, I was suddenly taken aback as Julie walked into the shop. Although I noticed her, I carried on filling the fridge, but I became nervous thinking about what my parents might say. And then I could be in danger if my uncle or aunty turned up. They would deliberately try to embarrass me.

Knowing my aunt, she would probably pull my tracksuit bottoms down or something similar. She was forever trying to show me up when I was younger.

Julie walked up to me and said, "Raj, I haven't seen you for a week."

I quickly asked her to come outside. We went out, and I looked around to make sure no one had noticed us.

"What's wrong, Raj? You haven't called for me this week or even stopped to wait for me after school."

I didn't want to make it a Barry issue because she would think I was jealous, so I answered, "I've been getting up late in the mornings and then rushing home after school to make it in time to get to the gym. Besides, you've got Barry to walk you."

I smiled, trying not to show my feelings.

"Damn!" I thought, "I've mentioned Barry! That's it! I've put my foot in it now."

I imagined her demanding, 'Is it Barry? Are you jealous?'

Having thought about it, I quickly said, "No, and I don't care."

"Care about what?" she asked. I didn't know what to say.

"You've started showing a lot of attitude recently. Are you sure you're not on steroids," she probed.

"What are steroids?" I asked, surprised.

"Drugs that weightlifters take to build muscles," she responded.

"I don't even know what they are, so how come you know about them?" I protested.

"Barry told me his elder brother takes them," Julie replied.

"Well, I don't, and I don't care whether Barry or his brother do or not. Just go to them and stay away from here," I said angrily.

"Is that how it is then?" she asked.

"Whatever," I muttered, to which she replied, "Well, suit yourself," and before she stormed off, she handed me a piece of paper.

I opened it, and it was another drawing of me with muscles. I stupidly punched the big metal bin outside the shop, which hurt quite a bit.

The next day, I ran home from school again and got ready for training.

As I walked to the gym, eating my kebab, hoping it would give me strength and muscle growth, I noticed Jindi from a distance.

I guess he had been waiting for me, hoping to get some of my donner kebab. I know he had only recently arrived from India, but I felt sure he was getting fed up here in the UK. I had heard that he was having problems with his wife, but this was only gossip from the other guys in the gym.

Without even asking how I was, he began to eat the majority of my kebab while telling me that I should eat a lot of meat for muscle growth!

I was already upset after arguing with Julie, and now this guy was making it even worse by eating my kebab! I suspected I was going to have a bad day with the weights as well now.

I walked into the gym. The smell of Ralgex used to get me in the mood to work out. A couple of our weightlifters would apply the Ralgex stick to their legs until they burned red! They insisted that it warmed up their muscles. I don't know where they got this theory from, but it never looked comfortable to me!

Once I was changed into my powerlifting gear, I always felt nothing could stop me, but I was getting nervous putting on this tight suit today. Maybe it was just adrenalin from the excitement of being about to lift weights that were about two and a half to five kilograms heavier.

I began to warm up and felt better. I am so glad that powerlifting came into my life.

By the end of the session, I barely remembered the fuss earlier, but when I got home to the shop, Julie's stepmother was standing there, complaining about her daughter being upset. Suddenly, I felt nervous again and didn't know what to say. On the one hand, she was going to accuse me of upsetting Julie, while on the other hand, my Dad would be questioning me about having a girlfriend.

Julie's mother walked up to me and asked if I knew what was wrong with Julie.

"No," I replied, trying to sound assertive.

"Are you sure?" she asked again with a hint of aggression, "Julie has been in her room crying."

When my dad heard this, he walked over and slapped the back of my head, asking, "Have you upset her daughter?"

"No!" I shouted.

"So why was she saying your name earlier?" Julie's mother retorted.

"Singh, Julie is a very sweet girl and very talented with her artwork. We have good hopes for her to become successful in art," she explained to my father.

"I don't know," I protested quickly, worrying that my dad was going to think something was going on.

"Maybe it was her boyfriend," I hastily added, hoping to avoid another smack around the head.

I couldn't believe I was getting hit for something I had no more than dreamed of happening.

"Boyfriend?" she exclaimed, and I nodded my head, "I thought the only boyfriend she had was you."

The shop went deathly quiet. My heart seemed to stop, the colour drained from my face, and my legs were shaking uncontrollably.

"This was it," I thought to myself, "I'm going to get the beating of a lifetime."

Then, from the shop entrance, a voice chimed in, "I told you he was going around with a white girl."

That was definitely it! I had seen it in movies and heard a lot of stories about girls being sent to India to date white guys, and now I was going to be the first guy to be sent there!

I didn't know what happened to them in India, but I knew that they were never allowed back. I began to stutter, and the words I spoke did not make sense. But Julie's mother was offended by my aunt's statement, and attention was suddenly diverted away from me. She asked my aunty what she meant by 'white girl' and what the problem was. I could feel that this was about to turn nasty.

Then Grandad walked in and saved the day by having a right go at Aunty Manjit for interfering with our customers and causing trouble. He also told Julie's mother that his bride was in India. I didn't know what that meant at the time, but I assumed that he was supporting the idea of me marrying an Indian actress!

Then Julie's mother completed my reprieve by saying, "When I said boyfriend, I just meant a boy who is a school friend."

Grandad said, "I know Raj wouldn't upset me."

Then he shook hands with Julie's mum, and she left the shop. I don't know how my grandad used to do it, but he really had a way with words. I guess that's why people used to call him the 'Indian Godfather'. He didn't come across as a violent person, but he was definitely not someone you wanted to upset.

I remember when I was twelve years old and walking out of the sports hall at school, I accidentally pushed the doors into an elderly pupil's face. He got angry and beat me up so badly that I ended up at the Eye Infirmary.

But that was not the end of it. My grandad and his construction workers went to the pupil's house, turned it upside down, and still had his parents apologising every day for a week! We did get the police coming round due to this, but my grandad was so good with words that he was let off with a warning.

Come to think of it, he also used his 'Gift of the Gab' to be a bit of a charmer amongst the ladies, too!

But that night, I couldn't sleep again. I was wondering how on earth I was going to face Julie now.

For the next few days, I avoided bumping into her as, luckily, we were not in the same subject groups.

Then, one day, I saw her walking up to me.

"Can't avoid her now," I thought, so I carried on walking, trying to think up some excuses to tell her.

But she walked straight past me without saying anything. In one way, I felt relieved, but at the same time, it was a little upsetting, as I didn't think I had done anything wrong.

When I came home, I thought I would watch my favourite film, 'Pumping Iron' and eat my favourite ice cream to cheer me up. I loved eating raspberry ripple ice cream and waiting until it melted.

While I was watching the movie, my aunty Baljit walked in, closely followed by my grandad, who asked her how she was.

Baljit saw an opportunity to get me in trouble, so instead of answering the question, she said, "Raj is so lazy. Every time I come in here, he is sitting in front of the television eating ice cream. I guess he's too clumsy, not like my Narinder, who is always helping in his father's shop or repairing stuff."

I was sure I was going to be told off, but the only thing I was thinking about was finishing my ice cream.

"Anyway," I thought, "What was this rubbish about her son helping out all the time."

More to the point, Narinder used to steal goods for his parents, which he then sold and made a clear profit. My aunt and uncle owned a shop in a council area with a high rate of theft. They would get a couple of kids coming in every other day to sell the stolen goods, and then they would sell them on to the local people for a profit. They couldn't see anything wrong with it as long as they were making a profit.

But they got so greedy that their son soon got involved in stealing goods, too, although this didn't bother them because they knew they were going to make a profit. I remember a time when Narinder stole a batch of top-brand sports clothing. My aunty made so much profit that she decided to give a percentage out as gifts. I remember her coming around and saying, "I've bought this new sports clothing for my nieces and nephews," clearly trying to get into my grandparent's good books. We all got excited as we never had branded clothing, and Grandad never saw the sense in spending money on things you can get the same locally for less than half the price.

At the time, I thought that my aunt had started to like me when I received a branded tracksuit, but coming back to the present situation, I know I was very wrong.

Grandad walked over to me and demanded, "Haven't you got anything better to do?"

I just looked at him guiltily. He continued, "Instead of stuffing your face and sitting around being lazy, why don't you make yourself useful? You're just a donkey and only worth lifting weights like donkeys. Get up and do some work in the shop."

As I left the room, I could see my aunty killing herself with laughter.

At first, when Grandad called me a donkey, I didn't know what he meant. Later, I found out that donkeys carry weights on their backs, and he was comparing me with donkeys. Initially, I was upset, mainly because I saw myself as an athlete, not a dumb animal. Thank God, this stopped by the time I was about twenty, as I finally gained recognition for my achievements in sports.

Chapter Eight

After a year of really hard training, my efforts would finally be rewarded. I was working out in the gym one day when my coach approached me.

"I think you are ready to compete now," he said.

"Really?" I gasped excitedly.

"Yes," he said, "so you will have to train even harder now! I'll send your application form this week for the Under Twenty-three West Midlands Championships, which will be held in ten weeks. You had better start stepping it up!"

In a daze of excitement, I assured him, "I won't let you down, coach!"

I trained hard for this competition. I didn't let anything or anyone bother me, as I knew I had to win to prove everyone wrong – and that I wasn't just a donkey! On the day of the competition, I was a bundle of nerves as I had never been to a competition before, and it was being held in an open prison! At first, my Dad was against this, as he didn't want me to be associating with criminals, but eventually, he agreed and even decided to come along with me.

That morning, my mother was even more nervous than I was and didn't know what to cook for me to give me strength. She eventually fixed me up with four boiled eggs and a glass of milk. I remember my Dad saying, "He is going to lift weights, not fight on the front line for the army!" My mum replied, "Well, it's his first time, and I only wish for him to achieve."

In the prison gym, there were some massive guys with huge muscles. Only being fourteen, these guys seemed like incredible hulks to me, not realizing that I was probably just as strong. It's ironic that my dad knew some of the prisoners. They knew my father from the nightclub he owned five years ago. We began to warm up.

Although I was nervous at first, I eventually calmed down as I thought about the success beckoning at the end. When I was called out, it was nerve-wracking. As I walked out onto the stage, the announcer stated, "Raj Singh is the youngest competitor to lift in competition history at just fourteen years of age – especially to enter prison to do it! Let's see how he does now as he opens with one hundred and sixty kilograms."

With all this information buzzing around my head, I was almost too excited to lift the weight! I approached the bar, got into position, and waited for the referee's signal. When he said, "Start," I performed the lift before carefully putting the bar back on the rack, as instructed by the referees.

We all waited for the judge's response, and I was given three white lights. I jumped up in excitement! I remember the announcer stating, "Raj, the youngest in his category, has out-performed men in their early twenties! This is remarkable, and if he carries on this well, he will soon be setting records."

All this information was encouraging. My coach approached me and asked, "Did you hear that you could soon be setting UK records? I want you to focus and stay awake."

I just said, "Yes, Sir!" He laughed and hugged me.

The competition was going well, and so far, I had been getting three white lights every time. But now I had come to my last lift, and Karam Singh had put in a weight request that would set a British record. The bar was ready, and I had everyone cheering me on, including my Dad, who I could see shouting in the crowd, "Come on, son!"

This was so encouraging! I looked at the bar and walked over to it with authority. I said a quick prayer and lifted. The weight shot up, and everybody cheered. I put the bar down to its starting position and waited once more for the judge's response. Three white lights! We all screamed, "YES!!!"

The announcer stated, "Raj Singh has set a new British record and is the strongest fourteen-year-old in the United Kingdom! We will have to check our records, but I believe he is the strongest and the only fourteen-year-old to compete in the World. As I heard this, my eyes filled with tears. I couldn't believe it! The strongest fourteen-year-old in the country! It sounded as if I was going to be awarded by the Queen! This was the most exciting day of my life. I got up on the stage and was awarded the bronze trophy for coming third in my category, but I was presented as the strongest fourteen-year-old. Awarded third place out of eight competitors was a huge achievement. I had out-lifted others a lot older than me. The announcer stated that if I went on lifting like I had done today, they could see me winning the British Championships in the coming year.

From that moment, the British Championships became my goal. My father walked up to me, hugged me, and said, "I'm proud of you, Son."

This was another special award; it was just to receive this love from my father. On the way back home, I couldn't wait to get in the house, show everybody my trophy, and announce that I was recognized as the strongest fourteen-year-old in the UK. I walked into the shop with my trophy and certificate. My mother was stacking the shelves, but when she saw me, she hurried over to hug me and say, "I knew you would win."

My Dad pointed out, "Actually, he came third."

But Mum replied, "He has won a trophy."

"Look, Mum, I was awarded the strongest fourteen-year-old in the UK," I cried triumphantly.

She kissed me on my forehead. "I'm so proud of you. It's your fifteenth birthday next week, so what do you want?"

All I could think about was training in the gym and becoming the British Power Lifting Champion, so I replied, "Training clothes!"

"You will get them, and you are on your way to achieving many awards and maybe from Her Majesty the Queen Elizabeth II." My mother says. She had probably said this because The Queen had visited a hat shop on our street the same week, and we were all excited and waited outside the shop to see the Queen drive past.

I'll never forget my fifteenth birthday. I recall my mum excitedly preparing food in the kitchen. She had hung balloons around the house and stuck a sign on the wall proclaiming my birthday party. She also made up another sign on which she handwrote with a black marker, "The Strongest Fourteen-Year-Old."

She was so proud. Aunty Baljit and Manjit walked into the kitchen and noticed my mother working hard. She said, "It's only a birthday party, not his wedding day. Is it worth working so hard? And have you looked out for my mother today?"

"She's fine," Mum replied sharply, "and she is perfectly capable of looking after herself. It's my son's fifteenth birthday, and on top of that, he has just won a trophy for lifting weights."

Manjit pulled a face behind my mother's back and said sarcastically, "You are so lucky to have a son like him?"

She always wanted everyone to make a fuss over her – just like her two sisters. Baljit and Manjit always had this competitive side to them, desiring only for themselves or their children to shine over everyone else. Sadly, as her children got older, they became more and more out of hand and eventually fell into crime.

Seeing my father and grandfather celebrating my success was too much for Baljit and Manjit. Manjit became a bit upset and walked over to her sons and told them off.

"You two should be ashamed of yourselves!" she shouted, "it should be you winning awards. Look at how your grandfather is so happy with Raj instead of you. You had better teach Raj a lesson!"

Navinder, Manjit's son, got excited and shouted, "Okay, Mom."

They walked over to me and said, "We've got a surprise for you in the garden, Raj."

With great anticipation, I went along with them into the garden and asked, "Where is it?" not knowing what they had in store for me.

Suddenly, I felt a whack on the side of my head, it was an egg, and then flour was thrown over me. I could see Aunty Manjit laughing in the corner, and I lost my temper. I grabbed the two of them and hit them a couple of times. They tried to fight, but their mother knew they were no match for me, so she got Uncle Ramdass and Aunty Baljit to hold me down while Manjit cut chunks out of my hair before running in to say that I was beating up her boys. I ran to my mum, who was shocked to see me in such a state. Then my Dad marched into the room demanding, "Why were you beating up Manjit's boys?"

Then he saw me covered in eggs and flour and with my hair cut up, and he changed his tune. My mother shouted, "I've had enough of that woman! Look what she's done to our son. She's always out to hurt him."

My Dad told her to shut her mouth as my aunty ran into the kitchen to defend herself. "No, brother, that's not right; I'll tell you what happened. Navinder, Ranjeet, and Kuljit smashed eggs and flour over him, but somehow, he got bubble gum in his hair, so I cut it out for him."

25

I jumped in to try and tell my side of the story. "No, Dad, she's lying. Uncle Ramdass held me down while she cut my hair."

"Ramdass wasn't even there; Raj is like a son to him. He wouldn't do anything like that," insisted Manjit.

Mum snapped, "She's lying!" but Dad told her, "Shut up! You talk too much. Go and finish the cooking!"

This made me angry. I said, "Dad! Are you seriously going to believe Aunty Manjit?"

"Stop fussing your hair will grow back; now go and get ready," he barked.

I never got any support when it came to battles with my aunties. What hurt most was that my mother never got any, either. I ran upstairs to my room crying and threw myself onto the bed. After a little while, I got up and looked in the mirror to see my mess. As that was the fashion, I had grown my hair long at the back, but now my aunty had cut it short. I heard a knock at the door but just shouted that I didn't want to cut my cake. My sister Shelly walked in and asked if I was okay, trying to reassure me that my hair would grow back.

"Come downstairs and enjoy the party," she pleaded.

"Dad always takes their side," I said angrily. "She cut my hair on purpose!"

Shelly tried to be supportive, "I know, but don't worry, God will punish them. You wash yourself up and get ready to cut your cake."

She left the room, also crying. I got up and looked in the mirror again, but the state of my hair made me weep even more. After about fifteen minutes, I went into the bathroom to take a shower. As I stood in the cubicle crying and stroking the back of my head, I suddenly heard a big bang on the door. Then I saw the lock being turned from the outside. It was one of those lock systems that you turn and lock from the inside but can open from the outside with a screwdriver.

The door swung open, and Narinder ran in with a Polaroid camera and took a photo of me. That was it! I screamed for my dad and told him to piss off. He eventually ran out shouting, "I got him on camera."

I managed to shut the door, but I couldn't believe what was happening to me on my birthday.

"What a life!" I thought. After getting ready, I walked back down to the living room to find everyone laughing at me. Mum walked up to me and said, "Blow out the candles and cut the cake; it's going to be okay."

"I've heard that many a time," I thought to myself.

I leaned forward to blow out my candles when my sister whispered, "Don't forget to make a wish, Raj."

At that moment, I wished that God would punish my aunties and cousins, and then I blew out the candles. For as long as I can remember, there has always been trouble on every special occasion, whether it was a birthday, Christmas, or even New Year's Eve. I used to ask myself, "When is this going to stop?"

26

Raj and Julie

The only time it was different was when we visited their homes for parties. Then, there was never any trouble. I took out a lot of my anger when I was in the gym, which certainly helped. My one dream was still to achieve the British title, and I had a chart in my bedroom on which I could record the progress I was making.

Months went by, but although my lifting was getting more powerful, my mind would still be forever returning to Julie. I would watch her from a distance and observe with a degree of hurt the bad habits she was picking up, such as smoking, and once I saw her with a bottle of alcohol in her hand. I wished I could tell her that the things she was doing were wrong, but there was no chance for that to happen as I had my pride, and anyway, she had ignored me the last time our paths had crossed.

Chapter Nine

Another year almost passed, and I was training regularly until one day, as I walked out of the gym, I heard a familiar voice behind me.

"Raj!" A tingle of excitement ran through my body, and my heart was pounding. After an intensive training session, I wasn't ready for this, but I didn't want to be anywhere else as I turned around and saw Julie running towards me. For a moment, I thought she had her arms wide open, like they do in the movies – but no. As she reached me, she extended her hand and enquired, "Friends?"

I held her hand and nodded, "Friends, "Why are your hands shaking?" asked Julie, to which I replied, almost suggestively, "Because I've just had a pretty serious workout."

"How have you been, Raj?" she asked.Hugging me at the same time.

"Fine," I replied, trying not to betray any interest.

"It's been a long time; where have you been hiding?" she asked.

"Nowhere," I replied.

Then, as if I wasn't already finding this hard enough, she grabbed my arms and screamed, "Look at the size of your muscles! You must've really been training hard!"

"Kind of," I admitted before adding, "And I have been awarded as the strongest teenager in the UK."

She looked shocked!

"Get out of here! Seriously?!" she asked in excitement. It felt so good to have made her face light up again. "Yep," I replied, with a hint of swagger. "That's so cool!" she stated. There was a pause for a few seconds as we walked, before Julie announced, "It's my sixteenth birthday this Saturday."

"Yes, I know" I replied.

"You remembered?" she asked, sounding surprised.

I nodded, and she continued, "My parents are holding a party for me in a hall next to the Grapes pub. Will you come?"

I felt my heartbeat rise slightly.

"Do you want me to?" I asked.

"Of course I do, silly," she quickly replied and gave me a reassuring hug before stating, "You're my best friend, and I've missed you."

I could have cried and wanted so much to wrap my arms around her, but I didn't want to risk being hurt again and resisted the temptation. "So, are you going to come?" she repeated. "Of course I'll come, how could I miss my best friend's birthday? I replied.

"It starts at 5 pm, so be there on time," she warned before adding, "Just in case I don't see you around the school."

I think she was hoping to hear me say that I would call for her in the morning, but I still didn't feel sure of how things stood, so as she looked at me, waiting for an answer, I just said, "I'll see you Saturday at 5 pm."

Raj and Julie

There were still two days until then, and I wondered whether I had just missed a really good opportunity. Was that a sense of disappointment in her voice I detected, when she replied in a low voice, "Yeah, see you Saturday?" I wondered.

She said she had to go, as she had a lot of things to prepare, but should I have walked her back to her house? I ran the last few meters home and up to the wardrobe in my room to see what I had available to wear to the party. I wanted to show off my muscles as well as look like the man for Julie.

Then, I dashed down to the shop to check out the card selection. I reached for a 'To my girlfriend' card but then thought, "Not yet."

Instead, I chose a card for 'A special friend' before grabbing a Dairy Box chocolate selection. I returned to my room, wrote the card out, and placed it with the box of chocolates. I was looking forward to Julie's birthday party.

The next day, I didn't see Julie in school, so I assumed she must have taken the day off to prepare for her party. Then, as I was walking back from school toward the forest area nearby, I caught sight of Julie with two white boys. They were all leaning against the fence and smoking, but as I got closer, I noticed they were trying to take advantage of her by feeling her legs and her breasts. She was shouting and telling them to stop, but as I got close to them, it became obvious that they had been drinking. I began running towards them and called to Julie, "Are you okay? Are these guys hassling you?" Her voice was slurred as she answered, "Yeah! Don't worry."

She sounded drunk, and I didn't think she was in the right frame of mind. One of the boys walked up to me and asked, "And what are you going to do about it, Paki?"

"Who are you calling a Paki?" I demanded.

The second boy stepped closer and sneered, "You. You fat bastard!" Perhaps I did appear fat in a school blazer, but what they didn't know was that I had arms measuring seventeen inches underneath, which was huge for a fifteen-year-old. Julie jumped in and said, "Forget it, guys. Raj, just go home. I'm okay, really."

But one of the boys said, "Yeah, go home, or we'll kick your curry head in," to which I countered, "I'd love to see you try."

The first boy tried to throw a punch, but I just swayed back before landing a firm punch to his jaw. He fell heavily to the ground. These guys didn't understand that I had the strength of an adult and had boxed many times in the ring against men often ten years older than me and always giving them a run for their money, so these two schoolboys had no chance. I think I cracked his jaw, and his face turned purple in seconds. Then the other boy came charging at me, so I slapped him three times, so he, too, fell to the ground in a daze.

"What do you think you're doing?!" Julie screamed.

"I was helping you out, and they were being racist," I protested, but she began to beat at me with her fists, which, although I could feel on my body, I felt much more in my heart.

"These are my friends; how could you do that?" she cried.

I was confused. They had been taking advantage of her, and then they had been racist to me. I know she was drunk, but on top of all that, I was supposed to be her best friend.

I said, "They're a bad crowd," and asked her to come home.

"Who are you to tell me what's good and what's bad?" she demanded.

This hurt even more, but worse still, she then broke my heart by adding, "Don't bother coming to my birthday party."

I just nodded my head and walked off. I felt I'd quickly fallen from hero to zero.

That night, I lay in my bed thinking about what had happened. I couldn't believe she had chosen these two guys over me, whom she had probably only known for a couple of weeks. In anger, I picked up the box of chocolates I had for her and threw it at the wall. The next day, I didn't go to school and told my mum I had a headache. I stayed in my bedroom all day. In the evening, I got ready to go to the gym.

"Are you feeling better now?" my mum asked, but before I could answer, my grandad chipped in with, "He would be now that he wants to go and lift weights."

I told them I was feeling better now and sensed a bit of a change in the atmosphere. Yet, at the gym, I was still full of anger and just wanted to lash out at someone. The question kept going through my head regarding Julie: "Why?"

For the last lift of my session, I asked Karam Singh to increase the weight by 10 kilograms. He looked at me strangely.

"I don't think you're ready for that amount yet" he stated. "Just put it on!" I snapped, "I am ready, and I'll lift it."

So, he did.

I got into position to perform the exercise, but then I heard Julie saying, "Don't come to my party."

I roared out, "Why???!!!" before lifting the weight easily.

My coach jumped up and shouted, "Yes! You are coming home with the title."

This brought a smile to my face, but I was still angry and hurt inside.

The next day, I was in the shop stacking the shelves when my mom walked in with a box of greeting cards and asked me to stack them. While placing these in the display, I saw the best friend selection. I still wanted to give Julie a birthday card, even though she had hurt me – after all; she was my best friend. I picked out a new card that looked more appropriate than the first one I had chosen and then ran upstairs and began to write it out. The next day, I got up early and told my parents that I was going for a run. Upon reaching Julie's house, I posted her birthday card through the door. Good timing, as the postman arrived just after me with the day's mail. I waited across the road, as I could see through the glass in the front door. I saw Julie walk down the stairs, and her mother passed her a handful of birthday cards.

She began opening them whilst sitting at the bottom of the stairs. The first card she opened was from her uncle John and the second was from her aunt Pauline, but then she came to mine. I could see her face, and I lipread. She was saying, "Love Raj, ah, he's a silly boy," and smiling affectionately.

***

But my musings were rudely interrupted by my aunt Baljit's chatter and asking how I was? I suddenly realised that all that had happened years ago, and I was back in the hospital ward.

"The doctor has said he is a lot better than before," my mother replied.

"He doesn't look any better," Baljit murmured.

"This lady has never seen anyone look better than her own kids!" I thought to myself.

***

I recalled an occasion when I was sitting watching my favourite Bollywood movie in the living room when Baljit walked in.

"Hello, Clumsy," she sneered.

"Hello," I said disinterestedly, not wishing to be disturbed. But then my sister Shelly ran into the room. Baljit grabbed her arm, and Shelly cried out that she was hurting her. Baljit told her off for the way she had run in, but then Aunty Manjit came in too. They took Shelly's glasses off and jeered, "Can you see without these?"

My sister began to cry and said, "No, I can't; give them back."

Then Baljit taunted her, saying, "No one's going to marry you. You wear glasses, and you're not nice-looking."

Eventually, Shelly managed to grab her glasses and ran out of the room crying. I got angry and stood up, saying, "Leave her alone."

"Sit back down before we tell your Dad you're back chatting!" threatened Manjit.

I reluctantly sat back down, knowing my Dad would take their side.

The next day was the last day of school before we broke up. That was it; our school days had finished, and we were all leaving to go to college or work. We all signed each other's shirts and were spraying shaving foam on each other. A few guys and girls were crying, saying, "We don't want to leave school! We will miss everyone too much."

Just then, it hit me that I wasn't going to see Julie again. Even as I was thinking this, two girls from the year came over because they wanted to sign my shirt. I had never even spoken to these two in my five years at secondary school, yet they wanted to sign my shirt! They both signed liked, fancied you for years and their names with three kisses. While they were writing, Julie appeared and asked if she could sign it as well. I looked up and smiled. She took the black marker and wrote, "All the best for the future. Best Friends Forever! Love you always, Julie."

"Forever?" I asked, and she smiled, hugged me tight, and said again, "Forever," and kissed me on the cheek.

I felt my knees go weak, and my heartbeat accelerated wildly.

Then she continued, "So what's your plan now? Are you going to college?"

31

I told her I didn't know and asked if she was.

"Yes," she said, "I'm thinking of studying an art or business course."

I said, "Art sounds good as you're good at it."

She glanced at me with a puzzled look on her face. "Really?" she asked.

"No, not really; business sounds better," I replied before adding with a smile, "Will you come and enrol with me?"

To my amazement and delight, I answered, "Yes!"

Chapter Ten

The holidays seemed to last forever, as I was looking forward to attending college with Julie. We didn't get to meet during this time as Julie had a job; in her spare time, she drew pictures from photographs for friends and families, and I was helping out in my father's shop.

On the first day of college, I was really excited. I put on the new clothes I had bought and my new after-shave before leaving home to call for Julie, only to find that her stepmother had decided to drop her off in the car.

I quickly ran to the bus stop and caught the bus to college. I was a bit nervous as this was all going to be new. I didn't know anybody or even what to expect from the course. To cap it all, my best friend Julie wasn't with me.

I walked down the path which led to the entrance. As I got closer, I noticed Julie waiting outside the doors.

"Hurry up!" she shouted, and I broke into a jog.

"You left without me" I complained.

"Yeah, my mom wanted to drop me off," she replied.

I told her it was okay; anyway, I didn't care as long as I was with her. As directed on the display board, we walked into the building and headed towards the student enrolment room. Both of us enrolled in the business course then walked into our classroom and sat down. Another girl, whose name was Preeti, came and sat beside Julie. Julie and Preeti became so chatty that I felt that she forgot I was even there. But we walked home at the end, enjoying the chance to talk about our first day of college.

On reaching the house, I told my parents I had joined college and was studying Business. I guess I thought everyone would be pleased, so I was a bit taken aback when my grandad angrily responded, "Business? We own businesses. We don't want you to go to college to learn the business and then come home telling us what we already know. I want you to study law and become a lawyer. All our relations in India are lawyers, and that's what I want you to become as well."

"Okay, okay," I said defensively, to stop this tirade, and told them I would change the course tomorrow.

In fact, I had no intention of doing this at all, and I continued studying business with Julie while my family believed I had switched to Law! Julie really got involved in the course, and we spent time together researching and doing presentations in front of the group. Preeti had become a close friend of ours, although more Julie's than mine, as they were both girls. Sometimes, she would drag Julie off and take her to daytime gigs. I was never invited to these, so I decided to go to one myself one day. I had made a few friends myself and reckoned they would gladly hang out with me as they could feel safer having a big, muscular guy around. So, we went to a daytime gig one Wednesday afternoon at a nightclub. They usually seemed to be held on either a Wednesday or a Friday. I walked in to find over 300 students dancing to Indian soundtracks. A high proportion of them were Asian, and I couldn't believe how the place was rocking.

My mate bought me a pint of lager.

"Sorry, but I don't drink this stuff," I informed him.

But he said, "Drink it. You'll find out how good it is after you've had a few sips."

They were all egging me on, so I just drank the whole pint glass in seven seconds. I was used to drinking liquids fast and was always trying to break my record of five seconds to drink a whole bottle of milk.

But after a few minutes, I started feeling dizzy. I didn't know what was going on, but it felt good. All my new mates began to laugh, assuring me that I would get used to it. I decided that I was more than willing to do that! I went onto the dance floor and began to dance. I had one girl after another dancing with me. I had never had this attention before, and it felt great. Then, this very pretty girl began to kiss me. After kissing her back, I said, "I love you, Julie."

She asked, "Who's Julie?" and I suddenly realised what I was doing.

I felt awful about kissing this girl, even though she was very attractive. I know I wasn't married to Julie or anything like that, but it still felt as if I was cheating on her. I guess I wanted my first proper kiss to be with Julie.

Back in school, when I was about thirteen, Julie tried fixing me up with one of her mates, Alison. We went for a walk together and were about to kiss each other when I stopped and said, "I can't," after which I just walked off. Even then, I couldn't bring myself to do it with anyone else.

The next day, Alison sent a rumour around the school that I didn't know how to kiss and that that was why I wouldn't date her. I became a laughingstock for almost a year. Sometime later, Julie and I were sitting on top of the hill by our school.

"Do you really not know how to kiss?" she asked me.

"Why? Are you going to show me?" I asked with a grin.

"If you want to know how, then yes, I will," she said seriously.

"After all, you are my best friend." I thought, "Great! This is the moment I've been waiting for!"

She leaned toward me, and I closed my eyes. However, as I moved forward to kiss her, she burst out laughing and asked, "Why did you close your eyes?" To which I said, "I don't know. It just happened. Can we try again?"

We went to kiss each other again, but she just began giggling once more.

"What is it this time? I asked, feeling confused and slightly embarrassed.

"It's you," she laughed.

"What do you mean it's me? What am I doing wrong?" I replied in frustration.

"I'm just finding it weird now," she answered. "That's great!" I thought before asking impatiently, "So, are you going to show me or what?"

"Nah, the moments gone now," she replied. And that was the closest I had ever come to kissing Julie.

34

Raj and Julie

So, I stopped kissing this girl at the nightclub, and she proceeded to ask repeatedly, "What's wrong?" and stated, "You're a delicious kisser," to which I answered, "Nothing, it's just...."

Then she asked if I was seeing someone else. I thought, "This is my chance to get rid of her," so I answered, "Yes."

She looked at me quizzically for a moment before saying sharply, "You're just a loser," and walked off. My mates came over to me and asked, "What happened? You didn't just blow that girl out, did you? You must be mad! Look how hot she is, man, and she was all over you."

I told them I had issues, to which they queried, "What issues? Are you gay?" to which I shouted back angrily, "No, I'm not gay. I'm seeing someone else."

I had to tell them this to get them off my back. I lay in bed that night wondering if anyone else had seen me who might go back and tell Julie.

The next morning, I awoke with a headache, as that was the first time I had drunk alcohol. Luckily, my parents hadn't noticed, as I went straight to bed after I came back from college. They were so busy working in the shop that they wouldn't have noticed anyway. Luckily, my aunty wasn't around, as she was bound to have realised and would have taken great pleasure in making sure everybody knew I had been drinking. I got myself ready the next morning and walked towards Julie's house.

On the way, I kept on asking myself what I could say if she found out about me kissing the girl at the gig. I reached her house and rang the bell. She came out looking as beautiful as ever. "What's wrong with you?" she asked.

"Nothing really, I just have a headache," I explained, "I drank alcohol yesterday at this Indian gig."

"You drank alcohol? I can't believe it!" she uttered in shock, "you're a health freak!"

"Thanks!" I said.

"You know what I mean," she laughed, "But what about your training and your goal to become the British champion? You won't able to achieve that if you become a pisshead!"

I thought about this, and she was right.

"I can't believe I got myself into this mess," I wailed.

"It's not a mess, Raj; you just don't drink again," she stated.

"Why are you so concerned anyway?" I asked.

"Look, Dumbo, you're my best friend and I know how badly you want to win the title. Besides, I can remember all the times you've lectured me on how bad alcohol is for me."

We began to laugh. I was so happy that Julie cared this much about my dream. My love for her grew even stronger. We got to college, and I tried avoiding my mates as I now felt they were bad company. Unfortunately, this was difficult. Julie, Preeti, and I were having lunch when Charan and Jas walked up to our table and asked, "How's it going, Gay boy?"

Julie looked at me before asking them, "Gay? Raj's not gay."

But Charan responded, "Well, he acted like one yesterday. A hot girl was hitting on him and trying to snog him, and he threw her off."

I thought, "Oh shit! That's done it now. My chances with Julie are ruined."

"What's this, Raj?" Julie asked accusingly. "You were snogging, and you never told me? What happened? Wasn't she good-looking?"

"Good looking! She was hot, hot, hot," butted in Jas.

"So, what happened, Raj? I thought you were well in there, the way you were snogging, but then the next minute, I looked, and she was walking off swearing at you."

"She wasn't swearing," I protested.

"So why didn't you follow through?" Julie asked.

It felt like she was a bit jealous and wanted to know more. I thought maybe it was about time I got my own back, but I couldn't. I just blurted out, "I only want you in my life, nobody else," hoping to get the right response.

"Aaahh, I know," she said reassuringly before adding, "And it better stay that way too!"

I wasn't sure whether she'd grasped what I'd said, but I think Preeti did, judging by how she looked at me. She nearly choked! Meanwhile, Charan and Jas walked off, muttering, "You're crazy, man!"

As Julie and I walked back from college that day, she asked, "Who was she?"

"Who?" I queried.

"The girl you were kissing yesterday," she replied.

"I don't know, I was drunk."

"But you must remember," she insisted. "And how do I compare to her?"

"She was my first kiss," I said quietly.

"She was the first?" said Julie, almost in disbelief.

"Why are you surprised?" I asked. "There have never been any other girls in my life."

"But you and I have never even kissed," Julie protested.

"Well, whose fault is that? I complained, "You never let me!"

"That's because you never knew how to kiss!" she responded and began to laugh.

"Ha ha, very funny," I replied.

She grabbed my arm and then asked me earnestly, "Am I really the only girl in your life?"

"The only one ever," I assured her. She hugged my arm and said, "You're such a great friend, Raj."

"Well, that's a start to being her husband one day," I thought to myself.

We stood, and she looked into my eyes, and we kissed for at least a minute.

"You're a delicious kisser," she said and walked into her house.

The next few months consisted mostly of studying and completing homework. We never discussed the kiss. But then Julie was put into a different group and soon spent a lot more of her time with Preeti. I started to spend time with Charan and Jas again and ended up going to the pub almost every other day. Bacardi and Coke became my favourites. There were times when I would drink it for breakfast! This went on for about two months, which was also the number of months I now had left to complete my course.

One evening, having missed training for two weeks through being too drunk, I decided it was time I went to the gym again. My coach was very upset with me when I told him what I had been doing. He took me to the mirror and said, "Whatever you do in life will be the picture and image of your life. If you think it's cool drinking Bacardi, then look at this," and he grabbed the fat around my stomach. I hadn't even noticed I was gaining weight from drinking. As I looked into the mirror, I could see myself becoming a fat drunk, but there was no way I was going to let that happen.

"I don't want to coach any drunks," Karam Singh stated firmly.

I turned around and begged him to keep me on and that I would stop drinking right now. Then he taught me a very important lesson for living.

He said, "In life, never be part of a circle but stay outside the circle and learn from other people – their achievements and mistakes. Don't be a follower but a leader, and you will always have a leader's character about you. Your so-called mates are in a bad circle, so don't be a part of that. Look in at them and see how stupid they look. Then you set an example for them to follow."

I gave my coach a hug and said, "Thank you, and I will."

The next day, I went to college and walked straight past my so-called mates. They called me, so I turned and said, "Listen, guys, I've got other plans, and going to the pub and shit like that is not part of them. We'll have to go our separate ways."

They just shrugged and said, "Suit yourself," and I walked on. I began to study harder and train harder than ever.

I hadn't seen Julie for the last two months or more because I was so involved in the wrong crowd. I looked for her but found Preeti in the canteen, drinking her usual hot chocolate while eating a Bounty chocolate bar. I walked up to her.

"Hi Preeti, how're you doing?"

"Great" she replied.

"Do you know where Julie is?" I asked.

"Oh, she's probably in the library, working on a group assignment with Shaun," she casually replied.

"Shaun?" I queried, "Who's this Shaun character?"

"He's that fit guy in our class," she replied.

Well, I never looked at guys thinking about whether they were fit or not, so I was none the wiser. But thinking about it now, I guess Shaun was quite a good-looking guy. Then Preeti pulled out a chair and said, "Sit down, Raj. I want to ask you something."

So I did. She looked straight into my eyes.

"Tell me the truth, do you like Julie?" she asked.

"Of course I do, she's my best friend."

"No," she said, "I mean, do you want it to be more than just good friends?"

"What are you on about?" I responded uncertainly.

She said, "Look, Raj, it's obvious that you like her more than just as a friend, and I think she knows that..."

"How does she know?" I interrupted, thinking maybe I'd let it out somehow, "What has she told you?"

Preeti started to lose patience, "Listen," she said, "stop beating around the bush and face facts. Come on, she's a good-looking girl, and you're not bad either, but you're fat, man."

"This is all muscle," I protested.

"Maybe that's true," she said, "but with your clothes on, it looks like fat – you're too big and bulky. And let's face it; you're no Jean-Claude Van Damme."

She could see I looked slightly hurt, so she quickly added, "Listen, man, you need to lose some weight and please get a haircut. Why on earth have you grown your hair like a rocker? It doesn't suit you at all; it makes you look even fatter!"

I was really listening in depth here as Preeti continued. "Look, I'm not trying to hurt your feelings or anything, but I don't think you stand a chance at the moment. Look at Shaun. He's slim and looks like he works out. But you look like the wrestler Ultimate Warrior off-season. I don't know what else to say. You're a good friend, and so is Julie. I don't want her hurt."

"Well, nor do I. I would never hurt her," I assured Preeti, "do you know how long our friendship goes back? We've known each other since junior school, from the age of ten."

"I know," she said, "and I don't want you to ruin it."

"Listen," I said, "nothing's going to be ruined. Julie is my best friend."

"Well, don't take my advice then," she said, "Keep just being a friend and not telling her how you really feel, but let me tell you, it's obvious."

I got up and walked off.

As I passed through the college corridors, I tried to think about what to do. Knowing that Preeti knew so much made it even more difficult. I heard a couple laughing around the corner and realised with horror that it sounded like Julie. I couldn't think where to run and hide. Preeti had me feel so embarrassed about the way I looked. I started to walk back, but it was too late.

"Raj!" Julie shouted.

I reluctantly turned around and said, "Hi," a little weakly.

She came towards me, holding Shaun by the arm.

"Hi, Raj. I haven't seen you for months. Where have you been? I thought you must have left!" she said.

"No, no. I just had a few things to deal with," I explained.

"This is Shaun," she said, and I shook him by the hand. "He's also into weight training," she added, which made me feel even more uncomfortable.

"Look, feel his muscles!" Shaun laughed, so I did so myself in an attempt to hide my hurt.

"He does martial arts as well," Julie continued.

"Hey, that's good," I said, hoping it didn't sound too insincere.

"Raj's muscles are huge," Julie told Shaun.

"What do your arms measure?" Shaun asked politely, and I replied, "Eighteen and a half inches."

"Wow! That is big," he replied. "We'd better go; we have a project to hand in," Julie interrupted.

As they walked off, Julie called back, "Speak to you later, Raj."

I noticed the way Julie was looking at Shaun. When she spoke to him, she would look into his eyes, rather like you see couples do in the movies. This was not good at all.

On the way home, I kept asking myself what on earth I could do. Then my thoughts returned to what Preeti had said before drifting back to Julie and Shaun. When I reached the house, I went straight to my bedroom. I picked up a bodybuilding magazine and noticed the heading, 'Lose weight for the summer and get the beach physique you've always desired.'

I quickly turned to the page of advice, read it, and made notes on the recommended types of training.

"Right, this is it. Starting now, I'm going to get in shape, and I'll show Preeti and Shaun what's what!" I thought to myself.

Chapter Eleven

That evening, I went to the gym. I wanted to change my training routine but knew my coach wouldn't approve. As it happened, he never turned up. I asked one of my training partners, Roger if he knew why Karam Singh wasn't here today.

"He's gone to China to work on a contract," he told me.

Our coach owned an engineering company and, being a professional at whatever he did, was going to be away for three to four months now. Now in his late fifties, Roger had been a World Champion himself – although in a different weight category than our coach. I told him about the situation regarding my bulk and weight. He advised me that I needed to do a lot more cardiovascular workouts. These range from boxing workouts, martial arts, and wrestling to running every day. It was good to have advice from Roger as he had a superb physique for his age and not an inch of fat on him. Roger was a Carrabein man and spoke about his childhood days in Jamaica. It was quite educational to learn about his native country and culture. Anyway, I worked on this plan. The dieting advice he gave me was the best I'd ever had. He told me to eat high-protein meals that were low in carbohydrates. I had read this many times before in muscle magazines but never actually put it into practice.

As soon as I got home, I began writing my workout plan and diet, and then I started to flick through my magazines. I picked up the first magazine I had ever bought, which had Sylvester Stallone on the front. It was when he was working out for the Rocky IV movie. I turned to the pages with his interview and read of the way he got in shape because his body had been an inspiration to many. He worked out every day, three times a day, and his diet consisted mainly of egg whites. So, this was the diet and training program I would use as well.

It was the last week of college, and I thought I would avoid Julie now so that I could surprise her with my new physique after the summer holidays. The plan was to get in shape over an eight-week cycle. As I walked through the college and approached the fitness room, I overheard a couple of guys complaining about their training session last night, which would have been a wrestling workout. I remembered Roger saying that I should add wrestling to my workout. The person who coached the college wrestling team was Khali Singh, and he was a Commonwealth wrestling champion. I decided to make this part of my training plan.

The following week, I went to the wrestling training session and met Khali Singh. He was a 6ft 6inch giant of a man. He must have weighed twenty stones or more, and his chest was massive.

I took part in the training session, and it was the hardest I had ever done! A two-and-a-half-hour cardio session was followed by half an hour of wrestling moves. Many who came to this session quit after the first day, but that was not going to include me. The training comprised movements including fifty press-ups at a time, fifty sit-ups, fifty squat thrusts, fifty free squats, and a lot more. This would be repeated four or five times. So, my program now consisted of working out with weights on Monday evenings, Wednesday afternoons, Friday evenings, and Sunday afternoons; then, Wednesday evening was for wrestling. That still left Tuesday, Thursday, and Saturday to fill! But as I was flicking through the weekly free newspaper one day, I saw an advert for Taekwondo Beginner classes on Tuesdays and Thursdays by second Dan Joginder Singh. This would nicely fill the gaps in the week while leaving Saturdays to practice what I had learned on Tuesdays and Thursdays. The program was complete. After a week into the program, it was getting hard as I loved my food. By now, I had lost nine pounds in body weight, which I thought was great. The egg white diet was hard, so I sometimes added chicken breast with salad. I also read that Sylvester Stallone ate burnt toast for breakfast with his egg whites, so I decided to try this, too. I was running on the road for twenty minutes each evening, before working out and then taking part in the wrestling and Taekwondo workouts. By the end of the second week, I had lost sixteen pounds. The workouts felt like they were getting easier, and I was enjoying them. The hardest of all was still the wrestling workout.

My father bought me a punching bag, so on Saturdays, I would work out by doing one-minute rounds on the bag, which soon progressed to two minutes. However, my interest in powerlifting began to diminish as I spent more time working out with Taekwondo movements. The instructor noticed my developing intensity in the sport. I remember the first occasion I took part in Taekwondo. I was a bit nervous when I got to the hall but found there were a couple of Indian boys from my school year working out there. These guys were quiet at school, and you would never have thought they would be involved in fighting sports. It put me at ease when I got talking to them, and when it came to sparring, these guys were very good. The fighting element was the most interesting part of the sport, as I had never really street fought and was never allowed to participate in boxing because my father was against it.

"Use your head for studying to become something, not for someone else's punch bag!" he would say.

Four weeks had gone by, and I had lost 30 pounds of body weight, but my family began to worry as they thought I must be ill. My mum would deliberately cook me my favourite chicken dishes and rice pudding, but I was determined to lose another two stones. I had read that my ideal weight was between 168 and 175 pounds, and I was determined to achieve this. I had scaled at 254 pounds, but now I was down to 224. I had another four weeks to go and still needed to lose another fifty-six pounds. I increased my training session by adding two sets of fifty crunches, two sets of fifty push-ups, and two sets of fifty leg raises every morning and every night. My body began to look sharper, and my physique looked very muscular. From a thirty-six-inch waist size, I had dropped to thirty-two inches. I was feeling great and began imagining the look on Julie's face when she saw me.

My training sessions continued to improve, so after five weeks, my taekwondo instructor said, "You should join our Sunday class as well."

I told him I didn't even know there was a Sunday class and was not happy that no one had informed me before. He said, "Don't worry, you can take part this week, but it's held at another venue, not here."

So that was why it had escaped my notice. Having added this third session on Sundays, I was down to 209 pounds by the end of the sixth week, but I was starting to feel weaker and fitter. My intake of energy-source food had dropped to almost nothing.

At times, I felt dizzy and had to drink lots of water. I sometimes began giving myself an apple or banana to give me some energy, but I avoided these as much as possible. I only had two weeks to go, and I was finding it hard to lose any more pounds. I reduced the number of heavy weightlifting workouts so that I would lose my muscle size. I started working out in another gym on Sunday mornings and noticed a bodybuilder with no fat on him at all. You could only see defined muscles and veins. I walked up to him and asked, "How do you get to look like that?"

"With a strict diet and hard training," he replied, "I'm at peak season and getting ready for bodybuilding competitions."

I asked what peak season meant. I had read about it in bodybuilding magazines but never understood how they did it. I just thought it was a well-kept secret. He explained how he was currently on a tuna, chicken, and egg white diet but with no fluids because he would be competing in two weeks.

"No fluids!" I said in surprise.

"That's right," he answered. "What happens is that when you starve your body of fluid, it will automatically start using the fluid in your muscles. That is when you will start seeing muscle definition and veins in your body."

"I need to lose another forty-one pounds in two weeks, so if I carry out this diet, do you think I'd be able to lose it?" I asked earnestly. He looked at me, probably thinking what an amateur and what an idiot I was.

He sighed and then said, "Okay! It's difficult, but if you train hard, you might be able to do it."

"Yes!" I thought. "This will be the new diet. I'm already training hard, so I need to be stricter with what I eat and drink."

I thanked this guy with forearms like Popeye the Sailor and noticed he even had a tattoo of an anchor on his forearm!

For the first week, just eating egg whites and tuna was really difficult. I found it hard to swallow tuna without fluid as it was so dry. I penciled that out of my diet after the first time I tried it. I stuck to ten egg whites in the morning and ten in the evenings. It wasn't easy, and I felt as if I had no energy. I became short-tempered with everyone and kept shouting while talking.

My parents told me off and said I was mad and taking this training too far. My aunts made up a story that I was on drugs, and that's why I looked dopey and had no energy.

"Look who's talking!" I thought.

Their sons were regularly smoking weed.

But during the last week, I passed out in the wrestling class and didn't know where I was. The only thing I can remember was my coach me giving Lucozade to drink. After taking this, I felt a bit better. I didn't want to drink anything, but I had no choice. I explained to my coach what I was doing, and he said I was crazy and told me I had to drink water at his training sessions as they were so intense that I was bound to dehydrate again. It made sense, and I realised how I had been creating problems for myself. I started consuming water again, but only enough to see me through my training sessions. I finally reached the end of last week, got up on Saturday morning, and weighed myself. 180 pounds; I was close to my target. I looked very lean, and you could see the muscle definition in my body. I had an abdominal six-pack. I stared into the mirror but felt something was still missing. Then I heard the voice of Preeti saying, "...and get a haircut!"

I didn't want to lose my hair, but for Julie to take an interest in me, it had to be done.

I got changed and then went down through the shop en route to the barbers. I asked my Dad for some money.

"What do you need money for?" he asked, puzzled.

"For a haircut."

He looked at me in shock and dropped the cigarette carton he was stacking on the floor. My mum overheard, too, and walked up to me, "When did you wake up?"

I said, "Leave it out, Mom!" but by now, my Dad was trying to make fun of the situation too and asked, "Do you remember the time you cried when your aunty cut your hair? Are you sure you won't cry again?"

"That was ages ago, so give me the money!" I laughed.

"With pleasure!" he said with a big grin. "Here, take twenty pounds, as it might cost four times as much to cut that amount of hair."

I just said, "Haha, very funny," took the cash, and went to get my hair cut.

Walking towards the town centre, I felt nervous and had half a mind to turn back, but I kept hearing Preeti saying, "Get a haircut."

I arrived at the hairdresser's but found it difficult to walk in. However, I eventually plucked up the courage and entered the salon. The lady at the front desk asked what exactly I had come for. She looked at my long hair and asked, "For a trim?"

"What's a trim?" I asked.

"About a quarter or half an inch of your hair length, just to tidy it up," she replied, laughing.

"Isn't it tidy now?" I queried. She looked at me with a 'Why don't you look in the mirror, you fool' expression on her face, but I had also put her on the spot. She replied, "No sir, it's fine, it's just a term that we use."

"Okay, I need a new look altogether – maybe have the whole lot off," I replied.

"Shave it all off?" she asked.

"No!" I said, suddenly beginning to panic, "Hold on, I'll be back in a minute!" and I dashed outside. I thought to myself, "What are you doing? You crazy guy, you're chopping off your long, hard-earned length of hair. It's taken you two years to grow this."

Then I heard Preeti's voice again, and I walked back inside.

"I don't want to shave it off clean. I want it shorter – a new look. Do you understand?" I pleaded.

"Yes, sir," she smiled. "please take a seat, and I'll bring you our photo album so you can get some ideas from there." I sat down, and she brought the book over to me. "Here you are, sir. Would you like a drink?"

I said, "No, I'm fine, thanks."

I wondered whether they were trying to pay back for my hair, which they were going to chop off and use for wigs. I was told once that hairdressers use all the hair they cut off people's heads for making wigs and how they made a lot of money that way. Maybe they should be giving me a free haircut for all the hair they were about to get from me! The receptionist came up to me again and asked if I had decided what I wanted yet. I said, "No, just give me a couple of minutes."

I was still working out how much money they were going to make from my hair! Anyway, I opened the album and began to flick through it. They were all good but rather short. Then I came across a picture that looked like Shaun. For a moment, I thought it was him! I walked over to the receptionist and told her, "This is how I want it."

"Are you sure you want it as short as this, Sir?"

"Yes, is that a problem?" I replied.

"No, not at all," she said.

She didn't understand how nervous I was about having my hair cut. I said I wanted it exactly like that, and then she asked if I wanted highlights.

"Highlights? What are they," I queried.

"You know, the blonde bits," she explained.

I thought, "If I am going for a change, I might as well go all the way," so I said yes.

She took me to the barber and told me, "This is Ben, and he will be cutting your hair."

I shook his hand and sat down in the seat.

"So you want to have this look then?" Ben asked, taking a good look at the picture in the photo album.

"Yes," I replied.

"You've certainly got a lot of hair here. Let's see what I can do," he said, but I was still thinking about how much money they were going to make out of me!

"I'm going to have my eyes closed through all this. Is that okay?" I asked.

"Yeah, sure," he said. "Why? Are you nervous?"

"Yes, I am, actually," I admitted.

"Well, you needn't be. You aren't the only one who has come in here with this amount of hair in the last few weeks. Long hair is out of fashion."

I told him it wasn't fashion I was concerned about but my strength when I was lifting weights. He looked at me strangely before asking, "Do you think you're Samson or something?"

"No, but I am the strongest teenager in the UK," I assured him.

He was so fascinated that I ended up telling him the whole story of my powerlifting exploits. He had even asked me if I was sure I wanted him to cut all my locks off! I thought, "You're the barber; why are you asking me? You should know." I just told him to get it over and done with as soon as possible, but he said it might take rather longer than I thought.

"First, I'll cut your hair, but then we'll apply a cap and put the highlights in," he warned.

"Okay, whatever, let's do this!"

I closed my eyes, and Ben began cutting. I could feel the hair being snipped and hear it falling on the floor. I cringed down into the seat until Ben asked, "Can you sit up straight, please, or I might not cut it straight."

I didn't want that, so I did as requested and kept my eyes closed. I thought about Julie and how shocked she would be to see me like this. I tried to picture myself walking down the pathway with her, but somehow, all I could see was Julie and Shaun. I decided to think about something else but couldn't seem to do so.

After a while, I thought I could feel a draft on the back of my neck, which felt weird. It sent a bit of a shiver down my spine. My head was feeling lighter as well.

Then Ben said, "Open your eyes."

I slowly opened them and looked into the mirror. I was shocked!

"Where is he?" I asked.

"Who?" said Ben, wondering what I was talking about.

"Me!" I said. "where did I go?!"

"This is you, the new you," he replied, laughing.

I couldn't believe it! I was looking at a different person. It was as if I had had plastic surgery. I could see my chiselled jawline, and my hair looked cool. My face looked super slim. The very attractive hairdresser next to me said, "Hey, handsome, are you seeing anyone?"

I got embarrassed and just smiled.

"Are you embarrassed?" she asked.

I smiled again. I couldn't believe how different I looked. She said, "You better watch out. You'll have all the girls after you!" I thought, 'I only want one, and that's my Julie'. The next stage was the highlights. This took a long time as the bleach wouldn't take to my hair; it was jet black and very thick. About three hours later, they had got it right. I looked in the mirror. The transformation was astonishing. It was as if I had been hiding behind a giant all this time. I felt really good and didn't have any more regrets about having my hair cut. All the hairdressers were looking at me and laughing. I walked back over to reception, and the lady said, "That will be fifteen pounds, please."

I thought, "What a rip-off and these guys are going to make a lot of money from my hair too."

"My dad isn't going to be happy," I said.

"It's a good thing I brought twenty pounds with me," I said, handing over the money and walking down the street confidently.

I walked past a shop that had tinted windows and could see my reflection in it. I kept going back again to see the new me. Walking back, I had a group of young women shout, "Hey, sexy."

This was the change I needed. When I got outside my father's shop, I took a deep breath, because I knew he would shout at me for dying my hair blonde. But then I thought, "Let's see if they recognise me,"

I walked into the shop. My dad was reading a magazine while Mum stacked the shelves.

"10 Embassy, please," I asked.

Dad glanced at me.

"Are you old enough, son?" He asked.

"Yeah, I'm seventeen years old," I replied, trying not to laugh.

Dad did a double-take, then said, "Raj?" rather uncertainly.

I nodded, and he asked, "What have you done to yourself?" although he did sound very happy that I had cut my hair.

He called my mom, "Look, do you recognise who this is?"

Mum came over, thinking it must be someone from abroad who she hadn't seen for a long time. But I couldn't hold it in, so I said, "Mom, it's me. Stop staring at me like I'm some stranger!"

"Raj, is that you? My Clumsy?" she cried in mock surprise.

"Mom, I'm not clumsy, don't call me that," I said crossly.

"No, you look very nice and really smart," she said. "Thank God you cut that mop of yours! Can you stop trying to lose weight now, too? I think you're thin enough. People are saying you look ill."

"Oh, Mom!" I complained.

"Now go inside and show your granny. She'll be very happy to see you," Mom said, hugging me.

I walked into the living room and tried to put an act on. Grandma was sitting on the sofa eating an apple. I touched her feet as Indians do to their elders, as a mark of respect. She looked jumped up and nearly jumped out of her skin.

"Who are you?" she said nervously. "You can't come in here. Get out!"

I was enjoying this. She shouted for my dad and said, "Come quickly. Some white man has entered the house."

Dad came running in to see what was going on and started laughing. Suddenly, recognition dawned in her short-sighted eyes.

"Raj!" she cried. "You monkey! What have you done to your hair? Where has it gone?"

I told her I had sold it, as there was a shortage of wigs. She looked at me and said, "Very nice, and now you can go to India and bring home a bride."

"No way! I'm not marrying anyone from India!" I replied.

"Well, you are more likely to get a white girl looking like that," she stated.

"I might just do that and bring a white girl home!" I said.

"I don't think so," Grandma warned. "Your grandad has promised his friend in India that you will marry his niece."

"No way," I said firmly, but I couldn't be bothered to argue with her, so I walked upstairs.

I went into my room and stood in front of the mirror. I could still hardly believe, how different I looked. I'd stared into the mirror many times before doing muscle poses, but I could see a transformation. I was so lean! I could do a six-pack abdominals pose, and see the muscle definition in my chest, shoulders, arms, and legs. I turned around to do a back pose, and there was muscle separation in my back. All the workout sessions, training, and dieting had paid off.

I thought, "I need something cool to wear back to college," so I went back downstairs into the shop and asked my mom for some money.

She asked what I needed that for, and I explained, "I'm going back to college on Monday, so I need some new clothes." She said, "You've got enough new clothes; wear them."

"No, Mom, I need something new to go with my new haircut. Remember you said if I ever cut my hair, you would buy a gold hand bracelet for me? Well, I don't want one of those, so can you give me the money for clothes instead?"

She gave me thirty pounds and told me there was a new shop that had opened in town called Komal's, and they had new men's clothing in there.

I said, "Okay. Thanks, Mom," and kissed her on the cheek.

I found the shop and discovered a lot of clothes I would like to take home for my wardrobe, but obviously, thirty pounds would only go so far.

"I love your outfits," I complimented the shopkeeper. "Where do you get them from?"

He explained how he had a factory where he had them designed and made.

"That's cool," I said. "Don't worry, you'll see me in here often!"

"You look like the younger version of Actor Karam Singh," he shared. This was a huge compliment.

After that, they became my regular shop for buying outfits because they made original designs and only made two of each style. The worst-case scenario would be that one other person was wearing the same clothes as me. I began to take pride in how I dressed again after I lost the weight. I believe it ran in the family as my grandad and father were always well-dressed. In the sixties and seventies, they were known to go out and spend their wages on new smart clothes every other week. My grandad is smart. He would spend a long time in the mirror combing his hair, tying his tie, and admiring himself. People used to love his hairstyle. He became known as the "Elvis Presley Hair Dude!"

When I got home with my new clothes, I found Aunty Manjit standing in the shop. She looked carefully and having recognised me she immediately called my Dad.

"Look, brother, look what Raj's done!" Then, turning to me, she sneered, "You're in trouble now."

"He already knows, and he likes it," I told her. "so, stop trying to cause trouble."

"Can you hear how he's talking to me?" she said as my Dad came out. "And this will just be the start of a whole trail of wrong things he'll do."

"No, it won't," I said angrily.

"It's okay, it'll grow out," my Dad replied.

"No, I'm going to keep it like this," I said confidently.

"Oh no, you won't," Dad said assertively. "I only allowed it this once because you cut that mop off your head."

"I'm going to have it done again," I angrily insisted.

"Listen to him answering back! Give him a slap, brother," cried Manjit, trying to inflame the situation.

"Just get inside and stop all this chat," said my dad angrily.

I went straight upstairs to my room in a rage. I was so angry, but when I looked in the mirror, I just saw myself going back to college and running up to Julie.

On Sunday morning, I went to the gym and trained hard. I was telling a guy there how I lost weight all my weight.

"Did you spend a lot of time in the sauna?" he asked.

"Sauna?" I replied.

"Yes," he said. "Sitting in a sauna can also help you lose weight. You don't have to go to a hot country to sweat off the pounds; you can do it sitting in a sauna!"

I told him I'd never even seen a sauna.

"Well, there's one in the changing room here," he said.

"There is? I said incredulously. "I don't believe it. I could've hit my target if I'd known about this, and it was right under my nose! I never take showers here; I always wait until I get home," I moaned.

I went into the shower room, took off my clothes, and sat in the sauna with just my boxer shorts on. I wasn't really supposed to do that, but I did. And what a feeling! It felt great, and I was getting really hot in there. I realised how much more I loved the heat than the cold! I sat in there for almost an hour and was sweating buckets! I felt lighter. I decided to stop for another fifteen minutes and skip a bit of sport, but then I began to feel dizzy again. I came out of the sauna and splashed some cold water over myself.

48

Raj and Julie

Then I dried myself down with my sweat top and left for home feeling wet and sticky. As soon as I got home, I had a shower, which felt better than usual. The sauna relaxed me, but I didn't feel up to going to the taekwondo class now – besides, I was looking forward to college tomorrow. I tried to sleep, but I was too excited. I did some push-ups and sit-ups at 2 am, and then I finally got to sleep.

Chapter Twelve

I was super excited when I got up in the morning. I walked into the bathroom, stepped onto the scales, and found that I was three pounds lighter. Feeling very pleased with myself, I looked in the mirror and noticed that even my skin looked better. I decided that I would start going to the sauna every week. I had a shower, got ready, and left the shop, taking some dinner money off my dad as I went. I walked down the street quite fast and was so exhilarated that I felt as if I was dancing down the street.

As I passed the flower shop, I noticed some roses for £2.99. I only had a fiver on me, and that was for my dinner, but then I thought that as I wasn't eating anything anyway, it didn't matter. I bought a bunch of dark red roses, and the smell of them further excited me as I anticipated giving them to Julie. I walked towards the bus stop, where two girls across the road whistled at me and shouted, "Hi, Sexy! Are those roses for us?"

I just smiled, and one blew a kiss at me, which I thought had to be a good sign.

I got off the bus outside the college, but as I walked down the path, I began to feel nervous and started worrying about what I should say to Julie. It felt rather like it would if I was about to ask her out – although I was going to do just that anyway, I told myself. I walked past four South Asian girls.

"How are you doing, sex machine?" one called out.

"I've never had this before!" I thought.

I walked into the building, still trying to talk myself into a higher degree of confidence. I approached the canteen, knowing that Julie would be in there with Preeti.

"I'll show Preeti as well," I thought.

I opened the doors that led into the tuck shop area outside the canteen, and there was Julie, hugging and kissing Shaun. My legs turned to jelly, and I found it hard to breathe. As I stood there in the doorway, a couple of guys pushed past me, knocked the roses out of my hand, and trod on them.

"Sorry mate," one of them said insincerely, "you shouldn't stand around in doorways."

I remained stationary as everyone who walked past me trod on the roses, smashing them to pieces. Julie turned around after hearing someone shouting, "The poor guy dropped his roses."

I spun around as my eyes filled with water and ran outside into the car park at the back of the workshop and cried. I had never felt this hurt, even after being horribly treated by my cousins.

After a while, I pulled myself together, but my hands wouldn't stop shaking. I walked around the college building a couple of times before going to sit in the nearby park. I didn't know what to do and kept telling myself that.

Raj and Julie

I looked at my watch and was shocked to see it was one o'clock. I decided to walk back to college, where I walked straight into the toilets to clean myself up. Then I walked into the canteen, passing right by Julie and Shaun, who were sitting eating their lunch. I felt like screaming. I glanced at Julie and found her looking at me. It seemed as if she was checking me out, and she had this smile on her face that I couldn't quite figure out the meaning of. I carried on over to where Preeti was sitting reading her Bollywood magazine. I sat at her table and looked at her, hoping to get some sympathy.

"Yes?" she asked, "did you ask if you could sit here with me?"

I looked at her blankly. "What are you talking about?"

"I'm not interested," she said assertively.

"Interested in what?" I asked, starting to feel strangely uncomfortable.

"If you have been put up to a bet or something, you had better go, because you're not going to win," she said emphatically.

"Bet?!" I cried incredulously, "It's me, Raj, you psycho!"

"Raj? No, you're not. Raj's big and fat!" But as she said this and made me feel even worse about myself, she suddenly realised it was me.

She screamed and yelled, "I can't believe it! You did it! Wow! You look good; I mean, you look sexy; you look, oh my God, let me snog you!"

"Get lost and sit down," I told her, fighting off her embrace.

"I can't believe you did it," she repeated. "What have you been doing over the holidays? Have you been on Ecstasy?"

"What are you on about?" I asked.

"Ecstasy or Speed tablets, those clubbers take and end up losing loads of weight'' she explained.

"No, I would never take drugs'' I assured her. "I just trained hard. I don't know why I bothered, though."

"You mean Shaun and Julie?" she said, nodding her head in their direction. "Well, you left it too late there, but I'm available!" she added with disturbing sincerity.

"Will you stop hitting on me? I'm not in the mood!" I insisted.

"You wait till Julie sees you; she'll soon change her mind about Shaun" Preeti assured me.

"Don't bother telling her anything," I warned.

"Why?" she responded disappointedly.

"Because I don't feel like talking to her," I said simply.

"But you have to!" insisted Preeti, "I want to see the look on her face!"

"Well, I'm not ready to talk to her" I replied.

"You can't take it out on her. It's not her fault. She didn't know you were going to come back looking this good," she protested, grabbing my biceps.

"Stop it, Preeti," I said before Preeti's expression suddenly changed dramatically.

"Lookout, she's coming," she whispered.

"Who?" I asked.

"Who do you think, Dummy? – Oh! Hi Julie," she said, and I looked down quickly. "Let me introduce you to my boyfriend," Preeti continued.

I looked at her, trying to indicate with my eyes that she should stop it.

"Boyfriend?" Julie asked in surprise, and she put out her hand to me and greeted me. "It's nice to meet you. Isn't she the lucky one?"

I took her hand, thinking how it was a hand I wanted to hold forever. I couldn't believe she didn't recognise me. Was I that different? No wonder she had looked at me strangely just now. I guess removing over five stones from my body weight had altered my appearance!

"You'll have to ignore him. He hasn't been in the country long, he's from India."

"You're from India?" Julie asked me. "Wow! Does that mean you're a foreign student?"

I nodded, still looking downwards and unsure whether I wanted her to recognise me or not.

"He's a bit shy," Preeti explained, putting her arm around me and kissing me on the cheek.

"So, what are you studying?" asked Julie.

"English," Preeti interrupted, hoping she could stop me talking and thus spin out this facade a little longer.

"I'm sure he can talk for himself," said Julie, trying to look into my face. "haven't I seen you before somewhere?" she added.

"Probably in a magazine, he also does modelling," said Preeti quickly. Under my breath, I told her to cut it out. Julie looked at her watch. "We'd better go. Are you going to take him to his classroom?" she asked.

"Yes, but don't you want to wait for Raj?" Preeti asked, trying not to smile. I glanced quickly at Julie to see her response. "I don't know where he is; I haven't heard from him at all over the holidays," Julie replied.

"Well, you've been so busy with Shaun that you probably didn't remember to call him," Preeti suggested.

"Shaun and I have been together every day of the holidays, so I never had time to go to Raj's Dad's shop," Julie explained. That was definitely not what I wanted to hear – that cut like a knife.

"Actually, he's already in the classroom. Let's go," urged Preeti. We all walked out of the canteen and up the stairs towards our classroom. As we reached our room, Julie asked why Preeti wasn't taking me to my English classroom.

"Oh, he's coming in here with us," said Preeti carelessly. "By the way, Julie, meet your best friend, Raj!"

There was a stunned silence. Julie stared at me in total disbelief as I finally looked straight into her face. She was completely lost for words. She clearly wanted to speak, but nothing would come out. Before anybody had a chance to say anything else, the teacher asked everybody to sit down, and we walked to our chairs. Instead of sitting next to Julie, I sat opposite her. She was visibly shaken and just sat staring at me while Preeti tried to hold back the laughter. Shaun walked in and sat next to Julie. She didn't even respond to him but tried to stop looking at me. Julie did her best throughout the lesson not to stare at me, but I caught her a few times, mainly because I hardly stopped looking at her either. The lesson ended, and as we walked out of the room, I felt someone nudge me in the back. I turned to see Shaun, who demanded to know why I had been staring at his girlfriend all through the lesson. I looked him right in the eye, thinking, "You've really picked the wrong moment."

I wasn't sure whether I was still feeling hurt or whether I was now happily optimistic. More to the point, I really wasn't sure what Julie was thinking. I did not wish to fight with Shaun, but I certainly didn't want to let him get one over me, either.

"So what are you going to do about it?" I said provocatively.

He went to punch me, and I blocked it easily. After all my martial arts training, he didn't have the speed to compete. He charged toward me and grabbed hold of my shirt. Before I could hit him, Julie came rushing out and shouted, "Let go of him! It's Raj."

"Raj?!" he said in surprise. "I thought you said he was fat and ugly?" he thundered at Julie.

I stared furiously at Julie, then back at Shaun, before stating, "Well, I'm not, and I would knock you out in seconds."

I walked off, giving Julie another look to say, "Don't even bother."

She screamed out, "I didn't say that about you!" but I was thinking in terms of who could lend me some rope.

I went and sat in the canteen, still fuming. Julie and Preeti followed shortly after and walked towards my table. I went to get up, but Julie begged me to hear her out, so I sat back down. "Honestly, I didn't say those things to Shaun, I promise," Julie assured me, trying to hold back the tears.

"He saw you before, and I often talked to him about you. I just told him what a good friend you were."

"And how fat and ugly I am?" I said sharply.

"No, I never said that," Julie insisted. "I just said you were big. I was talking about your muscles. He made the rest up himself. Raj, you know I wouldn't say anything bad about you; you're my best friend." She started to laugh, tears running down her face at the same time.

"What's so funny?" I asked.

"It's like I don't even know who I'm talking to! I mean, I do know, but – you know what I mean. What's happened to your big muscles?"

I just looked at her, and she gave me her 'Please forgive me' face. She could get around me whenever she gave me that smile.

"Hugs and kisses all around then, folks, and let's make up," Preeti chipped in.

"You can get lost, you can. You told me he was your boyfriend!" said Julie, and we all began to laugh. "Come here, you big bear, or should I call you match stick?" she continued.

"Watch it!" I said. Julie hugged me, and I could feel the hurt starting to drain out of me.

"Wow, feel this body!" cried Julie, "it's solid!"

"Let me feel!" Preeti said. "No, he's mine," Julie laughed.

"But am I, though?" I asked, looking straight at Julie, and she blushed.

"Are you blushing?" I said gently.

"No!" she protested in embarrassment. "Look, I'm sorry about what Shaun said."

"Okay, but what exactly is the situation with you and Shaun?" I asked.

Before she could answer, Shaun walked in with one of his mates.

"What are you doing, Julie?" he demanded, "get off him!"

"Shaun, stop it," Julie responded, "Raj's been my friend for years."

"So, what are you saying? That you are with him now?" he said almost sneeringly.

"No, Shaun," she answered meekly.

"Well, are you coming then?" he said impatiently.

"I'd better go," Julie said reluctantly, "I'll see you tomorrow, guys," and she walked away from my life once more.

In anger, I said, "It takes an army to take on Raj, and you still will lose."

"Please let it go," Requested Julie.

Back in my bedroom that night, I racked my brains, trying to think where it had all gone wrong. I had lost the weight, and other girls wanted me, but not Julie. I didn't know what else I could do.

The next day, when I walked into our classroom, Julie and Shaun were already sitting together. It hurt me to see that, but I couldn't do anything. I sat right at the back so they wouldn't see me. After the lesson, I walked out before anyone else. I had to get away from Julie and Shaun.

As I strode down the corridor, I heard someone shouting after me. I turned around and saw Julie and Shaun running towards me.

"Oh shit! What am I going to do now?" I thought.

As they caught up with me, Julie said, "Raj, it doesn't have to be like this. We can all be friends. Let me introduce you to Shaun." He put his hand out to shake. I quickly decided that I had better shake his hand, not wishing to be the villain in this situation. "Listen, mate, no hard feelings, and I'm sorry about yesterday," Shaun said diplomatically.

"Look, you guys can still be good mates," he added.

I nodded my head – to keep Julie happy more than anything else.

"I'm going to go now, so I'll see you later," Shaun said.

"Me too."

"What, you're both leaving me?" Julie complained.

"Okay, come with me then," Shaun suggested, and with a "See you later, Raj," they walked off.

I couldn't believe I had shaken hands with Shaun. It was like saying it was okay for him to be dating the girl I love. I went to my Taekwondo training session that evening, and because I was angry, I performed really well, according to my coach. My sparring partner couldn't keep up with me! At the end of the training session, our coach announced, "In three months, I'm going to Holland to take part in the International Taekwondo Championships, and I want to take a team with me. I have been watching you guys perform, and some of you are ready, while others need to work a bit harder. I'm not interested in those who are here just to pass the time; I want real performers, and I think you know who you are. If you don't want to perform, don't come next week, and I'll return your money."

Then he said, "I'm going to call out the names of those who will be in the team to represent Great Britain in the Championships. Can the following come out to the front: Wayne, Nigel, Raj, and Carl."

Wow! I'd been chosen for the team! We all came out to the front and were given a round of applause. The coach then said, "It's going to be a tough three months. We need to be training every day, with two hours each session consisting of sparring and a lot of cardiovascular training. You will be expected to run three miles before the beginning of each session."

We all looked at each other, thinking, "Wow! What a session!"

When I got home, I was so excited that I ran into the living room where my Mum, Dad, and grandparents were having their dinner.

"Guess what?" I said, and they all looked at me in anticipation. "I've been chosen to represent Great Britain in the Taekwondo Championships in Holland in three months!"

"But you've only just started; how can you be selected to fight in competitions?" my Dad asked.

"Well, the instructor said I was good enough," I replied, "And we have to train every day for the next three months leading up to the competition."

"And why wouldn't he get chosen?" said Grandad. "After all, we have athlete's blood in us!"

"Here we go again. He always tells this story," I thought.

"Do you know I was the best hockey player, footballer, and shot putter in my district in India?"

"Yes, Grandad, you've told us before!" I groaned.

"Well, that's where you get the sports skills from; it's in our blood," he insisted.

I guess there must have been some truth in this. He carried on telling his story.

"When I won the best footballer award, they celebrated by sitting me on a donkey and taking me around the village, announcing to everyone what a good player I was. My dad didn't approve of it, as he was a very simple, honest man and wanted to keep it that way. My college friends got me drunk, and when I got home, my father gave me a right telling off, and I had to keep promising that I wouldn't do it again. Then I broke the shot-put record."

"Yeah, I did that at school," I interrupted.

"There you go, you see; it's in the blood!" Grandad stated again. "Then, I was sent to play football in the State matches. That's when I broke my leg, and I never played again in India. I remember the whole village being concerned and giving me milk every day. That's when I thought of becoming a teacher." When he mentioned how he broke his leg, it occurred to me that it could be a family curse as I had broken my leg when I was knocked down by a car, and I remember my dad telling me how he got hit by a truck at work and a forklift blade went straight through his leg. He actually showed me the scar when I was younger. There was a hollow in the back of his leg where part of the muscle was missing. To some extent, this got me thinking. I carried on listening to my grandad.

"I came to the UK hoping that I would be able to play again. I came over as a student and began studying at Cambridge University, but due to a lack of finances, I had to quit the course and start work, as I was still expected to send money back home to India. I did eventually start playing again for a local football team, but unfortunately injured my leg once more, and that was the last time I played," he said ruefully.

Come to think about it, I remember my grandad used to go for a run around the block every night when I was about nine years old. Sometimes, I went running with him, and when we got back home, we would each drink a glass of milk with sugar in it. That used to be my Grandad's favourite.

"I believe you will reach the top in sport as well, son," he said. He took out his wallet and removed thirty pounds before asking, "How much money have you got in your pocket?"

"None," I replied.

"Here you go. You must always have money in your pocket. It doesn't mean you should spend it but always have it in case of emergencies. I'm very proud of you, Raj." He stood up and put his arm around my shoulder.

"Keep it up," he said.

I took the money and walked upstairs feeling really good. I sat on my bed and thought maybe I could be a champion in martial arts as well.

I leaned back against the bed rest and imagined fighting in the competition. I pictured Shaun as being my opponent. He was getting the better of me and saying, "I have Julie, not you." Angrily, I tried my best to fight him off. I was punching him, but clearly not hurting him.

I looked at my fists and thought, "Where's my power?"

I tried to hit him again, but he blocked my punch and then swung to hit me once more. But just before he struck, I woke up!

"Phew! It was a nightmare," I muttered to myself. "Thank God it wasn't for real."

I was sweating and shaking but still decided that I could use Shaun as a motivation for me to train.

After doing my mini-workout in the morning, I set off for college. I really wanted to tell Julie about the competition but convinced myself that she wouldn't be interested, as she had Shaun to think about. I bumped into Preeti on the way to class.

"You know when I told you that you were overweight and needed a haircut?" she asked.

"What about it?" I responded.

"Did you do it just to get Julie interested?" she probed.

"No," I said. "For your information, I lost it so that I could get accepted onto the British Taekwondo team. And guess what, I have been selected."

"Hey, that's really good," she said, sounding genuinely impressed.

56

"I start training today, and I'll be fighting in Holland in three months," I added.

"Wow! That's great," she exclaimed.

By this time, we had reached the classroom and sat down. I glanced over at Julie and caught her looking at me. She smiled, so I smiled back. Shaun noticed and decided to wave his hand to me as well. After the lesson, I tried getting away quickly, but Julie, Shaun, and Preeti caught up with me and asked, "Raj, we are going to the cinema this afternoon. Do you want to come?" I said I didn't, but they became quite insistent.

"Come on," Julie said.

"Yeah, come on, mate," Shaun chipped in.

"Yes, come on, Raj, I need a date," Preeti added, "I'm the odd one out. Please, Raj," she implored. I finally agreed as, luckily, I still had the money in my pocket that my grandad had given me. We took a taxi to the cinema from the college premises. Preeti was really trying hard to hit on me even though she knew that I was in love with Julie.

"What are we watching?" Julie asked Shaun.

"Anything," he replied, "something we can sit and make out to, I guess," he grinned.

"Oh shit, I don't need this!" I thought.

"Well, 'Doctor Hollywood' is on," he offered, but I had noticed 'Home Alone Two' was also on.

"What if you two guys go and watch your movie, and Preeti and I will go and watch 'Home Alone'? Preeti was more than ready to jump at this opportunity and quickly agreed.

"I'm up for that. Maybe you and I can make out, Raj," she added, grabbing my arm.

"No!" said Julie firmly. "We've come together, so let's watch the same movie."

"Thanks for ruining it for me," grumbled Preeti.

We bought our tickets and walked toward the screen. Shaun said he needed to go to the toilet, and Preeti said she did too, so they both disappeared to do so. Being alone with Julie felt a bit weird, this time. It was different. She came closer to me and said, "We won't make out," obviously referring to her and Shaun. I looked at her and just shrugged my shoulders.

"What's wrong, Raj?" she asked. I looked straight into her eyes, and my heart was beating fast.

"I, l love...." I began to stutter, but my words were drowned out by Shaun calling loudly. "We're ready!" he shouted as he and Preeti returned. We entered the auditorium and sat in the back row. I suddenly found myself sitting in the middle of Preeti and Julie. I wanted to sit on my own, but clearly, that wasn't going to happen. I couldn't concentrate on the movie. Even though I liked watching Michael J. Fox, I had Shaun holding Julie's hand on one side and Preeti trying to hold mine and stare at me on the other. She had long fingernails and was taking great pleasure in stroking me with them. I noticed Julie looking at me at one point and trying to smile.

For some reason, she decided to hold my hand as well. It felt good, but I didn't understand. Then, a naked girl came out of the water on the screen, and Shaun got up and started whistling. Preeti began to laugh and finally let go of my hand, but Julie kept holding on. She looked at me again, smiled, and squeezed my hand tighter. I didn't know what to do! What I wanted was to kiss her, but I gladly held onto her hand and enjoyed every moment of it.

As we walked out at the end of the movie, Preeti loudly asked if I'd enjoyed the film. I said yes even though I hardly knew what had happened. Then Julie asked me quietly if I'd enjoyed myself. It was as if she was asking me if I had enjoyed holding her hand. I smiled and nodded.

"Yeah, we enjoyed the part when she walked out of the sea naked! That was the best bit," Shaun interjected loudly.

I didn't bother responding, but Julie told him crossly to grow up. On the bus journey home, the only thing I could think about was what Julie had been trying to tell me by holding my hand. She was sitting towards the back with Shaun, but I didn't want to turn around in case I saw them kissing. Preeti was sitting next to me and still holding onto my arm. I wondered what I should say to let her know I wasn't interested. She asked many personal questions, including about my favourite movie, food, actors, and many more. Yet a few months ago, she was telling me I was fat and ugly. I really wanted to slap her, if anything, but I've always had this soft side to me that didn't allow me to hurt anyone – maybe it was because I had been picked on so much by my aunties. At the bus station, we all had to change buses to go in our different directions. Shaun caught his bus, and then Preeti got on hers, which left Julie and me waiting for ours. It began to get dark and a bit chilly, too. Julie nuzzled up closer to me.

"It's cold; keep me warm, Raj," she said and put her arms around me, hugging me.

"I love you, Raj," she then whispered.

I was stunned. That was what I wanted to say! She had said it before me, and I was happy that she felt the same way,

"But," I thought, "Does she feel the same as me?"

"I'm happy you've made an effort to get on with Shaun," she said as if to confirm my suspicions. I guessed when she said she loved me, what she meant was that she loved the way I could stay her friend and make her boyfriend feel comfortable, too. I said nothing. Then she looked at me and said, "You've been ever so quiet since we came back to college. Have you lost your tongue as well as your weight?" she laughed. I smiled and hugged her closer to me.

"You just don't know what I'm going through," I thought to myself.

Our bus finally arrived, so we jumped on and sat down together. Julie held on to my arm for the whole journey, but I wasn't complaining. After getting off at our bus stop, we went our separate ways, but for the rest of the way home, all I could think about was how I could tell her of my true feelings – or if I should tell her at all. I looked at my watch and realised I only had an hour to go before my Taekwondo session, so I quickened my steps. I was five minutes late for training, and my coach wasn't very happy. It was tough going as we ran for three miles before several rounds of pad work, kicking, and punching, followed by several rounds of sparring. At the end of the session, my coach came over.

"I'm not happy about you being late today," he said in a serious tone.

"It won't happen again" I promised.

"It had better not," he warned, "And your performance wasn't as sharp today either. Listen, Raj, I want to take a winning team to Holland, not a losing team. Get your act together because I don't want to have to replace you."

"Don't worry; I'll prove tomorrow that you haven't made a mistake," I assured him.

"You just make sure you do that," he said and walked off.

I sat at my study desk that night, swinging around and around in my chair, telling myself I had to get my training in order. I couldn't afford to let outside issues affect my training. I told myself that I would leave the Julie and Shaun issue until after the competition – by which time they would hopefully have split up or something! The next day, I tried to stay away from Preeti and Julie and spent most of my time in the library. This continued for several days, and my performance improved considerably in training. The coach came over on one occasion to spar with me. He worked me at a major pace and was super-fast, but I defended myself well, getting in a few good shots, which would be worth quite a few points in the competition.

After two one-minute rounds, he said, "Well done! You picked up the pace, defended very well, and scored some good shots too. Practice on your jumping sidekicks now; they will look good and show a bit of flash at the competition!"

I thanked him and left that night feeling very pleased with myself.

When I got home, I found a message from my power-lifting coach. My dad said he had asked me to ring him. I felt a bit nervous as I realised I had betrayed his faith in many ways. I picked up the phone and dialled the number.

"Hello," I started, "can I speak to the coach, please?"

"Raj?" he asked. "It is me!"

"Oh, hi, how are you doing?" I replied.

"I'm good" he responded. "Where have you been? I haven't seen you in the gym for ages," he asked.

I didn't know what to say. "I've been busy with a lot of college work," I said rather weakly.

"Oh, I see. I thought you'd lost interest," he said.

"No, no, I haven't lost interest," I insisted. "Anyway, I thought you were in China."

"Yes, I was, but I came back early and did not see you in the gym. I got a bit worried. Don't forget your dream," he stressed.

I suddenly realised I hadn't even thought about that for a long time now.

"I haven't forgotten," I said unconvincingly. "But you know I have to study as well," I explained.

"You liar, Raj," I thought to myself.

"That's right; you concentrate on your studies, but try and make it once a week if you can," he continued.

"I will," I promised. "Bye, coach," and we both put the phone down at the same time.

"Phew! That was tough," I said to myself. I didn't like lying to my coach, but I felt I had no choice. I know I had my dream as a powerlifter, but at the same time, I was excited about the Taekwondo competition. I told myself I'd take part in the competition and then go back to powerlifting. I trained hard every day, and I was getting fast and powerful. Our coach brought in some wooden blocks during one of the training sessions.

"In the competition, you may draw on points with your opponents, so to decide the winner, both fighters will have to break wooden blocks. You choose whether you want to kick or punch; it's entirely up to you, but we'll practise before we leave so that we'll know our strength in breaking the blocks," he stated.

He gave us a demonstration, and we were all amazed and became excited at the prospect of emulating him. Everyone had their turn at breaking one or two of these wooden blocks, which were about two inches thick. My coach asked how I was going to perform. I had been told I had a solid left sidekick, but I didn't want to risk embarrassment, so remembering how many times I'd knocked guys out in street fights with a punch, I said, "Front punch" with an air of confidence.

"Okay then," he replied, and they took their position, holding up the blocks, one on each side.

"Are you ready?" Coach asked, and I nodded. I carefully focused, then punched the first block, and it broke easily. So, then they set two blocks. I got into position and punched the two blocks straight through. I got excited, and the other guys cheered me on. Three blocks were set. "Focus!" my coach shouted at me. I set myself up, counted to three, and punched the blocks, once more breaking them straight through. Everyone cheered, but then my coach said, "Don't get over-excited," as they set up four blocks. I felt a bit nervous, but I had to break these four. I counted down, "Three, two, one and punched the blocks, but they didn't break.

"Three it is then," announced my coach.

"No, Coach, I'll smash them," I insisted.

"Well, you will have to wait until next week then," he replied.

"No! I must break them today!" I demanded.

"Okay then," he said, "let's see you break them."

One of the guys in the team said, "Think of someone you really hate and then smash them."

"But I don't hate anyone," I protested, so my coach told me to focus.

I got into position but then closed my eyes and saw a vision of Shaun and Julie. I counted, "Three, two, one," and punched the blocks, smashing them all and knocking one of the guys, holding them to the ground in the process! A great scream went up from those looking on, and Coach laughed. "Well done! So, it will be five next week then!" he roared with delight.

I got home thinking I had achieved something great. The first person I told was my grandad, but he just said, "You mind, you don't hurt yourself."

I was getting good at this sport, and I was doing kicks I never thought I could do. I was performing jumping roundhouse, sidekicks, and punching combinations that the other guys couldn't keep up with. With all this intense training, I didn't need to diet, and I was staying lean. My muscles were so hard and solid that I could even hear the power in my punches when I hit the punch bag.

Two months went by, and my attendance wasn't good at college as I was spending too much time training. As I walked through the corridor one day, I bumped into my Business Marketing teacher. Her name was Miss Jandhu, and she asked, "Where have you been, Raj? We've been getting rather concerned about your attendance, and none of your coursework has been handed in. Have you dropped off the course? We are in the process of writing to you and your family."

I realised I was in trouble.

"No, I haven't left," I said, "I just had to take some time off, but now I'm back."

"Well, I don't think you'll be able to catch up now," she said.

"Yes, I will!" I said determinedly.

"Follow me," she said firmly, and we walked into the office, where my other teachers all turned around and looked at me. I felt like a naughty little schoolboy who was about to get punished. Another lecturer came up to me and asked where I had been.

"You are way behind with your coursework," he said accusingly. But Miss Jandhu stepped in and said, "He'll catch up." She was a great help that day. She made sure that all of my teachers gave me copies of the assignment tasks I needed to complete. Then she said, "Listen, I didn't need to help you out and could easily have voted with the other teachers to have you kicked off the course."

"Thank you very much, Miss," I said, "I appreciate it, and I won't let you down."

"You have the potential, Raj, and I believe in you," she said reassuringly. " So you'd better complete the assignments and hand them in over the next four weeks, along with the other assignments you will be getting in that time. I promised I would."

Then she said, "Why don't you join up with one of your classmates? Two heads are better than one, and if you're teamed up with someone else, it can help you out, and you'll find it a lot easier. Don't you hang out with Preeti?"

I thought, "Oh no, not Preeti!" but answered yes anyway.

"Team up with her because her grades are excellent," Miss Jandhu continued. "Or else there's Julie, her grades are very good as well."

That was definitely not an option, as she would have Shaun hanging around her, so it had to be Preeti. I just wished she would stop making passes at me! I thanked Miss Jandhu again and assured her once more that I wouldn't let her down. I went looking for Preeti and found her in the library. She looked as if she was very busy writing.

"Hi, Preeti," I said, at which she jumped up and hugged me.

"Where have you been?" she asked. I told her that I had gotten carried away with my training, and she asked if I had lost more weight.

"Yes, another nine pounds, so I am at my ideal body weight," I said proudly. This was one thing I liked telling people!

"So what's that?" she inquired.

"I weigh 168 pounds," I replied.

"And what's that in stones?" she asked.

"Ten stone five, which is about sixty-five kilograms," I said confidently.

"That's lighter than me," Preeti complained. I felt great when she said this and asked how much she weighed.

"I don't want to say," she said meekly.

"Please tell," I begged, "I'll help you lose weight."

"Eleven and a half stone," she admitted reluctantly, "but bear in mind, I'm big-boned."

"What an excuse!" I said and mimicked her voice, "I'm big-boned."

"Stop it, Raj," she cried, "It's not long ago that you were in the same boat."

"I know," I admitted, knowing exactly how she felt. So, I said, "I've got a deal for you. If I help you lose weight and get down to your ideal body weight, will you help me with my assignments?"

"Deal," she said emphatically, and we shook hands.

After that, we spent a lot of time together, and she helped me a lot with the understanding of my subjects. At the same time, I helped Preeti with her diet and advised her to go for a walk every day for forty minutes. I persuaded her to cut out all the junk food and also reduce the amount of bread, cereals, pasta, rice, and potatoes she ate – everything she loved, basically! She found it hard the first week, but after finding she had lost four pounds, she came and gave me a big wet kiss on the cheek, which I didn't enjoy at all!

I was still training just as hard, but I was studying hard as well and getting closer to completing my assignments. My parents noticed that I would often stop up until two or three in the morning, typing things up. Sometimes, my Mum would come in and give me a glass of warm milk. On other occasions, it would be my Dad or even my grandad. They were all proud of me. My grandma was proud of me, too, but although she never had the energy to give me a glass of milk, she would frequently remind Mum to give me one! Preeti and I spent a lot of time in the library, and by the fourth week, I had completed all my assignments. I went straight to Miss Jandhu's office, walked in, and handed all my assignments to the relevant teachers. They were proud of me, too, and gave encouraging comments, exhorting me to keep it up. Then Miss Jandhu called me to one side and said, "Well done,

Raj, I knew you had the potential." I thanked her for believing in me, and she said it was not so much her as Preeti that I needed to thank her.

"We've noticed she's been working hard to help you," she said.

"I know, and I will," I assured her. I shook her hand and ran down the corridor to look for Preeti. She was talking to Julie in the tuck shop area, but it looked as if they were arguing. As I got closer, I heard Preeti saying, "You can't have the best of both worlds. You've got Shaun, so you can't have him as well."

I wondered who they were referring to.

"It's your bad luck if you've missed your chance," Preeti continued, but then she noticed me and stopped talking.

They both turned towards me, but Julie's look seemed to be saying that I had done something wrong.

"Hi, Raj," said Julie a little abruptly, but as I smiled in response, she just walked off.

I turned to Preeti and asked what had happened. She said nothing at first but then admitted that Julie was a bit jealous that we were spending so much time together.

"Why should she be jealous?" I asked, whilst feeling quite happy that she was. "She has Shaun."

"That's what I tried to tell her – and that we were getting close."

"Oh no, I've got to stop this," I thought. "Preeti's picking up all the wrong signals here."

"Listen, Preeti," I said. "First, I want to thank you for helping me with my assignments. If it hadn't been for you, I don't think I would have completed them in time."

"Yeah," she said, "but I want to thank you as well."

"For what?" I asked.

"I've lost almost a stone in body weight," she stated proudly.

"Hey, well done," I said. "But you need to know that you and I are just friends, and it can't be anything more than that. I'm in love with someone else." "Who, Julie?" she asked.

I didn't say anything at first. "Plus, I can't be involved with anyone at the moment as I have to concentrate on preparing for my competition. I'm leaving for Holland next weekend, and I need to come back with a trophy to give to my grandad," I finally said. "I know," she said, "and don't worry, I'll be praying for you."

I thanked her and put out my hand for her to shake. She smiled and shook it warmly.

I decided to run back home because my fitness level was super high, but all I was thinking about was that Julie was jealous! I thought it had to be a good thing, and I would talk to her when I got back from Holland or maybe when we went back to college after Christmas, as we would be breaking up next week.

Chapter Thirteen

Finally, Friday arrived, when I was due to fly to Holland. All my family gathered downstairs in the front living room to see me off. They hugged me and pronounced blessings over me to win. My sister grabbed me.

"Make sure you come back with the trophy," she said.

"He will. We have faith that God's hand is upon him," my Grandad replied.

My mother fed me a spoonful of yoghurt with sugar in it.

Dad drove me to the club, where I saw the rest of the team waiting to leave.

"All the best, son, and look after yourself and let me tell you that it doesn't matter if you win or not; we are just happy that you have reached this stage," he said.

"Thanks, Dad, but I am going to win!" I replied excitedly. "Okay," he replied, "any way you'd better go; I think they're waiting for you to join them on the minibus."

I got out of the car, walked over to the minibus, and climbed in. I shook hands with all the other guys and sat in my seat. I looked outside the window. I am sure I saw Julie and her stepmother in their car. The minibus was going to take us to the airport, and then we would take the flight to Holland. I felt that Julie had come to see me off. Her stepmom must have followed us to the sports centre, I thought. Julie's eyes kept on coming up in mind. I have seen that look in her eyes many times. It's when she's sad. She has sparkling blue eyes, and they sparkled more when they are slightly filled with tears.

I remembered a time when Julie and I were sitting in the park. We must have been thirteen or fourteen years old. She was missing her dad, who had to work away. Her eyes were filled with water, and the colour of her pupils sparkled even more. But they sparkled when she was happy, too. All those years and time we spent together, I always watched her eyes sparkle— something I'd treasure forever. We would race along the park path to see who was the fastest, and then she would grab my hand to get me to feel her heartbeat. Julie was always into her running. She just loved to run, which kept her in great shape. Back on the minibus, I also heard our instructor telling us about the fun we were going to have. I thought about coming home with the trophy, but soon, we were at the airport and boarding the plane. I was a bit nervous as this was the first time I had ever flown. It took about one hour and twenty-five minutes to reach Amsterdam, and from there, we caught a train to Eindhoven, where the competition was due to take place. We were collected from the railway station by the chairperson of the International Taekwondo Organisation. Our team stayed with two different families: three in one house and three in the other. The family I stopped with included two girls of about sixteen or seventeen years old, along with their younger brother, and thankfully, we all got on very well.

The next day, we were taken to the Netherlands Taekwondo Club. We all warmed up and practised sparring. The trainers here were very good, and they put us through our paces. It was a great session, which just added to the excitement as we looked forward to the competition the next day. That evening, the family we were living with arranged for us to go to a holiday resort where we were able to enjoy swimming and other indoor activities. The two daughters tried their best to show me they liked me by swimming and hugging me in the pool. I was too focused to get distracted.

The big day was here, and that morning, we hurried off early to the sports arena where it was taking place. We all weighed in, signed the relevant documents, and began to warm up. Exactly in time, an announcement was made that the competition was going to start. A wave of nervous excitement rushed over me. I prayed quietly and said to myself, "This one's for Grandad!"

When I was called to my first fight, I walked onto the mat and couldn't help noticing how tall my opponent was. The fight began, and he outscored me in the first round, using his long legs to his advantage.

My coach gave me some advice, saying, "This guy is good with his legs, so what you need to do each time he comes at you with a kick is to shorten it by performing an axe over his legs, get in close to his body and then score with your punches. You can beat him with your punches."

Once the second round began, I did exactly what my coach had told me. As my opponent came in with a kick, I kicked over his leg, and as I got close to him, I used him as a punching bag! He didn't know whether he was coming or going! That round was mine all the way, and by the end of the fight, the judge had decided that I had won. I jumped up and shouted, "Yes!" but my coach quickly reminded me that there were still many more fights. I was winning every fight, but my opponents were getting more and more difficult to beat. Nonetheless, it seemed that in no time at all, I was on the mat to contest the final. It had all gone so well; it was like a dream, but I knew that this was now it. I needed to put in hundred and ten per cent now if I was hoping to finish the job.

The fight began, and this guy was fast! He kept dancing around me, but my defence was also fast, and he didn't manage to score any points. Then, out of the blue, he decided to do a flashy kick, which didn't work at all, and I managed to get a good punch in, which dazed him. Obviously angry, he charged toward me with a barrage of kicks, and this time, he managed to get through and earn himself some points. The match remained very tight, but the then-coach shouted to me that I should look for the openings. It suddenly dawned on me that when he was kicking, he was leaving the rest of his body open for me to score. I picked up on his routine and got in a three-punch combination, which once more left him a bit dazed, enabling me to get two more kicks in quickly. The fight was incredibly intense, but I could hear my team members cheering me on. My opponent came at me again with the same kick, so I repeated the same combination and was now moving several points clear. I decided it was time to go for the kill, and a jumping roundhouse kick into his face, scored me six points. The crowd were going wild, so I followed that with a jumping-turning kick, which landed straight onto his jaw, and he fell to the mat. The referee blew the whistle shortly after and shouted time.

As we waited for the judge's decision, I felt confident but then wondered if the judges would see things the same way. My opponent was good and had certainly managed to get a few good hits in. Finally, they stood up, and YES!!! They gave the fight to me. I yelled out in delight and shouted, "Thank you, God."

This was a great day, even though my nose was bleeding and my eyes were bruised. Now, I could go home and hand the medal to my grandad. It was a brilliant day all around as every one of my teammates won first place in their weight categories, too.

It was a wonderful moment as we all stood to receive our medals and trophies, especially for representing our country, Great Britain, and I will never forget the feeling. Afterwards, our family hosts took us to the local bar to celebrate, and soon, we were all drinking and dancing—well, everybody was drinking other than me.

However, it soon became obvious that one of our team wanted to pick a fight with a group of guys in the pub. "It'll be like in the movie; 'Best of the Best.' he insisted. But Coach responded, "If you don't leave it out, you guys will get a beating from me!"

We all looked at each other and then jumped on top of him, punching and kicking him – but all done jokingly, of course, and he managed to get in a few kicks and punches himself!

Later, outside the pub, the mother of the family I was standing next to each other, who began to lean all over me, pretending she was drunk. It seemed she was trying to hit on me! I just looked at her and smiled, saying, "You haven't even had any alcohol!" She looked back at me with a face that seemed to say, 'You don't know what you're missing.'

She was very attractive, about thirty-five, but with the body of a fit eighteen-year-old. Back at the house, after brushing my teeth, I left the bathroom and encountered the young mother again. She leaned and kissed me, and I kissed her back. Then she stopped and walked into her room, leaving me confused. I walked into my room and found her daughter sitting on my bed. She stood up and walked over, kissed me and then began to giggle and began to take my clothes off. I stopped her and said sorry. She left the room upset, and then Wayne walked in, saying, "That was quick."

I laughed and reminded myself I was in love with Julie, so I wasn't tempted. We flew back to the United Kingdom the next day, and after singing victory songs all the way home, I was eventually dropped off outside my Dad's shop. I walked in to find Grandad standing there talking to his friend. I shouted, "I won!" and proudly showed them all my trophies and medals. Grandad held the trophy aloft and shouted, "Yes! We are proud of you, Raj," and he hugged me.

Mum and Dad did the same, and my grandma kissed me on the cheek.

Raj and Julie

I walked up to my sister. "Look, I won," I smiled. "That's brilliant, Raj. Well done," she beamed. "I'll show this to our aunties and tell them you'll kick their ass!"

While I had been away, they'd been picking on her. I later found out that as I had been spending so much time in the gym and at Taekwondo Classes, I had also missed a great many instances of my cousins tormenting my sister too. I asked her if she wanted me to go over and sort them out now, but she just said to leave it for the time being and just surprise them if they caused trouble again. Meanwhile, my family celebrated the victory with me, and my mother made my favourite meals – especially rice pudding!

Chapter Fourteen

The Christmas holiday began the day after my return, so I was off from college for two weeks. But I wanted to meet Julie and tell her about my winning the competition. I knew I would have to wait until we got back unless she happened to come into the shop, which I was hoping she would!

One day, I was working in the shop, helping my dad stack the shelves and wishing Julie would walk in. As I was getting older, he seemed less strict with me regarding talking to girls unless my aunties were there, stirring up trouble. The phone rang, and Dad answered.

"It's for you, Raj," he called.

"Well, that's a first," I thought to myself. I grabbed the receiver, and it was my Taekwondo coach at the other end.

"Hi, Raj," he said. "We have a photoshoot for local press tomorrow, so I need you to come an hour earlier than usual," I said that was fine, and immediately, the excitement rose as I always wanted to be in the paper; it was my claim to fame. I hung up and told my parents I was going to be in the newspaper for winning the championships. Dad turned around and congratulated me while I thought to myself, "I don't need to tell anyone now; they can all see for themselves."

Just then, Julie's stepmom walked in and said, "Hi, Raj."

I said, "Hi. Is everything ok with you and Julie?"

"Yes, why?" I asked.

"Julie has mentioned many times that she hasn't seen you in a while. She's always going on about your weight training, martial arts, and how much weight you have lost. I must say you look very good."

"Thanks," I replied.

"You know she draws your pictures all the time?"

"Really?" I asked.

"Yes, her art pads have many sketches of you."

Just then, Dad walked out of the storeroom holding a case of wine to put on the shelves, "Have you told her?"

Julie's mother asked, "What."

"He won the International Taekwondo Championships in Holland yesterday."

"Wow, Congratulations," she said.

The next day, I arrived at the sports hall early, and we all prepared for the photoshoot. We were each planning how we should pose, but then our instructor came in and decided on the poses for us. But I must say they were pretty cool. We all stood holding our trophies while Coach posed with a sidekick in front of us.

The next day, our picture was not only in the local paper but it was also on the front page! I couldn't believe it, but it was another step toward my plan for fame in the film industry. My mum cut about ten pictures out of the newspaper to hand out to relatives. She cut up the papers and said which could go to which relative whilst I served the customers. It was a bit quiet, and I kept staring towards the entrance, hoping that Julie would walk in. An attractive lady walked in and asked for ten Benson and Hedges cigarettes, and I turned round to take them from the display.

But as I turned back to hand them to the customer, I saw Julie walk in. My heart started beating so fast that I gave the lady the wrong change and had to correct it for her. Julie walked towards the counter.

"Congratulations on winning the championships, Raj!" she said. I thanked her and smiled.

"You didn't tell me you did martial arts," she continued.

"Well, you've not been around to tell," I protested a little weakly.

"I haven't been around. It's you who's been spending all your time with Preeti," she said accusingly.

"Do I have to go through this again – Preeti helped me complete my assignments," I complained.

"You could have come to me – I thought I was your best friend," she replied.

I had to be careful here. I didn't want to get into an argument. Otherwise, my parents would hear and get involved. I wanted to say a lot about Shaun but thought better of it. That would have to wait. So, I said, "You are my best friend, and next time I'll come to you."

"Second best, then?" she asked.

"No!" I said firmly. "You're always on top of my list."

She laughed and asked what I was doing for Christmas.

"The usual: help out in the shop, close up for a couple of hours to have Christmas dinner, and then back in the shop again."

"Don't you guys go to church or anything?" she asked.

"You know we don't – are you going?"

"Yes, I'll be going with my parents," Julie replied.

I pushed a little further. "Is Shaun going with you?" I had to ask that.

"No, he spends Christmas just with his family and then goes out with his mates," she explained.

"That seems a bit selfish, considering he's your boyfriend," I suggested, trying to open up an opportunity for scoring points over Shaun.

"Maybe," she said carelessly, "So, why don't you come to church with me?"

This was my chance! "Yeah, I guess I could," I responded quickly, "especially as I'm in my family's good books at the moment."

"That's cool," she said, "I'll see you then."

"But that's still a week away; don't you want to see me before then?" I asked.

"Maybe I will," she said mischievously.

"And maybe I will, too," I replied, and we both laughed.

"Well, I better go before your dad tells you off, or worse still, one of your aunts walks in," she smiled. "Bye, Raj."

I watched her walk away from the shop, but this time, it felt different. I didn't feel that she was leaving me this time, but more that she was with me. Julie came into the shop every day during the week leading up to Christmas. She never mentioned Shaun, and I certainly wasn't going to. I also explained that I had no interest in Preeti whatsoever.

Each day, we would talk about how time had flown through school and college so that we were nearly ready to go to university now. We talked about possible Universities we could study at and the courses we might follow. She also mentioned that she had an aunt in Canada whom she would like to go and visit and maybe find a job and live there. This rather upset me until she added, "…after we get married."

This I hadn't expected, and I wasn't sure quite how to take it. I thought she was still with Shaun, but it has all been good so far! I shot a glance at her, and she laughed, so I decided not to pursue it any further. She put her hand over mine and smiled.

On the morning of Christmas Eve, I was serving in the shop again when Julie walked in. This didn't make me feel nervous anymore; I was just happy. After I had finished serving the customers, she came up to the counter, slipped a card into my hand, and said, "Happy Christmas." I felt bad that I didn't have one ready for her, but I quickly assured her that I would bring hers to church tomorrow.

"So, you're still coming?" she asked.

"Yes, of course. Which one will we be going to?"

"The New Testament Church on the main road," she replied.

"Okay, I'll be there," I promised. "What time do we have to be there?"

"It starts at nine o'clock," she said.

"I'll be there on time," I said confidently. She left saying, "Have a very happy Christmas," to which I replied, "You too, and thanks for the card."

What I wanted to say was that I loved her, but maybe there would be an opportunity tomorrow.

A man walked in and asked if we sold gifts for women. I said that we only had boxes of chocolates. "Don't you sell bottles of perfumes or anything like that?" he asked, but I replied no, so he left. But it got me thinking that I should buy Julie some perfume. I looked at the time, and it was almost midday. I shouted to my mom in the living room and asked if she could take over the shop. She came through and asked what was wrong.

I said, "I just remembered that my mate is coming tomorrow to give me a present, so I need to get him one as well. Can I have some money, please?"

She asked how much, so I replied, "Oh, I don't know, about twenty pounds, I guess."

My mom looked shocked!

"Twenty pounds?" she cried, "You must be joking! Here, have fifteen and make sure you buy something worthwhile. I said, "Okay," and went off to town.

When I reached the town, it was packed with people doing their last-minute shopping. I couldn't believe the way some of them were acting. There were lots of couples I walked past who were arguing, and parents were screaming at their children. I thought Christmas was supposed to be the time of year for showing love, but people seemed to be doing just the opposite. Somehow, they all were missing the point. There was one man who was clearly drunk, and he was with what looked like his wife and son, but the only thing I heard from his mouth was f.....g this and f.....g that and every couple of seconds, he was slapping his son over the head. I couldn't believe it. Surely, as a father, he should be caring for his son and buying him gifts, but this poor lad was getting a beating. I felt sorry for both the boy and his mother. I found a perfume shop and began to check out the fragrances. It was difficult as the shop was really busy and I had no idea what to get anyway. I started watching other women see what they were buying and noticed that one brand was selling the most. I grabbed a bottle of that and sprayed it into the air, and it was nice. But then I felt a tap on the shoulder and turned around to see a black man, and he said, "All right, brother," in Punjabi.

At first, he surprised me by speaking in Punjabi, and I wondered what he wanted. Then he whispered in my ear, "I can give you any of these bottles of perfume for half the price."

I looked at him and decided he didn't appear to be a thief; in fact, he was very smartly dressed.

"Come to my car, and I'll show you!" he continued.

"Why not have a look, and if he attacks me, I can handle myself anyway," I thought.

I was very confident I could defend myself in this situation, having just won a fighting competition. We reached his car, and he opened the boot. There were dozens of bottles of perfume and aftershave in there.

"They're not stolen, are they?" I asked suspiciously.

He looked offended and protested, "No, this is my business. I sell replicas of the ones in the perfume shops."

"What do you mean by replicas?" I asked, still not sure whether I should trust this guy.

"Smell," he replied, spraying one of the perfume bottles. It was just like the one I had smelt in the shop.

"I've got all the same scents as that shop, except under a different name and at half the price," he assured me.

This sounded like a good deal to me! He took out a bottle of aftershave and told me to smell that as he sprayed it on me. It smelt good.

"Listen," he said. "You seem like a nice guy; I'll let you have two bottles for the price of the one you were going to buy in there. Take this one for your good lady and that one for yourself; fifteen pounds the pair to you, brother."

"That is a good deal," I thought to myself, but I tried to be a good businessman and said, "I've only got ten pounds on me."

"No, no," he said. "Are you telling me you went into that shop with only ten pounds? Get lost, I don't believe it! I know you Indian men are clever businessmen, but you're not putting one over me. Fifteen pounds or leave it."

I felt sure I could knock him down further but decided I could do without the hassle and just said, "Okay," and gave him the money.

"So where did this come from then?" he grinned.

"You Indians are clever, but I'm one step ahead." he laughed and handed me the bottles.

Then he grabbed my arm, felt my muscles, and said, "You work out, don't you?"

"Yes," I admitted. Then he told me how he wanted to start working with weights, so I told him where I trained and suggested he come along. Then, I suddenly realised I hadn't even been to the gym in months.

"This could be a way back in for me. I could take this guy along with me as a new recruit." I thought.

We agreed to meet in the New Year outside the gym.

I came home and took the bottles upstairs to my room. I left them on the bed and then ran downstairs to get some wrapping paper and a Christmas card. As I walked into the shop, my Dad said, "You left this Christmas card here earlier."

I realised, in horror, it was the one Julie had given me. I thought, "Oh shit," and quickly grabbed it from my dad, muttering thanks as I did so.

"It better not be of a girl," he said in a more serious tone.

"No, my mate Jas came in earlier and dropped it off. Do you think I would leave it there if it were from a girl?" I added, neatly getting myself out of trouble.

"It better not be," he warned again.

While he was stacking the shelves, I carried on looking for a card and spotted one saying, 'To the one I love'.

I grabbed it and quickly stuck it under my top before taking up some wrapping paper and returning to my room. I locked my door, sat on the bed, and opened the card Julie had given me. It had two bears hugging each other, and 'To a special friend' was written along the top. I looked inside, and it said, 'To my best friend in the whole world. Happy Christmas' and at the bottom, 'Love you always, Your Julie' followed by three kisses.

I took the card out from under my top and took it out of the wrapper. I sat at my table and began writing 'To my darling Julie, Happy Christmas', and at the bottom, I wrote, 'Love you always and forever, Raj'. I also put three kisses.

On the left side, I wrote a poem. I wrapped her gift with great difficulty as I had little experience in wrapping presents. Then I hid them under my duvet, where no one would notice them. I went downstairs into the living room and found my sister and my mum planning what to do tomorrow for Christmas.

Shelly was saying, "We should give all the gifts out first and then sit as a family around the table and have Christmas dinner."

"Yes, that's a good idea" agreed Grandad.

Then my aunty walked in and asked if they could join us for Christmas as her husband doesn't like celebrating it.

"He says it's an Englishman's thing, not Indian," she told us.

Shelly said we were getting together as a family and doing our own thing. At this point, my aunt got upset and stated firmly, "I am family, and as long as my mother and father are alive, no one can stop me from coming to my parent's house."

"She wasn't even saying that," insisted my mum, feeling slightly annoyed.

But then Grandad intervened, "That's enough! Don't start any trouble on special occasions like this," and told her she was welcome to come tomorrow.

Then I stated, "Well, I'm going to church in the morning." There were a few seconds of stunned silence before my grandad repeated, "Church?!"

"Yes, my mates are all going along to try and understand the real meaning of Christmas," I explained.

"So what time will that be then?" my mom asked.

"From about nine until around eleven, I think" I replied.

"Don't let him go to an English church!" my aunt blurted out. "If he starts going to church, you'll lose him forever to another religion. I've heard too many stories about how they take Indians to church and make them change their religion. Anyway, if you need to celebrate, you should go to the temple."

"So why do you celebrate Christmas?" I asked her. She didn't know what to say because she didn't even know what it was all about. I said, "Christmas is the celebration of Jesus' birthday."

"Ignore her, and you just carry on," said Grandad encouragingly and I thought "Yes! I've got Grandad on my side! He always supports me, especially when I've made him look good in the Indian community through my achievements in sport."

The next day, when I got up, I didn't know what to wear at first, but then I remembered how our customers would always be wearing suits when they came into our shop after church. My Grandad had bought me a suit for winning the championships, so I put that on, which meant the only thing I needed was a tie. I went downstairs and found my grandparents were there praying. I had to disturb them, but when my Grandad looked up, I mimed to him that I needed a tie. He pointed toward the ceiling and indicated that I could get one from his room. I ran up the stairs into my grandparent's room and was immediately hit by the smell. It smelt of the oil they wore in their hair. I opened his cupboard and went through his ties until I saw a red one, which I thought would be a good Christmas colour. I tried putting it on but couldn't get it right. I walked back down the stairs, still trying to tie my tie, but I couldn't seem to get it. Luckily, my Grandad had finished praying, so I asked if he could do it for me.

"Come here then," he said and began tying it, at the same time giving me a lecture.

"If you can't tie your tie, what are you going to do in life? Do you know? Your Dad and I have worked very hard to bring you guys to this stage. We both worked in a factory, but after we came back and had something to eat, we would work on the houses we had bought, all smashed up, and refurbished them to sell for a profit."

I looked at the clock, and it was a quarter to nine. I thought, "Get on with it, Grandad, I have to go!"

After a slight pause, he finished putting the tie on, then shook my hand and said, "Happy Christmas, Raj!"

"Happy Christmas, Grandad," I replied, "I'd better be going now."

"Have you got some money?" he asked.

When I said no, he responded, "How can you go to God's house with no money?"

I shrugged my shoulders, and he took out two ten-pound notes and gave them to me, saying, "Ten pounds for church and ten pounds for you."

I hugged him and said, "Happy Christmas" again.

I ran out of the door and down the street hoping I wasn't going to be late, but halfway there I realised I had left Julie's present! I sprinted back to my room, and as I passed through the shop, I told Dad I had left my card for the church. I ran as fast as I could to get to church on time. As I came closer to the church, my running speed was quite impressive, as I ran a mile within five minutes. I saw Julie and her mom waiting outside. Julie's mom, Mrs. White, pointed to her watch, and then she walked into the church. I ran up to Julie and gasped, "I'm sorry I'm late," but she surprised me by saying, "Wow, Raj! Don't you look smart?"

"And you look beautiful as usual," I responded, giving her the card and gift.

She grabbed my arm and said, "Thank you and Happy Christmas" before kissing me on the cheek. Every time she did that, it took me straight back to the very first time when we were about ten years old. We walked into the church, and I noticed there were people of all different origins, mainly black and white, but one Indian couple.

Julie and I walked a little way down the aisle, and I found myself imagining her walking down it to marry me! I continued picturing this for a while, even after we had taken our seats by Julie's mom, but I was soon caught up with the music and singing, which were quite loud. All the people were dancing and singing, enjoying what they were doing, and Julie joined in, too. I tried singing, too, but I was out of tune, so I resorted to humming and trying to move my body like the black guy in front of me. I watched Julie throughout the whole service. She was enjoying the singing and dancing, and it looked like her mother was also enjoying it. Julie looked beautiful in this light-yellow dress and a hat to match it. Julie's stepmom was a good lady and loved Julie very much. She never made her feel conscious of the fact that she was just her stepdaughter. I looked at the cross on the wall in front of me, and it took me back to the time I was in hospital with my broken leg at the age of nine.

Raj and Julie

One Sunday, a nurse who liked me and whom I fancied asked if I wanted to go to church and pray. I said yes. She pushed me in the wheelchair to the hospital chapel, and I sat and prayed. "Please, God, heal my leg."

My leg was fine a week later, and I was back home. There was this presence in the church, and I didn't know what it was, but it felt good. The service ended, and everyone was giving each other hugs, and shaking each other's hands, and there was a special atmosphere. Julie turned around, hugged me, and said, "God bless you, Raj."

I felt closer to her than ever and hugged her a little tighter, saying, "God bless you too, Julie."

Then, as I let go and looked into her eyes, I felt there was something else she wanted to say, but I wasn't quite sure. Then she leaned forward, shook my hand, and said, "Happy Christmas, Raj!" and gave me a lovely smile.

We both went around the church, hugging and greeting everyone. It felt so great that I didn't even think about going back home. Then Julie said, "I'm going to ask the pastor to pray for me."

"Can you just do that?" I asked, surprised.

"Of course, you can," she said. "Come up with me and see."

She went right up to the front of the church and asked, "Will you pray for me, Pastor?"

"Of course, my dear," he said. "What do you want me to pray for?"

"Can you ask God to bless me so that I pass in my college studies and also to bless my parents?" she requested. He began to pray for her, and after finishing, he looked at me.

"And what do you want praying for, Son?"

"Me?" I said, surprised.

"Yes, don't you also want to be prayed for on this special day? What do you want God to bless you with?" he replied.

I looked at Julie blankly, then back to him.

"Just to grant Julie's prayer," I suggested.

She looked at me and smiled. Then the pastor said, "That's good of you, but isn't there anything you want?"

I looked into Julie's eyes, and she looked so deeply into mine that the pastor asked, "Are you two a couple?"

Neither of us answered, so he said, "Let me pray for you."

He continued, "Father God, we praise and glorify Your Mighty Name on this glorious day you have blessed us with. I bring this young boy and the young girl before your altar and ask Lord, that you bless them with the desires of their hearts and fulfil all their needs. Bless them to do well in education, to serve their parents and to be able to understand Your Word and what you have in store for them. May they become champions in You, Mighty Lord, as You strengthen their walk with You. We ask this in your most precious name. Amen."

As he was praying, I experienced what felt like an electric current going through my body, and I fell back a bit. Julie fell back a bit or took a couple of steps back, too.

Then Pastor said, "The power of God just came over you two. You are truly blessed. Happy Christmas!" We both hugged him before walking out through the entrance. As we did, I felt a sense of relief or something as though God had blessed Julie and me to be together forever and ever.

"Did you enjoy church?" Julie asked.

"Yeah, it was something different" I replied. "Did you feel that force go through your body when the pastor prayed?"

"Yes," she laughed, "that was the power of the Holy Spirit."

"Oh. Is that a good thing?" I asked uncertainly.

"Of course," she said, "It's the power of God blessing our bodies."

'Wow!' I thought, 'that's something.'

"Is this where you are going to get married?" I asked.

"Maybe," she replied. "It depends when the right person comes into my life."

I looked at her and said, "I'm standing right here." She glanced at me and blushed.

"You're funny, Raj! I like it when you make me laugh," she said.

I said, 'I'm not trying to be funny. I'm being serious!' I love you, Julie. I love you as well, Raj. Before I could say anything else, Julie's mother walked up and asked, "Did you enjoy the service, Raj?"

"Yes, I did." I replied.

"You should try and come every week," she said before adding, "and bring Julie along with you as well."

"Anything to be with Julie," I thought and replied, "Okay, I'll see you here every Sunday."

She started talking to another lady, but Julie pulled me to one side and asked, "Are you serious? You're going to come every week?"

"Yes, if you're coming with me," I said assertively.

"No way!" she protested, "I like sleeping in and watching my favourite soaps!"

'Well, that's that idea out of the window!' I thought.

"Oh, come on, Julie," I begged.

"Let me think about it then," she said.

"I'd better go anyway," I said, "my mom and dad are probably waiting for me."

"And we don't want your aunties to cause any trouble," she said.

"No, we don't," I agreed. She hugged me, wished me Happy Christmas, and thanked me for the gift again.

"No problem, and Happy Christmas to you, too," I said and walked off feeling happy with life.

As I was walking, Julie shouted, "I meant what I said."

"Me too," I shouted.

Walking home, I walked past the library. I stood looking at the library building and thanking it for the time it allowed for Julie and me to meet there. Maybe I will buy this one day and turn it into mine and Julie's home.

Raj and Julie

When I reached home, I walked into the shop, and Dad approached me, put his hand out, and said, "Happy Christmas, Son."

"Happy Christmas, Dad," I replied, before continuing, "Guess what, Dad? In church, the Priest prayed for me, and while he was praying, God touched me, and I felt the power of God."

My Dad began to laugh and said, "Do you know how hard it is to receive the power of God? People spend years meditating in the jungle or the desert, and then they might receive the power of God."

"No, Dad, I felt it," I insisted.

"Don't be stupid, Raj, now go inside and open your presents," he said impatiently.

I walked through, wondering why he didn't believe me. Later in life, I realised that it was simply a case of wrong teaching within his religion. As I entered the living room, I found everybody there waiting to open their presents. I went around and hugged them all, wishing them Happy Christmas. We all opened up our gifts while my sister filmed it all happening.

Afterwards, my aunty, Manjit, turned up with her children and cried, "You started without us! Well, it shows how much you love us, doesn't it?" My grandad told her off, saying, "Not today, Manjit. Let's enjoy the day happily without any arguments." She pulled a face and then began giving her gifts out. Soon, we were all sitting eating Christmas dinner, once Dad had closed the shop for a few hours!

After Christmas Day, I didn't hear from Julie throughout the week, so on New Year's Eve, I told my parents I was going for a run and ran towards Julie's house. As I approached her house, I saw her hugging Shaun, and I quickly turned back. I was so upset that I sprinted back home, ran into the shed, and punched and kicked the punch bag until I could not punch and kick anymore. I was exhausted, and the only thing I could do now was to keep shouting, "How could she?"

I rested for a while and sat on my workout bench, but when I thought of Shaun hugging her, I got back up and began punching and kicking again. I hadn't bothered putting any gloves on, so as I was hitting the punch bag with full force, my knuckles eventually began bleeding. I looked at my fists and realised they were covered in blood. I went indoors and quickly washed them before my mother could notice, as she was bound to get worried and create a big drama out of it. I went through to the living room and found most of the family were sleeping or resting after having a big feast, so I went up to my bedroom and lay on the bed. Thoughts of Julie and Shaun just made me angry again, so I looked across the room and noticed my pile of muscle magazines. I picked one up, and the heading read, 'Dreams come true through bodybuilding'.

I began to think about my dream. What and who do I want to become? This question began to go through my mind over and over again.

Then I saw a vision of me standing on the stage receiving the British Power-lifting title. That was it; I was going to go back into powerlifting. I began flicking through the magazine and saw a famous bodybuilder holding gold biscuits in his hand. The statement read, 'Victory eight years in a row. I thought maybe I needed to start breaking records and win the championships year after year, like this bodybuilder. I grabbed a dumbbell, which weighed ten kilograms, off the floor and began to perform some dumbbell curls. I must have done fifty repetitions and then did the same again on the other arm. I tried to repeat this but could only manage another ten. I tried to do more, but my arms had had enough, so I stopped and stared at them. I couldn't flex my muscles as they were really tight, with the blood rushing up down my arm. I fell asleep feeling tired.

***

I feel a pain in my arm, and I wake up. I am back in the hospital room, and a doctor is pushing a needle into my arm. I look around the room and see that my mother and father are not there. Experiencing a sense of fear, I begin struggling to catch my breath. I can hear the beeping of the machine next to me getting faster and louder, and then I hear my mother asking the doctor what is wrong. Then I realize that both of my parents are standing behind the nurse, and I feel much more at ease and somewhat more secure. The beeps start slowing down, and I hear the doctor say that I have woken from my sleep and got scared for a moment. "He will be fine now; there is nothing to worry about," he assures them.

That makes me feel a lot better, and I can see the smiles on my parent's faces, too, as the doctor tells them this. After a couple of minutes, I feel pretty much back to normal – not as normal as I used to feel, but back to how I was before I went to sleep, anyway. I notice the door opening, and in comes my Uncle Daljit, who is the husband of my aunty Kuljit. He walks over and looks at me through his glasses. He has always had this look, which leaves me constantly wondering about his character. He comes across as being different in the way he speaks and acts, and in the message he gives through the lenses of his spectacles. From the time he married my aunt, I always felt something was not quite right about him.

It is a bit like seeing Superman and Clark Kent in the movies. That is probably an insult to Superman, and if Superman were here, I would apologize to him right now. It is more accurate to say he is hiding something behind those lenses that is more like Lex Luthor, the only difference being that Lex Luthor is rich.

In my uncle's case, it is the opposite, as was revealed a couple of years after his marriage to Aunt Kuljit. When she was forced into this arranged marriage, we were all under the impression that Uncle Daljit's family was wealthy and owned several successful businesses.

***

Daljit was supposedly operating one of these, but we later found that all of the family businesses were suffering such severe financial losses that one had already been lost to a bank. The others were soon to follow. It was realised too late that the only reason the matchmakers introduced Daljit's family to my Grandad was so they could screw him to pay off their debts.

At this time, Grandad was a very successful property developer. I heard that they tried selling him a piece of land in India, and he agreed, paying a deposit of eighty thousand pounds.

A week later, Grandad's assistant in India, who dealt with his property business over there, found a buyer who should have guaranteed double the amount of profit.

But before the paperwork was completed, they pulled out of the deal and stated they did not want to sell the land. Grandad had given them the money in good faith, but not going through the proper legal process meant he lost the lot. He was left in a very awkward position as this was his daughter's in-laws.

Flashback to when my grandfather's older son-in-law did the same. His third son-in-law did him over too financially. There was no third-time lucky here; this time, it was a bit more serious.

When my Aunt demanded that Grandad should be paid the money back, a series of arguments also brought out the truth of Daljit having an affair as well. All of his family knew about this but fully supported him.

As I said, I always knew that Uncle Daljit was hiding something behind his glasses!

I guess I first realised it when Uncle Daljit and Aunt Kuljit visited us one weekend. This was quite some time after that nightmare New Year's Eve experience. I was discussing my University course when Daljit decided to put me on the spot by asking questions that I couldn't answer.

He was a guy who thought he knew it all but had never done anything in practice. It was all 'bullshit'. The confusing thing was that the last time he had come over, he had been quite encouraging. But later, I found out that he never genuinely cared but was just doing it to get a buzz when he subsequently embarrassed me in front of the family. But although he made me look pretty stupid, the only thing I heard Aunt Kuljit say was, "You're just clumsy; you can't go to University because you'll fail."

She turned to my Dad and said, "Don't send him to University; it will just be a waste of three years. I suggest you stick him in the shop where he will be more useful. It's true what Father said: He's a donkey and only fit for lifting weights. He can lift stock and stack it on the shelves."

I looked at Dad for some support, but he still has a weakness for his sisters and merely said, "If he fails, I'll throw him out, and he can work in a factory."

I felt hurt at the time, although in reality, he had only said it to shut up his sister.

Shelly walked into the room and said, "Raj, your friend Julie is in the shop and asking if she can see you."

Feeling too hurt to consider the consequences of my actions properly, I leapt to my feet and hurried to the shop. Seeing Julie made me feel a bit happier, but I was still hurting inside. I also forgot that I had been avoiding Julie for the past few months.

79

As I walked toward her, she stuck out a hand for me to shake, and I obliged.

"Hi, Raj," she said.

"Hi, Julie" I replied.

"I haven't seen you for ages" she declared. "I've been coming in regularly, hoping I would bump into you. I didn't even see you on the last day of college."

I didn't feel capable of talking at this point and said quietly, "Look, it's a bad time to talk. Can I try and meet you tomorrow?"

I looked into her eyes and saw they were filling with water. I didn't know what to do. This was definitely not my day.

To make matters even worse, my Aunty Kuljit was listening behind me and said loudly, "You know he's not supposed to have a girlfriend."

"Girlfriend?" repeated Julie, "I'm not his girlfriend. Friend, yes, but not girlfriend."

I looked at Julie, trying to give her the signal to leave. But then my dad walked in.

"What's going on?" he demanded.

Kuljit answered quickly, saying, "I've caught him talking to his girlfriend." I turned around and said, "She's my friend; you know Julie." But Dad slapped the back of my head, which was embarrassing and said angrily, "What did I tell you about having girlfriends?"

"But Mr. Singh," Julie cried, "I'm not his girlfriend. I have a different boyfriend, and his name is Shaun."

This only served to compound my misery further, and I remembered why I had been avoiding her. But my Dad carried on.

"He can't have girlfriends; it's not part of our culture, and he will be marrying an Indian girl," he thundered.

Then Kuljit shouted out, "He's not going to marry any white trash."

Now I was super angry and ashamed. I couldn't believe they would say this. I shouted "No!!! Don't say that, you fucking bitch" to my aunty. Defending Julie. My dad slaps me across the face. Poor Julie burst into tears and rushed out of the shop, but I launched into a full-blown row with my aunt. Of course, Dad took Kuljit's side and insisted, "If she weren't your girlfriend, you wouldn't be defending her and speaking against your own family."

"She's just my friend," I shouted, thinking how this had to be the worst moment of my life. But suddenly, it deteriorated further as Aunty Manjit walked into the shop and joined the argument. You would think my father and his sisters really didn't care about the business, for there were several customers in the shop.

"White girls only use Indians for their money," stated Manjit, "she's going to ruin this family."

"Nothing is going on!" I yelled, and my Dad slapped me again before shouting angrily, "I don't want you talking to that white bitch again."

I could not believe what my Dad had said. My Aunts had put so much shit in his head about this that he had come out with that language and those comments about Julie. I stormed into the back of the shop but still heard my Aunty saying, "Don't send him to University because he'll end up with that girl, and then he'll leave home."

"Of course; that was it," I thought to myself.

All this fighting had come about because they were jealous of me going to university. It would be a long, long time before I was to see Julie again, but now I was not allowed to go to university.

Chapter Fifteen

I received a letter in the post. This was exciting, as I never received any letters! I looked at it and found that it was from UCAS, the University processing department. I got nervous, and I was afraid to open it, but I did a quick prayer and opened it. My eyes were shut tight, nervous about seeing the words 'University positions declined'.

To my relief, however, I opened my eyes, and I saw 'accepted in all chosen Universities'.

"Yes!" I shouted as I realised that the two Universities that Julie had also applied to had accepted me.

I got my letter of acceptance from the University of Wolverhampton. I was excited and wanted to rush out and tell Julie. As I began to step out the front door, I remembered how she was treated, so I stopped, went back in, and told my mother.

"Look, Mum, I've got accepted into University!" I beamed.

She was very happy and grabbed the letter before praying and bowing to a picture. I never understood why my parents did this, as I don't think God lives in picture frames! Anyway, she looked at the letter and said, "Well done, I'm very proud," before kissing me on the head.

Then my Dad walked through the door, shouting for my Mother to come and stand in the shop as he had to go to the cash and carry. He stood halfway through the door (which was the gateway between the shop and the house) and wondered why my Mother was looking so happy.

"Raj has got accepted into University!" she replied joyfully. My father said, "Well done, son," and put his hand out to shake. I shook his hand.

I wanted a hug but felt that he would think I was too feminine. I ran upstairs to my grandfather's room and found him deciding on which suit jacket to wear. He did this quite often - changing his suit jackets and sometimes the whole suit, although we never found out why.

As kids, we would mimic him! He would stare in the mirror admiring himself, combing his hair over and repeatedly until he got it perfect. He would also check his teeth and stare in the mirror for minutes as I grew older and wiser, though I realised that he was encouraging and motivating himself for the day.

I read many times that all successful businessmen did this around the world, and maybe this is why he was a successful property developer.

"I've been accepted into University!" I smiled at him.

"Great!" he shouted joyfully, much like when his favourite football team scored a goal.

"I am very proud of you, son," he continued. "You will make my dreams come true. I will tell all my family in India that my grandson will be joining them soon!"

I just shook his hand and thought not to say anything yet. On my first day at University, I was nervous. I usually had Julie with me, but this time, I was on my own. I was hoping to bump into her on my first day as I had not seen her in a while.

I walked into the University building, and my heart began to beat very quickly. It was the look and the smell that hit me – a similar feeling that you have when you visit the hospital or dentist. I walked for what seemed like ages, not knowing where to go, so I decided to follow a group of people, and luckily, I ended up at the right place. I walked to the desk. "What's your last name?" the lady asked.

I answered, "Singh."

"That's going to be a challenge as there are a lot of Singh's!" she replied.

After she had got my date of birth, however, she found me on the system. She told me the theatre room number and instructed me on how to get to the room. I walked out of the main hall and tried to find my room, but unfortunately, I couldn't find it. After asking again, finally, I found it. Outside, I took a deep breath and opened the door. I entered and found the theatre room full of students – there must have been about one hundred and fifty to two hundred students.

"Another one to join the group; find a seat!" the lecturer shouted as he saw me enter.

I looked around and found a seat. To my right, there was a good-looking black girl (Afro-Caribbean).

I said, "Sawhi," and she replied hello and laughed.

I then looked to my left and found a South Asian girl smiling at me in a way that suggested she liked me. I smiled back and quickly looked away. She was good-looking, but the way she looked at me was a bit weird! The lecturer started talking to the whole group about the course and the modules we had to pick.

At the end of the session, the lecturer said, "Look around, and you will see ninety-five per cent of these people in almost the same subjects for the next three years, so I suggest you make friends and get to know each other. You are more likely to stay friends even after university as well!"

I looked around and only saw the two attractive girls sitting beside me. The black girl put her hand out and said, "I'm Samantha."

I shook her hand and said, "I'm Raj."

We began to talk before the Indian girl next to me interrupted us. "I'm Sonam, and you guys are?"

We both told her our names, and we all began to talk. Then we found another Indian girl walking up to us, who said, "Hi, I'm Harj. Is it okay if I join you guys?"

We said it was fine and got talking when suddenly I felt this heavy hand on my shoulder. I looked around and saw a huge black guy with an earring in between his nostrils.

"I'm Teddy," he said. "Can I join you guys as well?"

We all said yes, so we set about introducing ourselves all over again. We walked out of the lecture theatre, headed towards the canteen, sat around the same table, and exchanged phone numbers. Towards the end of the week, Samantha, Sonam, Teddy, Harj, and I became good friends and decided to do all group tasks together, and over the next few weeks, we all had good fun.

Months went by, and one day, I was sitting in the canteen with Sonam and Teddy, eating our lunch. Suddenly, I felt a hand on my lap. I looked up and found Teddy smiling at me. He was chewing a sandwich, and pieces of bread were coming out of his mouth while he was smiling. His smile began to freak me out. I looked around – only to see students eating their lunch, people queuing up for their lunch, chatting amongst each other, and a couple sitting at the corner table looking into each other's eyes. The canteen was very loud, and everyone was occupied with what they were doing. I began to break out into a sweat, but then I saw his other hand on the table, which was a relief. I then looked over my other side at Sonam and found her smiling and looking at me in the corner of her eye.

At first, it was a relief that it wasn't Teddy, but then I thought, "Sonam? Why Sonam?"

I had certainly never looked at her in that way before.

I smiled back because I didn't know how to react. Luckily, at that moment, Harj walked in, and as she smiled and said hello, I felt the hand move away from my leg.

"Check this out, guys!" Harj said excitedly.

"What is it?" asked Sonam.

"There's a gig next week, and it has a major lineup with all the Bhangra bands!" she replied. "What do you say, guys? Are you up for it?"

"Yeah, I'm up for it," said Teddy.

"You want to come to a Bhangra gig?" I asked.

"Yeah, what's wrong with that?"

"Nothing, I just thought you wouldn't understand the songs."

"It's music, isn't it? We blacks can dance to any kind of music – we have the rhythm in us!" he smiled.

"True!" said Sonam, "look at MJ!" to which we all laughed.

"Well, you rock the floor then, mate!" I said to Teddy before we high-fived each other.

The following week, we are all at the daytime gig. To Teddy's shock, he wasn't the only black guy in the club. He was a bit upset as he wanted the limelight.

"Get over it, man. I don't think any girl will throw themselves at you with that crazy ring you have in your nose!" I tell him.

"Get lost, Raj. Watch! I'll show you that I'll be going out of here with at least three girls!" he laughed.

"Dream on, mate!"

We walked around the club and then met up with Harj and Sonam before buying drinks and moving onto the dance floor. The gig was hilarious as

Teddy was trying to dance in a Bhangra style. He could not get the moves right and looked funny. Whilst we were dancing, I felt someone pinch my behind. I looked around, and it was Sonam. I smiled, and she began dancing with me as the Band sang their slow love song. Sonam came closer to me, hugged me, and began to dance romantically, so I hugged her back whilst going with the flow. I looked over to Teddy and found him chasing Harj for a dance with his arms stuck out, but Harj dodged, and she ran away from him.

We then danced from one song to another until Harj and Teddy came over to us.

"That's enough, let's go," they said.

As we walked out, Sonam grabbed my hand, moved closer to me, and hugged my arm. I looked at her and smiled. As we exited the building, Harj spotted a guy she knew and shouted to him before running over. After a while, she returned. "I've got my life sorted. See you guys tomorrow!" she beamed before running off again.

"Looks like we are catching the bus!" I said.

Teddy looked at Sonam and me and said you're in their mate with his eyes. "You two hooked up early; make sure you don't let it mess with our group work," he said in a light-heartedly accusing manner. I smiled at Sonam and saw her looking up at me with her big eyes.

"No," I said before taking her off my arm. "let's catch that bus," I continued.

There was a long queue at the bus stop. Possibly, most of the guys from the gig were standing there. Most of them were looking at their watches, probably because they needed to get back home in time. Come to think about it today, most of the band performers were our parent's age, and they performed at daytime gigs. They must have known they were dragging out kids from schools and colleges from their studies to promote their albums and to make money.

Teddy, Sonam, and I got on the bus. Teddy fell asleep, with Sonam and I sitting behind him. Sonam went to grab my arm again, and as I turned to look at her, she looked at me and gave me that smile again. I grabbed her hand and moved it away from my arm. She looked at me, and for one moment, I thought she was going to cry. It was time to talk to her.

"Listen, Sonam, I'm not interested in you in that way. Don't take it the wrong way, but I only see you as a friend," I firmly stated.

"I thought we could be just more than good friends?"

"No, we can't. I'm sorry."

"Raj, I need someone in my life. You're big, muscular, strong, and a good listener. You can protect me."

"Protect you from what?" I asked.

"From my brother" she replied.

"And why should I protect you from your brother?"

"He beats me up and makes me do things I don't want to do."

"I'm sorry, I can't protect you from him. I can have a word with him, but you need to talk to your parents."

"They won't listen to me! You know how strict South Asian families are, and they are too embarrassed to bring the subject up with anyone."

"Well, I think you should go to the police. There's no other option." I replied. "Listen, if you need us to come with you to the police station, we can do that."

At this point, Teddy cleared his throat. So much for him being asleep.

We came to the main bus stop, where we were due to take our separate buses home. However, Teddy remained on the bus as that was the bus that would take him to his house. Sonam and I got off, but as we were, Sonam touched my arm and whispered in my ear.

"Don't hug me or stand too close to me, as someone might know me," she warned.

"So what are you going to do about your brother?" I asked, whilst looking straight.

"I don't know; I'll have to think about it or even talk to someone about it." She looked at me from the corners of her eyes and smiled before walking forward and boarding her bus that had just pulled up. I watched her get on and stand on the bus – it looked like there were no seats to sit on. She looked at me and smiled faintly as the bus drove off.

As I waited for my bus, I took a moment to look around and watch others waiting for their buses, and I began to think about how many people rely on buses. Would there be a time when there would be other types of transport which would carry passengers? This was my business studies mind thinking at the time - it happens when you study business! It was cold, and I couldn't wait for the bus to come quickly. Luckily, just then, the bus arrived. I got on with a struggle, due to other people rushing to get on at the same time. I decided to walk up the stairs and managed to get a window seat before a guy sat next to me and rudely pushed me into the corner of my seat.

"Isn't it freezing cold, mate!" he piped up.

I nodded. "Just a bit" I replied.

"I hate waiting for the bus, especially if it comes late. And that's guaranteed to happen every damn day," he remarked.

I decided to humour him and nodded my head, stating how disgusting I thought it was.

"I'm a car mechanic, and I have to catch two buses to get to work. Working under cars in the cold and then waiting for the bus in this cold weather really pisses you off."

"You work for a garage, and you don't have a car?" I thought to myself.

All the way until he got off, I had to listen to him moaning! It was a relief when he got off. I sat back and relaxed, thinking back about the day at the gig – how Teddy was chasing Indian girls around the club, and they were ducking and diving away from him! Then I thought of what Sonam told me. Before I could think anymore, however, the bus had stopped. I looked outside and saw a blonde-haired lady, who I was sure was Julie. Admittedly,

Raj and Julie

I only saw the side and the back of her, but it felt like it was her. I looked over the stairs bar, hoping she would come up the stairs, and to my pleasant surprise, she did. I could see more of her face, and I couldn't quite believe it - this lady was the spitting image of Julie. She walked toward me, and I looked away, nervous about her thinking I was drooling over her. She sat down next to me, making me feel incredibly nervous even though it wasn't Julie.

As she sat down, I looked at her, and she smiled. It was the same smile as Julie's! I smiled back. Her perfume smelled beautiful, and as I tried to think of its name, it reminded me of Julie's perfume. It had to be the same one. My stop arrived, and predictably enough, this girl got up to get off at the same time.

"Is this Julie?" I kept on thinking.

As we began to walk away from the bus stop, she looked at me and smiled.

"Bye," she said sweetly.

I smiled back, wondering if we had just had a conversation on the way and I had somehow missed it! I crossed the road and walked towards home, all the time watching her walk in the same direction Julie would walk home. That night at the gym, while I was training, I kept thinking of this lady smiling and saying bye. Because she looked like Julie, I began to miss Julie and wanted to tell her all about University and hear how she was doing too.

The next day, back at the University, Samantha, Teddy, Harj, and I were sitting at the canteen table having lunch. A couple of South Asian students were sitting at the next table, making a bit of noise.

One guy was wearing a white shirt, and black trousers, although that's what he seemed to wear every day. He was clean-shaven, about five foot ten, and had a scruffy hairstyle. The other guy was about six feet tall, wore glasses, and was very fair-skinned. The third guy was about six feet tall, had a moustache, and was always dressed trendily. I remember seeing him in the car park a few times, parking his sports car. He always seemed to be wearing a black sports biker's jacket.

"What's all the excitement about guys?" Samantha shouted over.

"Nothing, we are just talking about cricket," replied the one in the white shirt.

"What's your name?" she asked.

"My name? Oh, it's Ahmed," he replied nervously.

"My name is Khalid," said the guy wearing the glasses.

"Saeed," said the guy in the biker jacket.

"I don't believe you don't know our names, as we are on the same course and in the same classes as you!" replied Ahmed.

"Well, honey, I don't go to my lessons hoping to take down notes of names!" Samantha retorted.

He began to laugh. "I didn't mean it like that, sorry" Ahmed smiled.

"I bet you don't know our names!" enquired Harj.

"Of course we do," he replied. "you're Harj, she's Samantha, that's Teddy, and this big muscular guy is Raj. See, we memorise names as well as the class notes!" He said cheekily.

"Well, I don't need to memorise any names," Samantha said before getting up to take her tray to the tray rack.

"I'm not causing any trouble, just having fun," Ahmed said.

I have to say, Samantha was a very attractive lady. She dressed quite trendily for a mature student and had a cool, different hairstyle every week. This was probably because her parents were both hairdressers. The only funny thing about her was that she would wear short tops, which made her side love handles stick out.

"I could do with a fag now," she replied, having returned to the table.

"We're going for a fag," said Ahmed, "come with us."

"Can I ask a question? Every time I leave the building, I always find you guys smoking. You guys smoke a lot," said Harj. "Why is that?"

"We are in the fasting period, the build-up to Eid, and it's hard to stay without food. So, we use smoke to kill the hunger." Ahmed replied.

"Doesn't that defeat the object?" asked Harj.

"What can we do?" responded Khalid.

"We'll die if we couldn't smoke!" Saeed chipped in.

"Come on then, let's go and have a smoke," Samantha replied.

"Samantha, what did I say about smoking?" I said.

"Oh, shut up, Raj!" Samantha said, whilst laughing. She left the canteen with the three guys. She knew what I was on about.

"Well, we haven't got any lessons this afternoon, so I'm going home," said Harj.

"Yeah, I'm going to leave too," said Teddy.

"Well, I better go as well if all you guys are going," I replied.

A few weeks passed, and we found that Sonam had not returned to university. We all tried to make contact with her but failed. So, the last time I saw her leave on the bus a few weeks beforehand was the last time I saw her. I thought I saw her once in a clothes shop a few years later, but I couldn't determine if it was her. This person did see me looking at her but avoided me in such a way that made it clear she didn't want to be stopped to talk. That was the last time I saw her if it was indeed her.

We were one person short in our group. We struggled with the workload for over a month until we had the opportunity for another female to join our group. This girl was very bright and wanted to leave her last group as she found them not pulling their weight fast enough when it came to group projects. Her name was Jaspreet, and she was very attractive. She was from an Indian Punjabi ethnic background, but weirdly enough, she also had blonde hair – not blonde streaks like mine but all blonde, and to top that, she also wore blue contact lenses! She didn't look Indian at all, as she was very fair-skinned and looked more like an English woman. A lot of the guys referred to her as 'Blondie'. Jaspreet and our group hit it off very well, and as the days went by, it was soon a week before Christmas. It was Monday afternoon, and we were all sitting waiting for a lecturer to teach us economics. I loved this subject as I understood that it helped to explain economics, how economies work, and how economic analysis is applied throughout society, business, finance, and governments. Teddy and I were sitting together when Jaspreet walked in. As she walked past Ahmed, Khalid, and Saeed, they began to whistle and say, "Blondie."

"Grow up!" she snarled.

"Whoooo!" they jeered back at her.

Jaspreet found a seat next to Harj and sat down.

"Those idiots should grow up; they do this every time they see me."

"They need someone to give them a good beating!" said Harj.

The three guys carried on whistling and making remarks at Jaspreet, so I got up and walked over to them.

"What's the problem, guys?"

I saw a fear in their eyes – after all, I was standing there with my big muscles!

"What? We're not saying anything to you," answered Ahmed.

"Well, if you did, I would have broken your arm by now!" I replied confidently. Suddenly, I felt like Arnold Schwarzenegger or even Ranbir Singh from Indian films! "Listen, leave Jaspreet alone," I concluded.

"What are you going to do?" said Khalid.

"You guys want to know? Come outside - I'll give all three of you a good beating," I snarled.

"We don't want to fight," Khalid replied.

"Well, leave her alone then," I threatened.

Suddenly, a loud voice boomed from the other side of the room. "No one's going to be heroes in here!" It was Mr. Tall, our lecturer.

"Sit back down in your seat, Raj!" he told me.

Then, to make the embarrassment worse, Samantha began to laugh loudly and shouted, "Hero."

I sit back in my chair to hear Jaspreet whispering, "Thank you," at me and smiling. I looked back and smiled. Mr Tall was a West Indian man who then decided to speak about how he understood Indian culture because he was married to an Indian Sikh lady.

"I have taught and come across a lot of Indian guys who try to act the hero to impress the Indian girls!" he said.

The thing was, I wasn't trying to impress her, just to help her out. He then went on to talk about how Indian kids should act. The funny thing was that this guy wasn't even an Indian, and he was trying to teach us about Indian culture only because he was married to an Indian. I don't think the non-Indians and Pakistanis liked that guy as he went on about Indian cultures, even though there were only about ten non-Asians in the group and about fifty or sixty Asians.

After the lecture ended and as we walked out, some of my classmates approached me, saying, "Well done" and "Good, they needed telling off." I stood outside until the three guys in question walked out to show them I wasn't scared of them.

"So, what are you guys saying?" I asked.

"Na man, we don't want any trouble," said Ahmed, and he stuck out his hand to shake.

"Go on, shake his hand!" said Samantha.

I looked at Samantha. "You're only thinking of your free cigarettes," I thought to myself, yet I did proceed to shake hands with them. The good thing after that day was that the students in my class liked me more, and even the three guys gave me respect. However, I began to notice that Jaspreet became friendlier and clingier. She was also more open about her life and didn't speak too much about the subjects we studied. We learned from her that she wanted to live in Canada, where her sister lived.

A day before we broke for the Christmas holidays, we all went across to the pub, where we all celebrated achieving good grades. We all were having a great laugh, and even Jaspreet was having a drink. We played pool and darts – the challenging part was that we tried playing darts left-handed as we were all right-handed. Teddy walked over to the jukebox, put in a coin, and chose a soundtrack. The music began, and he walked over to Samantha, grabbed her hand, and pulled her to the dance floor. She laughed out loud, and they began to dance to the song 'Bump and Grind' by R Kelly. Watching them dance was really fun, and they acted in the dance moves very well. Teddy danced behind Samantha, holding her waist as she squatted down and back up, rubbing her behind against Teddy's legs. Then Harj and Jaspreet got up and began to dance, copying Samantha and Teddy. It was really funny.

Then the next song came on, and it was 'Baby I Love Your Way by Big Mountain. Harj grabbed me to the dance floor, and we all began to dance a reggae style. Most of the time, we copied Samantha, which was really funny. Then it was 'Oh Carolina' by Shaggy, and it was so funny as we performed the moves. Other students in the bar cheered us and clapped along to the song. Other students joined in, and the dance area became quite full. As we were all dancing and having a great laugh, Jaspreet moved closer to me. Just then, the song 'Save The Best For Last by Vanessa Williams came on. Jaspreet hugged me, and we began to dance to the soft, slow love song. As the song changed from that one to Mariah Carey's 'Vision of Love, ' Jaspreet's hug got tighter, and then I looked into her eyes. Even though she wore blue contact lenses, they reminded me of Julie. All through the romantic songs, I imagined singing and dancing the songs with Julie, yet as the song 'I Swear' began, Jaspreet and I began to kiss. The kiss lasted throughout the song until Harj pulled me away.

"What you guys doing?" she asked us.

Jaspreet and I looked at each other and laughed. We all walked out of the pub and headed towards the bus stop, Jaspreet holding my arm while we walked. I didn't say anything about kissing, and I didn't know where to take it from there. As we got to the bus stop, we stopped, looked at each other, and smiled. She kissed me on the lips and said, "See you after Christmas!" At that point, her bus arrived. Once onboard, she waved goodbye back at me whilst smiling, and I stood and smiled back.

I walked across the road as I could see my bus coming. Thinking of what had just happened, I walked out into the road without looking, when suddenly I heard a loud horn sound. I looked around to see a car heading toward me. I stupidly stood still, staring, causing the car to brake sharply and stop about two inches away from me. The driver got out of his car, swearing.

"Have you got a death wish?" he screamed.

"I'm sorry!" I shouted and ran across the road to get on the bus.

The bus driver was a Sikh Indian, as he was wearing a turban.

"Are you stupid?!" he screamed.

I looked back at him, shook my head, and walked up the stairs. I was shaken up, and my heart was still beating fast. I looked around the bus, and even people stared at me! I closed my eyes and saw myself kissing Jaspreet, which slowed my heartbeat down. However, the vision then changed to the car almost hitting me. I opened my eyes with a cold sweat across my forehead. This made me think that Jaspreet and I were not meant to be together and that the kiss was a build-up of my thoughts of being with Julie.

That night, I got myself into the gym and trained hard. Later, back home from the gym, I was exhausted, so I decided to take a shower before sitting on my bed. I looked up at the ceiling, contemplating the day that had occurred. Then I heard my mother calling me to have something to eat. I looked at my clock, and it was after ten. Come to think of it now, our tea or last meal was cooked after nine o'clock, due to the shop's hours. I forced myself up and staggered downstairs. My father was sitting at the table while my mother was running in and out, placing food on the table. This was my mother's routine day in and day out. She would wake up and make breakfast for everyone, then go and stand in the shop while my father went and looked after the other shops and work required for their property portfolio. Then, at around eleven, she would ask my grandma to watch over the shop whilst she cooked lunch. She was like a yoyo because she had to leave the kitchen when a customer came in. Then, my father would come back around six or seven and take over the shop while my mother began to sow clothes; she had to make food for family and relatives, so the day was nonstop for her.

I began to eat, but I was too tired even to lift the chapatti from the plate. My father looked across at me.

"It looks like you are draining yourself out with all training," he said. "Why don't you take a break from weightlifting and concentrate on your education? You have all your life to lift weights after you have completed your degree."

"I know, Dad," I replied, "But I want the British title as well, and in two months, I get to compete in the all-counties championships and get to qualify for the British."

"I know you are strong, but the other guys are really strong, and they have been training for years. You have not been doing it that long."

"I have! I've been training for almost six years. That is a long time, and many of the guys who have been training for almost twenty years can't lift the same weight I can!"

"Okay, fine, just take it easy and concentrate on your studies, is all I'm saying. You know, when I came to this country, I wanted to study, but due to financial situations, I had to work.

"I know that Dad, but you guys haven't done badly for yourself. Most people say you own our small town. Look at all the other successful businesspeople who never went to school and are successful. Look at Richard Branson; I've been studying him at University!"

"Calm down, stop dreaming, and come down to reality! Doesn't matter how rich you are, you only eat three meals a day, no more than that!" With that, my Dad finished eating and left to watch his Indian channel. I went back upstairs to my room, thinking that if I could concentrate hard, I could conquer both areas.

The next day, I spent time working on my assignments, breaking up the monotony with a walk. I walked past Julie's house, hoping to see her, but I never did. This happened almost every day, as the holidays consisted of completing assignments, training, and walking past Julie's house. A couple of days before Christmas, I thought I should buy Julie some perfume. I bought the fragrance from Winston at the gym but didn't know how to give it to her. I wrapped the present and wrote out the card sitting in my room. Would I be able to give this to Julie on Christmas Day? Whilst I was pondering this, I heard some music being played downstairs. It was my Grandad flicking through the television channels. He flicked on to the 'Songs of Praise' channels, and I heard a choir singing.

"That's it!" I thought. "I can give this to her at church; I'll make sure I'm there on Christmas Day... or should I post her the card and gift and go to church and wait for the response?" I decided to spend some time thinking about my decision.

On Christmas Eve, I walked out of the shop with the gift and headed toward Julie's house. My heart suddenly dropped, however, as I saw Uncle Ramdass and Aunty Manjit walking toward me.

"What do you have there?" my Aunty demanded.

At this point, I didn't care or fear what they thought. It had gone on too long, and my weight training had built confidence in me.

"It's a gift for my girlfriend" I replied.

"Girlfriend?!" Aunty shouted. "Does your father know?!"

"Yes, he told me to go and give her a gift," I calmly answered.

"I don't believe you. I will go and ask him right now!" she snarled.

She stomped off, causing Uncle Ramdass to pipe up, "Has your girlfriend got a good-looking mother for me?"

"You're just a dirty old man!" I replied, to which he laughed and walked off.

I decided to run towards Julie's house before my Dad called me back. There was no sign of her, so I quickly posted her gift and card and ran back home. I stepped back into the shop, knowing that my Aunty had probably stirred some trouble.

"Which girlfriend did you give a present to?" my Dad asked.

I decided to play it cool, not wanting my aunt to win again.

"You know, Dad, the one I introduced you to yesterday!"

He looked at me funnily. "What are you talking about? That one with a good-looking mother?"

"I thought so!" laughed Ramdass, "father and son going out with mother and daughter!"

I looked at my father as if to say, "Work along with me here," and funnily enough, he did.

"Oh, yes, Shirley or Helen?" he said.

"Helen and Shirley?" I queried.

"Yes, Helen, the daughter, and her mother, Shirley!" he continued.

"What are you talking about? This is disgusting?!" said Aunty Manjit before walking into the back as my uncle also walked out for a cigarette.

"What was all that about?!" asked Dad.

"Nothing, Dad," I replied, "I was just taking chocolates to the Chinese takeaway for Christmas when I bumped into them, and I knew they would make a story from it. So, I told them that the box of chocolates was for my girlfriend!"

Dad began to laugh and carried on serving the customers. I had got out of a tight spot there!

Chapter Sixteen

Christmas morning arrived, and I woke up and got ready in a new suit my grandad bought for me from India. It was dark blue velvet; I saw Lenny Henry wear one similar on Children in Need once! So, I had my grandad make two similar ones for me in India, which were a lot cheaper than what the celebrities paid for. I walked down the stairs and saw my grandad praying again. He looked at me and said, "Don't you look handsome? That suit looks nice!"

"Thanks, Grandad!" I replied.

"Where are you going?" he asked me.

"To church, as it's Christmas," I replied.

"That's good. It's not wrong to go to God's house, but I hope we don't lose you to the church?" he asked, "don't forget you are a Sikh."

"Okay, Grandad, I had better get going!" I said.

"Aren't you forgetting something?" he asked.

"What's that?" I answered, at which point he stretched out his hand to shake.

"Happy Christmas, Raj!"

"Oh, Happy Christmas," I said, and as I went to hug him, I found he had placed a £20 note in my hand.

"What's this?" I asked.

"Put it in the church basket," he smiled.

"Thanks, Grandad," I smiled and gave him another hug.

I walked down the street feeling like a star in the suit I was wearing. Even two Afro-Caribbean girls who walked past me complimented me on it - this was a good sign! I walked into the church and sat down, looking around for Julie and her mother, but I couldn't see them. The congregation all stood to sing. I tried to sing the songs, but for some reason, the songs came out in an Indian filmy song style! I carried on singing as I thought I could be the first to do this - I was singing a gospel song in a tone and style that a Bollywood singer would sing. The offering basket came around, and I put the money my Grandad gave me in the basket, with still no sign of Julie. At that moment, the pastor came up to me and hugged me.

"Happy Christmas, my son," he said, "Aren't you the young man who came last year with Julie?"

"Yes, that's me!" I replied, "But I can't see them today?"

"Didn't they tell you? They are spending Christmas at Julie's uncles in Wales." No, I haven't seen them in weeks or months. I'm sure you will when they return. Have a blessed day, son." he said

I walked back home feeling down and upset. I remembered Julie saying her mother had three brothers; one lived in Wales, one in Scotland, and the other in New Zealand. I walked into the shop and then into the house and found my aunties and uncles had arrived. After a snide comment of "Here comes the Christian!" from Aunty Manjit, we settled down for a family day together. This whole day was all about eating, dancing, and singing. The house was full as my father invited a couple of his customer friends and families. Luckily, my Grandad, being from a builder's background, had extended the house as far back as he could, as we had a sizable garden. We had a lot of space.

As we were dancing, my dad began to dance. This was the only time I think he got to enjoy himself. Then one of his English lady friends joined him and tried to copy his Bhangra dance moves! As this was happening, I saw Uncle Ramdass nudging Aunty Manjit, making her see what her brother was doing and trying to influence her thinking. She looked at my Dad with disgust, and soon after, there was a story rumoured that my Dad was supposed to be having an affair with this lady. But this was cleared when she and her husband were asked to stop coming to the shop. We finally found out that it was indeed Aunty Manjit and Uncle Ramdass who had begun the rumour. Unfortunately, my father lost customers because of it, but then again, come to think of it, I think that lady did fancy my father as she used to stand by the counter for at least four hours a day talking about anything and everything to him!

It was time to go back to University, and I had not seen Julie over the holidays. I looked at my calendar and thought maybe my next chance would be the Easter holidays instead. It had been a very busy two weeks back at University, doing nothing but assignments and weight training. I walked into the University lecture room and sat down, feeling good that I had completed all my assignments, especially my sales assignments. As I was sitting at the desk and others were walking in, Samantha came by, gave me a high five, and sat next to me. I poked her flab sticking out of her top, and she screamed, laughing, causing everyone to look at us. At this moment, Jaspreet came in and walked up to us, saying hello.

"Can we talk after the lesson, Raj?" she asked.

"Of course we can!" I replied.

She sat in her seat as I went into thought, wondering how I could forget what happened before Christmas. We met up after our lesson and walked along the corridor in a weird, uncomfortable silence. It was only when we had walked out of the building that we began to talk.

"So, how was your Christmas?" I asked.

"Fine, thanks. We don't celebrate as much, as my father is strong in his Sikh faith and believes we should only celebrate our religious days, she replied.

"Oh, that's weird. My family are Sikhs, and they don't think like that. They believe that we should respect all religions, and I am sure that is part of our religious teaching.

"I don't want to get into that; I had that all over the holidays!" she said. "Anyway, the thing I wanted to talk to you was about us."

"Us?"

"Well, I like you, but we can't carry on with what we started before Christmas. Listen, over the Christmas holidays, we had my sister, her husband, and their friends over from Canada. My sister introduced me to her husband's best friend, and they wanted me to marry him. I like this guy, and it has been my dream to move to Canada near my sister. So, what I am trying to say is that we can't date or anything; I'm sorry."

I looked at her. She was very good-looking, and I was disappointed that another girl had slipped out of my hands.

"Well, what do you think, Raj? You are quiet about this!"

"No, that's fine. If you are happy with the move to Canada and it's your dream, then hey, who am I to say anything? Plus, I didn't know where we were anyway as we only kissed, which was what... two weeks ago? Hey, you could have been drunk." I replied.

"No, don't be silly. I do like you, but I think if I let this opportunity go, I'll never get it again. Plus, it will make my parents happy."

I looked into her blue eyes and took a deep breath.

"I'll move to Canada with you."

"What Raj?!"

"Marry me, and I'll move with you."

She looked at me in a state of shock. Gobsmacked and speechless, she began to stutter and had trouble getting her words out.

"Well... if you are willing to move to Canada, that's fine by me!" she stuttered.

I moved closer to her, looked into her eyes, and saw confusion. Then I looked at her lips and saw her biting her bottom lip, and her breathing was faster than normal. I opened my mouth to speak, but at that moment, she leaned forward to kiss me.

"Woah, I'm only joking!" I admitted, laughing. She punched me in the arm.

"You twat!" she exclaimed.

"Listen, you clearly like this guy, and Canada is just the bonus. Come on, I wouldn't come in between you guys - I know what it is like to love someone." I replied.

"Are you in love with someone else?" Jaspreet asked me.

I nodded yes with my head.

"So why don't you tell her? Look at you; how can she say no?"

"It's a bit more complicated than that, Jaspreet."

"Does she come to this university? Because I can go and put in a good word if you want?"

"No, she doesn't. She goes to Manchester."

At that moment, I looked up into the clouds and silently prayed that she was doing fine wherever she was.

Weeks had gone by, and I was getting stronger, lifting heavier weights. It was also getting closer to the Easter holidays, and thankfully, all my assignments and presentations were out of the way. I always really enjoyed giving presentations. I always saw myself giving speeches to a larger crowd maybe I was destined to be in politics at the same time as my role models from the Hollywood and Bollywood worlds!

When Julie's stepmother walked in, I was helping out in the shop one day, working at the till and serving the customers.

"Has Julie come back from University?!" I asked.

She looked at me with a flash of anger.

"Are you sure you should be asking me that, Raj?" she said.

I was a bit confused.

"You had better ask your dad if you should be asking me about my daughter!" she continued.

"Sorry, I don't know what you are talking about," I replied curtly.

"What I am talking about is the time you and your family insulted my daughter and me," she briskly said.

"I am very sorry about that time." I said, "We didn't mean to hurt Julie. My aunties were having a go at me, and unfortunately, Julie walked into the shop at the wrong time. They don't have anything against you or Julie; it's me they don't like. Now, is Julie back?"

"No, she isn't coming back until the end of her last semester, around June/July, as she has settled into her part-time job," she told me before leaving.

Later that night, after my gym workout, I was thinking about Julie while sitting at my study table. I had a flashback of the moment when my family insulted Julie. I missed her, and I wanted to see her. I ran down the stairs, took my Grandad's car keys off him and took out the Great Britain A-Z book out of the boot of his car. Running back into my room, I worked out where Manchester was and how far it was from Wolverhampton.

"This is definitely a train job," I thought, "Looks like I'll have to wait until the end of the university year." This year's end wasn't far away; we were all running around completing last-minute assignments and revising for exams. It was a major time of panic, and we all had a lot to do. Finally, it was all over, and it was time to party. As usual, we all ended up in the pub across the road. We all danced and sang, and most were drunk. There was a daytime Indian gig on, but our group decided to party across the road.

Chapter Seventeen

The summer holidays were different this year. It happened when I dropped into Bilston Art and Design College to make sure the caretaker was going to open the college doors of the gym on time. Because of the holidays, the caretaker used to arrive late, which got all the powerlifters angry. For some reason, I used to get the responsibility of making sure I spoke to the caretakers. Luckily, they gave me a copy of the front door key this time and were told they would come at 9 o'clock to close up. I walked through the college reception and decided to look at the notice board to see if there were any fun courses to do over the holidays. I might sound like a geek, but it was to get away from stopping in the shop and bumping into my Aunty and Uncle. On the notice board, there was a leaflet on artists required for a college stage play. 'This is it!' I thought, 'I have to take part in this!' so I took the leaflet home and stuck it on my bedroom wall.

I went along to the audition on the day it was advertised for, a Monday evening. I got there excited and very nervous. I walked into the theatre room and found seats that were on an incline facing the stage at the front. 'Wow, I could be on that stage!' I said to myself.

"Hello!" said a man, bursting my thought pattern.

"Hi, I'm here regarding the play," I replied.

"Well, you're in the right place, sir." said the man, who I would later find out was called Chris and was the director of the play.

"Great, what do you want me to do?" I asked.

"Well, do you have acting experience?" he replied.

For some reason, I thought if I said no, I would never have a character part or even the main part, so I began to fib...

"Well, my Uncle is a film director in the Indian film industry, and he is launching me next year in a lead role. I'm here to polish up my acting."

"Hey, that's great! Why don't you come and visit some of the other cast members," he said.

"Wow, I got through that one easily," I thought. I walked to the front and found two young ladies and three other guys sitting in the front, flicking books.

"Guys, we have another cast member to join our team, and this guy has film experience. Sorry, what was your name?"

"Raj."

"Guys, as you have heard, this is Raj."

I stepped forward and shook the hands of Jason, Susan, William, Tracey, and Tim.

Jason had blonde hair which only went through the centre of his head. He was a rocker, and he was weird-looking. Susan was a beautiful blonde, six-foot-tall, and in good shape. Tracey was a brunette about five feet tall and had a sweet smile. Tim was a Hugh Grant look-a-like; he even spoke the way the film star did. William was a six-foot-two guy who resembled Tom Hanks, the actor. The group was certainly a mixture of different characters!

"Right, we have been going through a lot of plays to use since last week, and with you joining us, Raj, I think we should try 'The School Playground," said Chris.

"That's a brilliant idea!" said Susan.

"Right, let's have a read-through then. Tracey and Tim will play the lead of Samantha and John. Susan, you will play Tracey's best friend, Sandra, and Jason, you will play Carl. Raj, you will play Jindi, and William, you will play Andrew." continued Chris.

We began to read, and as my part came, I read very well and in time with the others. After the read-through, Chris said we would meet twice a week, Tuesdays and Thursdays. There are four weeks of rehearsals, and the fifth week is for making props and rehearsal before performing in the sixth week.

"Brilliant!" I thought, "It doesn't disturb my training at all." I looked at the stage and saw my dream come true.

The following week, Tim never turned up, and Chris had a call from him to say that he had changed his mind. I was gutted for a bit because, as I said, he looked like Hugh Grant, and this play could have been like Four Weddings and A Funeral! Luckily, Tim was replaced by Chris's nephew Richard, who looked a bit like Jeff Bridges. We were all almost the same age: I was nineteen, Susan was eighteen, Tracey was eighteen, Richard was seventeen, Jason was twenty-one, and William was nineteen. Chris would have been in his thirties. We met twice a week, and we all got along very well. I got on with Susan very well. Even though she had a boyfriend, she spent a lot of the time stroking my arms and feeling my muscles. I knew the other guys didn't like it, but they didn't say anything, probably because they felt intimidated by my muscles! The girls took a strong interest in my diet as I usually carried my protein drinks.

After rehearsal, the day before the show, I was in the changing room getting undressed when Susan walked in and grabbed me from behind.

"Shall I take my top off as well, Raj? So, you can feel how hot these are for you."

"Come on, cut it out," I replied.

However, despite my protestations, we then kissed a passionate kiss that must have lasted for at least two minutes. I opened my eyes to see her blue eyes and her blonde hair on the side of her face, and I was suddenly reminded of Julie, so I carried on kissing her. Eventually, we stopped kissing, but then she grabbed my penis and promised me a good time the next day. Needless to say, I was gobsmacked and completely in shock!

The evening before the show, we posted leaflets about the play around the local area. I purposely chose to post leaflets on Julie's road, and I was posting a leaflet through her letterbox when her mother opened the door.

"What are you posting through my letterbox, Raj?" she asked.

"Oh, it's a leaflet of the play I'm in. Is Julie back home at all?"

She looked up at Julie's window. "No, she planned to stay in Manchester and work full-time to save up some money."

I felt she was lying, but I wasn't going to argue with her.

"Well, if she happens to return tonight or tomorrow, could you please tell her about my play?"

"Well, don't hold your breath, but I'll take the leaflet," she replied. Before I left, I said, "Christians are forgiving people."

I got back to my father's shop to find my two Aunties talking to my Dad.

"Have you returned?" asked Aunty Baljit.

"It's none of your business," I replied in anger.

"You should not let him talk to us like that, brother!" she said to Dad, "This boy has no manners whatsoever and kids like him, you don't know what they get up behind your back!"

I couldn't believe what I was hearing. This was coming from a woman whose kids committed crimes and who had seen prison cells.

"Look, I'm starring in a play, and many people are going to see me perform on stage," I replied.

Before I could have the last laugh, though, Aunty Baljit began to berate me.

"You become an actor? Actors are like prostitutes in Punjab! They are with one person one day and another the next day. That's what you want to become?"

I looked at my dad, thinking, "What are these two talking about?!"

But instead of defending me, he said, "He'll get a hundred slippers slapped on his head before he does anything like that."

I looked at him with hurt before walking back into the living room. This comment came from the man who spent a couple of days in Bombay, the heart of the Indian film industry, hoping to get discovered before he came to the UK.

The next day, I was with the rest of the cast rehearsing before the show. We had two shows, one show in the afternoon and the other show in the evening. We rehearsed very well, and we had one run-through from start to finish before the afternoon show, and it rocked. The afternoon show was finally here, and even though we were all a bit nervous, we encouraged each other. Chris had us doing various exercises before the door opened. It lasted about thirty minutes, which helped us to keep calm. I believe all stage actors do these exercises to keep their nerves calm and to stop them from laughing. We all waited in the changing room and listened to all the people coming in and taking their seats. We all hugged each other and wished each other good luck.

"Don't forget tonight?" Susan said to me before pecking me on the lips and walking out. Then Tracey hugged and kissed me before sticking her tongue in my mouth.

"You have a choice to make, Raj!" she told me as she left the room.

I couldn't believe my luck! I walked out onto the stage and got in position, telling myself to concentrate. The curtain went back, and we began;

100

I stuttered on two words by repeating them a couple of times, but this didn't matter as we were playing characters who were ten-year-olds.

We hung around the college for the evening show. For some reason, Susan was no longer around, and it was only until later on, just before the show, that she returned with her boyfriend. I looked at her boyfriend, and I felt sorry for her. I never usually say this, but this guy was far too ugly for Susan. What was she doing with this curly-haired, ginger goggle-eyed freak?

Plus, Tracey wasn't around either. I thought she was probably with her boyfriend, but she turned up just after Susan and introduced me to her mother. The evening show was full, and I could see all my family in the audience. I heard my sister laughing at my comical scenes loudly! At the end of the show, we all stood to take a bow, and as I took a bow and came back up, I saw Julie, my Julie. She smiled at me and stuck up her thumb to say, "Chapeau! Good show!"

I smiled back and mouthed, "Thank you."

After we got off the stage, I tried running to get out, but Susan grabbed my arms and pulled me to the side behind the curtain.

"You better be coming back to Jason's flat and getting ready to make me happy!" she said.

"What about your boyfriend?"

"Forget him, we'll work it out," she replied.

"Okay, I'll see you at the flat."

But to be honest, I didn't care about the flat – I was full of the joy of seeing Julie. I ran out to catch up with her, but when I got outside, she was gone. I couldn't see her anywhere. I looked up in anger and saw the clouds changing direction.

Back at the flat, we had a lot to drink and were very tipsy. Even I, as a health freak, tried a drink recommended by Jason, which wasn't like other alcoholic drinks. It was called Dragon Stout, which was a Jamaican stout. It was really strong, but I decided to drink it anyway. We all began to dance. There was weed being smoked, which I didn't like the smell of. They tried passing the rolled-up rizla containing weed to me, but even though I was drunk, I refused. It was fairly dark in the room as they drew the curtains. As we were dancing, I felt Tracey grab my hand and place it on her breast as we began to dance very close. Soon, we were kissing, and our hands were all over each other's bodies. Just then, however, I felt someone hug me from behind. It was Susan, and she began to kiss my neck. I looked around the room to see where Susan's boyfriend was – he was asleep on the beanbag. Susan turned me around and plunged her tongue into my mouth before leading me down the corridor.

Tracey was holding my other hand as I was dragged into the bedroom. Susan's top came off, and so did mine as the two girls began to kiss my chest. I lay back on the bed, but the room stunk – it was definitely a dude's room, and the smell was really off-putting. Susan began to lick me all over my chest, and then Tracey kissed me on the lips as Susan kissed me between my legs. She then opened the button to the school shorts I was wearing for the play and unzipped my zip. I closed my eyes and suddenly saw Julie giving me the thumbs-up from earlier. I opened my eyes quickly, thinking of her. Before I could move, however, Tracey's stomach made a funny noise, and she was sick all over my chest.

"Shit! What are you doing?!" I shouted as I quickly grabbed the bedsheets to clean my chest, but they smelt worse than the sick. The buzz of being drunk was very much over.

"You bitch, what have you done?!" Susan screamed at Tracey.

"What are you doing here anyway!" Tracey screamed back, "Your man is out there!"

"Who are you to tell me who I should have fun with or not? What you going to do, shut me up, you whore?"

"Who are you calling a whore, you bitch!"

Susan reached over to grab Tracey's hair, meaning I had to intervene quickly.

"Hey, ladies, calm down! Let's clean ourselves up and leave."

"Leave?!" Susan shouted, "I haven't been sick. She can go, and we can finish off what we were doing."

I looked at Susan, thinking, "How stupid is she?"

I pointed at the sick over my chest.

"Really, Susan?" I asked. "Listen, ladies, chill out; I have to go."

I picked up my shirt and went into the bathroom, which also stunk. I cleaned myself with water before I put on my schoolboy shirt over my wet body and left. I walked home, and it was quite light for the time it was. I passed closer to the library where Julie and I used to meet. I was still a bit drunk, so I decided to jump over the wall and get over the gates. I walked down the slope, which led to the park area.

As I got closer to the park area, I began to have flashbacks of the time Julie and I used to spend in the park as friends. I sat on the bench, looked back, and saw the back of the library. I could see the room where we used to go and read and choose our books. I lay on the bench as the drunkenness drained out of me. I remembered the times Julie and I sat on this bench. I laughed and looked up at the sky and found the clouds moving from one direction to the other. Before I knew it, I fell asleep.

I could hear the tune from The Bangle's record 'Eternal Flame', which Julie used to hum, and I could feel someone stroking my hair. The humming began to sound like someone was singing the words, but when I moved onto my side, the singing stopped. I lay there for a while, waiting for the singing to come back again, but it didn't. I slowly opened my eyes, hoping Julie would be there – I could smell the fragrance of the perfume she used to wear.

"Could it be? Was she here? No, she couldn't be," I thought. "It's probably the smell and secondary smoke I inhaled that had gotten to me, making me think things like this."

I just stood up and went for a walk around the park, hoping that Julie was hiding behind a tree and was going to pop out any minute. I laughed and thought about whether I had done the right thing, leaving Susan and Tracey. I had two very attractive women who wanted me, and I ran out on them!

I walked home laughing at myself. I got home, walked into my room, and sat down on my bed, thinking about the play and the whole evening. I began to get unchanged, and while I was removing my trousers, something fell out of my pocket onto the floor. I looked and saw one of Tracey's hair bands, which she had worn in the play. I didn't know how this had gotten in my pocket. I looked at it and then smelt it, and I could smell Tracey. I could also smell the vomit on it, so I went and had a shower.

Chapter Eighteen

Starting back at University for my second year coincided with a very stressful time in my life. I had a load of assignments to do, and at the same time, I was preparing for the British Powerlifting Championships. Training sessions were getting harder, and I was under pressure to beat a specific competitor, Gurbir, this time. Because of this added pressure, I was consuming a lot more calories to increase my body weight. My group at university were back together doing our group assignments – the same people but one, however. We had some bad news: Harj had been involved in a car accident and was in intensive care. The evening the news broke, we all went to the hospital to see her. She was in a bad state – she had broken many bones, and her face was almost unrecognisable. Her mother was sitting by her side, crying her eyes out. We were all sad and speechless, and the only thing we could do at the time was to pray.

Our class friend Inderjit liked Harj and was planning to ask her out. I remember telling him to come and visit Harj as much as he could and spend a lot of time with her to create a relationship. But Inderjit was one of those characters who, when he faced disappointments and challenges in life, would drink a lot and smoke a lot of weed. He grew up wearing a turban, but in college and university days, he decided to wear a bandana. He always felt it necessary to communicate with people as if he were a leading gangster or a Godfather. When the accident happened, Inderjit decided to give up his studies and go into full-time work, and we didn't see him again. If my memory serves me right, he went into selling double-glazing windows.

We visited Harj as much as we could and saw her recover very fast, as she was a strong character. We also began to see a different light in her life. She believed that she almost died in a car accident and realised that she had not seen anything in life. She had quit University and had decided that she wanted to see the world, so she went backpacking with her sister. Like Inderjeet, we never heard from her again. I sometimes wondered if they ever crossed paths and if they both ever dated.

I was still training for the British Powerlifting Championships. I was eating more than ever and training more than ever. My lifts were getting stronger, and my muscles were getting bigger. I was sitting in the canteen one day having my breakfast as part of my mid-morning break. I sat up and flexed my chest muscles, which made Samantha, sitting nearby, laugh.

"Do that again!" she said, so I did, causing her to laugh even louder.

"You try!" I asked her jokingly.

She tried, but her breasts swung from one side to the other, which we both found funny. Just then, however, a South Asian girl walked up to our table.

"My mate fancies you!" she told me, pointing at her friend who was sitting across the canteen.

Raj and Julie

I looked over and saw an attractive South Asian girl. "She wants to thank you for giving her an orgasm when you flexed your chest muscles!" she continued.

I looked at her in surprised shock and was stuck for words to say. She walked off, and I looked at Samantha, and we both burst out laughing.

"You do have some effect with a huge chest like that," she said.

"Just think if it was pressed against yours!" I said flirtatiously.

She laughed. "Stop it!" she said, "and go and ask her out. Don't tell me you can't because of Julie."

I walked over to the girl and sat opposite her – luckily, her friend had left the table for us to talk. I looked at the girl and smiled. She was good-looking – about five feet one with a medium build - and wore blue contact lenses. After I said hello to her, she looked me up and down.

"What's your chest measurement?" she asked. I looked at her in surprise – certainly an interesting first question!

"About fifty-four inches," I replied.

"Wow, that's huge. How many times a week do you train?" she inquired.

"I do powerlifting sessions three times a week," I answered, wondering whether this was an interview about my training or her trying to figure me out before asking me out!

"Powerlifting!" she said in excitement, "I love powerlifting!"

"So, do you go to the gym?" I asked.

"No, but I use my brother's gym at home."

"You work out using weights?"

"Yeah," she replied, "I love lifting heavyweights. I might not look muscular, but I can lift some weights."

I was surprised and amazed by the enthusiasm of this girl.

"What's your name, sorry?" I asked.

"Oh, sorry, it's Katrina."

"Well, I'm Raj."

"So, are you seeing anyone, Raj?" she asked.

"I am kind of seeing someone, yeah," I replied, without even thinking about it. Her face dropped.

"Oh, that's okay," she said and got up and left.

I walked back to our table, where Samantha was eating her second breakfast.

"And?" she asked.

"And nothing!" I replied.

"Bloody hell, you told her you have a girlfriend, didn't you?" she shouted. I nodded my head, saying yes.

"You are fucking crazy!" she screamed whilst laughing.

We walked out of the canteen and headed towards our classroom.

A week before my competition, my training got intense, and it was nerve-racking. I had a lot of support from my university friends and family members, but every time I left the gym and walked back home, all I could think of was if Julie would walk around the corner and wish me good luck.

105

The day before the competition, I prepared my bag, adding all the clothing, boots, slippers, chalk, knee wraps, and belts for the competition.

"You all set for tomorrow?" my Dad asked, walking into my room.

"Yes, Dad."

"Don't worry about it, just do your best – I will still be proud of you. Where's the competition being held?"

I looked at the leaflet in my hand. 'Moss Side Sports Centre, Manchester.'

'Manchester? We had better go to sleep early then - it's about two hours from here.'

I said, "Okay," and then it hit me Manchester was where Julie was studying. I went to sleep early, thinking that not only would I come home with the trophy, but I might also get to see Julie as well.

The next morning, I woke up early and went downstairs to find my parents getting ready. Mum was also busy preparing all my food. Then my Grandad came down the stairs and began to pray for me before blessing me for the competition. My Grandmother began to rotate the scented stick around my face, telling me not to lift too much weight. She was always concerned that lifting too much weight may cause injuries. Then, there was a knock at the door. I opened it and found it was my friend Inderjit.

"Thanks for coming!" I said.

"How could I forget your big title event?!" he said before introducing me to his cousin, whom he had brought for moral support.

My mother blessed me and said, "May the Lord bless you with victory."

We all got into our cars and left for Manchester. When we entered the city, I looked out the window, hoping to see Julie. We got to the sports centre, and I began to feel nervous. We all walked into the building and found that the public was using the centre and the competition was held in the sports hall. My supporters walked into the hall and sat on the chairs while I went to the weighing-in room. I weighed in, causing one of the judges to remark that I had gained weight since the last competition! I then had all my clothing, footwear, and weightlifting belts checked for safety reasons.

I came out of the weighing room and entered the warm-up room. All the powerlifters were warming up, so I took a deep breath and told myself that this was it; this was the moment. I looked around the room but couldn't see my coach, Roger. Nevertheless, I put on my lifting suit and joined a couple of guys who were warming up. One of the referees came into the warm-up room and shouted to us to ensure we were all given our opening weights.

"Shit!" I thought, "My coach usually does this."

However, I had planned what I needed to lift, so I went and gave my opening lifts in. I came back into the warm-up room and found Gurbir warming up with his supporting team. There must be about nine of them! I noticed that none of the guys from my gym was there. I proceeded to warm up, looking back at Gurbir and getting focused. Just then, one of his mates passed me and said in a quiet voice, "You've lost."

"We'll see," I replied. It seemed like he was trying to break my focus.

Raj and Julie

The time had arrived, and the organisers began to call out names. I got my last warm-up lift in place, and then my name was called out. I got ready, walked out onto the stage, stared at the bar, and got focused. I lifted the bar before walking back into position and waiting for the referee's command. He shouted, "Squat! It was now Gurbirs's turn – he was lifting the same weight as me but went after me as he was a kilo heavier in body weight. He also got the lift in."

The competition went on, and it was neck to neck with me and Gurbir until we came to the last exercise and lift, which was the deadlift. Gurbir was supposed to be stronger than me with this lift. On our first lift, we lifted the same. Then, with the second lift, Gurbir lifted five kilograms heavier than I could. I knew I had to go for a twenty-kilo jump, which would give me five kilos more than Gurbir overall. I walked out onto the stage – I was so nervous at this point that the crowd in front of me seemed to be just one massive blur. I could hear a lot of the crowd cheering me on, as well as Gurbir's crowd making a barking noise to distract me.

I thought I heard Julie's voice, but I had to blank it out as I walked to the bar. I gripped the bar and thought of the first time I had ever gripped a bar. I got in position and began to lift the weight it came up very slow, and then halfway up, it got even slower, but I was determined not to give up. I held it at the top until the referee said, "Down."

I dropped the weight and looked at the three white lights, signifying I had done it. As I yelled out in excitement, I looked at the crowd, who were all clapping and cheering for me. But then it was Gurbir's turn. He decided to lift two and a half kilos heavier than me. He began to lift the weight and brought it up halfway, but then he got stuck and couldn't lift it any higher. He tried to hold onto it, but there was no way he was moving it any higher. His team was making a lot of noise, but to no avail – it began to move up, and the bar slipped out of his hands.

At the sight of three red lights. All my supporters jumped out of their chairs, and I was so happy I walked back into the warm-up room and screamed, "Yes! Yes! Yes! I did it!" as loud as I could. Gurbir walked in, looking disappointed, so I walked up to him and put my hand out to shake, telling him it was close.

Then, it was time to receive my trophy and medal. All the competitors' names were called out before my name was called out for first place. I came out onto the stage and received my award. Watching in the audience was my Dad, who was smiling with his eyes filling with water in happiness. He gave me a thumbs-up, and I smiled back at him. I got changed, but before I could leave, I was asked by the drug testing group to come and have a drug test. I walked into the toilets where they were carrying out the drug test. They usually randomly picked a name out of a hat, but I believe they targeted me as I had won. Just as I had given them my urine sample, an Afro-Caribbean man walked into the toilets and began to shout out. You could tell he was high on something! The security men ran in, grabbed him, and took him out.

We later discovered that Moss Side was a rough area where a lot of shootings and drug taking took place.

When I heard this, I immediately thought of Julie and the dangers she could be in. On the way out of the building, I looked around, hoping to see her, but again, I left feeling upset.

It was singing of joy all the way home. We reached home, and my mother was waiting by the door with a bottle of oil. I got out of the car and walked towards the entrance where Mum had poured oil on each side, a tradition I had never understood. Then my Mum gave me some sugar to eat, which was another tradition which I was told was to sweeten the mouth in happiness. I walked into the front room with my trophy and medal and showed my Grandad, who was so happy. He began to bless me and then asked me to pray to the picture of my great-grandad.

Again, I didn't know why this also had to be done, but I obeyed his command. The day went well, consisting of partying and celebrating. I noticed that none of my cousins and Aunties had come around probably because they never joined in with our celebrations unless they had planned to ruin them.

A week after my triumph, I was in for a big surprise. The local newspaper contacted me and asked if they could run an interview with me. I agreed to it, and I was interviewed and photographed holding my trophy and medal and posing with my muscles! I could finally see my dreams coming into place.

The following week, two other papers called and interviewed me, and this time, I had my grandad and Dad in the pictures. The week after that, I had the BBC Asian Network call me, and two radio presenters interviewed me on two different occasions. I remember the first interview I had, my dad drive me, and I was nervous about the radio station.

I walked through the doors and entered the reception area, where there was a smell that made me more nervous – it was the same feeling you get when you walk into a dentist's or a doctor's surgery. After giving the receptionist my name, my father and I waited until we saw an Asian lady walking down the corridor.

"Hi, I'm Sharonjit. Are you Raj?" she asked while putting her hand out to shake mine. I shook her hand, and we followed her to the security doors. Sharonjit took her card, attached it to her waist, and swiped it for the doors to open, which reminded me a lot of the time when I went to my first competition at Featherstone prison.

"So you've just won the British Weight Lifting Championships?" Sharonjit asked me.

"Well, it's powerlifting..." I tried to correct her, but she showed no interest. She walked us into the room and asked us to sit down. It was a small room which led into the studio. I asked her if there was a set format of questions, but I was told that the presenter would ask me the question that popped into his head. This made me more nervous, added to the fact that I couldn't remember the presenter's name. I was sitting waiting and could hear the music being played by the presenter, before he began to speak, which felt weird!

"After the next track, we will be speaking to British Powerlifting Champion Raj Singh!"

I followed Sharonjit into the studio and was introduced to the presenter.

"Hi, I'm Gurdev," the presenter said. I shook his hand and said, "Raj."

"So, British Powerlifting Champion! What exactly is powerlifting, Raj?" he asked.

"It's weightlifting of three different exercise events," I replied.

"Excellent!" he said, "say exactly that when we go live!"

Gurdev then faded the music and began to speak through the mic.

"Right, we have the British Powerlifting Champion Raj Singh with us. Welcome to the BBC Asian Station, Raj. Now, British Powerlifting Champion—that is something. Tell us what powerlifting is."

Well, powerlifting is a sport which entails three weightlifting events, which are The Squat, the Two Knee Deep Bend, and the Bench Press and Deadlift, which is performed by lifting the bar from the ground to just over the knees.' I replied.

"So how much did you lift then to win the British Championships?"

'Well, on the Squat, I lifted two hundred and fifty kilograms, one hundred and sixty kilograms on the Bench Press, and two hundred and eighty kilograms on the Deadlift."

"Wow, that's a lot of weight, Raj! How much is that in total?"

He had put me on the spot there, but luckily, I had my certificate by me.

"Six Hundred and ninety kilos," I replied confidently.

"To lift that amount of weight, a lot of preparation must have gone into preparing for the championships, Raj. How many times a week or day did you train?"

"I trained three times a week, and I've been preparing for the Championships for the last two years. But I have been doing basic Powerlifting training for eight years now."

"Eight years? How old are you then, Raj, if you don't mind me asking!"

"I'm twenty years old and began training when I was thirteen years old."

"Wow, thirteen years of age? So you have had the dream of becoming the British Champion since the age of thirteen?"

"Pretty much, yes. It began when I was awarded the title of the strongest fourteen-year-old and then fifteen-year-old in the United Kingdom. Now, looking at the world records online, it seems I was the only teenager in the history of powerlifting to begin competing at the age of fourteen.

"Wow!" he said again. "So you're a history maker? What do you eat during your preparation?"

"Well, my diet consisted of chicken and pasta, mainly." Annoyingly then, however, my mind went blank, and I forgot what I had eaten to train. Dev saw I had gotten a bit nervous, so he cut the interview short. I wanted to say that my diet consisted of six to eight meals a day.

On an average day, I would be eating three Weetabix's in full-fat milk, two slices of toast, and a pint of orange juice for breakfast, a protein shake two hours after, pasta, tuna with rice for lunch, then another protein shake two hours after lunch, and a bowl of fruit salad before a workout. After the workout, I would have another protein shake. Then, for dinner, I would have two chicken breasts, vegetables, baked potatoes, and probably another protein shake before bedtime with my favourite raspberry ripple ice cream.

On the way back from the studio, I kept thinking I could have said a lot more. The 'chicken and pasta' comment kept on going through my mind. We pulled up outside my father's shop, and when I walked in, I found almost every member of my family sitting in the living room – even Aunty Kuljit was there. My Mum praised me for a good interview, but Aunty Kuljit walked over to the stereo and pushed the play button, playing my interview again. On the tape, I was saying 'chicken and pasta', then she stopped it and rewound it so that it played that comment again. She burst out laughing.

"All this time, and you have only learned about chicken and pasta?" she laughed. "No wonder everyone calls you clumsy!"

I just looked at her and walked over to the stereo, where I pulled the tape out and walked out of the room and up the stairs.

Chapter Nineteen

The next day, I was driving back from University when I had a call on my mobile.

"Hello, Raj. My name is Richard Sailor, and I'm the editor of the Wolverhampton College magazine. We want to have a piece in our paper on your Powerlifting success if that's okay with you?" he asked.

I almost jumped with joy and had to pull over to concentrate!

"Of course, that'd be great!" I replied.

"If you can come tomorrow to the college campus at three o'clock, I'll greet you in the reception area," he said.

"Okay, see you tomorrow at three!" I replied excitedly. I then prayed to God, asking him to please make this one of many more to follow.

The next day, I pulled into Wolverhampton College and found, to my surprise, that they had knocked down the old building and built a new modern building in its place. It was hard not to miss it, as the old building was your old traditional building, and now it was an all-glass, futuristic-looking one. I looked further away from the college and saw the same pathway that Julie and I had walked down many times. However, before I could dwell on Julie, a screaming noise by a gaggle of students walking past my car woke me up from nostalgia. I walked towards the entrance, looked up and was surprised to read it said 'Wolverhampton College'. Again, this was another difference as it used to be known as 'Bilston College'.

Looking at the changes, I did a full circle around the reception area when I felt a tap on my shoulder. I turned around and was greeted by a man.

"Hi Raj, I'm Richard," he said.

I wasn't sure how he recognised me, but he answered that question before I could speak. "I recognised you from the pictures in the newspapers!" he told me.

That answered that. He walked me to his office and offered me a seat.

"I'll be taping this interview, Raj, so try to answer as much as you can. If you want to have a break in between, please feel free to do so," he told me.

I was fine with that, and when I'd settled down, he began to fire away. The interview lasted about an hour and a half. At the end of the interview, Richard told me that he had enjoyed talking to me and had found it inspiring listening to my story! He also told me something very interesting.

"Raj, I have a friend who owns an Asian magazine, and I believe he would like to interview you," he told me.

"That would be great!" I replied enthusiastically.

"If you want, I can call him today and pass on your number to him, so lookout for a call from him. His name is Satvinder, and his magazine is called 'Asian Spice.'"

The name came across as an Asian porn magazine, and I began to think this guy was perhaps having a joke with me! Nevertheless, I shook his hand and thanked him. When I got into my car, I decided to drive to the nearest newsagents. I looked in and found that the owner was South Asian, so I drove to the next shop. I did this so I wouldn't get embarrassed or even judged if the Asian Spice magazine was pornographic. I walked into the store and walked over to the magazine rack, and for some reason, I began to look right at the top shelf of pornographic magazines. I saw the owner looking at me, so I asked him where the Asian magazines were kept.

After he directed me, I looked and found the Asian Spice magazine. I picked it off the shelf and flicked through it, finding it was a normal magazine with information and interviews with Asians. I smiled and put the magazine back. I walked towards the shop door when the store owner called out to me.

"There is another Asian Spice on the top shelf if that's what you were looking for?" he asked me.

I looked at him, a bit embarrassed at first, but then said, "No!" before laughing and walking out.

Just two days later, I had a phone call from Satvinder, the owner of Asian Spice magazine.

"I spoke to Richard earlier, Raj, and he told me all about your success. I was wondering if you wanted to appear in my magazine?" he asked me.

I told him I would love to.

"Great! I only need you to come into my studio for a photo shoot this Sunday, as I can get a copy of your interview from Richard if that's okay with you?" I told him that was fine, and he gave me the address for his studio. It was in Birmingham city centre. A day before the photoshoot, I sat in the sauna and worked out to get a muscular pump.

The next day, I drove to the studios where Satvinder had asked me to come. I walked out of the lift onto the eighth floor to find just a big empty room. I felt like this was a set-up for something like you find in Jackie Chan movies! Then I saw a guy setting up the lights and camera.

"Hi, welcome to Spice," he said when he saw me. "You must me, Raj. Give me five minutes, Raj, and then I'll be ready to start photographing you. Meanwhile, you can take your top off and get ready to pose with your huge muscles for me." The first thing that came to my mind was whether this guy was gay. Anyway, I did. Then he asked, "Could you do some push-ups to warm up." I looked at him, feeling a bit uncomfortable, but decided to do so anyway. I got into the push-up position and began doing my push-ups when I heard him say, "That's it, pump those muscles!"

That was when I got worried. So, I got up and told him I had done enough, so he told me to pose, and he began photographing me. He must have taken about fifty photographs, after which he told me that I could put my top back on and that Spice would get the photographs the next day or the day after. I thanked him and left. It was a bit weird being photographed by a guy on his own in a studio, but on the other hand, it felt great being

112

photographed for a magazine. I was a bit confused that it was doing bodybuilding poses as I was a powerlifter. I thought they should have had weights, a weightlifting bar, heavy chains, or large wheels as props in place.

The following week, my interview was in the College paper. I had a call from Richard asking me to come and collect a copy. I remember how I rushed to the college, taking two steps at a time on the stairs leading up to Richard's office. I walked in to find the paper on his table.

"Hello, Raj. Thanks for coming," he said. "Here you go. Have a look at the copy of the paper."

I grabbed the paper off Richard and turned to the back to see my picture – it was me in the Hulk pose! This was my favourite pose. The whole page was about me, with my picture in the centre.

"What do you think, Raj?"

"Brilliant!" I replied. "Can I take this one?"

"Sure you can, and take a few more!" Richard answered. He pointed toward his cabinets, and I saw a pile of papers. I walked over to the pile and grabbed a handful.

"Not that many, Raj – we have to sell them, you know!"

"Sorry!" I replied. "How much are they?"

"Twenty-five pence each."

I put my hand in my pocket and took out a five-pound note. "Give me five quid's worth then," I said.

"That many? What are you going to do with that many copies?" he asked.

"I'll give them to all my cousins and relatives," I answered.

Richard gave me twenty copies, and I rushed home to show my parents. As I got towards my father's shop, I thought I would go and post a copy in Julie's letterbox. I drove to Julie's mom's house, got out, and posted a copy. I paused there for about ten seconds, hoping she would come to the door, but no luck. I got back into my car and drove home.

I pulled up outside the shop and grabbed the papers, but as I was doing so, I looked out of the window and saw something going on inside the shop. I got out of the car and walked into the shop. I found my mum, dad, grandad, and Aunty Balbir standing around her son, Narinder. He was getting told off for something, which was no change.

From the age of eleven, he had always been in trouble with the police, often for stealing cars and joyriding. He had spent most of his time in and out of Detention Centres and prisons. What was it about this time? I was excited to show my parents the college paper, but I knew that the ongoing situation ruined it.

"Is everything all right?" I asked.

My Aunty looked at me and told me that I had better listen as well.

"Narinder has got caught drink driving, and he will lose his licence," she said.

"Why are you telling me off? I don't drink and drive!" I replied.

"Raj is studying and doesn't have time to go out drinking," said my Mum.

"Well, we know what they all get up to!" my Aunty replied.

"What are you trying to say? For your information, I have just come back from college, picking up these college papers with my interview in!" I said, showing her the paper to make her go quiet.

"This is not the place to discuss these matters!" my Grandad suddenly piped up, "The customers are probably wondering what is happening. Let us all walk back in there, besides your Mum and Dad, Raj."

At that moment, I got the opportunity to show my parents the paper. They looked at it and congratulated me – Dad shook my hand and said well done, whilst my mother kissed me on the cheek.

"My son, you are going to achieve much more in the future!" she told me, "Now go and show your Grandad how to change the atmosphere in the house."

I said, "Okay, okay," and walked down through the shop and into the house. I walked into the living room and found my Grandad, Grandma, Aunty, and her son sitting there. They went quiet when I walked in. I walked up to my Grandad and showed him the paper.

"I'm very proud of you, Raj!" he told me. He then looked at Narinder and asked him why he couldn't do stuff like that. However, my Aunty leapt to his defence.

"He is very clever and very hard working when he puts his head to things!" she said, "This is nothing, what Raj has achieved, nothing! Narinder can achieve a lot more!" she claimed before they both got up and left the room. After they left, my Grandad shook my hand and said well done, I also left. I walked up the stairs, looking at my picture. I walked into my room and sat on my bed when suddenly, I realised that I hadn't even read what was written in the article, as I was too busy looking at my picture. I settled down to read it. However, I was soon disturbed by my Grandad shouting my name.

"Raj, come down here!" he shouted. I got up quickly and walked down the stairs, wondering what was happening. I got to the bottom of the stairs, which led into the living room, and saw my grandad, Grandma, and Dad sitting having tea.

"Come down, son, take a seat!" my Grandad said. I sat down, wondering what I had done wrong!

"I am going to India in two weeks, as you all know," he began, "And I have planned to take you, Raj, a gift for winning the championships."

I got up and hugged him, completely stunned by this news.

"Could I visit Bombay as well?!" I asked.

He laughed and told me that, of course, I could. Just then, however, my joy was interrupted by Aunty Manjit walking in.

"Please take my son as well!" she said.

"Okay!" said Grandad, and my heart sank.

Then, unbelievably, my Grandma told us that she may as well come along with us! The list had just gotten bigger within five minutes; I couldn't believe it. I had two weeks to get ready. I told my lecturers at the university that I would take my assignments with me. They were fine with this, and I managed to get all the books I needed to take with me. Two days before I left for India, I wrote a note to Julie, telling her my news and that if anything happened, she should never forget that I loved her. I went for a run that night, and as I ran past Julie's parents' house, I posted the letter. The day before, we all got our luggage ready. I think I was carrying more than I needed, and I don't think I needed to take my books with me as I wasn't going to get any time to complete my assignments.

The next day, we all travelled to the airport. My father had hired a minibus as there were a lot of us – especially as my Aunties had come with us, wanting to see us all off at the airport. We got to the airport and queued up to have our luggage checked in. We put our suitcases down to be weighed – as a Powerlifter, I had a fair idea of what all our cases weighed individually, and they were definitely over the weight required. However, when I looked at the screen to see the weight, I found that they were lighter than I thought, which was weird. I then looked down to see my Grandad having his foot underneath each suitcase, to make it lighter! Once we had checked our luggage in, we all had a Burger King meal and then walked towards the gates. I remember that it was an embarrassing experience, as every time I walked through the metal detector, it bleeped! As I did not have much room in my suitcase, I stuffed a load of my toiletries into my coat pockets. I walked through the detector the first time, and it bleeped, so I took out my deodorant bottle. The second time around, I took out my aftershave bottle! Eventually, my Grandad got fed up with this and ordered me to empty my pockets. Out came my soap dish, gel, loose change, and toothpaste, causing the people doing the checking to laugh! My Grandad looked at my items and warned me that I'd have to use my Grandma's herbal wood pieces to replace toothpaste.

I thought, "Oh no, my teeth will go orange like my Grandma's!" but he told me not to worry, as they had everything in India that we had here. We walked through the gates, and I sat on the plane next to my cousin, readying myself for the long flight.

Finally, we arrived at New Dehli airport after an eight-hour flight. We got off the plane and queued up for the immigration point. When I walked up to the counter, the official looked at my passport and began questioning me.

"Is this you?" he asked. I answered yes. I had wanted to say no, and that it was my twin brother, but I didn't want to get in trouble! He looked at me strangely.

"Is this your first time in India, sir?" he asked me.

His accent was very bad, and I only just about understood him. I answered yes, starting to get a bit worried that I was going to be arrested for something! Luckily, however, I could go, and we all went to retrieve our luggage. Suddenly, we were struck by a really bad smell. I didn't know what it was, but it was not pleasant at all. My cousin Ranjeet decided he wanted to go to the toilets while we were waiting for our luggage, and I went with him. Entering them, we discovered that it was these toilets that were causing the bad smell. We opened the toilet doors and found no toilets, but just holes in the floor.

"Oh crap, these guys haven't even got toilets here!" said Ranjeet as the smell overwhelmed me.

"What have I got myself into here!" I thought to myself.

"Why are you not saying anything, Raj?" he asked.

"I'm trying not to breathe in this smell!" I replied before I left the toilets as quickly as I could, finding my Grandad outside.

'Don't they have toilets in this country?' I asked him.

'No, you have to go out in the fields where we live!' he laughed, "No, don't worry, I have built a house with all the same facilities as we have back in England."

"Thank God for that!" I thought to myself.

We collected our luggage and walked towards the exit. As we walked out, I saw a load of people standing around, waiting to collect their relatives - it was like being at the Asian Fair back home.

"Stay very close to your stuff," my Grandad warned us.

We pushed the trolleys with our luggage on, and then my Grandad noticed his nephew, who had come to collect us. He came over and showed his respect for my Grandad and Grandma by touching their feet.

"Follow me," he told us, "the minibus is over here."

Stepping outside, I noticed that the air was very polluted, and the heat was overpowering. The worst thing about that was that I had my coat on! While I was pushing the trolley towards the minibus, a guy dressed in red came over and put his hand on my suitcases. This guy's we're known as coolie's who carried luggage for tourists.

"What are you doing?" I asked him.

"Helping," he replied.

"I don't want your help, so get your hands off my suitcase," I told him.

The guy wasn't listening, however, and I felt like slapping him.

"Do you want a beating?" Ranjeet asked the man.

"I just want my fees for helping," he replied.

I told him again that we didn't want his help, but my Grandad told us both to go and sit on the minibus. We got on the bus, and I saw my Grandad giving the guy some money and tapping him on his shoulder.

"These guys get together and cause scenes; it's their regular job," he later told us. "Plus, it was only twenty rupees."

I looked at my watch before asking Grandad how long it would take to get to the house. He told me it was going to take a while, so I should try and get some sleep. It was dark at this point, so it must have been time to go to sleep. I asked my grandad and nephew the time, and he replied that it was 10:43 pm. I changed the time on my watch and clicked the stopwatch. I stared out of the window, hoping to see some historical buildings, but it was too dark, plus I hadn't come with a traveller's guide to help me recognise buildings from the pictures. I stared out the window for a little while before I found myself drifting off to sleep.

116

Raj and Julie

I remember dreaming about being lost in New Delhi. I saw the mad crowd coming out of the airport, but this time, they were all grabbing onto my suitcases. It broke out into a fight, but just as I was smashing the guys up like my hero Karam Singh from Bollywood films, Ranjeet woke me up.

"Wake up, Raj, we are here!" he said. I opened my eyes, looked out the window, and saw that it was morning. Motorcycles were driving past, as were people on bicycles and trucks. I looked at my watch, and it was 06:48 am. Ranjeet and I got off the minibus and began to stretch our legs. I looked around and saw a row of badly built units that seemed like shops.

"Come and have some tea!" my Grandad said to me. I looked at the area where they were serving the tea and found that it didn't look hygienic at all.

"Is it safe to drink or eat here?" I asked him.

"Don't worry," he laughed, "The tea is boiled, and all the germs are killed; nothing is going to happen," he assured me. 'We are only an hour away now, so a cup of tea and we'll eat at home.'

A young kid came up to me and handed me a small glass with tea in it. However, when I looked at the cup, it had about two sips of tea in it. I took a sip and asked my Grandad what they called these places.

"Dhaba, " he replied before pointing at the board with "Shinda's Dhaba" written on it.

"Dhaba?" I asked.

"Yes, that's what they call these fast food cafés over here," he replied.

It was too early to take all this in! We got back into the minibus and set back on the road towards the house. As I stared out of the window again, I noticed that the streets of Punjab were getting busier. I saw many motorbikes, including one with a man driving, his wife sitting behind him, and two children sitting behind her! The road had many potholes, which the driver clearly didn't believe in missing. We drove past beautiful fields and saw women carrying pots on their heads and kids in their school uniforms. The view was becoming more like the India that I had seen in the movies. Eventually, we drove away from these beautiful sights and instead entered a busy town with a lot of smoke.

"Where are we?" I asked Grandad.

"Ludhiana," he replied, "This area is the main manufacturing town for the region."

We drove down some side roads, where the standard of the road went downhill dramatically – in some places, there was literally no tarmac on the ground. After what seemed like a long time, we reached our destination.

Chapter Twenty

We pulled outside this massive mansion. We got out of the minibus, and I looked up to find a three-story building with an open rooftop and two massive gates guarding the front entrance.

Suddenly, the gates were flung open by a lady who walked out to us holding a tray. She grabbed the bottle of oil off the tray and poured the oil on both sides of the gates before welcoming us. She also touched the feet of both of my Grandparents. She then came over to me, touched my shoulder, and asked how I was. After also greeting Ranjeet, we all walked into the huge house. My grandfather's niece began the tour of the house. Grandad's niece was the caretaker of his house. First was the living room, then the bathroom. I was very impressed as there was a British-style shower and also a proper toilet. The kitchen was also very similar to ours back home – in fact, I felt this one was better. There were three bedrooms, which I found weird as they were all on the ground floor. The bedrooms were fully fitted with air conditioning, wardrobes, and Televisions. We went up the stairs, which were made out of stone and looked like they needed completion. The first floor had another three bedrooms, one with an ensuite attached. The second floor had another two bedrooms with fully kitted out showers and a large which also had a large open space.

I chose my room on the ground floor before settling down on my bed and dozing off for a nap. However, I was soon woken up by a strange lady sweeping the floor with a broom.

"What are you doing in here?" I asked her. However, before she could answer, my Grandma walked in.

"That's Rani," she told me, "She cleans our house every day for us."

"No privacy at all," I thought! My Grandma left, but just then, Ranjeet walked in.

"Checking her out, are you?" he asked me.

"Get lost, Ranjeet," I replied.

"She's fit, isn't she? I'm going to have sex with her before we go," he smirked.

"Don't you think about anything else?" I asked him.

"I'm a guy. What do you think I think about?" he replied.

I couldn't be bothered continuing the conversation, so I left Ranjeet and went to have a shower. After I had washed, I heard a loud knock on the front gates, a continuous knock that sounded as if the person trying to get in was either panicking or excited. My Grandad's niece opened the gates, and I saw two elderly ladies walk in and a man who walked in with great authority.

"Who's this – Hitler?!" I thought to myself.

He did have a weird-looking moustache! My grandma and grandad came out of their room and welcomed the guests, offering them a seat in the living room. Grandad's niece brought out some food for us – two plates, with a Paratha – thick Chapati, on one and yoghurt on the other.

"What's in the Paratha," I asked.

"Aloo and Gobi," she replied. This was my favourite!

I took the tray off her and walked into my room to sit on my bed. I broke off a piece of paratha, dipped it into the yoghurt, and raised my hand to put it in my mouth, but before I could eat it, my Grandad called me. I went into the living room to find the guests all sitting on the leather sofas, with one of the elderly ladies smiling at me with some incredibly nasty, orange, and ugly teeth. The man with her was sitting in the main leather seat. My Grandad asked me to sit down, so I did so, noticing that the other lady was also staring at me. Boy, was this an uncomfortable situation!

"Raj, this is one of my best friends, DSP Daljit Singh," my Grandad began. "His wife is from the village next to the village where I was born."

"Your Grandad tells me you are studying law?" he began.

"Oh no!" I thought.

"Yes, I am," I replied.

"What area do you want to specialise in?" he continued.

"I don't know yet, but maybe business," I replied.

"Business is not a bad area," he said, "My brother is a judge, and his two daughters are also lawyers," he carried on telling me. "My daughter is studying law, and she will also become a lawyer."

Then my Grandma started to speak, "She is very beautiful, Raj, well-spoken, good height, and very fair-skinned like you."

"She is very bright, a clever girl, and we all like her very much," my Grandad said.

He quickly added this in before my Grandma said anything else to embarrass us. I told them that was all very nice, as I didn't know what else to say.

"She will be coming over tomorrow, and she will take you around to show you the shops," the lady with the orange teeth said.

'Okay, that's good' I replied. At that moment, Ranjeet entered the room.

"What's up, people?" he asked. He looked around before hugging the lady with the nasty teeth.

I walked out, hoping to finally eat my Paratha as I was really hungry. I walked into my room to find that my food had been eaten. I walked out of my room and stormed straight towards the kitchen to my Grandad's niece.

"Who ate my food?" I asked her.

"I don't know, I just gave the food to you," she replied.

"If you want some more, just ask; you don't need to lie about your food being eaten by someone else," Ranjeet suddenly piped up from outside.

I knew then that he had eaten it. We broke into an argument before Grandad's niece, Shindi, told us to stop, telling me that she had made loads more anyway. She was trying to be super nice to me. Shindi was married and had no children – her husband worked abroad in Dubai. My Grandad felt sorry for her, and when he had the house built, he put her in charge of it. She

119

looked after it while my Grandad was back home in the UK. She prepared the tray again, this time adding three Parathas. I ate them in the kitchen, during which time I heard our visitors leaving.

The next day, I woke up and found the cleaner cleaning my room again. For some reason, she wore a lot of makeup – it seemed like she was trying to impress someone. I hoped that it was Ranjeet and not me. I got ready and went downstairs to find that my Grandad had gone out and that Ranjeet had also gone out, with my Grandad's nephew, Joga, to the shops. Probably to buy some cigarettes. I sat back in my room. The second day of the holiday, and I was already bored! I shut the door and began to do some press-ups and sit-ups. However, after about ten minutes, there was a knock at the door. It was Shindi.

"A guest is waiting for you in the living room," she said.

"Guest?" I asked, "I don't even know anyone here! Who is it?"

"Go and have a look for yourself," she told me, before walking away grinning. I walked to the living room and found a girl sitting on the sofa. She was wearing a traditional Indian outfit with a headscarf covering her head.

"Hello," I said, "Have you come to see me?"

She looked up, and I saw her very light brown eyes. She stood up and said, "Yes."

With her headscarf falling off her head down to her shoulder, I could see her properly. She was very good-looking. She had short hair with a brown tint to it, and she was about five feet and five inches.

"I am Madhu," she said.

"Madhu? I'm Raj," I replied. "Do I know you?"

"No, you don't, but my mother and father visited you last night. Do you not remember?"

"I am sorry, I do remember. So, are we going to visit the shops today, then?" I asked.

"Well, I thought I would show you our local city, Ludhiana," she replied.

"Okay then," I replied before calling Shindi and telling her I was going out. She came over and handed over some rupees to me.

"My Uncle told me to give you these," she said as she handed them over.

"How much is here?" I asked her. It seemed a lot.

"Five hundred rupees."

"Is that enough?"

"More than enough!" she replied, "There are families here who earn that in a month! If you want more, I can give you some more," she said before putting her hand down her top and taking out some more rupees.

"Here's another five hundred," I was suspicious. I reckoned that my Grandad had given her a thousand to give me, and she was trying to keep half. I put the money in my pocket, and Madhu and I left.

Madhu was very chatty. We walked out of the gates, and I immediately suffered from the extreme heat. We walked around the corner, and I found that all the buildings were different, and many needed refurbishing. We then came to the main road, and it was incredibly busy—I saw cars, bikes, and rickshaws, the last of which Madhu waved down.

As we sat down, she said, "Chora Bazar," and we were off.

"You don't have a car?" I asked.

"Of course we do, and drivers," she replied. I thought you probably wanted to experience the local transport first. I looked at the guy who began to cycle the rickshaw and noticed that he was skinny. I stared at his legs, wondering how he was able to pull our weight – I was seventy-five kilograms all muscle, and Madhu must have been about fifty kilos. He was pulling us, and the only thing I could think was that this guy could be a good powerlifter! If someone sponsored him, he could be able to compete in the world championships. I saw a cinema which had massive posters of my favourite actor Karam Singh's son's first movie, called "Rain."

I quickly pointed at it to Madhu.

"You like Hindi films?" she asked.

"Like? I love them!" I replied.

"We have something in common then – I also like movies," she said.

"Have you seen this movie?" I asked.

"No, but we can come and watch it tonight if you want. My dad will call the cinema and get us a private cabin."

"Your dad can do that?" I asked.

"Yes, of course he can," she smiled.

We then came to the actual high street of the town. We got off the rickshaw, and I offered to pay the eight-rupee fee. I took fifty rupees out and gave it to him, remembering what my Grandad told me about fifty rupees to one English pound. The man went to get out some change, but I told him to keep it. He looked at me and thought, "sucker," but I didn't care as he had put some serious effort into riding us on that rickshaw.

"That's too much," Madhu said.

"Don't worry, it's okay. Back home, we would payloads more in a taxi for the distance he cycled us here." I told her.

"Up to you," she said, "Just don't do too much of that, as they take whatever they want."

"Do I look like a sucker to you?" I asked her.

"A sucker? What's one of them?" she asked.

"A person who gets taken advantage of," I said.

"Oh no," she replied, "I'm just saying be careful, that's all."

We began to walk down the high street, which was incredibly cramped with all the people and rickshaws. Guys were standing outside the shops trying to get customers to enter, saying things like, "Please, sir, come. I'll show you," which I found odd.

"Anything, in particular, you want to buy?" asked Madhu.

"No, I'll just have a look today, I think. I am here for four weeks. After all, I can do the shopping in the last week," I replied.

"Well, you had better take me with you then, or all these shop owners will charge five times the amount, and I know you'll end up handing it over as well!" she laughed.

We walked past some shops, and I saw some nice female outfits.

"Those are really nice," I said, thinking about my sister, Shelley, who had given me a big list of outfits to purchase for her.

"Don't worry, give me her sizes, and I will get them for you," said Madhu, "I thought you were looking on behalf of a girlfriend!" she exclaimed, looking at me from the corners of her eyes. Just then, however, I looked through a shop window, and I saw a beautiful pink Asian bride's outfit. The more I looked at it, the more I saw Julie wearing it and standing in the window waving at me. She looked so beautiful. I picked up my hand and waved back.

"Who are you waving at?" Madhu asked me.

"Oh, no one," I said, suddenly feeling very embarrassed. We walked towards the end of the long high street towards a roundabout which had a big clock in the centre of it.

"This is the Clock House Point."

"Clock House Point?" I asked.

"Yes, this is what we call it," I looked around to see a sign for a Chinese restaurant.

"Let's go and have lunch over in that restaurant!" I said.

"Lunch, Raj? It's only eleven o'clock!"

"Don't worry, we'll have an early lunch," I said, so we headed to the restaurant. A man was standing outside the door, welcoming customers. He opened the door for us, and we entered after thanking him. We walked into the restaurant, and I was surprised to find that the setting was exactly the same as the Chinese restaurants in the UK.

"What would you like?" I asked.

"I haven't eaten here before, to be honest. I'll need to see the menu. Don't you need to see the menu?" Madhu asked.

"No, I'll just have my regular, no worries."

The waiter came over to our table and handed us the menus. I told him that I didn't want any starters –to tuck straight into the main course!

"I'll have chicken fried rice with chicken curry and chips for me, please!" I told him.

"That's a lot of food for one person, you know," Madhu stated.

"Look at me, Madhu! My muscles need the fuel!"

"Fuel?"

"Yeah, I need food for my muscles to grow!" I said.

"Oh right," she laughed.

"What would you like?" I asked her.

"I am a vegetarian, so that limits me a bit," she told me whilst looking down the menu.

"A vegetarian, why?" I asked.

"What is wrong with that?" she retorted.

"Nothing, just I never have any meals without a meat content," I replied.

"Anyway, I'll have a vegetable curry with rice," she said to the waiter before turning back towards me. "I am a vegetarian because of my faith. We believe it is cruel to kill animals."

"I'm sorry, and I respect your faith, but I think God put animals on the earth for us to eat," I replied. As I said that, I suddenly had a flashback. It was a time when Julie and I were sitting on the bench at the back of the Library. It was when Julie and I had just begun college, and I was slightly surprised to find her sitting on the bench reading a Bible. I later found out that she would read the Bible to understand where her mother had gone, and she wanted to know all about Heaven. I remember her reading about how the Earth was created, and what she later told me rang far more true than what Madhu was now saying to me. Fortunately, the waiter soon arrived with our food, with the names of all our dishes on display.

"Let's tuck in!" I said.

"Tuck in?" she asked.

"Let's eat," I said before I got another flashback involving Julie. This time, I remembered her praying before she ate her meals, so I put my hands together and said a quick prayer out loud. Madhu looked at me with a big smile on her face.

"You're religious!" she almost squealed in excitement.

"No, I'm not!" I exclaimed, which seemed to wipe the smile off of her face. I noticed that she looked good, whether she was smiling or not.

"I know God exists, and even though I don't know in what form, we must always give thanks to Him for the food we get to eat," I told her.

"Well, as you know, there are a lot of children here in India who don't get any food to eat," she replied.

"Where did that come from?" I thought to myself before reflecting on my Dad and Grandad, who, at times in their youth, were both close to poverty and so had to come over to England to become wealthier. We soon finished our lunch, mainly because the food was absolutely beautiful, and so we decided to leave. I paid the bill, like a true gent, whilst leaving a twenty rupee tip. Madhu thought that this was too much! We came out of the restaurant, and Madhu suggested that we catch a rickshaw from there back home. We passed the cinema again, and this time I caught the name of it – "Shringar Cinema."

"Shall we find out what time the films are showing?" I asked Madhu.

"No, I'll get my father to call them," she replied. She did come across as a bit stuck up and a bit proud when she said that. Eventually, we came to her house. Wow, I thought her house was a massive mansion with two guards standing outside. They were in police uniforms.

"Please come in and have a drink with me, Raj," she asked.

"No, it's fine, thank you. Maybe another day," I replied.

"It's up to you," she said.

"Could you just tell him where to drop me off, please?" I asked her, referring to the rickshaw driver. She leaned forward and addressed him, telling him to drop me off at a place that sounded like "Atam Nagar."

"I will get my father to book the film "Rain" tickets if you want, and he will pick you up," she told me.

"Okay, that's cool," I said.

She walked into the side gate, with the two guards saluting her, and we rode off. I was a bit nervous about getting home safely, but I went along with the ride – I guess I had to! I decided to start a conversation with the guy cycling the rickshaw.

"So, how long have you been riding the rickshaw?" I asked him.

"About twelve years," he answered.

"Do you make a lot of money?" I asked.

"No, sir, but it does pay for the food."

"Do you know you could do very well in the Olympics, competing in the cycling competitions," I told him. He laughed, and I realised he probably didn't even know what the Olympics were. He pulled around the corner.

"Do you know which house you are going to?" he asked.

I began to panic, as I didn't know, but suddenly I saw a dog get up and begin to bark at us. I remembered seeing that dog yesterday and also when we left this morning. He barked at us as if he knew me. So I told the driver to turn the corner. He did so, and I instantly recognised the house, which was about five houses down. We pulled in front of the house, and I asked him, "How much for the fare?"

"Twenty rupees," he replied.

"Seriously? This morning, another guy only charged us ten rupees!" I told him.

He realised that I had clocked on to his game, and he tried to defend his reasoning for wanting to charge twice the amount.

"Sir, we had to drop off that sister who was with you first!" he exclaimed.

"Surely that was on the way," I replied sternly. He then put a sorry look on his face, so I took twenty rupees out and gave it to him, telling him that he had just missed out on a tip. I walked into the house and up to my grandparent's room. My Grandma and Shindi were sitting next to each other, with Shindi sorting through a load of dry lentils which were in a dirty tray on her lap.

"How was your day, Raj?" my Grandma asked.

"It was okay, thanks," I replied.

"Did you like Madhu?" she asked.

"She was okay."

"Where is she?"

"She went back home, and we're going to the cinema later on."

"That's good news!" she said.

I walked out of their room and walked into mine, falling onto my bed and taking the opportunity to have a quick nap. After a while, I heard the door knock, which woke me up. It was Shindi.

"Raj, Madhu just called and said they'll come round in one hour," she told me. I was really tired, and I felt like changing plans. I got up, walked out into the big space outside the rooms, and looked up at the sky. It was dark, but the sky was not black; it was this nice dark blue. You could see the stars shining, and it was very beautiful. Then I heard Ranjeet walking down the stairs.

"Where have you been?"

"I was in my room," I replied. "Where have you been?"

"I had to go to my Dad's brother's house. It was massive, man! Better than this place!" he said.

"So why didn't you stop there then?" I asked.

"Nah, dude, I've got things happening here."

"You want to come to the pictures with me?" I asked him. "I'm going with that old lady with the orange teeth!" I said.

"No way, man. Are you crazy? I'm working on the fit girl across the road!" he told me before walking off.

I showered and got ready, looking at my watch to find that there were fifteen minutes until they were due to arrive. I went to see what Ranjeet was up to on the second-floor landing and heard him singing. He was sitting on the wall of the house, looking across at a very small house opposite. From the second floor, you could see straight into their kitchen, which looked to be very small. I saw an old woman sitting next to a young girl who looked about sixteen years old.

"You trying to impress her?" I asked.

"You bet she's fit," he replied.

"Is that her daughter?"

"No, that's her daughter-in-law."

"Daughter-in-law? So she's married! Leave her to her husband, you idiot."

"No way. I'm having sex with her before I leave. They've only been married a month, and she looks depressed already."

"Just be careful."

"Be careful? Of what? Him? I'd knock him out!" he asked me whilst looking at her husband, who had just pulled up to the house on his motorcycle. I looked at the guy; he was a small, skinny character, and Ranjeet probably would have knocked him out. I felt sorry for the guy. Then, a white car stopped outside our house. I looked over at it and saw the lady with orange teeth.

"There's your girlfriend, Raj. The lady with the orange teeth," Ranjeet said.

"Get lost," I said.

I walked down the stairs and shouted to my grandparents to let them know I was going. My Grandma came shooting out of her room, demanding to speak to them. We walked out of the gates together, and Madhu's mother got out to hug my Gran.

125

"I thought we would take the kids to the cinema to show them a movie. Why don't you come as well?" she asked my Grandma.

"No, no, it's fine; you guys have a good time. Just take care of my grandson; he's a bit clumsy."

Their driver opened the car door for me. I stepped into the car to sit down and found Madhu sitting in the centre with another girl sitting at the other end, who I found out was Madhu's little sister, Kajol. We pulled up outside the cinema, and the gates opened to let us into the car park. We got out of the car and went into the cinema, which smelt strange inside. A man came running out of the box office towards Madhu's father to shake his hand. I looked at his badge, and it read "manager." We followed him into the screening room, and he led us to a private cubicle. We all sat down, and I found Madhu on one side of me and her mother on the other. I leaned over to Madhu.

"I thought it was going to be just you and me?" I asked her.

"I thought the same, too, but my mother was adamant she was coming with us," she said. "I think she was a bit nervous about you, coming from England and all!"

"What?" I whispered, "You had lunch with me today!"

But then we had to be quiet as the movie started. Before I knew it, we had reached the interval.

"Raj, do you need to go to the toilet?" Madhu's father asked me. I did, so we walked outside to join the lengthy queue. Eventually, we walked inside, and the smell was unbearable. I could hardly breathe in there and had to hold my breath for a bit! They needed cleaning. We washed our hands and walked out, thankful that I could breathe again. Madhu's father walked over to the popcorn stand where the manager was standing. I followed him, and the manager handed over five bags of popcorn to us, which I thought was odd. What was even strange was that I didn't see Madhu's father pay for anything. It looked like he had some authority over this cinema manager. We walked back into the cubicle and sat down to watch the movie as it had started again.

I ate my popcorn slowly, which was in direct contrast to Madhu's mother, who munched her's at an alarming rate. She did not waste any time at all! I looked up at her and saw her looking at my popcorn.

"Would you like these?" I said, sighing quietly.

"Don't you like them?" she asked.

"I'm not a huge fan of popcorn," I replied.

"You should have told my husband; he would have bought one box less," she said sharply. I gave her my popcorn, realising the irony of him not paying for them would have been lost on her. A few minutes later, the movie finished, which pleased me – I couldn't wait to get out of there. I had been looking forward to watching it, but the lady with the orange teeth had ruined it for me. We set off back to the house, and eventually, we arrived.

"Would you all like to come in for a bit?" I asked.

"No, it's too late, and I have to go to the police station tomorrow," Madhu's father replied.

"Okay, well, thank you for taking me to the cinema."

"You're welcome," Kajol said and giggled.

"Goodnight and sweet dreams," I told them, and then they drove off.

I went to open the front door but found it locked, meaning I had to bang on the gate and try to wake up my Grandad. The dog ran up to me and began to bark. Luckily, Shindi opened the door, walked out, and told the dog to clear off.

"Did you enjoy the film?" she asked.

"Yeah, it was good" I replied.

"Madhu's mother didn't talk too much, did she?"

"Just a bit!" I said, causing Shindi to laugh.

"She's a bit loud, isn't she? Anyway, I'll get your dinner for you, as your grandparents have gone to sleep," she told me.

While she was putting my dinner in, I stood up and looked up at the sky to see the stars shining. Shindi bought the food for me, and I ate it sitting on the bench, which was called a Manja. After I finished eating, Shindi brought me a cup of milk, which I took with me into my room.

After drinking the milk, I sat on my bed, leaning up against the headboard. I couldn't sleep, probably because the place was alienated. I took my homework folder out and tried doing some homework.

After a few minutes, I lay on my back and tried sleeping again. It was now 1 am. I thought back over the day I had had, and I remembered the outfit I imagined Julie was wearing. She looked beautiful. Suddenly, however, I was woken from my dream by a loud bang on the door. It was my Grandad.

"Wake up, Raj, you need to come with us!" he shouted.

I slowly walked over to the door and opened the lock. My Grandad walked in as I lay back on the bed.

"Don't go back to sleep, Raj; we're going to the police station where DSP Singh works. Get ready, and he will show us exactly what he does!" my Grandad said.

I slowly walked into the bathroom and got ready. Ranjeet was already up and ready, clearly excited. I slept on the way there. We got to the police station, which was a small building surrounded by fields. I stepped out of the car to find all the police officers staring at me, probably because I had decided to wear my vest and show off my muscles a bit. Madhu's father greeted us, and he gave us a tour around the prison cells, where we got to see the criminals. It was a bit shady. We walked past one cell where a prisoner was just staring at Ranjeet, and I. Ranjeet noticed this and began to swear at him, asking him what the fuck you looking at? This guy couldn't understand English but realised that Ranjeet was swearing at him, so he began to swear back at us in Punjabi and be very aggressive, which resulted in the other officers taking him out of his cell and handcuffing him before taking him out into the yard and belting him with a big, thick belt. The guy was screaming with pain. While this was happening, I noticed Madhu's father looking at me. It looked like he was trying to tell me something.

"I wouldn't take crap like that off a police officer!" Ranjeet stated.

"If you got in trouble in India, you would," I told him. Ranjeet was a bit of a troublemaker back home, and he got into trouble with the police a few times. Madhu's father walked up to us.

"This is the way they learn; there's no other way," he said solemnly.

"I came to show them the police station and what you do," my Grandad said to him.

"This is nothing," Madhu's father said.

"Anyway, we had better go, as I have a meeting I need to go to," my Grandad replied.

We stayed in the station for about two hours before we left and returned home.

Chapter Twenty-One

The next day, we decided to visit Khan Khanna, the village where my Grandad and father were both born. As we entered the village, I saw lots of new, developed houses in the middle of fields. The first house I saw must have had at least ten acres surrounding it.

"Whose house is that one?" I asked Grandad.

"That belongs to a friend of mine. He now lives in London, and his brother lives in Canada. They have had their house rebuilt and spent a lot of money on it," my Grandad told me.

A short while later, we pulled up outside the house my family had lived in. It was nothing special, to be honest with you, and was considerably smaller than the houses located near it.

"How come this house is small and the others are massive around here?" I asked.

"We built this house ten years after we left India to go to England," my Grandad replied, "But for the last fifteen years, as we have been living in the city of Ludhiana, we have not needed to extend this building."

The entrance led to a small corridor which had two rooms on either side of it. One seemed to look like the bedroom, and the other must have been the living room, as it had an old television set on a table.

"That television is the first black and white television I bought my brother," my Grandad told me.

"Your brother?"

"Yes, he lived here too, but he passed away five years ago."

"Five years ago? No one told us!" I protested.

"You children were too young to understand at the time. I bought this land and built this house in 1969. Your dad was born in the house across the road."

We walked out of the house, and I saw a very old building right opposite. It was slightly bigger than the one we had just visited. I walked in to find cobwebs everywhere and bare brick walls. There were two small rooms and one room that had a kitchen area attached.

"We all slept in these two rooms, and this is where your dad and your two aunties were born," my Grandad told me. I looked around and saw an old statue of a Hindu.

"What's that statute doing there?"

"Your father bought that many, many years ago. When he was about six years old, he used to talk about how he used to feel something crawl over his body when he slept at night. Eventually, we discovered that it was a snake, which used to slide down a hole in the corner over there. Since that day, your dad thought that he was blessed and imagined that the snake would lead him to treasure under the house!" my Grandad laughed. I walked outside into the garden, and it was fairly big. There was a staircase that led onto the flat roof of the house, so Ranjeet and I decided to walk up and see the view, which turned out to be stunning. I felt my Grandad's hand on my shoulder.

"You see that massive field? That's ours. And that building over there is a school where I was taught, and then when I became a teacher, I taught your dad there," my Grandad told us.

"Did my mom go to that school as well?" asked Ranjeet.

"No, in our days, the girls didn't go to school!" Grandad replied.

We walked down to the school, and I looked at the village well. A high percentage of the buildings were still really old. On the way, we came to a water well, and I got to experience pulling water out of the well. We came to the school, which was also clearly old but had had repair work done on it. The school was quiet. I looked around and saw students sitting outside in the playground, probably because the weather was warm and nice for them to have their classes outside. One of the teachers who was not teaching walked up to us; he shook my Grandad's hand and touched his feet.

"These are my grandsons, and they are here on holiday," my Grandad informed him. The teacher nodded his head towards us.

"This is one of my ex-students who now is one of the teachers here at this school!" my Grandad continued. "He was one of my favourite students."

"Did you teach Dad as well?" I asked my Grandad.

"I did, much to my regret. One time, when I marked his paper, I found he had everything right, but I failed him so he wouldn't be in my class again the following year."

"Why?" I asked.

"I didn't want people to think I was favouring him in my classes, so he had to repeat the year," my Grandad smiled.

We walked into the next building, which was the canteen.

"I sponsored this canteen!" my Grandad said.

I filmed the whole school and the teachers teaching on my camcorder, getting footage of everywhere I was visiting. We left the school and walked back to the fields. Some of the village people gathered together and came and greeted us.

"You're supposed to be the British Powerlifting Champion, aren't you?" one of the locals asked me.

"I am, yeah."

"Well, let's put your strength to the test then."

"Lead the way," I said.

Just further up the road, there was a cart. About five locals sat on the cart and urged me to try lifting them.

"Be careful, son, you don't have to do it if you don't want to," my Grandad said.

"I have to. Now I took on the challenge!" I replied.

I took off my shirt and wrapped it around my waist tightly to give support to my back. I gripped the handles and closed my eyes before I pushed the cart up. All the locals shouted with joy! I then asked Ranjeet and Grandad to sit on the cart as well, and I then proceeded to lift it another two times.

Ranjeet got off and filmed me pulling the cart down the street. The guys on the cart all got off and shook my hand. We then returned to our field and went to the water container that went out into the field. Ranjeet took his clothes off and jumped into the water.

"Sod this!" I said, taking my clothes off as well and jumping in. The water was cold, and we were both in our boxer shorts, yet we were having a great time and throwing water at each other. The people in the village thought we were crazy! Eventually, we got out and went under a shelter to dry ourselves down and put our clothes back on. We headed back to Ludhiana.

Two days later, I woke up and walked out of my room to find Madhu and her mother sitting in the living room. I looked at my watch – it was only 8:30 am. I walked into the bathroom, got ready, came out, and looked back into the living room. There were a lot more people sitting in there! I went back to my room, splashed on some aftershave, and stuck some gel in my hair. I walked back into the living room, and this woman jumped off the sofa and ran toward me.

"Is this my nephew?" she cried, "Isn't he handsome!"

"This is my nephew's wife," my Grandma explained excitedly, "She'll be stopping with us for the rest of the time we are here," she told me.

I looked at her, and she had a massive grin on her face. Then, the lady with the orange teeth suddenly jumped up and grabbed my other arm.

"This is Raj, my son-to-be!" she squealed. "Son, to be?"

I thought to myself. She pulled me away from the other lady and sat me on the sofa beside Madhu.

"Meeting all these new crazy relatives is all too much for me," I told her. She laughed.

"Too much for you? There's a lot more to come and visit you yet! The message has not reached everyone yet!" I looked at Madhu, wondering how it could get any worse.

"I went to your dad's police station the other day," I told her.

"Yes, I know, my father told me. He said you looked afraid whilst they were hitting the prisoner."

"Afraid? No, I wasn't afraid; I thought they were getting punished a bit too much, that's all."

"This is how they deal with the criminals here. Otherwise, they would think the police force here was a joke. I am sure the police in the UK treat the criminals the same way."

"I wouldn't know!" I answered.

"I didn't mean that you had experienced it, Raj."

At that moment, I looked up and realised it was quiet. My Grandma and the other women had stopped talking. I saw them staring at Madhu and me with massive grins on their faces. It was freaky, especially Madhu's mother, with her orange teeth.

"We have planned to show you the local theme park tomorrow, so be ready!" she told me. I got up and walked out of the room, looking back to see my Grandma and Madhu's mother hugging.

The next morning, Ranjeet, Grandma, her nephew's wife, her two kids, two kids from the house across the road, my grandma's niece's son, and I were all up and ready for 9 am to visit the theme park. After waiting for about twenty minutes, a car pulled up outside. It was Madhu and her mother. She walked into our house, apologising.

"I am so sorry for being late. We were waiting for the minibus driver to turn up, but he never did, so we will have to go in individual cars," she claimed.

"What a liar," I thought.

It was so obvious she was lying. Finally, though, we got everyone into three cars. Unfortunately, I was stuck next to Madhu's mother. We arrived at the theme park to find Laurel and Hardy printed on the entrance board, which was weird! We entered the theme park, and I realised that the set-up was the same as we would find back home. We walked around and went on a few rides. It was good to see that the kids were having fun.

"You love children, don't you?" asked Madhu, gripping my arm as if we were a couple.

"Well, these children probably don't get the opportunity to come to these parks so often," I replied. Ranjeet noticed a big waterfall in a garden area.

"I'm going under there!" he shouted.

"Don't be crazy. You'll get hurt," I warned him, "Plus, there's a wall blocking the access.'

"I don't care," he called before climbing the wall and running under the waterfall. I have to admit, it looked like great fun, so I climbed up the wall and also ran underneath the waterfall. It was really cold, but the feeling of the water falling on me was great! Eventually, we climbed back down, as several members of staff were shouting at us. I took my sodden top off, at which point the ladies screamed and covered their eyes. Madhu's mother slapped my back.

"That's disgusting, put a top on!" she shouted at me.

"This is disgusting? This is all muscle!" I told her. She didn't have a clue what I meant. She quickly took off her cardigan and told me to wear that. I put on her cardigan to find it stunk of bad body odour. I had no choice but to keep it on. I looked at my watch, wondering when I could go home and have a shower. Luckily, my watch read 4.50 pm, so it was time to go as my Grandad had told us he would be waiting outside for us at 5 pm. We all walked toward the exit, and luckily, my Grandad was indeed waiting in the car park area. Unfortunately, I had to sit in Madhu's parent's car. All the way home, all I could see was Madhu's mother pulling faces at me for making her car seat wet. I just wanted to go home and take off the horrible-smelling cardigan! We pulled up outside our house, and I got out. I quickly took off the cardigan, gave Madhu and her mother a double bicep pose, and then ran in to take a shower.

Nevertheless, I hadn't trained for a few days, and I felt I was getting a bit soft, even though I was doing press-ups and situps every morning. My grandfather's friend lived near a gym, and he offered to take me to it. I went into the gym and found it was cramped, yet they had all the Machines and equipment I needed.

"How much is one session?" I asked the gym owner.

"We don't charge daily fees, but only monthly charges," he told me.

"Okay, how much is it monthly?"

"One hundred and twenty-five rupees," That would work out to the equivalent of one gym session back home; I worked out after using a calculator.

I filled out the form to join and walked into the gym. I looked around to see all kinds of guys working out. There was one guy who was chewing gum and didn't seem to be taking his eyes off of me.

At first, I wondered if he was gay, but then I realised that he probably just had an attitude problem! I went to the bench to carry out my bench presses. I warmed up to sixty kilograms and then loaded the bar to one hundred kilograms. I carried out the exercise, but when I got to fourteen repetitions, I found two guys standing on either side of the bench. I completed the set by doing sixteen repetitions. I planned to do twenty repetitions even though my record has been twenty-two repetitions. I got up and looked at these guys staring at me.

"What's up, guys?" I asked.

"You have been training long?" one of them asked me.

"Yeah, about seven years," I replied, "Why, what's wrong?"

"Nothing. We've never seen anyone do that many repetitions with one hundred kilograms. The owner of this club can only press one hundred and twenty-five kilograms!" the same man replied.

"Well, thanks, but I'm sure there are stronger weightlifters in Punjab!"

"Yes, there is, but not in this gym, though!" he answered. Just then, I saw the owner of the gym walking over to us.

"What's the most you have benched?" he asked me.

"One hundred and sixty kilograms in competitions," I replied.

"Show us!" he asked.

"It's been a couple of months since I last lifted at competition level, guys, to be honest. But I'll try."

They loaded one hundred and sixty kilograms onto the bar. I got into position and gripped the bar, and they lifted the bar over to me. I brought the bar down to my chest, touched my chest, and pressed the bar upwards. It was a slow move, and I struggled as the bar got halfway. For a moment, it got stuck at the halfway point, but I screamed out, "Come on" in a loud and aggressive voice, and that inspired me to finish the press.

"That was awesome!" one of the two guys said.

"Can we train with you?" the other one asked.

"Why not?" I replied. So we all trained together, working on the muscle groups in our chest, shoulders, and arms. They were exhausted towards the end of the session! I completed my session and walked out to my Grandad's friend, who had just pulled into the car park area. As we were driving home, I saw my Grandad's friend turning his head and looking at me. This became a bit uncomfortable as I began to realise that I didn't know this guy. He was my Grandad's friend, but how well did my Grandad know him? Then he began to question me.

"How are you finding India, Raj?"

"I'm enjoying it so far, thanks."

"Would you like to live here?"

"No, I like the UK better," I answered.

"Oh, I thought you were enjoying it here? Your Grandad told me something different."

"I do like it here, but it's a big step to move here."

"How about if you found a partner here?"

"A partner?" I asked.

"Wouldn't you want a bride from India?"

"Bride?! I'm not ready for marriage! I'm still studying."

I closed my eyes and wondered what was going on. I saw Julie dressed in the Indian bride's outfit again, and then I saw myself lying on the floor with blood all over me. I began to panic.

"That's okay. You can finish your studies. You know I am a retired judge," he told me.

"My Grandad did mention it, yes," I replied. My throat had gone dry.

"Well, when you complete your studies, I can set you up here. You can open your practice here in Ludhiana. I have all the contacts, and setting up your business will be easy," he told me.

"It's something I can think about," I told him, just to get him off my back for a minute. Thankfully, at that point, we had reached the house. I showered, had something to eat, and then went to sleep.

A couple of days later, we travelled to a beautiful city called Chandigarh. It took almost three hours to get there, and we had to hire a minibus as Madhu and her mother also came with us. When we reached Chandigarh, I was shocked, as it was a massive difference from what I had seen before. It was the same as the UK, almost. The roads were properly tarmacked and had pavements to walk on, and the houses were built in the English style. I felt like I was home. The driver took us for a tour around the area.

"That building there is Tara Singh's studios," he told us. "This is where he makes his movies!"

"Great! Let's go there!" I shouted.

We drove around the massive building but found nothing was going on there, so instead of hanging around, we drove on and headed towards the beautiful and historic Rock Garden. It was a unique garden consisting of various art objects and styles, with my favourite section being the area dedicated to the artwork made solely by using industrial & urban waste.

On the wall there, I scratched Raj loves Julie. After lunch, we went to the beautiful Sukhna Lake, which is unique in India because it is man-made.

People like to visit the lake in the mornings to enjoy the cool breeze and its beauty, but also at lunchtime when several designated picnic areas are allocated around it. When we were there, I saw the lake area as a perfect place for meditating. I looked up at the sky, and the colour blended perfectly with the lake - it felt peaceful, and you could hear birds humming. Sadly, however, we had to leave after a little while, as my Grandad wanted to show us two properties.

We drove to the first property, which was situated in Chandigarh, Sector Eight. It was nice but wasn't comparable to the second one, which was located just around the corner.

"Why aren't we living here?" I asked my Grandad. It was that beautiful and majestic.

"This is an investment, Raj. I bought this place six months ago, and I have a buyer paying more than double the rate to live here," he informed me. " Besides, all our family lives in Ludhiana," he stated while smiling at Madhu.

Again, we didn't stay here long. It was certainly a whistle-stop tour! Next, we went to visit Madhu's cousin, who lived by the University. He was the professor there, and his wife, Madhu's cousin, was a lawyer. My Grandad arranged so that we would stop at theirs for the night and leave for Shimla in the morning.

We walked in, and the house was beautiful. Each room had a very distinctive Indian cultural theme. One room even had a hammock hanging from one room to another! We sat down and had a cup of tea. Madhu sat opposite me next to her cousin Sandeep. Whilst they were talking to each other, in Indian, they giggled and looked over at me, which freaked me out a bit. Then, Sandeep picked up her cup of tea and looked over at me.

"How is your studying coming on, Raj? Law, isn't it?" she asked.

"Fine, thank you," I replied, dreading the conversation which was about to take place.

"You know, Madhu is studying Law as well?"

"Yes, I do," I replied, nodding my head.

"You two could open a practice together as partners, you know!"

"Not a bad idea," I replied, trying to sound as enthusiastic as possible.

Sandeep grabbed Madhu's arm and squeezed it tight, but thankfully, I was spared any more of this conversation as it was time for bed. We shared rooms, and I had to share mine with Grandad, as Ranjeet had already decided that he wanted to sleep on the hammock. I was lying in bed when my grandad suddenly walked in and lay beside me. I knew it was him as I could smell the oil off his head and the whisky off of him.

"Son, you have made me very proud. It'd be great if you could become a partner with Madhu and open a law firm. It doesn't have to be here—you can do it back in the UK if you wish. You know, I wanted to become a lawyer when I was younger, but I was not able to afford to complete my degree," he stated.

135

I was confused. Was this about becoming a lawyer? About being part of a law firm partnership or becoming part of their family? I decided not to worry about it at the time and instead asked him what he meant in the morning. I fell asleep.

Chapter Twenty-Two

I woke up in the morning to find my Grandad sitting up and praying. I looked at my watch – it was only 6:40 am. My Grandad opened his eyes.

"You're awake! Good. Get up and get ready to go to Shimla," he told me.

"It's too early!" I protested.

"You have half an hour to get ready. We will leave about nine," he warned me.

We all got ready and went downstairs to eat breakfast before we piled into the people carrier and set off for Shimla. The drive to Shimla was quite exciting and dangerous, as the roads had many bends and slopes. At one point, I looked out the window to find a bus that had flipped over on its side.

"Look, there's a bus tilted over!" I shouted.

"Yes, that happens quite regularly, sadly," our driver replied.

We started driving up a slope. We were going into a semi-circle, and the cars and buses coming from the other direction were whizzing past, missing us by inches. One car got so close that I thought we were bound to collide!

"Wow, that was close!" I shouted, to which the driver just laughed. He seemed crazy.

I looked out of the window again to see that we were on the road incredibly high up, overlooking the woods down below. It was a major drop-down from here to there! Finally, however, we reached the town of Shimla safely.

The people in this area seemed to be a lot fairer-skinned than the people I had encountered previously. Their dress sense was different here, and many looked Asian-Chinese. We pulled up outside our hotel and checked into our rooms. I was stuck with Ranjeet this time, but for some reason, he was a lot quieter than usual.

"What's wrong with you?" I asked him.

"Don't tell anyone, but I think I've fallen in love," he told me.

"You?! Love?! To whom?" I asked.

"You know who. The girl who lives in the house opposite our house," he replied.

"But she's married!"

"I know, but her husband is never there for her, and she hates it there."

"How do you know all this? We've only been here a short while!"

"I saw her mother-in-law leave, so I sneaked over to their house."

"What?! Was she not scared?"

"No, she has been smiling at me for the last few days."

"So? What happened?"

"We got talking, and she told me she was forced into the marriage. Her dad did not have any choice because he was poor. Her husband is fifteen years older than her, and he works away four days a week. She's stuck with her old mother-in-law, and she hates it there."

"So what did you say to her?"

"I didn't say anything!" he laughed.

"You did what?!"

"I gave her what her husband wasn't giving her!"

"Ranjeet! You're fucking crazy. What are you going to do now?"

"I don't know. I feel sorry for her, and I would love to take her back home."

"You know that's going to be very difficult. She is married, man. Don't fall into the trap and become a target."

"A target?"

"Yes. You could be the target, which enables her to get a passport to get away from here and her life. She could be using you, man. Just think about it. Besides, your dad would kill you."

"I know."

"Listen, let's go and check out the town, and you can sort it out when we get back to Ludhiana."

This talk enabled me to feel close to my cousin for the first time. He had shared something personal with me, and I felt happy as, over the years, we had only had arguments and fights. We walked out of our room and down into the lobby, where we found our group waiting for us. Madhu walked up to me.

"Let's have a walk through the romantic mall," she suggested.

We walked away from the hotel and into the market, buying many souvenirs in the process. I came across a shop that sold outfits similar to what Rajiv Singh wore in his first movie role as an adult, "Rain." He wore long, knee-length gowns, and I bought fifteen different types of outfits, some of which were in his style, all in different colours. I also bought some short-sleeved Nehru-style jackets, which reflected the culture of the Shimla area.

"You have made that shopkeeper's day!" Madhu told me. "He probably earned that amount in a month or two, the amount you just spent in there!"

We walked towards the church. It was good to see the church, as it reminded me of the time Julie and I went to our local church together. Just outside the church, a man hired traditional clothing for you to wear while he took photographs of you, so we all wore these traditional robes and had our photos taken.

Madhu and I sat down a bit later to decide what we wanted to see the next day. However, we were to be disappointed.

"Sorry, children. You have to have an early night as we have to leave early tomorrow," my Grandad informed us.

"We're leaving tomorrow morning?" I asked.

"Yes, I have a very important meeting I have to attend. We can come back next week, though," he answered.

I looked at Madhu.

"We'll have to see these areas next week then."

138

"Okay," she replied, and she left to go to her room.

I opened the door to my room to find Ranjeet in bed with one of the women from a shop we had stopped at earlier.

"What the hell do you think you're doing?" I seethed at them, trying not to look.

"Just give us another twenty minutes!" Ranjeet whispered.

"Another twenty minutes?" I asked, "I thought you were in love with that woman across from the house?"

"I'll talk about it later; just let me finish off here. Come back in about twenty minutes or so."

I grabbed my coat and walked out, disgusted with my cousin. I decided to walk to Madhu's room. I didn't know why, because that would be the last place I would like to go, but there was no one else to talk to. I knocked on the door, expecting to find Madhu, but instead, it was opened by her mother. When she realised it was me, she began to smile widely, like a clothes hanger lodged in her mouth.

"Oh, son, what brings you here?" she asked me.

"Is Madhu here?"

"Yes, yes, do come in!" she replied.

"No, no, it's okay. Can you just get her for me, please?" I requested.

"Alright, just one minute."

There was a brief pause as Madhu's mother closed the door quietly and went inside to get Madhu. After what seemed like a long time, she opened the door and slipped silently outside the room.

"Hi Raj, what's up?" she asked.

"Hey! What are you doing?"

"Nothing. Just watching television."

"Why waste the last night here? We should check out the evening view from the top of the hotel. Would you like that?"

"Of course, let me just get my coat," Madhu smiled at me.

We walked out and up to the top of the hotel, to the sitting area that overlooked the hills and mountains. We sat down, and I looked at my watch, hoping that Ranjeet would finish quickly.

"Nice view from here, isn't it?" Madhu said.

"Yes, it's very beautiful," 'The British Raj built this whole area, and it hasn't changed since they left. Everything is the same.

"So Raj, tell me about the UK."

"What can I tell you? What do you need to know?" I replied.

"Anything! About London, Scotland, anything at all!"

"Well, mainly it's cold like this and, normally, colder!"

"Well, in London, we have Buckingham Palace, St. Paul's Cathedral, Big Ben, Westminster, Leicester Square, Piccadilly Circus, Trafalgar Square, Oxford Street, London Zoo, London Bridge, Museums, and think that's the lot. You have seen all these?"

"Yes, it was on a school trip."

139

Raj and Julie

I remembered a time when we had a school trip to London, and Julie and I took many pictures of us outside many of the tourist attractions.

While Madhu spoke about how she has fantasised about visiting London, I drifted back to Julie and being on the coach to London.

I sat in the coach, waiting for Julie to join me. She was busy talking to the art teacher outside the coach. One student after another asked, "Is anyone sitting next to you?" and I kept saying yes. Just then, Julie walks on behind, saying to the other girls. "That's my seat," and she sits next to me.

"About the time," I said.

"Sorry, I just had to speak to Mrs. Shore for some advice," She said.

"Hey, look at that."

"What?" I asked

"There was a time when nobody wanted to sit next to you cause of your smelly hair, and now they all want to sit next to you," She laughed whilst saying it.

"Ha, Ha," I replied.

"At least you don't use the oil anymore. Come here, let me smell your hair," she continued jokingly.

Now, back to Punjab.

"What about Scotland?"

"I haven't been."

"You haven't been to Scotland?"

"Nope. Never had the opportunity."

"My friend visited the UK last year, and she toured Scotland," Madhu said.

"Many tourists who visit the UK tour Scotland. But you will find a lot of people who live in the UK have not seen many parts of the UK away from where they live," I replied.

"Whys that?" she asked.

"People are too busy! Like you guys – how many times have you been here?"

"This is my fourth time."

"See? There you go."

For some reason, I felt uncomfortable talking to Madhu about why I hadn't travelled much to neighbouring countries and places in England. I decided to change the tack of the conversation.

"So... do you have much planned after you graduate?"

"Well, I plan to join my sister in her firm and learn to become a successful lawyer. Either that or, you never know, I might be joining your firm!"

"You never know...but I only need a secretary!" I replied jokingly.

"What do you mean?"

"Take it easy! I'm only joking!"

"Oh, sorry. I felt offended. I am going to study and work hard to be a secretary. No way."

140

Raj and Julie

I looked up at the clouds to find my face getting wet. It wasn't raining, but it was actually snowing. I stared at the clouds, thinking, I hope Julie is also looking up at the clouds and it's snowing in England.

"It's snowing!" I exclaimed.

"Oh wow! I thought it was rain!" said Madhu, looking up and letting the snowfall on her face.

"Is this the first time you've experienced snow?" I asked her.

"Yes! It feels nice; it is soft and cold," she replied.

Madhu moved closer to me and held my arm.

"You are going to open your Law firm, aren't you?" she asked, looking deeply into my eyes.

"You have light-coloured eyes," I smiled at her.

"You haven't answered my question, Raj!" she replied.

"Well, let's complete our degrees, and we will look into it closer to the time. Anyway, maybe it's time we went back inside."

"Yeah, okay."

After saying goodnight to Madhu, I made my way back to my room, hoping that Ranjeet had finished doing what he was doing.

"Are you guys decent?" I shouted out before I fully opened the door.

"Yeah, come in. She's gone," Ranjeet replied.

"And how did you manage to pull her?"

"Man, she was easy! I just told her that I'm here looking for a bride and that she's the best-looking girl I've ever seen.."

"How old is she?" I asked.

"Same as me, sixteen."

"I thought the girls here were well strict due to their culture?"

"Well, this one was easy. I told her that I was involved in my dad's business, and we are planning to set up a factory here in Shimla."

"You liar! Your dad's unemployed and scrounges off my dad!"

"Get lost! He doesn't scrounge off anyone."

"Listen, I don't want to argue with you. But what happens if this girl comes round with her parents?"

"She isn't coming back, Raj. I told her that I'm coming back next week with my mother."

"You crazy fool. What about the girl back in Ludhiana?"

"What about her? I was playing with you. I'm not really in love with her. I just wanted to see your response."

"You're a fucking idiot. Messing around with these girls' lives and embarrassing my Grandad! I'll give you a fucking beating and a half."

"Relax, dude, relax! Don't worry about it; I've got them all under control."

I got changed into my pyjamas and got under the duvet, wondering how all these girls were being duped so easily by Ranjeet. However, I didn't worry about it for too long as I soon fell asleep.

We all woke up at seven o'clock in the morning to eat breakfast and left the hotel. As we were leaving, we drove past the shop where Ranjeet had met that girl. She was waiting outside the shop, and she jumped up with joy and waved at Ranjeet as we drove past. Ranjeet waved back and laughed. I felt the evilness in his laughter and felt sorry for the poor girl. The trip was very tiring, so I slept on the way back.

Chapter Twenty-Three

Three days later, we got ready to go to visit Bombay. Only Grandad, his friend, the retired judge, and I got ready to go. In the beginning, Ranjeet was excited and then changed his mind to go.

Probably because of the girl across the road. Then, I thought, "Is she a girl, or do I address her as a lady as she is eighteen?"

It was early morning, and we had to be at the train station at 6:30 am. Our driver drove us to the railway station. It was cold in the mornings. The driver dropped us off, and we waited at the platform for our train.

The train arrived, and we got on board. We sat in our reserved seats.

This was not a normal train. My grandad said, "It's a fast train which should get us to New Delhi in half the time."

I thought it was great because I couldn't sit through the experience of travelling nine-plus hours again.

The service on the train was very good. About thirty minutes into travelling, we were served breakfast. I opened the tray and found it was an egg omelette. I finished my breakfast and went to sleep.

I woke up and found us reaching the New Delhi train station.

"That was fast," I thought.

We got off the train and caught a taxi to the domestic airport.

We then boarded the aeroplane, which flew us to Bombay. We arrived at Mumbai airport. I think the flight took one hour and thirty-five minutes. We came off the aeroplane and went through the security checks. I had that nervous feeling again walking through the airports, especially thinking of the news I had heard of bomb blasts, etc. The smell wasn't as bad as the smell in New Delhi.

My grandad's friend went and booked a taxi for us. Then we went outside the airport, and I felt a different atmosphere in the air. It was a lot hotter and less polluted than New Delhi and parts of Punjab. I looked around and found palm trees, and it was warm.

We sat in the taxi, and the driver asked, "You want to go to Juhu?"

"Yes, Juhu! Sea Princess Hotel," replied my grandfather's friend, Mr. Pyare Mohan.

We drive away from the airport to our airport. As we travelled to our hotel, I recognized a lot of the landmarks used in movies. We finally pulled up outside the hotel. It was called the Sea Princess Hotel. The hotel was lit up with lights and had so many floors high.

We got out of the taxi, and the bellboy carried our suitcases in. Mr. Singh, wearing a red turban and a white outfit, greeted us and opened the door for us. I walked in, and there were spotlights above the ceiling, which gave off a lot of light which was bouncing off the mirrors on the side. This was a good idea. It doubled the light in the area. Mr. Pyare, Grandad, and I walked to the reception area.

"Hello, sir. Welcome to Sea Princess Hotel," the receptionist greeted us.

"Hello, we have booked two rooms," Said Mr. Pyare.

"Two deluxe rooms, I hope," my grandad asked.

"Yes, Sir, Two deluxe rooms. One with two single beds for five thousand five hundred rupees per night and one with a double bed for six thousand five hundred rupees per night," She answered.

"How will you be paying?"

"I can pay in cash or by card," Said my Grandad.

"Whatever you prefer, sir."

Grandad passes over his credit card.

"Thank you, sir. We will charge the card for today's payment, and you can settle the rest on your departure."

"Ok, that's fine," he said.

"We would also need to leave your passports with us for your stay here."

"Ok, that's no problem," Grandad gave her our passports and signed the forms.

She gave Mr. Pyare the card, which opened the door.

"The bellboy will take your luggage up to your room," said the receptionist.

The bellboy led us to the lifts. We walked into the lifts, and they were full of glass and mirrors again.

We were on the fifth floor. The bellboy led us to our room. We entered the room, and it was nice. I looked out of the window and thought, "What a view." I saw the beach and the swimming pool area.

"Let's freshen up and get a couple of hours of sleep," my grandad said.

"I'm not tired. We are here only five days. We need to see as much as we can," I said.

We will. Just freshen up. Take a shower," said Grandad. I went, had a shower, and got ready within an hour.

I put gel through my hair and applied some aftershave.

I looked back and found my grandad asleep, snoring.

I grabbed the key and walked out of the room.

I thought I'd check out Bombay myself.

I went down into the lobby area. I walked around and came to a lounge, then walked out and saw the pool area.

I walked out to the pool area and thought swimming in the morning would be a good idea. I walked to the edge and looked over the view of the beach area. The water was filthy, and the sand area was full of people selling goods. I even saw a kid taking a toilet and human feces on the sand. I felt sorry for these guys who had to live like this, but at the same time, it was horrible to look at.

I walked back into the hotel and walked into the shopping arcade. I bought some swimming trunks and postcards. Then I went back up to my room. Walked in and found Grandad still sleeping.

"Come on, Grandad, wake up," I said.

144

My grandad got up, sat up, and began to pray. He finally got up and went to the bathroom to get ready. I sat down on the bed and flicked through the TV channels. I came across a channel playing one of my favourite Bollywood films, Andaz Apna Apna.

I love this movie. It stars my favourite actress, Sabrina Kumari. There was a knock on the door, and I opened it. It was Mr. Pyare.

"We will have a walk around the beach area tonight," said Mr. Pyare.

"Is it safe to walk around here?" My grandad asked.

"It should be," he said.

"We all get ready and go down to the reception area," Mr. Pyare said.

"I'll go and book a car and driver for tomorrow."

"Grandad and I sat in the lounge and waited for Mr. Pyare.

He walked back over to us and said, "The car and driver are all booked for tomorrow."

"Let's have a cup of tea before we set off," my grandad said.

"Not a bad idea," said Mr. Pyare

I thought, "Why are we wasting time?"

We walked to the restaurant and sat down. The waiter came over and asked, "What may I get you, sir?"

"Three cups of tea," answered my grandad.

"Anything else, sir?"

My grandad looked at the menu and said, "The prices are very expensive. The tea is fifty-five rupees a cup. That's more than a pound a cup."

"Just the tea, thank you," he said. "We are not stupid to pay these prices. We'll eat out at other restaurants."

"We can leave the tea as well if you want to," Mr. Pyare asked.

"No, it's ok. I need a cup of tea before we go. It's never bothered me in the UK, but it's only eight rupees in other cafés here."

The tea is served, and my grandad toasts the cup of tea, which is a pound.

Grandad, being successful and not being short of money, was always wise. Mr. Pyare, who I gathered was rich, didn't like to spend either.

We finished our drink and headed towards and exited the doors with Mr. Singh, who was wearing a red turban and opening the door for us. I have relatives who wear red turbans, but I found this man wearing them to be a bit strange. I didn't know what it was.

"Sir, would you like me to call a taxi?" Mr. Singh asked.

"No, thank you. We are going to have a walk," My grandad answered.

"What are the best places to visit around here?" I asked.

"Behind the hotel are Juhu Beach and Chowpatty; they are popular places to spend time in the evenings and enjoy appetizing local snacks. You can nibble the spicy Bhel Puri or gobble the appetizing Pani Puri at the local kiosks out there. It becomes an extravaganza in the presence of vendors, toy sellers, horse and donkey rides, dancing monkeys, acrobats, and cricket matches," He explained.

He continued to explain, "Juhu Beach is frequently visited by a lot of people around the year. It has been portrayed in many movies in the Indian film industry."

"Do actors come to the beach?" I asked.

"Yes, sometimes," he answered.

"Let's go there then."

"You can go this way," the doorman said.

He pointed towards the side of the hotel.

This led to the Juhu beach. The beach was really busy and noisy. I could see people selling goods off their trollies, selling snacks, a man getting money doing backflips, donkeys, and much more happening on the beach. It seemed like I was at a fair. It was the same as I have seen in movies. Wait a minute, this is the beach I have seen in many films. I couldn't believe it. I was on the famous Juhu beach.

We walked up one way and ended up in the stalls where they sold various goods, food, and drinks.

There was one stall that sold fresh juice. We all had two rounds of fresh orange juice. We walked onto the main road and saw loads of traffic passing.

"If we walk around, it should take us to the front of our hotel," my Grandad said.

We carried on walking and came to a row of shops. We walked a bit further up, and I then saw the major movie billboards.

"Wow, this is great. Look, those are the billboards we see in the movies," I exclaimed.

I took out my camera and photographed these billboards. We continued walking around the bend on this busy road. We came to another row of shops and then to a couple of restaurants.

"We can come back here and have dinner in one of these restaurants. They'll be a lot cheaper than the hotel menu prices," Said Mr Pyare.

We carried on walking to see what was on this main road. We came outside a hotel called Ajanta Hotel. My Grandad was curious to find out how much they charged per night. He was a typical businessman always looking for the best deals.

Mr. Pyare went in to find out how much it was per night. As My Grandad and I were waiting for My Pyare, I saw someone who looked familiar walk out of the hotel. I could not believe it; it was Sabrina Kumari. I stood, hoping that she would notice me. I quickly took out my camera pocket and began to snap. Then, a lady shouted, "Please ask before you take photographs."

I looked, and it was Radha Rai telling us off.

I couldn't believe it. I just got told off by Radha Rai. Radha Rai was one of the leading actresses of the sixties and seventies Indian movies and was married to the biggest superstar, Vijay Rai. He dominated the film industry as an actor in the seventies and the eighties.

Then Sabrina looked at me and smiled. I couldn't believe it. Sabrina smiled at me. I was a huge fan of Sabrina.

"You want a photo taken with them?" my grandad asked.

146

I looked and saw that they had already sat in their Jeep.

"Na, it's ok."

Their Jeep drove past us, and Sabrina looked at me and smiled.

I still couldn't believe that we had just seen Sabrina, and she smiled at me.

Mr. Pyare came and said, "It is not much of a difference. We should stop at the hotel we are at."

I didn't care where we stopped. I just saw Sabrina.

I began to daydream, and my grandad asked, "Are you ok?"

"Yes, I'm fine. I hope I got a photograph snapped of Sabrina."

We left the car park area of the hotel and carried and walked further up. We then went to a hotel called the Hotel Royal Garden. My Grandad noticed there was a bar area in there.

"Let's go in there to have a drink. I need a couple of pints to wash down the pollution stuck in my throat," said my Grandad.

This was just an excuse. He needs his drink every night.

We walked into the hotel bar. My grandad orders two pints of larger for himself and Pyare.

And asked, "What do you want, Raj?"

I looked to see what they had and said, "Diet Coke will do."

We stood at the bar area and drank our drinks. Then I looked across the room and recognised a famous singer from the UK.

I looked and saw my grandad and Mr Pyare finishing their first drink and ordering the second drink.

We left the club and began to walk back toward our hotel. We walked up to the row of shops and restaurants. Mr. Pyare said, "Let's eat in here."

We walked in and sat at our table. Then, an Indian film song came on, and we saw women get onto the tables and begin pole dancing. My grandad got up and said, "Let's get out of here."

The man by the door asked, "Where are you going? This is a restaurant with good food and nice ladies dancing for you at your table."

"No thanks," my grandad replied.

The man began to laugh as we walked out and said, "They got scared."

We walked out and went to the next restaurant further up the road. We ate and went back to our hotel.

The next morning, I got up and got ready to swim.

I went down into the swimming pool and began to swim. It had been a while, but I managed to get back into a routine.

I stepped out of the pool, walked over to the deck chairs and sat down. Then, I saw this huge, muscular guy jump into the pool.

He caused a big splash, which was very funny. I saw a guy filming him coming out of the water. At first, I thought he was part of a film crew, but then I realised they were just tourists.

I went back to the pool and carried on swimming. After a few lengths, I came back out and sat back on the deck chair. Then I saw the big guy walk towards me. I thought, "Why is he coming my way?"

147

He stood opposite me, stretched his hand out to shake, and said, "Hi, you all right, mate?"

I recognised the accent.

"Are you Raj?" he asked.

"Yes, how do you know?" I asked.

"I'm Guru Singh from Wolverhampton as well. I've seen you in the paper for winning the powerlifting championships," He said.

He sat on one of the deck chairs next to me.

"Do you work out?" I asked

"Yes, just a little. I train at the Atlas gym," he answered

"Atlas Gym. I know of Atlas Gym. It is near East Park, isn't it?" I asked.

"How long have you been training?" I asked.

"About five years, he said."

This guy was huge. His chest must have been about fifty-five inches, and his arms about twenty inches big.

"That's cool. Have you ever thought of going into Powerlifting?" I asked,

"Yes. When I read about you in the paper, I thought of starting, but no one teaches powerlifting at our club," He answered.

"Why don't you come to my gym?"

"Where's that?"

"We train in the Bilston Art College basement on Monday, Wednesday, and Friday from 7 pm to 9 pm."

"I'll come and check it out when I'm back in Wolverhampton."

"Are you here on holiday?" I asked.

"Yes, I've come with my uncle. We went to Punjab for two weeks and spent our last week here in Bombay. My uncle and I are both fans of Bollywood films and actors. That's why we are here. Hoping to meet some actors. How about you?" He asked

"I'm a fan of Bollywood films, too, and I hope to bump into actors. I bumped into Sabrina Kumari last night," I said.

"Sabrina Kumari? You lucky sod. What was she like? Was she hot?"

"Hot," I answered.

I saw a lot of people rushing around, arranging the tables and making space.

"What is going on here?" I asked.

Guru Singh called one of the guys who worked at the hotel.

"Yes, sir?" the worker asked.

"What is going on here?" Asked Guru

"It looks like a film shoot, sir," He replied

"Let's have a look, Raj," he asked.

"Don't you think we should have gotten changed?" I asked because we were in swimming trunks and topless.

"Let's have a quick look," said Guru Singh.

He walked over to where the trailer was set up, and a couple of guys were sitting on chairs discussing.

"It's Aryan Khan!" he shouted.

He ran towards this Aryan Khan actor. I stood still where I was as I didn't want to embarrass myself.

This actor, Aryan Khan, jumped out of his seat and shouted, "Stop him!"

The other two guys also jumped up with him and stopped Guru Singh.

I would get scared seeing Guru Singh running toward me, as he was huge and packed with bulky muscles. Guru Singh walked back towards me.

"Did you see who that was? That was Aryan Khan," he said.

"I don't know who Aryan Khan is," I replied.

"You don't know who he is?" he asked. "You must have scared them the way you ran towards them."

We laughed.

"What film are they filming?" I asked.

"The guy said it's called 'Fauj'."

"I think we should get changed and come down with some clothes on," I suggested. "Let's meet back in the reception area in the next thirty minutes."

"Ok, I'll get my autograph book," said Guru.

We walked back to our rooms.

I entered my room and found my grandad and Pyare sitting and having breakfast.

"Had a good swim?" asked Grandad.

"Yes, Grandad. Plus, I met a guy from Wolverhampton."

"Wolverhampton?" he asked.

"Yes, he's here to see actors. Plus, there's a film being shot downstairs."

"A film? Let's have a look. They might want a Karam Singh look-a-like to play a part," said my grandad.

My grandad did look like the famous actor Karam Singh, and I was always stopped by people thinking I was his son Ranbir Singh. I did resemble him quite a lot.

We all got ready and went downstairs into the restaurant area, where we found the whole area set up with filming equipment and junior artists of the film. We were not allowed to sit in the lounge area.

Then I felt a tap on my shoulder. I looked back, and it was Guru Singh. He carried on talking about how excited he was to meet actors.

Then we saw an actress walk out of a trailer, and it was the brilliant actress, Sridiya. Now I knew her.

"That's Sridiya," I said.

As she walked through the doors, Guru Singh quickly asked Sridiya, "Can I have an autograph, please?"

She gave him an autograph.

"Can I have a photograph, please?" I asked.

Sridiya stood against the wall next to me, and we snapped a couple of pictures.

"Me too," said Guru Singh. He stood beside Sridiya and his uncles as I clicked the camera for them. With great excitement, we watched the two actors perform the scene. It seemed like it was a song scene.

Then, when Aryan Khan was walking towards us, Guru Singh stopped him and asked for an autograph and then for a photograph.

"Raj, could you take a photograph of us, please?" asked Guru Singh.

They all stood next to Aryan Khan. At the same time, I got ready to take a photograph and asked them all to smile. Then, Aryan Khan said, "Listen, take the photo or leave it."

I thought, "Who is this guy?"

I took the photograph. Then Guru Singh ran up to me and said, "Your turn."

"Na, it's ok," I said.

Then, Aryan Khan walked off.

"Didn't you want a photograph with him?" asked Guru Singh.

"I don't know him, plus he has an attitude problem." This actor went on to become the biggest actor in the Indian film industry, and I didn't take a picture with him.

"What's your next plan?" I asked.

"We are leaving tomorrow afternoon. So, we plan to try meeting Karam Singh before we leave," he shared.

"Can we come with you?" I asked.

"Yes, we are leaving at ten o'clock in the morning to his house, which is around the corner from here," he said. "Great. I can't wait to see Karam Singh. I'm a big fan," I said.

"Are you doing anything this afternoon?" I asked.

"We plan to visit Film City," he said. "Can we follow you in our taxi?" I asked.

"We can hire a people carrier, and all go together," said Guru's uncle.

"I'll ask my grandad, who is sitting in the reception drinking tea with Mr. Pyare."

"I know your grandad," said Guru's uncle.

"You do?" I asked.

"Who doesn't know your grandad? He's a well-known businessman in Wolverhampton. In the seventies and eighties, he was the voice for the Asian community in Wolverhampton."

"OK, that's the plan then. We'll go to Film City."

In the evening, we all met in the reception area. We all got into the people's carrier, a Suzuki. The driver was a Sikh, which made it easy to communicate.

He drove us around the Juhu area, where most of the actors lived. He pointed at the house where each famous actor lived.

We drove through the streets of Bombay. There was a lot of traffic, and it was congested. We drove through a high street, which was congested. There were nothing but shops and stores along this road, which was called Linken Road.

150

We finally got on the main road towards Film City. It was all uphill, with nothing but green on the sides and a few small huts selling goods. We came outside the Film City studio. The driver, Sukhi, said, "These guys have come from the UK and would like to come and view the studio."

The guard said, "Let me go and find out."

He came back and said, "You would have to pay one thousand rupees at this gate, and this will allow you to get to the next gate, and I can't promise how much they will charge."

Then Mr. Pyare said, "I know these types. They'll charge us from one gate to another, and in the end, we will not see anything."

"It sounds about right," said Guru's Uncle.

"Just pay them and find out," said Guru Singh. He was excited to see the film studio.

"Don't be silly," said Guru's uncle.

"We don't know these people; my friend Pyare is from here. He knows what they are like. You have to be smart when it comes to things like this," said Grandad.

The driver also agreed. "I don't think they will be able to see anything. These guards don't have any authority to make decisions," said the driver.

"See, this driver is good," stated Mr. Pyare.

"I'll take you to Surinder Batra's studio," said Sukhi.

We drove to the next studio, which was SB Studio. Sukhi got out of the car and knocked on the gates. The guard opened the gates and talked to Sukhi.

Sukhi came back and said, "Nothing is happening at the studio."

"I can't believe it," said Guru Singh.

We all travelled back to our hotel.

The next morning, we all met again and sat in Sukhi's vehicle. We came outside Karam Singh's house. We all went out, and I noticed Guru and his Uncle wearing sweat tops printed with old film magazines cut out of magazines of actors printed on the tops. These were printed on the front and back of the sweat tops with most of the pictures of Karam Singh and Ranbir Singh.

Sukhi asked the guard, "These people have come from the UK to see Karam Singh. Could they see him?"

The guard came back with another guy who looked like Ranbir Singh but wasn't. He tried speaking English, "What's the problem?"

Guru's uncle said, "Brother, we have come from the UK and would like it if we could meet Karam Singhji. We are big fans."

He looked at his top and laughed a little. Then he said, "Karam Singh is not here. He is out shooting and will not come for a few days."

We all sat back in Sukhi's Suzuki.

Guru Singh was worked up and said, "What are we going to do now?"

"We have until seven o'clock until we have to be at the airport," said Guru Singh's uncle.

151

Then the driver said, "You guys have been trying to see actors for the last few days and haven't seen Bombay properly. If you guys want, I can show you the main spots in Bombay."

"That's a good idea," said my Grandad.

We headed back to the hotel and waited for Guru and his uncles to check out.

They checked out, and we had a tour of Bombay. We headed towards the main City; the driver parked outside opposite the famous Taj Hotel.

"This is a Taj hotel, and right over the road is the Gateway of India. I'll stay in here while you guys walk around and have a quick look," said Sukhi.

We walked across the road and walked into the Taj Hotel. With the air conditioning in the hotel, it was really cold compared to outside.

The building was beautiful. We spent about a couple of minutes looking around.

Then we walked across the road and looked around the Gateway of India. There were two police constables outside the Gateway of India.

For fun, Guru's uncle asked the constables to arrest Guru for a laugh so they could film it on their camcorder.

The policemen walked up to Guru and grabbed him from his shirt. He looked around them. I could see these two skinny policemen scared of Guru Singh's muscular size. We began to laugh. Then Guru realized it was a joke, and he was set up.

Then a man asked, "Do you want to visit the Elephant caves?"

We looked at the time and said, "No, it's fine."

We later dropped off Guru and his uncles at the airport and headed back to the hotels.

We tried seeing Karam Singh the next day, but unfortunately, he was shooting outdoors as told. We spent most of the day at the poolside.

We had an early flight back to New Delhi on the fifth day. Meanwhile, went back every day to Karam Singh's house to see if he was back. He wasn't, so we spent the two days by the poolside.

We reached back home to Ludhiana after a long journey. We flew back to New Delhi and caught a train back to Ludhiana.

I walked into our house and greeted my grandma. What I found was a woman talking to my grandma. Two other girls were sitting next to this woman. They must be about sixteen and seventeen years old.

They looked at me, putting their hands together, both greeted me and said, "Please visit our home one day."

It was night-time, and I was lying on my bed thinking of my experience in Mumbai. Then Ranjeet walked in.

I sat up and said, "You missed the opportunity to visit Mumbai. What did you do here?"

"What do you think? I did those two girls who were here earlier." Meaning I had sex with them both.

"Those two as well?" I asked.

152

"No wonder they were asking me to visit their house," I thought. "No way, I would have sex with them."

"I had them on their backs naked on your side of the bed," he carried on sharing.

"You bastard," I said and moved over to that side of the bed.

The time in Punjab was flying past fast as we spent most of the time shopping.

Four days before we were going to leave back for the UK, my grandad said, "We are having a party before we leave, so I suggest you get all your packing done earlier."

"Are we having the party here at the house?" I asked. "No, we have the party in two days at a new banqueting suite which recently opened up here in this city."

So, I finished all my packing the next day and kept out only the clothes I was going to wear.

Chapter Twenty-four

On the day of the party, I wore a blue suit my grandad had made for me. My grandad had booked minibuses for relatives to attend the party. We all reached the banqueting suite. I looked at my watch, and it was noon midday. We walked into the banqueting suite, and I saw that there must have been about five hundred chairs laid out, all facing the stage. The food was along the sides, and waiters served the guests.

Mr. Pyare walked up to us and said, "It's your party, and you have come late."

"Late? I think it is our party, and we come when we please," I replied.

My grandma and aunties went and sat in their reserved seats. Ranjeet said, "I'm going to check the girls at the party."

Mr. Pyare took me and my grandad around, introducing me to people I had never met and I didn't think I would ever meet again.

My Grandad and I sat in our seats and watched dancers performing their dances and acts.

Then, I saw Madhu and her parents walking toward us. Madhu was dressed up and looking nice.

My Grandad stood up and said, "Stand up."

I stood up, and my Grandma and grandad hugged Madhu's parents. Mr. Pyare, with his wife, stood next to Madhu's parents. They also got a hug. Then, one by one, they hugged me.

Then my grandad said, "Sit down."

My grandma seated Madhu next to me. I wondered, "What's happening here?"

Mr. Pyare got on the stage and grabbed the microphone from the DJ.

He began to talk, "Good Afternoon, ladies and gentlemen. We would like to thank you all for coming on short notice today. Today is a special day for our family, and we would like to share it with family, relatives, and friends. Firstly, I would like to introduce you to all my dear friends, Gurjeet. Please come on the stage."

As my grandad walked towards and stepped on the stage, Mr. Pyare continued to speak, "We are not just friends but also business partners and will become family today. He is a kind-hearted, successful businessman who has been operating his business in Ludhiana for the last five years. He has developed a very successful business not only here in Punjab but also operates a successful business in England, UK."

My Grandad took the microphone and said, "Thank you for the wonderful introduction. Again, thank you for attending a special occasion. It is nice to see family and friends to share the good news. Mr. Pyare and I have been very good friends for many years. We became business partners three years ago, and today, I am glad to announce we will become related.

Ludhiana, over the last five years, has become very close to me. I have enjoyed the growth I have gained and the challenges it has thrown at me. Mr. Pyare is a strong community member of this city and a very successful businessman. I wanted to become closer to the two as family members. Today, God has blessed me with this opportunity to announce the great news of the engagement of my grandson and Mr. Pyare's niece."

I looked around, thinking, "Which grandson?"

I looked at Ranjeet, who was too busy chatting up one of the dancers. He saw me looking, and I lip-synced, asking, "You?"

He pointed back, saying, "To me?"

"Oh no, this can't be happening," I felt my heartbeat so fast that it was going to shoot out of my body. I looked at my hands, and they would not stop shaking.

"Who is his niece?" I kept asking myself.

Mr. Pyare took over the microphone and said, "Raj and his grandma, please, come on to the stage."

I looked to my side and found Madhu smiling. Then she realised that I wasn't smiling.

"What's wrong?" she asked.

"Nothing," I replied.

My grandma stood up, grabbed my arm, and said, "Get up then."

I stood up, and my grandma kissed me on the cheek.

We both walked to the stage. My grandad put his hand out to shake. I shook his hand, and then he hugged me. Then, Mr. Pyare did the same.

Then, Mr Pyare continued on the microphone and said, "Can DSP Dhillon come to the stage with his wife and their beautiful daughter?"

I thought, "What a setup. They all knew besides me."

They walked to the stage, and everybody in the hall was clapping.

I looked towards Ranjeet, and he was on the floor laughing. He was laughing so loud that we could hear him on the stage.

I didn't know if to cry or to laugh because the way Ranjeet was laughing, I wanted to laugh. I couldn't even run off.

They made me stand next to Madhu in the centre of the stage. My grandparents stood next to me, and Madhu's family was next to her.

Mr. Pyare said on the microphone, "The engagement begins. Can Raj put the engagement ring on Manjit?"

"Manjit? Who's Manjit?" I thought.

My Grandad took the ring box out of his pocket, took the ring, and gave it to me.

I thought, "What do I do with this?"

I never thought this was going to happen like this.

I looked at Madhu or Manjit, whatever her name is, and thought, "I always thought that Julie would have been the girl I would be putting this ring on."

I began to envision Julie standing in front of me, and I said, "I have loved you from the first moment I saw you," and placed the ring on her.

Madhu stretched her left hand forward, and I placed the ring on her finger. While she put the ring on my finger, she dug her fingernail into my hand. Again, I thought she was showing aggression, and the pain got worse.

***

I am disturbed and wake up back in the hospital. A lady is trying to take off my wedding ring. I look closely, and it is my father's cousin's wife, Sheela. There is nothing sweet about her as it gives us the creeps every time we meet her. She comes across as very nice and innocent, but after all the stuff my father found out about her was scary.

Having faith in God since childhood, I never believed in witchcraft or its effects of it. But this woman got caught dropping gifts off with death curses on them to kill my father. I heard once that maybe she was behind me, ending up here in the hospital.

Her husband, my father's cousin, and my grandfather's brother's son, is a successful businessman, and that is because he never paid taxes to inland revenue over the years.

Until one day, they caught up with him. However, he is the stingiest man you could ever come across. He would try not to pay for anything in life. People eventually saw through him. Even though the two have never had an input in my grandfather's or father's business, they still believe they should get fifty per cent of the inheritance. This is because my father borrowed money from them once, which my father paid back. The property had a significant growth, which my father bought.

She continues to dig nails into my hand.

"They shouldn't leave jewellery on him as a patient," Aunty Sheela says.

"It's ok to leave it on him," my mother says.

"He doesn't need that anymore," says Uncle Rupinderjit, My father's cousin.

"What do you mean?" asks my mother.

"Who knows if he will survive?" says Uncle Rupinderjit.

"How dare you say that. It's because of people like you he is in here. You have always been jealous of his success. Be it Raj's success in sports, business, and movies."

"No, we haven't," Aunty defends herself.

"Yes, it's true, especially in movies, Rupinderjit. You always wanted to work in movies, and because my son got in there before you did, you couldn't bear it. You always advised him wrong so he would miss out on opportunities."

"That's enough," Rupinderjit shouts.

"I'm not going to shut up now. You have always been jealous of my husband and children. You never liked the fact that your father treated my husband more like a son than you."

Just then, my sister Shelly walks in with her husband Jaswinder. She asks, "What's going on, and what are these two doing here?"

"We are here to see your brother, our nephew," says Sheela.

"Nephew? You don't care about us!"

156

"It's because of you two, both Jaswinder and I almost lost our lives," says Shelly.

Again, without any proof, all fingers are pointed at Uncle Rupinderjit and his wife. My sister Shelly was in hospital like me four years ago with an illness that the doctors didn't understand. She had lost all of her hair, and two years after she got better, her husband ended up in hospital with TB in his spine and brain. He has partially recovered but has severe memory loss and has to use a walking stick to assist him in walking.

My father had a Hindu lady from a Hindu temple visit and cleanse his house and my sister's. This lady found items that contained formulas of witchcraft, and all these items were given from Aunty Sheela. Aunty never explained why she took uncooked chicken mixed in spices to my sister Shelly's house.

"Get out of my brother's room. I bet he is here because of you two," screams my sister. They both stormed out, with Aunty saying, "Your children all deserve to be in the hospital and die."

I want to applaud my sister's bravery.

***

Back in India, everybody in the hall clapped and cheered.

I didn't know what had just happened. I felt like I was falling down a deep hole and with no one there to help me. I could physically feel the drop.

I looked down at the stage floor to see if I was falling. Everybody was cheering and clapping in the hall. Madhu's mother came and hugged me, and so did her dad.

The only thing I was thinking was, "How am I going to get out of this?"

I looked at Madhu, and she was looking down and smiling. She was good-looking and attractive, but I didn't love her. The feeling was not there. We were then asked to take the centre of the dance floor.

I thought, "Oh no, this can't be happening. I have to dance with her as well."

"Come on, son," my grandad said.

I walked down to the dance floor. Madhu followed me.

I stood with my back to Madhu, and then Mr Pyare walked over to me and turned me around to face Madhu.

I thought, "What dance move shall I perform to get out of this? To make Madhu think she made a mistake."

"Shall I do the moonwalker or Karam Singh dance, or didn't know what to do?" It was all happening too fast. She grabbed my hands to dance and pulled me towards her.

Then, the DJ played a romantic Bollywood song. As we began to dance, I felt Madhu squeezing my hands and digging her nails into my hands.

I reacted by looking at her and asking what she was doing.

"Just dance," she said.

That tone of voice was angry, and I had not seen this side of her.

We carried on dancing. I thought, "I better go with the flow, and I'll ask my grandad about all this later on."

157

I smiled at her, and as I smiled, she released the pressure. But her eye was saying something else. Guests came and blessed us by waving rupee notes around our heads.

Then Madhu spoke, "You looked surprised at this celebration."

"Aren't you?" I asked.

"No, I knew all along. Didn't you know?"

"No," I thought, "I don't want to get my grandad in trouble. So I had to think quickly."

"I knew, but I didn't think it was going to be here and in front of this many people. People I don't even know," I said.

"Don't worry, you'll soon get to know them all."

"Do I have to visit all these people one by one at their homes?" I asked.

"Maybe," she said and laughed.

"Raj doesn't seem too excited. Let's put some English music on for him," said the DJ. Then he put on "I Swear" by Boys II Men.

We finished dancing, and I showed a bit more excitement.

"You two follow me," said Mr. Pyare.

We walked over to a table with two large chairs decorated like it was for a married couple on their wedding day.

"Sit here," he said.

We sat down, and people rushed to feed us Indian sweets. They were too sweet to keep tasting.

"I'm feeling a bit sick," I said to my grandma, who was standing next to me.

"Drink some water," she said.

"Get some mineral water for him," Grandma said to one of the waiters.

He brought me a glass of water, and I drank it, which removed some sweet taste from my mouth.

"I have to leave," I said to my Grandma.

"Sit right there. You will embarrass us in front of these people," she instructed.

I looked around the hall and found people eating and dancing on the dance floor. The whole experience made me feel a bit dizzy like I was about to pass out. I sipped on the water, hoping to understand what had just happened.

The party was over, and I couldn't wait to get back home this was back to the UK. I never missed home as much as I did today. I felt alone even though my grandad and grandma were there, but they were only there for their friends.

Madhu and her parents hugged me before they left. Madhu said, "I'll come and see you before you go."

I nodded, saying okay, thinking, "What else could I say?"

Grandad came and joined us. "How are we all doing? Isn't this great? I am so happy."

I couldn't believe he was saying this because I wasn't happy. Madhu's mother added, "We are so happy that our daughter will be joining your family. Come here." She said to Madhu and pulled her towards me. "You two had two days more to get to know each other. Don't spend it standing apart from each other."

"That's right, come round tomorrow, and we'll have breakfast tomorrow," said my grandad.

"Let's go then, and thank you very much for today," said Madhu's dad. "See you tomorrow morning," said Madhu.

They walked out of the hall. "We better go as well. Let me tell the owner of this place we are going," said my grandad.

As my grandad left to look for the owner, Mr. Pyare walked up to me. He put his hand out to shake. I shook his hand.

"Do you know this new relationship between our families is going to create many business opportunities? You never know; your grandad and I could be the leaders in this city," He said. "There you are, Mr. Pyare," shouted my grandad. They shook hands and hugged. "Come, let us go."

We left the hall and headed back home.

Chapter Twenty-five

I walked into my room and sat on my bed, and for the first time, I missed my parents. My grandad walked in, sat next to me, and said, "I knew you were upset and probably angry. You probably don't like me so much at this present moment. But I did this for you, my son. This family is respectful. They all have strong career roles. You won't realise that yet, but later, you will realize what I mean and appreciate what I did for you. If you are dating someone else back home, then tell me. I will call all this off. I know you are not seeing anyone because you love me too much to hurt me."

I wanted to say it was Julie, but I didn't know if Julie felt the same way.

"If you give this a chance, I know you will like this family. With our businesses operating in the UK and India, you can live six months in the UK and six months here in India. Who am I doing this all for? You are my only grandson, and this will be all yours after I pass on. Are you going to let this new relationship happen?"

I was cornered up at this point and agreed by nodding my head and saying, "Yes."

He put his hand on my shoulder, said, "I am very proud of you, my son," and hugged me.

Hugging my grandad, I closed my eyes, and a tear fell down my eye. Just then, as my eyes were closed, I saw Julie and saw tears in her eyes. Grandad walked out of my room, and I was left thinking about Julie.

Ranjeet walked in and said, "You crazy idiot. How can you agree to marry a girl from India? My mother and Aunty Baljit are right. You're just a clumsy idiot."

"Hey, the other week, you wanted to marry the girl across the road," I said.

"No, I didn't. I was playing with you," he replied.

"You messed your life up," he continued, destroying my mind.

He walked out laughing. I laid back in my bed, thinking, "Have I made a mistake?"

The thing is that Julie did not like me in that way, and I could be waiting for a long time. Or she did like me, and I could go back and find Julie and myself getting together.

All night, this was the only thing I could think about.

The next morning, I woke up and found my grandma waking me up.

"Get up, son," she shouted. "Your in-laws are coming for breakfast in the next half an hour. Get up and get changed."

"In-laws? I'm not even married to her yet," I thought.

"I'll get up in five minutes," I said.

"Don't take too long," she said and walked out.

I was drained from all this; I just didn't feel I had the energy to get up. After about ten minutes, I woke and just about got ready.

I was asked to sit in the living room. I sat in the living room with my grandad and grandma. I was too tired to sit up, so I decided to lie down on the sofa. Then we heard a car pull up. I knew it was them as I heard Madhu's mother talking loudly. I think she was making it a point to our neighbours that her daughter has got engaged to me. A guy from England.

The lady with the orange hair, and orange teeth, who could be my future mother-in-law, came charging in.

I couldn't get the thought out of my head of her being my mother-in-law. It was horrible, and I felt sick.

Then I remembered someone telling me that ninety per cent of young women grow old looking like their mothers. I couldn't be married to someone looking like that. My stomach wasn't feeling too good. I drank a cup of tea, and I felt sick.

I quickly ran out, running past Madhu and her dad. I went straight into the bathroom, and I puked up. I felt a lot of strain on my stomach as I only had a cup of tea.

I cleaned up and walked back into the living room.

"You okay, son?" my grandma asked.

"I have just been sick," as I said this, I looked at Madhu's mother, and she pulled a face, hearing the word sick.

"It's the food we ate yesterday. I feel the same," Madhu's mother commented.

I think she complained about the free food she ate, which was paid for by my grandad.

"You need some fresh air," she said, "Why don't you and Madhu go to the top of the house and sit on the landing? Enjoy the fresh air, and you both can talk."

"What fresh air?" I thought.

Madhu and I walked out of the living room and walked up to the second floor.

As we walked up the stairs, Madhu in front of me looked back at me and smiled as she climbed the staircase.

It was like a romantic scene out of an Indian film. Well, it was for her, but not for me. I walked onto the landing and towards the wall, which looked over the whole area.

I looked over and saw people walking in the streets. A man was struggling to ride his bike while delivering milk.

"So, how do you feel about us being engaged?" Madhu asked.

I gazed into the neighbours' kitchen, thinking, what do I say?

I carried staring into the neighbour's kitchen. I noticed the lady whom Ranjeet was dating staring back and smiling.

"Oh no, what is she thinking? I am not Ranjeet," I thought

I turned around and asked, "How do you feel?"

"I'm excited and happy that I'll be related to your grandad."

"Brilliant excuse to marry someone," I thought.

"How long have you known my Grandad?"

161

"We have known your grandparents for a very long time. As I can remember, I was very young when they visited our house and my uncle's house. He has been a big inspiration in my life. I watched how confident and smart he is, and he is very good at giving speeches."

"She's in love with my grandad, not me," I thought.

"Right. Do you think you will ever be able to come and live in the UK?" I asked, changing the subject.

"Yes, I love what I have seen in videos and read in books about the UK. Plus, my best friend recently got married and moved to the UK with her husband."

"Was he from the UK?" I asked.

"Yes, he lives in Southall London. She called me once and said it was great in London. How far do you live from London?" She asked.

"About two hours away," I replied.

"That's not far then," she said.

Then, my grandad's niece brought up our breakfast.

"Have something to eat?" She said, placing the tray on the table and leaving.

"Have you had any girlfriends?" Madhu asked.

"This is a bit out of the blue," I thought, "And a bit late."

"Don't look shocked. I have to know these things before we get married," she said.

"You are late to ask this question. I could have or not have a girlfriend now that I am back in the UK," I replied.

Her face dropped, no more smiling.

"So what's the truth?" She asked.

"It's complicated," I thought.

"Why didn't you ask this question before we got engaged yesterday?" I asked.

"I trusted your grandad, who said you did not have a girlfriend as you were too simple for these kinds of things," she stated.

"Well, I don't have to have a girlfriend to be in a relationship; there could always be the same sex."

"Are you gay?" She shouted out.

"Calm down. I am only joking. ," I said.

"Come on, tell me the truth. Are you straight, or do you have a girlfriend?"

"Well, let me assure you that I'm straight, and can I ask you if you ever had a boyfriend or even loved someone?"

"Yes," I thought. I reversed it around.

She looked down and took a long pause.

"She had been in love," I thought.

"Well, have you been in love with someone?" I continued to ask.

She looked back up and said, "I thought I loved someone."

"Thought? You either did or didn't."

"I liked this boy at college, and we studied in the same class. We had a lot in common. He also liked me and asked me to marry him. But the only problem was that my parents did not agree to it."

"Why wouldn't they?" I asked.

"He was a different cast. I thought I loved him. But when I told my mother, she said that it's not love. Love is what you build on. You marry the person we chose for you and build and grow in love."

As she went on and on about being in love with this guy, I remember a time when Julie and I were in our usual park talking about life partners. Again, we must have been in our early teens.

"What's your ideal partner, Raj?" Asked Julie.

"Partner?" I asked.

"Yes, your future girlfriend and wife?"

"I don't know," I replied.

She took out her notepad and pencil and said, "OK, let's make a list," she insisted.

"A list?" I asked.

"Yes! I saw my mother and her friend do it once. It's about all the things you like and what you want your partner to be like. What's your favourite food?" Asked Julie.

"All types of Fish, Chinese food, rice pudding, and fig biscuits," I replied.

"What do you like to do or want to do?"

"I like weight training – so sports, I love movies, writing, reading, praying, comedies, poetry, music, scuba diving – so water sports, and Julie."

Julie laughed.

"Ok, now your turn," I said.

"Ok, I like fish too. I love rice pudding, fig biscuits, drawing, music, running, church, reading, fruit, and travelling. I would like to go skydiving, and Raj.'' We both laughed.

"So, if you and I like all the same things, should you be my partner?'' I asked.

"A good question, Raj."

And just then... Back to Punjab.

"Are you listening, Raj?" Asked Madhu

"Yes, please carry on," I said.

"I knew too much about this boy, and after marrying him, there would be no excitement and adventure."

"I won't be able to love you. All the love I have is for Julie, and I don't have any more to give," I thought.

"Do you still love him today?" I asked

"No, he is married in the United Kingdom, I think."

"Are you sure you don't want to marry me to get with this guy in the UK?" I asked.

"Of course not, and how can you ask such a thing?" I am sure she mumbled, "I thought he was clumsy."

163

I was stuck in a funny situation.

"When do you plan to get married?" I asked.

"I plan to get married soon after we graduate, and the rest is up to your grandad. That's just over eighteen months away. Will you be able to wait that long?" I asked.

"Of course, we are not getting married before we finish our studies. Let me tell you," she protested.

"A girl who lived near us got married to a guy from Canada last year. She is still waiting for him to take her over. I don't want to be left in an awkward situation. You understand," she said.

"Calm down," I said. "I'm not suggesting we get married right now anyway."

"Eighteen months," I thought, "It is too soon anyway. Let's make it exactly two years," I said.

"Why don't you make it three years?" She suggested.

"Why three?" I said.

"Why not four years?" I replied.

She began to laugh and said, "Eighteen months is fine."

"But the thing is that I don't know you," I kept on thinking, standing and talking to her. She came across as a very simple, nice, career-oriented lady. But there was something else I was hearing in her voice. I couldn't put my finger on it, but I would have to work it out.

"How much alcohol do you drink a week then?" She asked.

"I don't drink alcohol at all. I hate the taste of it," I replied.

"That's good because my friend's husband goes to the pub every weekend. This is the only thing she hates about her husband," She said.

I thought that was a moment to find out more about her. "So, tell me what you like and dislike."

"Food-wise, I like butter chicken, but I don't like fish or dairy products. Truth, even though I was born in India, I don't like Bollywood movies or even Bollywood songs. I dislike the heat; hence, why I live in the air conditioning, which I am privileged to have."

"What have you always wanted in a woman?" She asked.

I thought and thought about Julie's character and mine combined, as we were so similar.

"I had never wanted anyone who was jealous of others, got angry, not someone who always criticized, someone who was honest, genuine, ambitious, someone who had similar values to mine, loved jazz music, loved reading, loved sports, loved movies, loved poetry, water sports, and someone who respected her partner."

"That's a big list. Let me see," she said.

"I can't help that I am short-tempered and easily get angry, and if you don't give me a reason to get jealous, I won't. We both will be lawyers, so criticizing is in our nature. I don't like sports, and you get respect if you give it to me first," she answered.

"So very much the opposite of my list," I said.

164

"They do say opposites attract," she stated.

"That's a myth, I think. If both have the same interests, life would be simple and easy," I replied.

"Unfortunately, it won't be in our case," she said.

"So, will you and your family come with us to the airport tomorrow?" I asked quickly, changing the subject and wanting to get away from this nutcase.

"No, I think you will be leaving very early hours of the morning. We won't be able to wake up so early and travel eight to nine hours to New Delhi."

I thought, "Great, they are not coming with us, but I wasn't looking forward to the eight-hour trip to New Delhi at all."

"So, how many times are you going to call me a week?" She asked.

"Why would I need to call you?"

"To talk to each other and share our daily experiences," she said.

"I don't know. I think when something exciting happens, I'll call you."

She laughed and said, "You are funny."

"You better start packing and get some rest for the trip back."

"I know."

I put my hand out to shake and said, "It was good talking to you and thanks for all the tours."

"The pleasure was mine," she said.

She moved forward and hugged me. My arm was still stretched out to shake her hand.

"You can hug me as well," she said.

I hugged her, and then her face moved up, and she kissed me on the lips.

"This was a bit soon," I thought. I froze, thinking, "I am not going to lead her on."

She stopped and said, "I hope you don't mind."

I didn't know what to say, but...

"Have a nice day," I replied.

She walked downstairs smiling.

"How do I tell her that I don't feel the same way?" I thought.

Chapter Twenty-Six

A month later, I sat in the university canteen talking to classmates. My phone rang, and I answered.

"Hello," I said.

"Hello, this is Satvinder from Asian Spice Magazine. I called to let you know that the magazine with your interview in it has been published. You can either go to any of the Asian stores in Wolverhampton and purchase one, or you can come into the office and collect copies from me."

"That's great news. I'll come and collect copies this afternoon."

"OK, see you later this afternoon."

"Cool, and thanks," I said.

I put my mobile back in my pocket.

"Guess what? My interview in the magazine was published today," I told the group.

"What magazine?" asked one of the twin sisters of three young ladies sitting at the table with me.

"It's the magazine I was interviewed for winning the British Powerlifting Championships."

"Powerlifting championships? You? We don't believe you."

"I'll bring the magazine in and show you."

I skipped my afternoon lessons and drove to Satvinder's office. I met Satvinder outside his office when he came back from lunch.

"Sorry, we just went on our lunch break," he said.

I shook his hand and said, "So, how did the pictures turn out?"

"Very well, I must say. Have you gained some weight?" he asked.

"Yeah, just a little. I've been to India for a month, and due to a lack of training and constant eating double-thick chapattis, I gained the weight."

"I thought you probably moved up into a heavier category, as you won the British championships in the previous body weight," he said.

"That's a good idea," I said.

"Take a seat," he said, walking into his office.

He picked a magazine from a large batch and said, "Here you go. Have a look at the contents page."

The front cover had a picture of a Bhangra dancing group celebrating a Punjabi festival.

I flicked over the page and saw my picture on the contents page. I couldn't believe it. I had only seen Arnold Schwarzenegger doing this pose in the bodybuilding magazines. Now I was seeing myself in the magazine.

My story was printed on page twenty-one. I flicked over the pages and came to my pages, and there were two pictures of me. On one side, there was a picture of me wearing a suit with the title saying, 'I will be the world's strongest man one day'. On the other side, I was topless with my arms folded, with the title British Power Lifting Champion written.

I turned over the page, and on the back of the previous page was my story with small pictures of me doing bodybuilding poses.

"Do you like the way it has turned out?" asked Satvinder.

"Yes, of course, I love it."

"Have a read of the write-up about you later on and call me if there are any mistakes or left anything out. Can't do a lot about it, but would like to know if I left anything out."

"Don't worry, I will," I answered.

"I have another meeting to attend, so I'll have to end this one."

"Can I take a couple more to give to my relatives?" I asked.

"Well, they should be buying them. Take two more."

I grabbed another two. "Thanks."

I shook his hand and rushed home to show the magazine to my family members.

I reached outside my dad's shop, ran in, and said, "Look, my interview is out."

I waved the magazines in the air, showing everyone in the shop.

My father, mother, and grandma were in the shop.

"Let's have a look," my mother said.

I quickly opened the magazine to the contents page.

"Look, I'm on the content page."

They all came around to look at the message as I spread the magazine across the sweet chocolate bar stand. I turned the pages to my interview and photographs.

"Look, what do you think?" I asked.

"Where's your shirt?" my grandma asked. "I'm showing my muscles, granny," I said.

"Very good son," my father said and shook my hand.

He took twenty pounds out of the till and said, "Here you go, son, and treat yourself."

"This is very good, my son," said my mother while putting her hand on my head and blessing me.

I ran into the living room to show my grandad.

"Hi, Shelly, look, my interview is out in the magazine."

"Wow. This is great. Watch! The movie industry will give you a call," she said.

"I hope so," I said.

I took the magazine to my grandad, who was sitting on a single sofa in front of the television, watching a John Wayne movie.

"Grandad, my magazine is out."

"Your magazine?" he asked.

"No, not my magazine. I mean, my interview is in this magazine," I replied.

He took the magazine and said a small prayer.

"Have a look at the contents section," I said.

He flicked open the magazine.

"Just a small picture?"

"No, that's the contents pages. Go to the actual section. Here, let me open it and show you."

I took the magazine back and opened it on the page with my interview.

"Here you go."

He flicked through the two pages, just looking at the pictures.

"Well done, son." He shook my hand.

"Aren't you going to read it?" I asked.

"I'll read it later," he said.

I was a bit gutted, "I'll read it out to you."

"Ok, carry on," he said.

I began to read the interview, and I made sure I highlighted the fact that I began training to make my grandfather happy.

At the end of the interview, he got up and hugged me.

"Thank you for mentioning me," he said.

He took out his wallet, gave a twenty-pound, and said, "Treat yourself, son."

"It's ok, Grandad. Dad has already given me twenty pounds."

"It's ok, you enjoy yourself. It's not every day we get blessed with our children mentioned in magazines."

"Give me one of these magazines; I'll post one to Madhu's family. You have three here; I can also post one to Mr. Pyare."

"You can send this one to Madhu, and I need the rest. I'll get another one later this week, which you can send to Mr. Pyare," I said.

I kept a copy for myself, one to show my university friends and one for Julie.

I stepped into my bedroom and grabbed the first bodybuilding magazine I ever bought. I then opened up the page with the interview and said, "I did it."

I sat and read my interview again and again.

I wanted one other person to read my interview.

I got changed into my workout clothes and headed out for a run. I ran towards Julie's first so I could post her in the magazine. Luckily, Julie's stepmother was outside her house talking to another lady.

"Hi. Sorry to disturb you, ladies."

"Hi, Raj," said Julie's mother.

"Could you give this magazine to Julie, please?"

"Yes, what is it about?" she asked.

"My interview is in it," I replied.

"Interview, and what is it about?" she asked.

"It is my powerlifting success," I said.

"Oh yes, Julie did mention it. She did?" I asked. "That's cool," I said.

"I'll give it to her when she comes to visit."

"When is she coming back?" I asked to find out.

"Don't know. She did say that her manager said he would offer her full-time after she completes her degree. So I think she may be stopping in Manchester. That's if she gets a place to rent."

"Oh, could you ask her to come and see me when she does, please?" I asked.

"I'll mention it to her," she replied.

"Thanks. See you later."

"Bye," she said.

I carried on with my run, but before I began, I overheard the other lady speaking to Julie's stepmother, asking, "Is that him?"

Chapter Twenty-Seven

A week later, on a Saturday morning, I was in bed sleeping when I heard my grandad calling my name from downstairs.

"Raj, Raj, wake up," he shouted out.

I looked at my watch, and it was only 8:17 am. I was really tired from the training session last night.

"Raj, come downstairs. There's someone on the phone who wants to talk to you," my grandad carried on shouting.

"Oh, do I have to?" I thought.

I got out of bed and strolled down the stairs. My grandad was talking on the phone with a big smile on his face.

"Here he is," he said and passed me the phone. "It's Mr. Pyare."

"Hello," I said.

"We have not heard from you in weeks. We received the magazine this morning. We are very impressed and very proud of your appearance in the magazine. Here, talk to Madhu's mother."

"Hello, son, how are you?"

"Fine, thank you."

"We saw your pictures, and they are very nice. We are all happy. Here you go, talk to Madhu."

I totally forgot about these guys in India.

"Hello, Raj."

"Hi, how are you?" I asked.

"I've been waiting for you to call me for the past three weeks."

"I'm sorry; I have been busy with university and other things."

"What's that showing off your magazine and your body?" she said.

"What's that supposed to mean?" I asked.

"I've been waiting here to hear from you, and I only get a communication by receiving your magazine. Your grandad probably sent us the magazine, not you."

"So? What are you saying?" I asked.

"I want a full commitment. I am going to leave a lot behind here when we get married, so I expect you to take some responsibility as well."

Things began to heat up. I could hear a side of her that I didn't see in India.

"Well, I didn't sign up for anything. We agreed we had eighteen months, and this gave us time to know and understand each other," I said. "And one thing, I am not being pressured into anything."

Then my grandad started poking me and whispering in my other ear, "Tell her that you'll ring her once a week. Be fair."

I didn't want to lead her on; I just wanted to see if it went anywhere over the next eighteen months. I didn't really know if I had a chance with Julie.

"Well, you won't get to know me if you don't call," she said.

"I know. How about if I call you once a week?" I asked.

"I would prefer twice, but to start with once a week is okay. And you better call; otherwise, you will know about it."

"Know about what?" I asked angrily.

"After all, I'm a daughter of a DSP."

I didn't want to create an argument, so I passed the phone to my grandad. He carried on talking to them.

"Hello, don't worry about him. It's really early in the morning. You have to give him some time as it's all new for him. You know the British children here don't understand culture, tradition, and values."

I was sitting on the sofa, thinking, "Yes, I do."

I stayed downstairs because I knew I was going to get called back again.

This time, Grandma carried a scented stick, waving the smoke around the room and rotating it in circles around my face.

Grandad put the receiver back on the phone set.

"What did you say to her?" he asked.

"She was crying."

"I didn't say anything. You were here next to me all the time."

"Would it hurt you if you called her once a week? It's not that you have to pay for the calls. I don't want you to say anything wrong to her again. Listen, you won't get a girl like this again. She is a very bright and very attractive girl. You should count yourself lucky that she's said yes to marriage to someone clumsy like you."

"I don't want to marry her anyway," I said.

"What do you mean you don't want to marry her anyway? What about the expenditure on the engagement party? Do you know how much I spent?"

"I didn't ask for it. I was thrown into a corner and had no say in it."

"Do you hear what he's saying?" he said to my grandma.

"Do you know how much embarrassment there is going to be if you call this off now? I won't be able to go to India again."

"Girls from India are very bright and clever; you won't get a girl like Madhu in England," my grandma said.

"I've just spoiled you a lot. If you had to go out and earn your own money like I did, you would know about it. People dream of having marriage offers like this one, and you want to throw them into the dirt?"

"Have you seen you? Your energy is wasted lifting weights like donkeys all week. Do you know how much money I have invested in India, and it will all be lost with one wrong step you take?"

"What's wrong with her? She is pretty, educated, and the family is very good."

"I don't love her," I screamed.

"Love her?" he asked.

"You will get to fall in love with her after you get married. Do you think I loved your grandma before we got married? We didn't even see each other. The same with your mom and dad."

"That's you guys, and you don't even get on with each other," I said.

171

"Do you think love marriages are the best marriages? I know many families who have children who have had love marriages, and none of them lasted more than two years."

"You work on the development of this relationship and love after you get married. It's the process of life. You get married to someone you fell in love with before you get married; you have had all the fun before you got married. It leaves no surprises and takes the spice away in the marriage."

"Why can't I marry someone here in the UK?" I asked.

"I had promised my friend Mr. Pyare that I would marry my grandson to his niece. Plus, this marriage will benefit the two families in many ways."

"Business?" I asked.

"Yes, and our business in India and maybe in Canada."

"Canada?" I asked.

"You don't need to know."

Then, my aunty Manjit walked in, saying, "Good morning."

"How are you, Mom and Dad?"

They said, "They are fine."

"Listen to this. Raj doesn't want to marry Madhu," my grandma said.

"What's wrong, Raj? Why don't you want to get married?" Aunty was trying to sound very concerned because my grandad was here.

"Raj, you don't understand that we are trying to secure your future. A relationship and family like this will never come again," my grandad said.

Grandad walked out of the front door to have a cigarette.

"Raj, you won't get a girl from here in England, so we suggest you marry a girl from India."

"Why won't I get a girl from here?" I asked.

"For a start, you are too clumsy. Who would want to give their girl to you in this country?" Aunty Manjit said.

Then, my grandad walked in.

"Why don't you get your son to marry her?" I asked my aunty.

"I would love to, but she is too old for him."

"How about Narinder? He's a year older than me," I said.

"He can't get married; his English girlfriend is expecting a baby," Aunty Manjit said.

"What nonsense is that?" My grandad asked.

"She said I'm too clumsy to get married to anyone," I said.

"It is what I heard and saw. I was walking through the town centre, and I bumped into Narinder and his girlfriend, and she was showing a bump," my aunt shared.

"Who knows whose that is; girls like this sleep around with anyone," my grandma said.

"What is happening? I have great plans for my grandchildren and built respect within the community," Grandad shared angrily.

"Narinder, we will get married into a family I have spoken to here in the UK. They operate building yards and DIY stores."

"But he's got a court date next week, and they say he could be facing two years in prison," said Aunty Manjit.

"Hopefully, it doesn't come to this. He's a bright child; children like him should be doing business," my grandad said.

"What brightness, I think. He has spent most of his teenage years behind bars and got expelled from school for beating the teacher. Only because he does some building work when he's out helping my grandad, and that's if he gets up on time."

"The issue here is not them but Raj not wanting to marry Madhu," Aunty Manjit kindly reminds everyone. "The blessing our mother will get if you get married to Madhu will be a lot. Girls in this country do not cook for their in-laws," Said my Aunty.

"We don't need her to come and do the cooking or anything. She has servants doing that for her in India," my grandad stated.

"Listen, Raj, you need to get in your head that you are marrying Madhu," said Grandad.

He said this and walked out of the room.

"This is all I needed on top of assignments to hand in and exams to focus on."

Chapter Twenty-Eight

Almost a year went by, and I had spent almost every week speaking to Madhu, training harder than ever, and completing assignments for my final year at university, and there had been no sign of Julie back in my life.

Oh, also, Narinder had a baby son. Which was a blessing to his girlfriend as she was severely beaten by Narinder's sister for dating her brother Narinder.

One night, six months ago, Narinder had sneaked his girlfriend into his bedroom. While he was having sex, his mother busted into his bedroom. Unfortunately, she saw them having sex and naked. His sister grabbed his girlfriend and began punching her in the face. The only thing his girlfriend screamed was to let me get changed. I was told by her later in life. I bet Narinder thought he wished he got sent down a few months ago instead of being embarrassed like this. His sister gave his girlfriend a serious beating, which resulted in black and blue bruises on this poor girl's face. But thankfully, the baby she was carrying was not harmed.

I remember him also telling me this before another court case he had a month before he got sentenced. This time, he believed he shouldn't have been sent down. He was driving under the influence of alcohol and was pulled over by two policemen. He was driving with his girlfriend, who was due at any time.

The two policemen pulled him over, and as he told me what happened, the policemen walked to the car. One policeman knocked on the car window, asking him to wind it down.

"Do you realize you're driving recklessly?" Policeman asked.

"No, I was driving fine," Narinder answers.

"Well, according to us, you were."

The policeman looked at his girlfriend, did something to his walkie-talkie, and said, "So I see another paki makes a cheap white trash pregnant."

"You what?" Narinder asked.

"Get out of the car," the policeman told Narinder what to do.

Narinder, under the influence of alcohol, got out of the car, and there was a lot of verbal abuse.

Then, one of the policemen punched the other policeman in the face, turned around to Narinder, and said, "How dare you hit me."

Then, the two policemen began to hit Narinder. He tried to hit back, but they outnumbered him by hitting him with truncheons. I could vouch for this as I saw all the bruises on his body when I went to visit him in prison.

Chapter Twenty-Nine

The final year of university was challenging. Along with doing assignments, revising for exams, and compiling end-of-year dissertations. This project drained me with all the research I had to carry out. What made it interesting was that I based it on Marketing Gym equipment towards the Millennium. This idea was an extension of the marketing section of a business plan for a health and fitness centre I compiled for my second year. Researching for these projects gave me a great buzz as I saw myself owning a fitness centre one day.

I could see this because after returning from India last year, I was given the opportunity to take over the gymnasium I trained at. As my coach was too busy to operate the business funded by the local college, I put myself forward. I remember I jumped at the chance and took a weekend course to become a weightlifting instructor. Luckily, I was successful and became a certified weightlifting instructor.

I then had to sit for an interview with the college department, which would employ me to operate the gym and run courses.

I had the privilege of forming a qualification and helping the students carry out a basic weight training course.

The interview was a success, and I became the person who ran the gymnasium. This was a great feeling.

Assignments, dissertations, exams, and operating a gymnasium were all demanding. Time began to fly, and I couldn't believe where my time was going.

Towards the end of university, I was stressed out about typing my dissertation, and I typed for three days, running with no sleep and living on king-size Snicker chocolate bars and Mars bars.

I finally completed my project. I printed two copies to hand in before the deadline. I drove to the university and quickly entered the library to bind my dissertation. I managed to bind my two dissertation projects and handed them in at reception. The receptionist gave me a reference number. Phew, the pressure was off.

I couldn't believe it; all assignments were handed in, exams were out of the way, and now my project was handed in. It was like some kind of weight had been lifted off my shoulders.

The last week, there is no more university after this," I thought to myself.

The feeling was good. The only two things I could think about were getting back into the gym and training hard to compete at the West Midlands Championships. I hope Julie completed everything she needed to for her degree. I did not train at a competitive level and did not compete for over a year because I wanted to concentrate on my degree.

I walked out of the reception area into the car park. As I walked, I could feel my body feeling weak. I just needed to go home and sleep for three days.

175

I heard the mobile ring. I took my mobile, and it was a number I didn't recognize.

I answered it.

"Hello."

"Hi, Is that Raj Singh?" The caller asked.

"Yes! Can I ask who I am talking to?"

"Yes, my name is Vijay, and I am calling from Sonu Films. We got your number from the Asian Spice Magazine.

We saw you in the magazine and were wondering if you were interested in coming and auditioning for a film."

I could not believe it. The weakness had shifted; I could feel the joy inside me.

"Yes, Yes, I can come and audition."

"Excellent.

Have you got a pen and paper at hand?" he asked.

"Just a second," I said.

I ran to my car, opened the doors, and pulled a writing pad out of my bag and pen.

"Hello," I said.

"Hi, right? Can you come to the following address and make it this Saturday?"

I wrote down the address and said, "Yes and thank you very much."

"So I'll see you on Saturday," Vijay said.

"Yes, you will."

I got out of the car and jumped three times, screaming yes, yes, and yes. I quickly took my phone and called my dad.

"Hello, Dad."

"Hello, Raj, what's wrong?"

"Guess what?"

"What?"

"A film company just called and asked me to come to give an audition this Saturday."

"What's an audition?" Dad asked.

"It's like an interview. They want me to come and sit for an interview for an acting role," I explained.

"That's very good news, son. Come home, and we will talk about it."

I could not believe what just happened, but it was a great feeling. I was driving in excitement. It was Wednesday, and I could not wait until Saturday.

Chapter Thirty

My father could not drive me to London, so he asked his cousin Uncle Rupinderjit to drive me to London. Rupinderjit drove me to the audition. We followed the instructions given to us. We came off the motorway and followed the road around, and we found ourselves in an industrial area.

We pulled over and asked some South Asian people walking in the area if they knew where this office was.

"Excuse me, my friend, do you know where the offices of Sonu Films are?" I asked.

"No, sorry, we don't. But the offices to Zee TV are in the units turning to your second left. They might know where these offices are."

"Thanks," I said.

We drove further up, turned left in the block of units, and followed the sign to Zee TV. As we approached the Zee TV Studios, we found a couple of trucks standing outside opposite the Zee TV studios entrance.

I got out of the car, walked into the Zee TV office reception, and asked, "Hi, can you tell me where the offices for Sonu films are, please?"

The receptionist pointed across the room and said, "Right opposite us."

I looked out of the window and found a sign on the units above saying Sonu films.

"Thanks," I said and walked out.

"They are across the road, Uncle," I said.

My uncle parked our car and came out while I walked across the road. We walked up the stairs to the office. At this point, I was nervous but excited at the same time.

I opened the office door and saw a poster of Rajiv Singh's new film, "Pyar Hogea (We Fell in Love)." There were posters up, and there were posters of Ranbir Singh's film, "Vijay." These were all their home-production movies. I could not believe it; we were standing in the offices of the actors we are big fans of, and these guys are my role models.

"Hi, how can I help you?" The receptionist asked.

"Hi, my name is Raj Singh, and I have come to see Vijay."

"Please take a seat, and I'll give him a call," she replied.

We sat down while the receptionist tracked down Vijay.

I just gazed around the room, looking at the posters on the wall.

A Spanish-looking guy walked in and said, "Hi, I'm Vijay," and shook our hands. "You're Raj Singh?"

"Yes," I said. "I'm the assistant director, and I'll be telling you what you'll be doing, etc. Follow me," he said.

I got up and followed him. We walked into the next office, with my uncle staying at the reception. I looked at people working on their computers.

Then I saw my picture from the Asian Spice magazine cut out and put on the wall. Wow, I could not believe my picture was on the wall among many other famous actors.

This lady walked up to me and shook my hand.

"Hi, I'm Surinder Mankoo, the director of the film. Thanks for coming."

I nodded my head and didn't say anything as I was nervous.

"We were impressed with your pictures and your story in the magazine."

"Thanks," I said. "What we would like to carry out is an audition. If you come into this room."

I followed her into another room where there was a camera set up.

"Have you done any acting before?" She asked.

"Just stage work in my summer holidays," I replied.

"Good, do you remember any movie dialogues?"

"I can think of some."

"Well, I'll give you a couple of minutes, and I'll come back."

What can I say? Nothing was coming into my head. Then I remembered dialogues from my favourite movie, which also ironically starred the producer of this movie I was auditioning for, my favourite actor, Karam Singh.

"Come on, think of the dialogues," I told myself. They weren't coming to me. The director came in with another person.

"This is Peter, my husband and the co-writer of the movie."

I shook his hand, and he said, "Let's see what you got."

He asked me to look into the camera.

"What is your name? Age? The town you live in?"

I answered all these questions.

Then came the dialogues. I delivered them as well as I could and all that I could remember.

"That's fine, thank you. Take a seat outside," said the director.

I went back into the reception area and sat down next to my uncle.

"How did it go?" My uncle asked.

"I don't know. Not very well," I said.

Vijay then walked out and said, "Well done, and you'll be playing the part. Follow me, and I'll introduce you to the rest of the cast."

I could not believe it. I was jumping with joy inside.

"Are you his father?" he asked Rupinderjit.

"No, I am his uncle."

"You can go now as Raj will be staying for a couple of days. Did you bring a change of clothes for three days? As I asked you to?"

"Yes, I did."

"Good. If you can get stuff out of the car and bring it up here, then we will start." I went down to the car with my uncle. I took out my bag, containing a change of clothes for three days and my toiletries.

"You're very lucky you got the part. I heard your audition, and if I were the director, I would never have hired you," said Uncle Rupinderjit.

He always had to say something negative, especially criticizing Indian actors and films, as he was an award-winning filmmaker.

I walked back into the office. Vijay was standing there waiting.

"Put your bag on the side there, and I'll introduce you to the rest of the cast," said Vijay.

I walked into the room and saw three other people sitting on the chairs, flicking and reading through a manual.

"Guys, let me introduce you to a new member of the cast. This is Raj Singh, The British powerlifting champion. He will be playing one of the villains."

"You look like a villain with huge muscles," said one of the guys.

"Hi, I'm Suresh. I'll be playing one of the good guys."

"Then go round the room and speak to the others."

"Hi, I'm Anil, and also playing one of the good guys."

Then I say hello to the third guy.

"Hi, I'm Amit, and I'm playing the lead bad guy."

"Take a seat and talk amongst yourselves and get to know one another, as you will spend at least eight weeks together."

I sat down and thought about it. Then I remembered I'd seen Suresh and Amit somewhere.

"So, have you done acting before?" Asked Suresh.

"Just stage work in the summer holidays," I replied.

"Well, this isn't anything like that, as you will see. I come from a theatre background."

"So you have no acting background?" Asked Anil.

"No," I replied.

"Lucky you. We all have had to go to acting and theatre schools to get this far."

"Cheers. I'm as lucky as Arnold Schwarzenegger was," I said.

"Don't get too carried away," said Amit.

Then, they all talk about how each of them got into the film industry.

I then discovered that I had seen two of the actors, Suresh and Amit, in two TV movies. It was interesting to listen to their stories on how they came into showbiz and their work.

According to his parents, Suresh's story was similar to mine, in the fact that he went to university to study economics. He went along to an acting class with a friend and found it interesting. He joined the acting course and ditched the economics course. This was similar to the fact that I was supposed to be studying law, according to my parents, but I was studying business studies.

Then another actor walked in.

"Hi, everyone, I'm Sachin," he said.

This guy had loads of energy and a larger-than-life presence about him.

We got talking, and Sachin was funny. Sachin also later acted in one of the UK's most famous TV soaps. I tried not to say much because they all made fun of my accent every time I did. I know it was a typical Birmingham Black Country accent.

After about twenty minutes, the main actor walked in. I looked, and it was Rajiv Singh. The actor whose film I watched in India was standing in front of me. He shook everyone's hand as we all introduced ourselves. Vijay, the assistant director, also gave a brief introduction to all of us.

The director walked in, and she gave us all a copy of the script. So, the manuscript I thought the actors were reading was the script.

She gave us a brief rundown of the storyline and explained each character we would be playing. I was hoping that Rajiv's father, Karam Singh, would also come to the office. It would be a dream come true. I got talking to Rajiv and found out that he has visited Wolverhampton.

He asked, "There's a Beatties store there, isn't there? I remember I was about eleven when I visited that store."

Then he asked, "Why are you wearing an earring in both ears?"

"I watched one of your father's films, and he was wearing earrings, so I went and had my ears pierced as well."

''They were clip-on," he said while laughing. "They look cool, though," he stated.

The director stated that we all should go out for a meal. Rajiv suggested that we all eat at his favourite Thai restaurant.

We all sat in a people's carrier and left for this restaurant. Then I found us driving past the famous Harrods store. We were in the heart of London, and the restaurant was near Harrods.

We all went out and ate at this restaurant. The food was great, and we were bonding very well. Rajiv and I were chatting like we had known each other for years.

All the London actors went their way to their homes. Rajiv and I were taken to our hotel.

On our way to the hotel, we stopped at a paan (Betel leaf) shop, which Rajiv enjoyed eating.

"Do you want one, Raj?"

"No thanks, I don't like them," I replied.

I remembered my experience in Shimla.

We were then dropped off at the Hotel. The driver, Mr. Singh, was a cool guy. He must be in his late forties.

The hotel was called Flyways Hotel. We walked into the reception, we were given our room keys and were directed to where the rooms were.

"See you in the morning," Rajiv said.

"See you in the morning, Brother," I replied.

I walked into my room, stared around, and could not believe I was there. I fell asleep thinking about what just happened that day.

I had a wake-up call at 7 o'clock. I woke up thinking, "Is it a dream?"

I pinched myself to see if I was dreaming. I quickly got up and showered, and I was ready for the day. I went out into the reception and found the crew team loading up the coach.

180

Then, I saw Rajiv Singh standing inside the reception area drinking tea.

"Have a cup of tea, Raj," he said.

I went and got myself a cup of tea from the restaurant area. They had an Indian buffet set up.

Luckily, there was fruit there, so I grabbed some fruit and a cup of tea.

I walked back into the reception area. Rajiv was still there, and so was the famous Tara Singh. Tara Singh was a former world wrestling champion and a successful actor. Rajiv introduced me to him. I touched his feet to give him respect and receive his blessing.

"Did you get something to eat?" asked Rajiv.

"Yes, thanks, some fruit."

"For a famous actor, Rajiv is the nicest character I have ever met."

We were then all collected by Mr Singh, our driver. Rajiv and I went in Mr. Singh's car, and Tara Singh was to stay at the hotel as he was not required today.

We set off and drove to another industrial estate. We got out and walked into the block of the office. We got the elevator to the second floor and were asked to sit in the boardroom.

We sat down and watched every other actor walk in and take their seats. This was a dream come true. All the actors playing the character were there beside the main female actor.

"She'll be here in about ten minutes," the director said.

I thought, "Who could it be?"

The director had a call on her mobile and was told she had arrived and was making her way up to the boardroom. Then she walked in, and I could not believe it. It was my favourite beautiful actor, Sabrina Kumari. I felt like rubbing my eyes to make sure it was her. I couldn't believe it; I saw her in Mumbai just over a year ago, and now I'm working with her on the same movie.

She said, "Hello, everyone, and sorry, I am late."

That was so nice of her and professional.

We were all introduced to her, and then the director said, "She has just come off the aeroplane and came straight here."

I was a big fan of hers, not just of her acting and not because she was beautiful but because she was hardworking. She has made over forty films in the last five years. This took a lot of hard work.

She was asked if she wanted to eat first. But she answered, "No, it's fine; let us get on with it."

We began to read the script, and I nailed the timing by saying my lines. While we were reading, I saw Sabrina looking at me, and I was hoping that she recognised me from the time we saw each other outside Ajanta Hotel a year and a half ago.

I then looked at her feet and thought she had nice feet with sky-blue nail varnish painted on her toenails. I know it sounds weird, but I had a slight fetish about women's feet. She saw me looking at her feet and pulled them back.

At the end of the road, we were told to go back to our homes and hotel beside Rajiv and Sabrina as they had to stay back for photoshoots.

Back at the hotel, I was bored and had nothing to do. I was hoping Rajiv and Sabrina would come soon so we could hang out. Then again, I didn't know if Sabrina Kumari was going to stop at the same hotel. I felt like the fan child was coming out. I had to tell myself to be professional.

I walked to the local service station and bought myself a sandwich and a couple of drinks.

I walked back to the hotel and found out that Sabrina Kumari was staying there. This was great news, and the best news was that she was staying in the same block of rooms.

Chapter Thirty-One

In the morning, I woke up at 5:30 am, and while I was showering, I looked in the mirror and said Sabrina Kumari inspires me. Got ready fast so I could catch Sabrina walking down the stairs.

I thought Sabrina had to get up at 06:30 am every day and work on many projects. I was inspired by this, and I could hear the director saying she had just got off the aeroplane and had come straight from the airport.

I walked down the stairs and found Sabrina walking out of her room with her mother.

"Good morning," I said.

They both looked back and said, "Good morning."

I got closer and saw Sabrina without makeup. She was more beautiful without make-up.

"You guys must be jet-lagged."

"No, I'm okay because I'm used to it now. But my mom is jet-lagged."

"Hi, mom," I said.

She looked at me, thinking, "What the hell is he talking about?"

She just about smiled and said, "Hello."

Sabrina laughed.

As we walked towards their car, one of the hotel waiters came out and handed Sabrina a pint of milk.

She said, "Oh no, no milk."

"Come on, drink it," Her mother said.

She drank a pint of milk within seconds. I thought my type of girl. My record of drinking one pint of milk was five seconds.

She got in their vehicle, looked at me, and noticed her beautiful blue eyes. She said, "See you later."

I smiled and said, "See you later."

She replied, "I'll see you later."

I wished my school, college, and university friends were here to witness this. I strolled happily towards the coach, who was taking the rest of the cast and crew to our first location. On the way, the crew sang songs in Hindi, and I was already living in a Hindi Bollywood film. I sat in my seat, thinking I was so pleased to have met Sabrina Kumari.

The day started great, and I knew the rest of the day would be amazing. We all were asked to go to a fitness centre to practice the fight scene. The fight choreographer choreographed the fight scenes. It was good to watch him put the whole concept together. The fight we were practising was actually for a nightclub scene in the movie. It was fascinating the way the whole thing was coming together. The most interesting point was that the fight choreographer was the man on the team who was part of successful Hollywood films.

We practised and mastered the fight actions, and unfortunately, one of the floor mats moved out of place. I was thrown onto the mat and whacked my elbow on the floor. Within minutes, my elbow swells up into a golf ball. The first aider quickly assisted me, and I thought she had always been an American actress. She was the spitting image of Andie McDowell. While she was treating my elbow with an icepack and spray to ease the pain, she was trying to tell Rajiv Singh about all the areas in which she was qualified. She seemed to be trying to get a permanent job with the celebrities. Unfortunately, I later found out that I had chipped pieces of my bone and had to have an operation. I felt this was a journey similar to Jackie Chan's. Which later in life caused me a lot of pain.

On the way back to the hotel, I was looking forward to meeting Sabrina. But unfortunately, Sabrina was out shopping.

The next day was my last filming day until the following schedule. I didn't want the filming to end, but I'm sure I had no choice as I wasn't required every day for filming. I met Sabrina again in the morning during the same process of drinking the milk. This time, I ordered a pint of milk, too. I wanted to set up a competition to see who could drink the milk the fastest, but Sabrina had to leave early due to the time. So, drinking the milk challenge never happened.

The day we spent practising the fight scenes, and I was asked to join the good guys in the movie instead of the villains. The filming of the scenes was excellent, and one of the actors on the villain's side was funny. He later appeared in Eastenders and became very famous. I think most of the British Indian actors in this movie I worked with appeared in Eastenders, the TV soap, playing different characters over the years after this movie.

I returned to the hotel, and my dad had arrived to pick me up, and I had to leave. I was hoping to introduce Sabrina to my father, but I was told that she was out shopping again.

On the way home, I only thought of what I could have spoken about with Sabrina. It was a dream come true even though I had only been watching her movies for the past seven years, and I remember watching her first movie.

My dad asked, "So, how was it? Did you meet Karam Singh?"
"No, he didn't come, but Tara Singh did."
"That's good; what was he like?"
"He was very nice."
"Guess who else is in the film?"
"Who?" "Sabrina Kumari."
"That's nice; what was she like?"
"It's the girl I want to marry, dad."
"Marry Sabrina Kumari? Would she want to marry you? They are a different league altogether, son. She'll probably marry someone from the Film Industry. Did her mother come as well?"
"You like her mother, don't you?" I asked
"In my days, who didn't like her?" We laughed and spoke about the film shoot on our way home.

I went back home and had a week before returning to London.

Chapter Thirty-Two

Back home, I had to focus on training and getting Sabrina out of my head as I prepared for the West Midlands Championships. I didn't feel like training as much as I wanted to be in London. But the competition is not too far away, and I have always dreamed of winning and re-qualifying for the British Championships. The training sessions were very intense as I hadn't trained regularly. I was introduced to block deadlifts and was amazed by the strength I obtained.

The week after, I was back in London. I got there the evening before the day of the shoot. As I was walking up to my room, I bumped into Sabrina.

"Hi," I said.

She smiled and said, "Hi."

"How have you been?"

"Okay," she said.

"Do you enjoy filming in London?"

"It's not the first time I've filmed in London."

"Oh yes, sorry. You have."

"What have you been up to?

"I went back home to operate my gymnasium."

"Do you own a gym?"

"Yes, I do."

"So you must be a fitness instructor? So you can give me tips?" she asked with excitement.

I looked at her, thinking, "You don't need any tips. You're in fabulous shape."

"What sort of advice do you need? On your diet or workouts?" I asked.

"A mixture of the two, if possible," Sabrina replied.

"Well, it seems like you work out regularly. What do you do?"

Then, she talked about her workouts. The different types of diets she had been on. It was just great just listening to her speak.

Then, her mother walked out and asked, "Where have you been?"

"I was just talking to Raj."

"Raj!" she remembered my name. Someone wake me up. I thought I was dreaming.

"He's a fitness instructor," she told her mother.

"A fitness instructor? You must advise me on my diet and workouts," her mother demanded.

"No problem, I can do that for you," I replied.

"We better go. We will see you later," said Sabrina's mother.

They both left, with Sabrina turning back and smiling at me.

I walked into my room thinking, "Is this crush or love?"

The next day, Sabrina and I met on location. I was eating my breakfast, which was a bowl of fruit salad. Sabrina was again without makeup and looked beautiful. She was in a pink tracksuit, and her blue eyes stood out.

"That looks very healthy," she said.

"Try to be," I replied.

"Get some breakfast," I said.

She went over and got a bowl of cereal and a plate of fruit.

"Is this healthy?" She asked.

"Yes, very healthy," I replied.

We got to learn about each other while we were talking. Our birthdays, horoscopes, favourite colours, favourite foods, and favourite songs.

I asked her the number of films she had made and when she got time to sleep. She answered on the way to the sets or travelling abroad to film.

I found this inspiring, and she became my role model.

Back in the nightclub location, we carried out the fight scenes, which was exciting. The underground nightclub was huge, and there must have been about four hundred background junior artists waiting for the filming. It was a hot and humid day. Throughout the filming, the weather that month was probably the hottest it had ever been.

While waiting for the next shot to be filmed, I began talking to Sabrina's mother about a new diet and workout combination. I added that she starred in a movie with Karam Singh.

"Oh, you have seen my movie," she asked, getting excited. She continued telling me about her role in the film and how great it was to work with Karam Singh.

We carried out the next scene. Then we took another break.

Then, a couple of the junior artists called me over and asked me, "How long have you been training?"

So I told them the story of me and powerlifting. They were very impressed.

Then Sabrina walked over to me with a piece of chalk in her hand. She began to chalk my chest, which made it easy as I was wearing a netted t-shirt.

I thought she was flirting with me.

"The guys in the crowd, and we're mouthing what's going on?"

I shrugged and said, "I don't know myself."

I then took the chalk off her and began to chalk her arms and shoulder. Then, the costume department lady came over to us and said, "You'll ruin her costume."

She smiled, thinking clumsy.

I was stuck thinking, what can I do here? I could get myself fired if I did anything wrong. Just then, two background dancers asked me if they could take a photograph with me, and I said okay.

They asked me to lift them in my arms. I lifted them both in my arms while another person out of the crowd snapped the picture. These two dancers must have been about five feet and three inches and weighed about seven stones each.

When they left, Sabrina said, "Very strong," squeezed my biceps and walked off smiling.

It was a successful day of filming, with all the scenes happy with the director.

Many of us got together that night in the private room allocated to the cast and crew. There was no sign of Sabrina Kumari. I asked around and found out that she was out shopping again.

"She loves her shopping," I thought.

On the way back to the hotel, I thought if she made a move again, I must act on it.

That night, I went to my room early because I was tired.

After about an hour, I heard the noise of someone arguing outside. I quickly got ready and went outside. There were police officers, crew members, and hotel staff outside.

I came towards the reception area and found Rajiv standing by the entrance.

"What happened?" I asked.

"One of the crew got attacked by a drunken customer of the hotel. The funny thing is that he came to attack one of our guys but ended up getting beat up," replied one of the crew members.

Tara Singh came out to see what was happening. I shook his hand to pay him respect.

Then, the guy who got attacked walked up to Rajiv.

"You, okay?" Rajiv asked.

"Yes, but if I had the opportunity, I would have beaten him even more," he replied

"Don't worry about it. Get over it now, and calm down," Rajiv said.

This crew guy was full of adrenaline and excitement at the same time.

"What happened?" I asked

He went on and on to tell the story, "I was sleeping on my bed, and the other guy was sleeping on the additional single bed. I heard the door open and thought it was the other going out for a cigarette or something.

Then suddenly, the man wrapped the duvet around my face and said, 'I'll kill you, you paki.' I quickly got out of the hold and thrashed him across the room. Then I gave him a couple of punches in his face and head. He then got away. I chased him down the stairs, but he got away."

"Okay, calm down," said Rajiv.

"Are you still alive? He didn't kill you," said Tara Singh.

"They were lucky they didn't enter Tara's room because his room was next to mine. Tara would have done some serious damage," I thought.

Tara was the undefeated world wrestling champion in the sixties.

"Go and get some sleep then. We have an early start tomorrow," Tara said.

"That's right, We have a 5 am wake-up call, So, I better go to sleep as well," I replied.

Chapter Thirty-Three

In the morning, we were driven to a park where the football match scene was to be filmed. I got changed into my vest and shorts. I thought I'd show off my muscles. Come to think about it, I used all my own personal clothes in this movie.

While we were waiting for the cameraman to set up his camera, Rajiv and I challenged each other to test our strengths by doing the bear hug. I was shocked that an actor who hardly worked out had enormous strength. In the genes, I imagined.

We carried out our football scene most of the day, and the weather was a scorching hot day. The make-up lady noticed I caught a deep tan. My suntan was dark red with a severe sunburn.

We packed up for lunch, and after lunch, while we were waiting, I heard Sabrina singing to me. I thought I was the only one there, but Rajiv turned around and said, "Hey, Toughie, what's going on?"

"I didn't know myself."

Then I thought. "Toughie, who's Toughie? I asked. "Is that a pet's name?"

"No, Raj," he said. "You look tough with all these muscles."

"Oh, that's okay then; otherwise, I would have knocked you out," I said, joking whilst showing my bicep muscles.

Then I saw Sabrina staring at me. I smiled, and she smiled back. I got a bit confused and didn't know what to do. I did feel like talking to Rajiv Singh about it, but I didn't want to get embarrassed. Then, when I got a moment, I walked over to Sabrina and said, "Hi, how are you?"

"Fine, thank you," Sabrina replied. "You, okay?"

"Okay, thanks," I replied. "Hot, isn't it?"

"Just a bit, but we're used to this weather," she replied.

"Oh yeah, that's true."

Then she screamed, "Sareena."

I looked back, and it was a girl running toward her. She hugged her. They began to chat, and their mother was also there.

Then, as I waited to talk to Sabrina, she introduced me to Sareena.

"Sareena, this is Raj, and this is my baby sister," said Sabrina.

I shook her hand and said hi.

Then Sabrina was called for her shot.

"You guys talk, and I'll be back soon," Sabrina said and left.

"So, are you an actress as well?" I asked.

"No, I'm studying at Harvard University in America," Sareena replied.

"Oh, that's excellent. What are you studying?" I asked.

"I am studying information technology and software design."

"Wow, so you are going to be the next Bill Gates for India," I asked.

"No way! I want to become an actress."

"That was strange. Why was she studying Information Technology and wanted to become an actress?" I thought.

"Maybe it was a backup plan," I thought.

Come to think about it, Sareena later became one of the most successful female Indian actors.

Then Sabrina Kumari returned and said to her sister Sareena, "They finished with me for today. Let's go shopping."

"I needed to talk to Sabrina," I thought.

"Do you love your shopping?" I asked.

"Oh, yes, definitely, and I can't get enough clothes when I am in London."

"You can come as well," said Sareena whilst giggling.

"I don't think I can; they probably still need me for the film scenes," I said.

"No, you guys still have a lot of filming to do," Sabrina said, teasing me and blinking at me at the same time.

"So, are you guys coming back to the hotel?" I asked.

"Oh, no way; we moved to another hotel last night after hearing what had happened with one of the crew members."

"That was that, then. I wasn't going to get to talk to her about this thing happening between us," I thought.

"Okay, I'll see you guys tomorrow then," I said.

"You bet," she said and laughed.

After the shoot, I was back at the hotel, exhausted. Rajiv Singh also checked out of the hotel into another hotel.

I showered up and went to sleep.

I heard a knock on the door in the morning while I was getting ready. I opened the door, and it was Sabrina.

"Hi, what are you doing here?" I asked.

"Are you not going to invite me in?" She asked.

"Sorry, please come in," I said.

She stroked the bed when she walked in. She sat down and patted the bed, hinting for me to sit down next to her. I closed the door, moved over to the table, and leaned and sat on the table. My heart was beating fast; it felt like it was going to come out of my chest.

She stroked the bed blanket and said, "Come and sit down next to me."

I walked over to the bed and sat next to her. She looked deeply into my eyes.

Her beautiful, stunning blue eyes made me nervous even more.

"Why haven't you been reading the signals?" She asked.

I stuttered, saying, "I didn't want to embarrass myself, thinking I might be wrong."

She stroked the side of my face, looked at my lips, and kissed me.

While kissing me, her voice changed, and she began to sound more like Julie. I opened my eyes and found myself kissing Julie. Then the phone started ringing, and I thought, "Not now."

191

The sound woke me up, and I found it was the wake-up call. I then realized it was a dream. I sat up, asking myself if I was in love with Julie or Sabrina.

This played on my mind all morning. There was this beautiful, successful actress who I might have a shot with, and on the other hand, there's Julie, who's never shown any interest. But I've loved her since the age of ten.

We were back at the football scene filming other scenes after the match, which led up to a fight scene.

While we waited for Rajiv to get ready for this scene, Sabrina and I walked into her make-up van.

She sat down, and the make-up artist began to put more makeup on her. Then, out of the blue, Sabrina asked me, "Who is your favourite actress?"

If I had said her, I could be leading her on, and I can't be doing this as I love Julie.

Just then, Rajiv walked in and whispered, "Katrina Rai."

"Why?" I asked.

Her family produced a film last year and didn't have her in the movie but had Katrina Rai instead. So she was super angry about this.

"I don't want to piss her off anymore," I said.

"Go on, say it," he kept on saying.

Out of the Blue, I said, "It's Kusum Ganga."

I didn't even know who this actor was, but it came out as I flicked through a magazine earlier with Kusum interviews in.

There was no way that I liked this new actor over Sabrina.

She asked, "Do you like Kusum?"

I could see this sad look on her face and eyes. But an excellent actress she is, she managed to cover it up in seconds. She's human, after all, and we all experience all the emotions. Regardless of a good actor, it's hard to cover up pain at times.

I nodded my head, saying yes.

She looked away and let her make-up artist finish off her make-up.

I walked out of the trailer thinking, "What have I just done?"

That afternoon, she ended up arguing with the UK makeup artist and decided not to work the rest of the day.

Chapter Thirty-Four

I returned home and ran my gym, which I had left in the hands of a couple of guys who used the gym.

This was risky as I could have been fired if the college knew about it.

I spent the next couple of weeks preparing for the West Midlands Championships. I had not trained for a couple of weeks and wasn't feeling as strong as usual.

I visited a health shop one of the days to find out which new energy drinks were out to give me an energy boost. I found a new drink imported from the USA called Orange-Orange. Before my workouts, I forgot to start drinking this new orange-orange drink, and it remained on top of the kitchen cupboard.

During my competition week, I had a call from the film production assistant director saying they had finished filming and were holding a party to celebrate the completion and to thank everyone for their hard work. He asked if I could come to the event.

I thought this was an excellent opportunity to see Sabrina and give her a gift. I bought her an ab roller. An ab roller helps to exercise the stomach muscles and trim it down. I managed to buy these at wholesale prices and sell them for a profit.

I decided to go and had my dad drive to London. Again, I could have pushed myself as I had passed my driving test. But my dad, being a protective parent, wanted to drop me off.

I took five ab rollers with me, hoping to sell them to other crew members. I got to the hotel and checked in. I introduced my father to actors who played character roles, which made him happy.

The party had started, and it was very basic and boring. They had an open buffet and drinks for artists and film crew members. There was no sign of the main actors, especially Sabrina. Then, finally, she walked in and said thank you to everyone and bye.

She approached me and said just bye.

I said, "I have a gift for you."

"Have you?" She asked.

"Give it to my hairdresser, and she will bring it with her."

That felt like a slap in the face, No offence to the hairdresser, but I was expecting a little appreciation.

I said, ''Okay, if she wanted to play that game."

Sabrina left, and the party became a bit more depressing. After about twenty minutes, as soon as I thought I should call it a day, Rajiv walked into the room with his elder brother Ranbir. Ranbir was the biggest action hero in the Indian Film Industry. He was the equivalent of Arnold Schwarzenegger with box office hits. Rajiv introduced me to Ranbir and said, "Raj is a big fan of our dad."

'Thanks, and you're in good shape; keep it up," he said.

"It's all inspired by watching your and your dad's films," I replied.

"Thank you," he said and shook my hand. I was a fan of Ranbir as well.

He then walked around the room, greeting people. The night got a bit better, and we all danced bhangra on the dance floor for the rest of the night.

My dad came to collect me the next day, and we headed back to the Midlands.

"Driving back?" My father asked.

"So, are they going to have you in more films?"

"I don't know, and they said we must wait until this film is released," I replied.

"Let's just hope they have you in their other films," he said.

"I hope so," I replied.

"Did you meet Barbara?" Dad asked. Barbara was Sabrina and Sareena's mother. She was from a mixed-race background, with her mother being French. Plus, Barbara was very good-looking and a big star in the seventies.

"Yes, just to say bye as they were no longer stopping at the hotel."

I reached home and rested the last two days before the competition. I wasn't up to competing because I kept thinking that if I told Sabrina that I liked her, I might have gotten a different response.

On the morning of the competition, I remembered that I had a new energy drink. So I mixed this drink and poured it into a sports bottle.

I went to the venue along with seven gym friends. Two out of the seven guys were also competing. I always had good support from my friends who trained in my gym.

I got changed and began to warm up, and as I was warming up, I drank this new energy drink. Unfortunately, this drink felt like it had the opposite reaction. I felt a lot drowsier and weaker. I had not performed to the best standard. There were a few boos and name-calling from competitor family members.

I thought I had lost the competition, but in the end, we discovered that I just scraped the first position by five kilograms. At the end of the competition, the drug test asked me to give them a urine sample, which I did, and I went home with my first-place trophy. This was another happy day of my life, not just winning first place but also qualifying for the next British championships and coming home as a proud coach. The two guys from the gym I coached also won first place.

The next day, I called the local papers and asked them to print the good news that the local powerlifters had won the West Midlands championships.

A couple of days later, the journalist took the photographs, and we appeared in the local papers holding our trophies. I had the two other lifters sitting on either side of my shoulders as we held our awards.

A couple of weeks went by, and I carried on training and working part-time for the college teaching powerlifting. We carried out a strongman strength session in the gym during our training. One exercise was to hold out a twenty-kilogram dumbbell for some time, and each lifter had to beat the other's record. I held the weight out, and my time came close to forty-seven seconds; my shoulders and arms became heavy, and I began to strain.

***

I was woken up in the hospital with me leaning on my arm, which had a needle in it and was hurting me. I looked around, and I was the only one in the room. I looked at the door and visualised Sabrina Kumari walking in, asking, "How are you, toughie?"

I saw the door open, and it was a blonde lady in a nurse's outfit. For a second, I thought it was Julie.

"You woke up, Raj?" She asked.

I nodded my head, indicating yes.

"That's good, as a guest is sitting outside with your father. 'Shall I send them in?" She asked while checking my monitor.

I nodded, saying, "Yes."

She left, and my father walked in with this man. To my surprise, it was Ranbir Singh's UK manager. I was excited to see someone from the film industry.

"Hi, Toughie," he said, "What are you doing lying in bed ill? You're a strong man. Get up, lift weights again, and get back into movies and stuntwork."

I nodded and smiled.

He said, "You could have been a big star. In the first film, you worked with the biggest action star of the Indian film industry, followed by starring opposite the biggest actress of the late nineties. Your first movie was one of the biggest films of the year two thousand."

"Your muscular body was a revelation to the Indian film industry. You need to get better, get back into powerlifting and back into movies. Do you hear me?" He said.

The nurse walked in.

"It's Raj's dinner time," she said.

"I better go. Raj, Ranbir and Rajiv Singh send their best wishes," the UK manager shared.

While he was sharing this, I was still trying to remember his name, but at the same time, I was happy to hear my favourite actors send me their regards.

"I'll be back," my dad said and walked out.

"Do you want me to put your favourite film on, Raj?" asked the nurse.

Luckily, I was in a private room with my TV and Video recorder. So I nodded yes, and she put on 'Pumping Iron'.

Chapter Thirty-Five

One Saturday morning, I sat in the living room watching my favourite film, Pumping Iron. I thought to myself, "It's been almost ten years. I have watched this film nearly every day. The movie has been a great motivation in my life involving sports."

Then, the house phone rang while I was watching 'Pumping Iron'. I looked around and found no one else to answer it, so I had to answer it.

"Hello, Have you forgotten about me?" the caller asked.

"Who's this?" I asked.

"Looks like you have. It's Madhu, you idiot."

"Hi Madhu, how are you?" Thinking, "Shit, why did I answer the phone?"

"Not happy at all. It's been almost three months since we last spoke, and every time your grandad calls or we call, you are never there. We receive another picture of you posing nude in the paper again," she said.

"It's not nude, just topless," I said in my defence.

"Well, that's nude here in India. So why do you have photographs taken like this? Is it to impress the women?"

"No, I'm happy with my muscles and like to celebrate it by posing topless."

"You never called to tell me that you worked in a movie alongside the Kalirais. So when were you planning to tell me?" She asked angrily over the phone.

Kalirai was the surname of my actor role models Karam Singh, Ranbir Singh, and Rajiv Singh.

"Well. I get stuck for words."

"That's right. I have nothing to say. Did you manage to find yourself an actress girlfriend?" she asked.

I wanted to say, well, I almost did. But it wasn't appropriate.

"Do you want to get married to me or what?" she asked.

"Well, I wanted…." I began to say.

While I was trying to tell her, her mother came on the phone.

"Hello, Son, how are you?" she asked.

"Fine, thank you. How are you, Aunty?" I asked.

"We are perfect, and you don't need to call me aunty anymore. You can call me mom now. Listen, you've completed your degree, and so has Madhu. I think we should set the wedding date very soon. Don't you think so?" she asked.

"You have to ask my grandad," I replied.

"I know you are a good boy and do what your parents tell you, but this is your marriage. You should force your parents to speed up things now. You understand where I am coming from and what I am saying," she protested.

"Yes," I said.

"Do you want to speak to Madhu?"

"It's okay. I think we've had our chat," I said.

"She is very heated up," she said. "Ask your grandad to call us."

"I will," I replied

I placed the phone receiver back on the stand. I walked up the stairs thinking, "How do I get out of this?"

I sat in front of my computer and browsed the net. I typed gyms in the search bar. A complete list of gyms came up on the screen. Then, I noticed the World's Gym franchise. I quickly opened this page and found information about the famous gym in California, USA. This is where all the famous Hollywood stars worked out. It comes to me that I should open a bigger gym. And having a franchise of the World Gymnasium would be a great idea. I type in all my details and request an information pack regarding their franchise deal.

I got pretty excited and pulled out the business plan I had compiled in my second year of university and thought I could use this business plan. I remember my lecturer saying this was a great business plan, and if it was implemented, it would be a great success.

I made many notes and looked at the possibility of where I could have this gym. Then, it occurred to me that my father had an empty office block in the town centre that could be turned into a gymnasium.

The plan became very clear, and I decided to talk to my parents about it. Luckily, my father thought it was a great idea. After two days, my father called his architect, and we discussed the changes needed to get approval from the local council for the change of use.

The architect drew up the plan, and I handed it to the council.

Meanwhile, I continued teaching part-time at the college and found that the class turned out great, with my success celebrated in the papers. In addition, the club had more than doubled the number of people who wanted to learn about weight training. This was very encouraging, and I wanted to open a new gym or fitness centre.

Also, around that time, I was asked to host a Diwali event at the City town hall alongside famous singer Amardeep Sandhu. The event was super successful, with more than five hundred audience members. However, women from the crowd were throwing flowers at me. So I threw the flowers back into the crowd, where the women screamed, "We love you, Raj."

After six weeks, I received a reply from the council stating that my application was approved. This was surprising as I would become a competitor to the council leisure centre.

197

Chapter Thirty-Six

I had the builders visit the site to go through the plan and how I wanted them to refurbish the building. My bank manager was there, too, as my father said he would support me being as the guarantor. I wanted to pay back the loan and didn't want to borrow the money from my father. This was going to be my journey of success. Luckily, the hourly rate paid by the college was reasonable, and the fees paid to me from the film were excellent as I got an equity rate. This helped me pay for the start-up.

I was on the site explaining the critical path analysis to the builder, who I felt laughing behind my back. John, the builder, asked, "Have you just finished college or something?"

"Yes, I replied. "I thought so."

He said, "Listen, you have to be working in the building sector to understand how it works. Leave it to the professionals," he told me. I was trying to tell them about working within the timescale and the budget.

While trying to calm me down from getting angry with this builder and firing him, I got a call on my mobile.

"Hi, is this Raj?" the man asked on the other side.

"Yes, this is Raj, How can I help?" I asked.

"This is George. I'm a film director in Hong Kong."

"Hi," I said.

"Raj, I have a film offer for you."

"For me," I asked in excitement.

"Yes, can we meet for a coffee?" he asked.

"Of course we can," I replied.

"How about tomorrow?"

"Of course I can," I replied.

"Okay, I'll text you all the details and time."

"Great, I'll see you tomorrow," I shared.

I got home and shared the good news with my family. My grandad was unhappy and said, "Don't forget you are marrying Madhu and setting up your law practice."

I couldn't be bothered with all that now as I was excited about meeting this Hong Kong filmmaker.

I drove down to Reading, which is a town in Berkshire. The first time I visited this town, I couldn't believe its beauty. The town building architecture was something new and beautiful. No wonder this town was busy.

I walked into the bar, where I was asked to meet George. This bar was like the bars you see in American movies and sitcoms. This was feeling good already. This guy tapped me on the shoulder.

"Raj?" he asked.

"Yes," I replied, and I saw it was a caucasian man. I was expecting a Chinese man.

"Please come and take a seat," he said, guiding me to my seat.

"What drink would you like?" he asked if I'd have some.

"Orange juice," I replied.

"A good choice," he said.

He ordered the drinks and sat back at the table.

"The waitress will serve the beverages," he said. "Waitress."

"I never had that service in England before," I thought.

"So, Raj, you have become this new craze with your type of physique and acting ability," he shared.

"That's good to hear, and thanks for the compliment. I have only done one film, which is still to be released. When did you see my acting?" I stated and asked.

"Good question. I was told about your acting and shown your pictures by one of the artists of the film you worked in," he shared, before continuing, "Please don't ask me who, as they didn't want their name mentioned."

I thought this was a bit bizarre.

"That's nice of them, but how can I thank this person?" I asked.

"You can thank that person when the film is released," he said. "Okay," I replied.

"Share the concept with me," I asked.

"Excellent, this will be the first cross-over movie done in two languages. We will film in Hindi and the same scene in English. The story is a love story between your character and Kusum Ganga," he explained.

"Kusum Ganga?" I asked.

"Yes," he replied, "And it will also star the former Miss Australia, an actor from Hong Kong, Bollywood actors playing character roles, and a TV games show presenter from the USA. Nothing like this has been done before. Eighty-five per cent of the filming will take place in the United Kingdom and the rest in India."

"Will I be in the scenes filmed in India?" I asked.

"These are the flashback scenes of your grandfather's character's younger days." George shared.

"Wow, this sounds amazing. When do you roll the camera?" I asked.

"This will all start in three to four months. Are you interested?" George asked.

"Of course I am," I replied.

"Great, so I will have my production team send you all the contracts tomorrow. Sign them and send them back," George instructs.

The waitress served us the drinks, and George ordered food. We spoke for most of the afternoon about the type of fight scenes that would take place, many stunts, dialogue delivery, locations, and songs.

"Songs, George?" I asked."

"Yes, Raj, there is a Bollywood version, too, as I mentioned earlier, and don't worry, I have explained what I am looking for to my team, and they are liaising with the Indian music director," he explained.

"Guess what?" he asked.

"What?" I asked.

"My production manager and assistant director are from the Indian Film Industry and have worked with the top actors in the industry. So don't worry. I have a whole team around me, not just a white guy trying to make a Bollywood film. Plus, you will get to have a say, too," he explained.

"Me?" I asked.

"Of course, you're the lead actor so that you can add as much input as possible," said George.

"Thanks," George. I said.

I couldn't believe how my dreams were coming together on another level. I was starring in a Bollywood film and a Hollywood one, too. It felt a bit like Bruce Lee's life. I was nowhere near and never would be, but I remember watching a movie called 'Dragon' based on Bruce Lee's life, and in one scene, he was approached by Hong Kong filmmakers. Even though George was Caucasian, I still was approached by someone from Hong Kong. I had to ask, though.

"George, you're caucasian, and how are you from Hong Kong?" I asked.

He laughed and said, "My parents are both English teachers in Hong Kong, and I was born in Hong Kong."

"Oh, that explains it," I said comically. We both laughed at the same time.

Back home in the living room, I told family members, my grandad, grandma, and dad. Luckily, my mom walked in, bringing my grandad's cup of tea. It was late at night, and he had to have milk tea every night if he wasn't getting drunk in the pub, so it must have been after ten o'clock in the evening.

"So, you want to do this film as well. How about your career as a lawyer?" asked my grandad.

"Grandad, I will become a lawyer but also want to do this."

"What am I going to say to your inlaws in India?"

"They are not my inlaws," I thought.

"Grandad and everyone, I can get married after this is finished. Many students have a year out before they begin work. Let me have my freedom before I get married and start our law firm."

"He's right," my mother said.

"Not interested in your advice," my grandad said to my mother. "I have a lot at stake here."

"Is it always about your interests," said my grandma. "Let him have his freedom for a bit longer."

Everyone was staring at me, and my grandad said, "Okay. Have your freedom, and you're getting married as soon as you finish."

I hugged my grandad and said thank you.

200

I spent the next few days training, doing bag work, punching, breaking bricks, and working at the new gym site. Watching the builders do the jobs bored me, so I called the World's Gym franchise team in the USA. The lady took my call and told me they gave the UK franchise full rights to a businessman in London. As London is the capital of England, they felt that the first franchise would be ideal in London.

This was heartbreaking. My grandad walked to enter the site and asked, "What's wrong, Raj?"

I told him, and he said, "That's not a problem, but there's always a solution to every problem."

This was one of his famous sayings.

"What's the solution?" I asked.

He asked whether I had the gym layout of the gym in the USA.

I say, "Yes."

"And the floor designs?" He replied.

"I do," I said.

"That's it. Copy the layout, and the rest will work the same way."

I loved it when he gave me wise advice.

Driving back home, I got a call on my mobile.

"Hello, Raj!"

"Hi, who is this?" I asked.

"This is Vijay, the film's assistant director if you recall," he said.

"Yes, I do, and how are you?" I asked.

"I am good, and I just wanted to let you know that the film premiere will be in two months, and you can bring a plus one," he shared.

"Excellent, and is it in Mumbai?" I asked.

"Yes," he replied, "And I will send you all the details closer to the time."

"Thanks," I replied.

We both hung up.

Walking into the shop, all excited. Thinking I have had two excellent outcomes to the day. A solution and invitation to the film premiere. I noticed Julie's stepmom in the movies section of the shop. I walked over to her, "Hi, Mrs. White."

Before I could finish saying hello, she said, "Oh, hello, Raj. How have you been? Your mother told me about your film success and that you're opening a fitness centre in this small town."

"Yes, thank you," I said.

"I can't wait to tell Julie," she said.

"How is Julie, and is she ever coming back to Bilston?" I asked.

"She is doing very well. She has also finished her degree and got a job up North. So, is she coming back? I don't know. The last we spoke about this, she said if she gets a job up north, she will rent an apartment," she shared.

"Rent an apartment?" I asked, and I thought I would buy a home for her in my head while her stepmom went on about how she's tried convincing Julie to return home and get a job here in our town.

"Can I give you my number to give to Julie?" I asked.

"Of course I can, Raj," she said.

I quickly wrote down my number and gave it to her.

Those were three areas I was happy with today. First, I walked in singing a Bollywood song' translated as 'I'm on top of the World' in my head. Then I see Aunty Manjit speaking to my grandparents.

"That's it. She is going to say something to ruin my mood," I thought.

"Grandad, guess what?"

"What, son? He asked.

"I have been asked to go to my movie premier in Mumbai, and I've been asked to bring a plus one with me. That's you, Grandad," I said.

I didn't think about what I said; I just wanted to gain a few brownie points.

"That is good, and congratulations, my son," Grandad said whilst shaking my hand.

"That's a great idea to let all go together, meet the actors, and Raj can get married simultaneously," my aunty said.

"No, Grandad and I have a deal," I said.

"It's not a bad idea," said my grandad.

"But grandad," I moaned.

"When is it?" he asked.

"In two months," I replied.

He took out his pocket diary and flicked the pages.

"Isn't it your graduation in two months?" he asked.

"Oh, Yes, it is," I replied.

"I bet he's failed anyway," my aunty said.

"That's enough," my grandad said, telling her off.

"Grandad, I am sure I can attend the ceremony next year, and it would be better because Madhu would be with me too," I quickly added Madhu's name to the equation.

"That would be a good idea," he said. "Can you find out if this can be done?"

"Yes, I will call the university tomorrow."

The next day, I called the university and got confirmation that I could attend the ceremony the following year. I would send this confirmation in writing via post.

Chapter Thirty-Seven

The time of the film premiere was coming near. The house had colossal excitement, and my grandad went shopping for new suits for the event. Grey was the year's new colour, and we bought two suits to wear almost identical for the premier. I trained very hard, and my diet was strict to look leaner in muscle size and sharp for the movie premiere. Daily, as part of my run routine, I would run past Julie's parent's house. I hoped we would bump into each other and I could share with her that her friend Raj's film was being shown worldwide at all cinemas. I not just worked in one film but also on my second film as the main lead too.

As much as my parents were happy for me, I knew they were culturally bound and thought this was just a hobby; after I graduated, I got married, and Madhu and I would run our law practice together.

It was eating me up inside that I couldn't share the good news with the girl or woman I love. I often imagined that Julie met me at our Bilston Library park, and I shared my achievements with her, and she told me about her journey since she's been away—more in a song than conversation.

I think it was in my head. I often wrote songs for her, explaining how I felt and missing her. As Julie and I stared at the sky when we were young, I thought about the clouds when I wrote my song. It always began. "Every time these clouds changed direction, you either made me happy or broke my heart. 'Stuck to understand where our relationship is?" It rhymed more in Hindi.

Well, the first song I wrote was 'What's Happening? Why is this happening? Why is my heart beating so fast? I don't know why, don't know why. ' I felt Julie and me singing and dancing in the park. More lyrics about flying in the air, in love with her, who has stolen my heart from childhood to adulthood, I can't live without.

I often felt I should have my songs produced, and maybe Julie gets the message through the songs.

Then again, that would have been difficult as the songs would have been sung in Hindi.

Only if I knew someone in Manchester to pass on my message or locate Julie.

***

"Wake up, Raj," and I wake up from my thoughts. My mother says, "Look who's here?"

I open my eyes and see one of my dad's friends, who is a regular customer of my father's shop. Next to him is his son Sandeep.

"Hi, Big Raj. It's Sandeep. Are you okay, son? I hope you are feeling better," his father asks.

"Hi," I slightly smile to indicate yes.

"He's a strong lad," says Sandeep.

His voice is different and calmer than what I remembered. He also works out with weights and is about seven years older than me. He is always in good shape; if I recall, he is into rock music, and his voice was aggressive about five years ago. He would always speak with an aggressive tone and stick his tongue out.

***

I never knew why. I remember serving in my dad's shop once, and he walked in.

"Hey, Big Raj," he said in his aggressive voice.

I think he was the only person who called me Big Raj.

"Hi, Sandeep, how's it going?"

"Of course, it's all going well," he replied.

Now, as I remember, most of his answers were also defensive. He referred many times to the rock songs he listened to and their deep meaning and related them to life.

"What have you been up to?" I asked.

"You don't know?" he replied and asked.

I didn't answer.

"I've been living in Manchester, man," he replied.

A light bulb moment struck in my mind.

"What are you doing in Manchester?"

"I'm a teacher, Man."

I was thinking, "How?"

I'm not saying he didn't have the abilities; I remember once him telling me he studied economics. It was his aggressive tone, which I'm sure would scare students.

"That's awesome," I said.

"Of course, it's incredible, man," he replied.

He continued, "Anything can be better than living in this town; nothing for me here, man. Hence, I went to the university in Manchester and decided to live and work there."

"That's great," I said.

"You bet, man," he replied.

"Would you be able to do me a favour?" I asked.

"What's that?" he asked.

"I need to find and get a message to someone from here in Bilston who now lives in Manchester," I said.

"You crazy, man?" he asked. "If you don't know where they live, you will never find them, and who will do that for you, man? No one cares about you in this World, and you must do it all alone, man."

He laughed and walked out of the shop.

***

Back at the hospital, I look at him, and he still has that smirk but is not chewing gum. Somehow, the tone of his voice has changed.

"Let's go," his dad says, and they leave.

***

Back in the shop, I stood, thinking I needed to get a message to Julie without hassling her Stepmother," while customers waited to be served.

Chapter Thirty-Eight

The day came to fly to Mumbai, India, and I felt nervous but excited again. Then, as I put the suitcases into the jeep, my phone rang.

"Hello," I said. There was no one speaking on the other side.

"Hello," I said again.

Then, the person hung up, and I continued to put the bags into the jeep. I had packed extra if I had to stop longer.

Everything was packed, and we began our journey to Heathrow airport. My phone rang again while we were driving.

"Hello," I said, and again, with no response from the other end.

This time, the number the person's number came up. So, I rang the number back. Before the person hung up, I was sure I heard Julie's mother's voice in the background.

This made me smile and happy. So, I saved the number under Julie.

"Couldn't they book the tickets from Birmingham Airport"? "My grandad asked.

"I don't know, Grandad, they booked everyone's tickets from the UK from London," I replied

We reached Heathrow Airport, and I found Ranbir Singh's UK secretary waiting for all the actors who took part in the film. We all greeted each other and boarded the Air India flight to Mumbai.

On the flight, we all discussed which actors we wanted to see at the movie premiere. Finally, we reached Mumbai airport and were collected by drivers sent from the producers. The smell hit me again, but the excitement was a lot more.

I travelled through the same area only a couple of years ago, and it brought back memories.

We checked into our hotel, which was across the road from Juhu Beach and not too far from the hotel I stopped at last time.

We all went to our rooms and decided to meet in a couple of hours. So, we all met in the evening in one of the other actor's rooms.

I walked into Vicky's room and found they all were already drinking with bottles of Bacardi open.

"Come in," said Natasha, one of the UK actresses.

It seemed she was drunk.

"Don't you look hot?" She continued to speak. This actress went on to become a huge British television celebrity. She was only five feet tall and very talkative.

Vicky, Vicky's girlfriend Rita, Polo, Natasha, Soniya, and I walked down the road from the hotel and found a Chinese food restaurant.

We were walking back to the hotel from the restaurant. Natasha was super drunk and said, "Raj, you better have sex with me when we get back."

"Aren't you married?" I asked.

"So, what's that got to do with anything?" she answered.

We got back and put Natasha to bed first, and then we all went to our rooms.

The following day, I woke up early and went along Juhu beach, wearing two sweat belts, a t-shirt with a black bin liner on top, and another t-shirt in this hot country. I ran for forty minutes along the beach, drenched with sweat. This was to get rid of the access water around my body. Before I had left, I weighed sixty-eight kilograms.

I was surrounded by hotels. I ran to the end hotel and thought I'd see if they had a gymnasium as part of the hotel. I walked into the Sun and Sand Hotel, and the receptionist guided me to their gymnasium. It was perfect, with weights, cardio equipment, a sauna, and a jacuzzi. I paid for the monthly membership, which was around twenty-five pounds. I worked out with weights and did another run on the treadmill. My energy levels were about low, and I wasn't feeling great. I sat down and sipped lemon water.

***

Back in the hospital, I felt unwell, and the room spinning. The machines began to bleep. Finally, I focused and saw my mother panic. The nurses injected something into my drip, making me feel better.

"His Sugar levels dropped," said the doctor.

"His sugar levels have dropped?" my mother asked.

"The other day, you said his liver wasn't working correctly last time," so continued my mother, speaking loudly in a concerned voice.

"You have nothing to worry about, as we have this under control," the doctor explained.

***

In the Sun and Sand Hotel gym, I was feeling super weak. I had just walked out of the sauna wearing my bin liner and T-shirt. I was soaked with sweat, and my heart was beating super fast. I sat and explained to the instructor how I was feeling. A man on the treadmill walked off and walked over to me.

"What have you eaten today? he asked.

"I've had five egg whites," I replied.

"Just five egg whites," he screamed at me.

"I am a doctor, and it looks like your sugar levels have dropped," he said.

On the side were a couple of jars with powder in them. He mixed one of them in water and gave it to me.

"This glucose drink will help you," the doctor said.

"Get him a sandwich to eat," he instructed the fitness instructor.

Then he said, "I'll be back in two minutes."

I sat there, worried about what was happening to my body. Finally, the doctor returned, holding a bag. He took out a kit, pricked my finger, put my blood on a strip, and checked my blood sugars.

"So, what have you trained today?" He asked.

"I ran on the beach for almost an hour, did weights, did forty-five minutes of cardio, and did thirty minutes in the sauna," I explained.

"All this training and you have only consumed egg whites?" he disgustingly asked me.

"I'm trying to stay lean for a movie premiere," I shared.

"Stay slim? You won't stay alive. Look at your blood sugars. You should be dead," he shared.

Just then, the fitness instructor walked in with a sandwich. He gave it to the doctor.

"Eat this, and bread should boost your blood sugar back up," said the doctor.

"Actually, get him one more," he instructed the fitness instructor.

"Has this happened before?" he asked.

"I have been on an egg white diet for the past couple of months and eat other foods when I feel weak. Almost passed out in my gym and fell down the stairs twice," I shared."

You are silly, boy, for taking these health risks. You will end up killing yourself," he explained.

We talked for another twenty minutes, and the instructor bought me another sandwich I consumed with a full sugar-based fizzy drink. He did another test after another five minutes and showed me.

"Look how eating food helps," he explained.

We laughed.

"Listen, my brother is a casting director and runs an acting school," he shared. "This is his number," which he wrote down.

"Give him a call because I feel you have the look and the face to be a star," he said.

"Thank you," I replied.

"But eat and live," he shared.

"Put the sandwiches on my bill," he said to the instructor.

"No, it's ok," I said.

"It's ok," he said and left.

The day after, I stupidly had egg whites only, but this time, I had two toast with them. I did the same workout and sipped the glucose drink with lemon in the gym. I did feel a bit weak and dizzy, but I increased the quantity of powder in the glucose drink. I don't know if it was wise, but I did.

The day of the movie premier came, and we were told that taxis would pick us up at 5 pm to get to the cinema. So, I went for the last run and sauna on this crazy diet, stepped on the scales, and weighed sixty-four kilograms. This was the lightest I have ever been. I couldn't believe it. I looked in the mirror and looked lean but not so muscular, lean but skinny. I looked more ill. Just then, the gym instructor told me to put my T-shirt on.

"What's wrong with me posing?" I asked.

"One of the other members doesn't like it with your top off," he said.

I looked at the member, and it was the famous actor Ravi Singh. In respect, I put my top on and smiled at Ravi Singh. I was star-struck and was stuck for words to say anything.

Raj and Julie

We all got ready and waited for our taxis. We got in the taxi and were driven to the cinema where the red carpet was. We pulled outside the cinema, and the area was heaving with people. At least fifty police officers guarded the red carpet. We stepped outside, and the fans were screaming the actors' names. I felt like a star walking down the red carpet. For a laugh, I waved at the fans and shook hands. They didn't know who I was, but the feeling was incredible. We had entered the cinema and stood as close to the movie stars. I couldn't believe my luck. I was in the presence of all the Bollywood film industry I grew up watching in movies. One film star after another was walking past us, shaking the lead actors' hands. It was a seven-year-old child's dream which came true.

My grandfather couldn't believe his luck either. He was surrounded by actors he also grew old watching. My grandfather was known to look similar to my role model. It was a moment in history when two of my role models were snapped for a photograph. We were all seated in our seats in the cinema theatre. I looked around and saw Mr. Vijay Rai, one of the most influential actors in the history of Indian cinema, sitting two rows behind me, and it reminded me of a scene from his film. I looked across the other side and saw Mr. Karan Kumar, who has given us great performances since the 1940s. I was surrounded by all these famous actors, including my favourite actor, Karam Singh, known as the "He-Man" of the Indian Film Industry and one of the most talented actors the industry has ever had. I looked around to see if Sabrina Kumari was in the cinema. But I could not see her anywhere.

The film started, and as everyone's names appeared on the screen, they whistled and clapped. Then my name came up, and my grandad clapped. Then I saw myself on the big screen, and my eyes filled with joy. I looked at my grandad, who was wiping his tears. So he looked at me and put out his hand. We shook hands.

"Thank you," he whispered.

After the film ended, we all exited the theatre. I was hoping to see all these actors at the party. As I walked out, a stunt director put his arm around me and congratulated me on my work in the film. Then, I looked back and saw the famous award-winning actor Richi Batra. He is the son of actor Surinder Batra, who worked in films from the late 1930s to the 1980s.

Surinder Batra was known as the Charlie Chaplin of Indian Cinema. His performance in Gumrahi was ranked as one of the "Top-Ten Greatest Performances of All Time in World Cinema." This was in the 1950s. I quickly used this opportunity to shake his hand, which he did.

That evening, we ended up at the Taj Hotel for the party. We danced and drank. My grandad enjoyed the moment and hugged me, saying, "Thank you, son."

"Also, please eat," he said. "Do you think I haven't noticed you haven't eaten properly since we have been here?"

He continued to tell me off in a loving way. So I ate food to make him happy.

209

Raj and Julie

Sabrina walked into the party area and looked beautiful. She walked around greeting everyone, and then I saw her walk towards me. I was standing with my grandad. He noticed her and said, "Doesn't she look beautiful, like her mother."

I looked at my grandad, thinking, "Not you, too."

"Hi, Raj," she said, putting out her hand to shake my hand.

"Hi, Sabrina," I said and shook her hand.

"How are you?" I asked.

"I'm good, and how are you?" she asked.

"I am good, thank you, and this is my grandad," I said, introducing her to my grandad.

"Hi, Dadaji," she said.

"Hello," my grandad said.

"Your mother not with you?" he asked straight out with it.

"Yes, she is, Grandad," she said. "Over there," she pointed.

We saw her, and my grandad said, "I'll go and say hi to her."

He walked off to introduce himself to Sabrina's mother. One thing I liked about my grandad was that he never lacked confidence. I have watched him close business deals, flirt with women, give speeches at events, be a voice for the black and Asian communities in Wolverhampton towards equality, and dictate to his lawyers and accountants.

"Did you enjoy the film?" Sabrina asked.

"I did, and you were amazing," I said.

"Thank you," she replied.

"I didn't see you in the cinema theatre," I said.

"I was there and saw you looking around," she replied.

"She was watching me," I thought in my head, "Wow."

"Are you going to stay in Mumbai?" She asked.

"I would love to, but I have a business in the UK to operate," I replied.

"You have a gym, don't you?" she asked.

"Yes, you remember?"

"Of course," she replied.

"You could coach actors and business owners here and make a lot of money," she suggested.

"That would be a good idea," I replied. "I will definitely think about it."

I said, "I also have another film I will be working on shortly."

I continued to tell her.

"That's right, how's that going?" she asked.

"Very good," I said, then I thought, "How did she know?"

"We hear about all films being produced," she said before I could ask how did she know.

"Oh, ok," I said.

It also stars Kusum, doesn't it?" She asked.

"Yes, as far as I know," I replied.

"Would you like to star in it?" I asked.

"Me?" she asked.

210

"Didn't you say you like her?" she continued to ask.

I stutter, saying, "I like your performances, too."

She laughed.

"I know the producer," she said, "And maybe I'll do a special appearance in it."

"Ok, and that would be nice," I said.

"Raj, I don't speak much in public, and this is very much out of my comfort zone, but I was wondering if you and I could meet for a coffee."

I looked surprised and stuttered, saying, "Yes. Of course."

"Ok, do you have your phone?" she asked.

"Yes, I do," I replied, taking my phone out of my pocket.

She gave me her number, and I saved it and gave her a missed call so she could have my number.

"Call me, and I'll tell you where and when."

"Ok," I replied, and she walked off.

This felt like a dream. I just had the biggest female actor in Bollywood asked me on a date. I saw her leave the building, looking back at me and smiling. I was surprised, and that night, I danced in excitement. I even picked up actors on my shoulder and danced with them sitting on my shoulder.

All the British cast came out of the hotel around midnight. We sat along the wall next to The Gateway of India. We shared how we all were lucky to have had the opportunity to be part of this great movie. I was also excited that I was going to go on a date with Sabrina Kumari.

The next day, we all woke up late afternoon. I walked along the beach and thought how blessed I was. I looked at the big billboards with the film poster of the film I was in.

I sat on a wall near the beach and popped into the costume designer Seema's of the film house. She greeted me, and we talked for almost two hours. Seema's sister Reena was a huge star in the seventies and eighties. She walked in and said Hi, and I was hoping her daughter Beena would also pop in. Unfortunately, there was no sign of her, and I wouldn't ask to stay professional.

She was the daughter of not just Reena but also one of the superstars of the 1970s, Suresh Kumar.

After a long conversation about weight loss programs, training regimes, and healthy eating, I left to return to my hotel. If I recall correctly, there was a rumour in the film industry that I dated Seema. I only coached her a few times and didn't know where that came from.

The next day, the rest of the British artists and crew members returned to the UK and Grandad and I stayed another week.

I called Sabrina, and I believed it was her who answered it, but she said the wrong number. I then thought I was wrong-numbered. I tried again later that day.

"Hi, is this Sabrina?" I asked.

"Hi, Raj," she replied. "Sorry about earlier. I was with someone and had to say the wrong number," she explained.

"No problem," I said.

"I think it will be difficult to meet in public, so it's best if you come to my apartment," she said.

"Ok, no problem," I said.

"Where are you staying?" She asked.

I told her the address.

"I will send my driver to collect you at 6 pm, is this ok?" she asked.

"Of course it is," I replied.

I was picked up by Sabrina Kumari's driver that night and driven to her apartment. I walked into her apartment, and it was beautiful. It had a very cultural theme with a lot of paintings on the walls. One wall was allocated to pictures of all her family members. It was a history wall of all family members who have worked in the film industry. She gave me a bit of a tour.

"What would you like to drink?" she asked while I admired her awards in her display cabinet.

"I'll have a soft drink," I replied.

"You don't drink alcohol?" she asked.

"No, I don't," I replied.

"Oh, yes, I remember you. You're healthy."

"Do you drink?" I asked.

"Moderately," she replied.

"I love red wine," she shared.

"That's nice. I have tried wine in the past, but it's not my cup of tea," I shared.

"It's not everyone's cup of tea," she said.

"Are you ready for the next film?" she asked.

"Hopefully, I am," I replied.

"Not hopefully, but you should be certain and positive. I'm sure the producer has strong hopes of signing you up," she said.

"I am ready but only share the confidence when filming and when projects finish." I shared.

"That's one way of looking at it," she said.

We spoke about the film project in detail, and I felt that she knew more about it than I did. She sat next to me, and I looked into her blue eyes. I felt the colour of her eyes change from blue to green at times.

In a heartbeat, we began to kiss. We kissed for at least five minutes, and before you knew it, our clothes were off, and we ended up in her bedroom.

Even though this was my first time, it seemed like she had a great time. I, on the other hand, enjoyed it. It was hot and sweaty and fast and slow. We tried many positions, and being a competitor at heart, it felt like a workout for me.

"I can hear my heart beating fast," she shared.

I was a bit out of breath, and I looked at my watch and I realised we must have had sex for at least seventy minutes.

"Women must love you in bed," she said.

I didn't know what to say at first, as she was my first.

212

"I hope so," I said, trying not to embarrass myself.

"I hope you have used protection in the past, and this was safe; what did we do?"

"Can I share the truth?" I said.

"What? You have something," she asked concerned.

"No, I'm super safe, as you are my first."

"Your first?" she asked.

"Yes," I replied.

"I don't believe that. You were damn amazing, and if it was your first time, how did you know what you did?" she asked.

"I followed your lead," I replied.

"I don't believe that one minute," she said.

"Up to you what you want to believe," I said, but at the same time, I didn't want to ruin any opportunity to work with her.

"Can I say you were amazing, too?" I shared.

"Thanks," she replied.

We began to kiss, and before you knew it, we were back at it again. The noise she made was a real turn-on.

"Wonder what the neighbours thought," I thought.

She had beautiful eyes, a great smile, and a great body, and the sex we just had was amazing. I thought I could be the next son-in-law in the famous family of the film industry. She was really beautiful and a talented actor.

As I was getting ready, I noticed blood on the bed sheets. She saw me notice and said, "It was my first time as well, and I just don't sleep around either. I felt a connection when we met in London. I know the world expects me to marry someone in the film industry or some successful businessman. But I felt something in my heart. Did you feel the same?" She asked.

I looked at her in shock and felt this feeling in my heart that this might be right.

"I do like you, and I did mention it to my dad when we worked together in London. He said you and your family were in another league. Truth, I have never seen anyone different in our lives. Even though we live simple lives, my family is worth seven million pounds. My uncle, my mother's brother, is probably worth double that. So, financially, you could say we are wealthy. I know you and your family are worth a lot more, maybe ten times or a hundred times more. I also have to point out that this is my parents' wealth, not mine. I have only just graduated from university and run a local fitness centre," I shared. "You, on the other hand, have worked in fifty films to date and earn your own money."

She looked at me and didn't say anything for a minute or two.

"Listen, we still have to get to know each other as characters, and we will see where it goes. Deal?" she asked and shook my hand.

"Please don't go to the press with this story," she said.

"Of course I wouldn't," I said. "I have to convince myself that this happened first."

I said, and she laughed.

Driving back to the hotels, I kept thinking about what just happened. My life was going to change, and I may have to relocate to India. Did I want this? Will this relationship remain for long, or was it a one-off?

When I got back to the hotel room, Grandad was on his phone as usual and making some deal. While he was talking, I remembered a time when I was ten years old and being tortured by my uncle Ramdass. Just then, my grandad, grandma, and Aunty Baljit walked in.

"What's going on?' my grandad asked.

"Nothing, just playing with Raj," answers Uncle Ramdass. "I don't know what Raj will do when he is older; he's just too slow."

My eyes flipped up with water as a ten-year-old child. He always tortured me and put me down because of my learning difficulties.

"Did you get him to check to see if he had some kind of autism when he was born?"

"What was autism?" I thought as a ten-year-old child.

"Of course, he hasn't got autism," my grandad defended me. "All of you behave as I have my nephews coming in the next hour from Bradford. One of them is a retired lawyer in India who, in the late 1970s, was one of the advisors to the prime minister of India."

"Well, you better not introduce them to Raj as he will embarrass you," said Uncle Ramdass.

"That's enough, Ramdass," said my grandad.

I remember being introduced to these distant relative uncles. One brother lived in Bradford, whose two sons were lawyers, and the other brother lived in New Delhi. The brother, who lived in New Delhi, was the advisor to the political party in India.

As my grandad was on the phone, I thought, "All these years, I had been told that I was slow and may have had some illness growing up. And now I have the biggest actress, Sabrina Kumari, who wants to marry me."

Grandad came off the phone.

"Do you know who that was?" he asked.

"No, grandad," I replied.

"It was your uncle, a retired lawyer in Dehli. He said he has a house here in Mumbai in the main part of the city. Why are we stopping in a hotel? He asked if we should go and stay at his house," Grandad shared.

But I couldn't think of anything else but just about what happened between me and Sabrina.

***

I wake up in the hospital, and I can hardly see. Through the blurred vision, I see and hear that uncle from Bradford's wife crying. The more she cries, the more pain I go through. Everything is becoming more of a blur and dark.

***

I found it hard to wake up and open my eyes in the hotel room. I may have been drained out with training, diet, travelling, and all the partying. I sat up, and my grandad was reading the newspaper as usual.

214

"You ok, son?" He asked.

"Don't know," I replied. "I feel drained and like I have a hangover."

"You have had a busy few days, and your body is probably in shock," my grandad said. "I knew you were tired as you snored loudly and then spoke to yourself."

"Talking to myself?" I asked

"Yes, first you said, 'I love you, Julie,' which rang alarm bells, and then you began to say, 'I love Sabrina.' I concluded it was an actress you were dreaming about. Who is Julie?" he asked.

I quickly thought on the spot and said, "Julia Roberts. She's a big film star in Hollywood."

"Oh, ok, it's natural," he said. "What have you got planned today? I have a meeting with one of my friends who has flown over from Punjab."

"I don't know yet," I replied. "Ok, don't stay out too late."

He left the hotel room.

I got out of bed and drank a whole litre of mineral water. Sat at the desk and thought about Sabrina. I then think about my dreams and remember I was also dreaming about Julie. I was so confused, I think. Only if Julie would pick up my phone and speak to me. I grabbed my phone and called Julie. The phone rang, but there was no answer. I waited for her to call me. I lay on the bed thinking about my whole journey to date—Julie, sports, family, Madhu, and now Bollywood. Then I remembered I needed to contact the Doctor's brother. I quickly called him and arranged to meet Ashok Kapoor, the acting coach.

Two days later, I met him in Chembur and discussed the possibility of him coaching me and opening doors to other movies.

"You have a face to be a star, and your dialogue delivery is very powerful. Of course, I feel you will take the media by storm, similar to my other students, Ricky Roshen, Josh Abraham, and Farooq Khan," he said. "All three of these have great potential to be box office success, and I feel you will also have the same potential."

This encouraged me even more, and I began to plan to stay in Mumbai after the next film shoot. "Just get a set of professional photographs done for me to pitch to my circle of director and producer friends," Said Ashok Kapoor.

"I will," I replied.

I left and went back to the hotel, and sitting in the hotel room, I brainstormed about my career moves. Called the Assistant director of the movie I just worked on and asked him for details of a photographer. He gave me details of a well-known photographer who was also the niece of my role model. I called her.

"Hi, is this Beena?" I asked.

"Yes, this is Beena." She replied.

"This is Raj, and I was in the movie," I began to say.

"O'yes, I remember you," She said.

"I was told you are a photographer," I asked.

"Yes, I am, and you need a set of pictures done to hand out to agents," she said.

"Yes," I replied.

"It's going to cost ten thousand rupees," she said.

I quickly calculated that in my head, and it was around one hundred pounds, which I felt was super cheap. "Yes, that's ok. Let me know where I need to come," I asked.

She told me the details, and we planned for the shoot.

I got ready to go for a workout, and just then, my grandad walked into the room. He stopped me to go training and said, "I have a surprise for you."

"Surprise?" I asked.

"Yes, come downstairs to the lobby."

I walked downstairs and found Madhu and her mother sitting and drinking tea in the lobby. Madhu's mother saw me, jumped up, came running to me – well, trying to run – and hugged me. "My son, how are you? You got skinny and look ill."

"Hi," I replied.

We walked over to Madhu, and she got up and went to touch my feet in respect, and I stopped her.

"What are you doing?" I asked.

"She is giving you respect," said her mother.

"It's ok," said Grandad.

"It's not respect I believe in, but love," I said.

So, Madhu gives me a short hug.

We all sat down.

"So, Raj, you were very busy filming the past year. Are you going to be the next Ranbir Singh?" asked Madhu's mother.

"I'm just enjoying the experience at the moment. Yes, that's it; it's an experience," said Grandad.

"He was going to open their law practice in the UK."

"I hope so," said Madhu.

"Well, we both had to do our LPCs anyway before that happened," I replied.

"Of course, you can both do these at my lawyer's firm. I have spoken to James Roger, and he will arrange with you both to have jobs within the firm and help you both with your LPCs."

"Why are we disturbing these two?" said Madhu's mother.

"Why don't you take Madhu for a walk and dinner?"

"Good idea,' said my grandad, taking out his wallet and giving me three thousand rupees.

"Go and treat her," he said.

"Come on, then," I said. I knew I didn't have a choice, so I went along with the whole madness.

We walked along Juhu Road, and Madhu got excited about seeing Juhu Beach. "Is this the beach we see in many movies?" she asked.

"Yes, it is," I replied.

"Can we walk there?" she asked.

"Of course, we can."

We walked over, and she soaked in all the area by just staring at the beach, the sand, the shops, and the activities on the beach.

"What are the beaches like in the UK?" she asked.

"A lot cleaner, I mean a lot cleaner," I replied. 'That beach is very filthy, and most of the beaches in the UK are clean and blue, especially the beaches in Cornwall."

"Blue?" she asked.

"Ok, that's where we will spend our honeymoon," she said.

"Ok," I said, "But I would like to go to the USA and the Caribbean Islands."

"The Caribbean Islands?" she asked.

"Yes, like Jamaica, Bahamas, and Barbados."

"I know about the islands, but why there?"

"They are beautiful, and the seas are something else."

"How will I be able to travel?"

"I'm sure you will be able to, and if you can't, I'll go on my own," I said with a short laugh.

"Very funny," she said. "So, can I confirm you are serious about our marriage?"

"Well, it is all planned, isn't it?" I asked.

"Yes, but it seems like you're unhappy with the marriage," she said.

"What gave it away?" I asked.

"Come on, Raj, be serious. I do want to marry you and begin my life in the UK as a lawyer. Ever since your grandad has become our family friend, he has only spoken about us two getting married, and ever since then, I have dreamed about moving to the UK," she shared.

"Madhu, my grandad, has planned our marriage, and I love my grandad, so I can't ignore his wishes."

"But is it your wish?" She asked.

"Does it matter what?" I said. "Plus, you made it quite clear when I was in Punjab that if I didn't invite you, you would have your friends in England beat me up," I stated.

"I am sorry about that. I have a short fuse and get hot-tempered quickly. I didn't scare you, did I?" she said comically.

"Scare me? You're having a laugh, aren't you?" I asked.

"I'm sure Grandad has told you and your family about his journey. He came to the UK and managed to stand up against racism in the seventies and eighties. From the mid-eighties, he built himself a brand of someone people shouldn't pick a fight with, known as a godfather and also known for owning half of a town. I followed suit by taking no crap off people. Not in a gangster way but standing up against the wrong people. I'll give you an example; last year, a couple of African men came into our shop holding a plastic gun and demanded my mother give them the money out of the till."

"An armed robbery?" she interrupted.

"Yes, you could say, and my mother slapped the gun out of the guy's hand and told them to get out before her husband and son came back. They got away with nothing, but when I came back and checked the camera footage, you know what my grandma said?"

"What?" Madhu asked.

"She gave me the crowbar and said go and teach them a lesson. I found out where these two men lived and went to their flats and beat them both up. I used an axe and crowbar to smash through their flat door to get in. After I beat these two, I decided to go around beating up all the bad guys within a three-mile radius."

"Yes, there were meetings held, and many wanted to shoot and kill me. But due to Grandad's money and reputation, they all backed off. So, to your question, 'Am I scared?' The answer is no."

"I didn't mean anything by it when I said it," she defended herself.

"So, local thug, a rich man's son, a sports star, a businessman, and now a movie star. Are you telling me you never had women asking you out? You are telling me you never slept or had numerous dates as a gangster's child? And I'm joking about the gangster bit," she said laughingly.

"You must have a fan base in your hometown," she asked.

***

"Wake up, Raj, look who's here."

I slowly open my eyes and see a group of ladies who are my father's customers. There is Jan, Lesley, and Kerry, a woman whose name I never knew but who is the spitting image of Catherine Zeta-Jones; Diane; and Lianne, who is the spitting image of Felicity, the new pop artist, and Julie's stepmother. I smile at Julie's stepmother, and she smiles back.

"Oh my god, look how skinny he has gone," says Kerry.

"I know," my mother says. "Come on. Raj, we need to get you well and back into shape. All the women are missing you and your muscles in the shop."

I smile. "Thank you."

The pain from my kidneys and constant headaches make it hard to talk. I am also too cautious as I get essential tremors of my body shaking while talking.

I look at Julie's stepmother. "I hope Julie is well, and tell her I love her," I say in my head.

She looks at me, and I hear, "She loves you and misses you a lot. Get well soon, so you both can get together."

I imagine telepathically. I hope for what she is thinking or saying.

"Raj, you will get well. You need to stay strong and believe," Julie's Stepmother says.

"So many people love you and are hurting for you to be this ill. You know all those who love you. Remember when you told Julie that your grandad told you once that there is a solution in your mind?"

Raj, the power is in your mind," Julie's stepmother continues to say. I smile to thank her. My mother walks over to Julie's stepmother and hugs her to thank her.

"Thank you," my mother says.

"He'll be okay, Prakash, and there is more than one person waiting for him to return home," says Julie's Stepmother.

"Get better soon, Raj," they say while leaving the room.

Mum and Dad walk them out.

"Listen," Dad says to Julie's stepmother as she walks out. "I know my family has upset you and Julie in the past. Please accept my apology on behalf of all of us."

"Oh, please, it's all water under the bridge, and we haven't even remembered any of it," Julie's mother says.

"I haven't seen Julie in years, but if she could come and see Raj, I know it would make a difference," asks my father.

"I will ask, but she has been busy with her job and touring Europe with her artwork."

"Artwork?" Dad asks.

"Yes, she is very talented and had her work displayed in galleries."

'That is amazing, and well done to Julie,' he says. "Give her my congratulations, and please request if she can come to see Raj."

"I would appreciate it," Dad is persistent in his voice.

"I will ask, as I said, and trust me, she will be really happy that you have asked her to come and see Raj. She has a lot of respect for you," she shares.

"Tell her she is no different from my kids, and I've always seen her the same."

"Okay," she says, and she leaves.

A tear falls down my face, hearing my dad asking Julie to come and see me.

Mum walks in, saying, "They all had a crush on Raj."

I am just happy that Dad had asked for Julie to come and visit me.

"Don't know if and how long I'm going to live, but it would be great to see Julie," I think.

"I am sure Julie fancied Raj too," shares my mother, and Dad says, "I think it was Raj who liked Julie. Am I right, Raj?"

He asks me with a smile and gives me a thumbs up. I smile in my response and close my eyes.

***

"So, you haven't answered the questions, Madhu. There might be many who have liked me but never asked me out or showed an interest. In the town, I live in an area where many other Caucasian women live. But they never showed an interest in Indian or Asian men in general, I've always felt," I said.

"Probably due to Indians being too religious in our faiths or even the curry smell," I shared.

"Curry smell? What?" Madhu asked.

219

"I'm only joking; it's a joke about us Indians smelling of curry all the time. Isn't that a bit racist? Maybe it is, but it doesn't bother me anymore."

We continued walking along Juhu beach, and she held onto my arm.

"So, do you like India?" she asked.

"It's okay, but why?"

"You have been here twice now in the last couple of years. Just asking."

"If you're asking if I would move here, the answer is no."

"If it was for Bollywood?" She asked.

"Still no," I answered.

"I love England too much even to consider moving." I saw her thinking for a moment as she walked, and she asked, "Do you like English women?"

"I like all women," I answered.

She thought again, "But you must find English more attractive."

"I see English women, Afro/Caribbean women, Indian women, Chinese women, and European women in the city, and I like them all."

I walked her around the Juhu area, where many of the actors lived and pointed out their houses. Two days later, I had my photoshoot. Madhu and I went to the photoshoot that morning. It was the first and the worst photoshoot of my life. We first went to the city library to take pictures outside the building, as this building is used many times in Indian movies as criminal courts. From there, we went to local streets and then a local park. Madhu was angry and upset throughout the whole photoshoot, probably because the photographer complimented my body and kept on stroking my arms. Even the photographer felt the tension. We finished off filming outside a new hotel being built, but this time, there was a model present who was Swedish and very attractive. The photographer had the model kiss me on the cheek, which didn't go well looking at Madhu's face.

Later that evening, back at the hotel, Madhu was fuming again.

"So you loved the photographer stroking your arm and that blonde model kissing you?" Madhu asked angrily.

"It was part of my photoshoot, and if you didn't like it, why did you come with me?"

"So, that's how it was going to be: you having fun behind my back at modelling shoots?' she said.

"Listen, I'm not going to apologize for something that is part of this new journey in Bollywood."

Just then, her mother and my grandad walked into the hotel room.

"How are your kids doing?" Her mother asked.

"All good," Madhu replied.

I looked at Madhu and thought, "How did she just switch from being angry and then calm?"

"We have to get ready for tomorrow's flight," said her mother.

"That's right, and I was thinking that we should fly to Punjab with them, Raj. What do you think?" my Grandad asked. I looked at Madhu, and she was grinning, and I looked at her mother, who was also grinning.

This freaked me out inside.

220

"What, Grandad?"

"I think it's a good idea." He replied.

"It is a good idea, but I have to be back to work on the next movie," I quickly thought on the spot, which was good for me.

"That's a shame," said Madhu's mother.

"I know, and I wanted to spend more time with you," said Madhu.

"Can't you go a week late?" Asked grandad.

"I can't, grandad. I committed to the filmmakers," I replied. He gave me this angry look.

That night, my grandad got drunk and began to swear and tell me off in Punjabi. I decided to drink a bit of alcohol that night, too, to ignore him, but it got me angry, and we both were in a heated argument. Madhu and her mother, who were sleeping in another room, heard the argument and came running to us. My grandad and I said things that I vaguely remember. We both were asked to take this argument into the street, and we did.

After a while, my grandad left by getting into an auto-rickshaw, and I got into a different auto-rickshaw. But I don't remember what happened after this.

I woke up the next morning and just about opened my eyes and had this terrible hangover. I saw my grandad sitting at the table having a cup of tea.

"You all right, son?" He asked.

"Yes, grandad," I replied.

"Drinking alcohol isn't definitely for you," he said.

"Do you remember what happened last night?" I said no.

"I did end up in an autorickshaw," I thought.

"I don't, either," Madhu's mother said. The autorickshaw guys brought us back after an hour. They earned a lot of money last night," he shared.

"Are we taking Madhu and her mother to the airport? I already took them with the driver two hours ago. They were too angry to speak to us," he continued. A day before we were leaving to come back to England, I had a call from the photographer.

"Hi, Raj, I managed to get you an advert," she said.

"An advert?" I asked.

"But I am leaving back to England tomorrow," I shared.

"I thought you wanted a career here in Bollywood," She said.

"I do, but I have to go as I'm starting a film next week in the UK," I said. "Oh, okay, but you may not get these opportunities again," she said.

"Couldn't I come back in 6 weeks' time?' I asked.

"Let me find out and get back to you," she said.

The next day, we flew back to England.

Chapter Thirty-Nine

Two days before filming, we were all called in for a meeting with the director and cast of the film. I was super excited as I was the main lead, and I got to meet the actress, Kusum Ganga, who was launched opposite the biggest rising star of Bollywood, Aryan Khan.

Day one of filming was awesome, and I met the crew members. We began filming scenes for one of the heartbroken songs. Scenes were filmed walking sadly along the canal, along an old railway track, a park, and streets.

On day two, I worked out with other fellow actors in the gym. On day three, we had additional training scenes with bag work and sparring.

After six days of filming, there was no sign of this beautiful actress.

At the end of our filming of day six, the director called me for a bite to eat in the evening.

I was sitting in the restaurant of the hotel where all the cast and crew were staying, waiting for George, the director. George walked in and said, "Raj, sorry to keep you waiting; last-minute changes to a couple of scenes for the filming for the next few days. Hope you're enjoying it."

"I'm loving every second of it," I replied.

"Great," he said. "Listen, I thought you would love all the training part of the scenes first; hence, I decided to schedule all your training and fight scenes first. Get you comfortable in front of the camera, and then the drama and love scenes will follow."

"Awesome," I replied.

"I just need you to give me a little on your performance. I want you to imagine you're in the 'Rocky' movie, and you're Sylvester Stallone."

This got me excited.

"You got it," I replied.

We ate and spoke about how George wanted me to perform in each scene we were filming in the next couple of days.

For the next couple of days, I gave it my all and did a scene with me skipping, martial arts training, running through the town centre, working out at the gym, and looking in the mirror to motivate myself. What made it interesting was that one of the co-actors was a former American gladiator training me in the scenes.

Day seven was a rest day, and I spent time going over my lines. I got a call, and the assistant director called me and asked me if I was around to meet in the lobby of the hotel. I walked down to the lobby and found Kusum sitting there. The assistant director introduced us, "This is Raj, your co-actor and lead of the film, and this is," and I quickly said, "Kusum. It is very nice to meet you."

We shook hands.

"Let's discuss characters and scenes," said the assistant director. We all sat down and went through the scenes.

I had a night shoot the next day, which was going to be a huge fight scene. I tried to sleep during the day as I needed the energy. The late evening scene was set up to be filmed. I was taken into the makeup van to get ready. I went on the set, which was within a location of abandoned garages, lighting up the area. I had already walked out of the makeup van to do the fight scenes. I looked around and saw two white Caucasian guys. One of them was a muscular character, and the other a slim character. Both skinheads had tattoos painted on them by makeup artists. I went and introduced myself.

"Hi, I'm Raj," I said. They both shook my hand.

"So, you're who we have to beat up?" said Hench Man one. I think his name was Cuban.

I laughed and replied, 'I think according to the script."

George, the director, invited us onto the set.

"Right, guys," he said. "I will be choreographing this fight scene."

He explained the fight scene. We carried out the fight scenes, and most of it was my character being beaten up. Then I fell on the ground when the henchmen kicked me in the ribs. Unfortunately, they made contact, which caused a lot of pain.

***

Back in the hospital, I was in a lot of pain. I was screaming in a lot of pain.

"What's happening?" my mother asked.

She was crying at the same time, trying to comfort me from the pain. I heard my father crying loudly outside my room, which made me cry. I thought I wanted it to all end so that I wouldn't put my parents through this daily. The nurse came in and injected me, which eased the pain.

***

I was on sets, and these two men were both kicking and going at it at full force. The padding was not helping at all. We finished the scene. I took off my top and found all of my rib cage areas bruised and in pain.

The director said to everybody, "Let's have a thirty-minute break, and we will come back to this same scene."

I began speaking to these two guys and asked what other work they had done. Cuban answered, "This is the first film, and I have appeared in TV shows. I have walked celebrities down the stairs in the Graham Norton Show."

"I think I've seen you on the show," I replied.

The other guy said, 'This is the first for me too. I have done background extra work."

"Like?" I asked.

He said, "Drama series like the famous Eastenders."

"Oh, that's great," I said.

We were back on the sets, and the director surprised us this time. He played the taxi driver who saved my character from the thugs. He shocked me with his martial arts moves and stunts. To look at this guy, you wouldn't think he could do the moves he was doing. It definitely was an element of surprise. We finished the scene with George driving to the garages, jumping out, and thrashing these two henchmen. We finished all the fight and training scenes over those days. Then, it came to a romantic song scene. Usually, actors from the Indian film industry would practice the dance scenes in the dance studio. Due to the budget, they couldn't afford this and kept the dance choreography simple.

Kusum arrived on the set and went straight into the makeup van, and after her makeup was done, I was called to have my makeup done for the scene. We were on the sets, and we began performing the song. It is a great song with Hindi lyrics: 'This is true love'. We danced around the park area and drove to other locations, filming the song all in one day. Kusum and I got on like we had been friends for years. We shared many life stories while waiting for these scenes to be filmed. We connected, and the choreographer applauded our performances, which came across as very real on the small TV screen. She said we looked like we were in love.

After packing up for the day, we headed back to the hotel. We were both tired and we grabbed our food from the restaurant and headed to our room. Kusum was so friendly that she put the food on my plate for me. I felt this was nice. The next morning, we began our other scenes. The following weeks contained college, family members, trips, cinema, a kickboxing competition, two more fight scenes with Kusum in the scenes, a coach, and a dance number with many background dancers' scenes. The song was amazing—someone who has stolen my sleep.

Kusum had to leave for another film shoot two days before the film's wrap-up. We had completed all our scenes. We exchanged numbers, and she said, hopefully, we will work together again. For the last two days, we have been filming another song, which was part of my dream. We were in the park, ready to roll the camera, when George asked for the actress to play the role opposite me. I did notice a separate makeup van. The doors opened, and it was none other than Sabrina Kumari.

I couldn't believe it. She walked onto the set.

"Hi, Raj, how are you doing?"

"I'm good," I stuttered to say. "How are you?"

"I'm great," she replied. "Are you ready to do this?"

I said, "Yes."

"Make sure you look like you're in love with me."

"I will," I said.

The choreographer talked through the season, and we completed the scenes for the day. During the whole filming of the song, I felt we were in love. George thanked Sabrina and said, "Raj, let me introduce you to the producer of the film."

I was lost for words. Sabrina and I walked to the side while the whole crew was packing up.

"So, you're the producer?"

"Yes, and is that a problem?" asked Sabrina.

"Not a problem, but confused," I replied. "We had that moment in Mumbai, and then you produced this movie starring me."

"Don't flatter yourself. I did this for myself as I'm testing the whole British and Indian filmmaking collaboration," she explained.

"Oh, plus you said you like Kusum. Well, you had your chance to get close to her and date on this film set. Well, did you?" Sabrina asked.

"Firstly, I was nervous when you asked me last time. Secondly, it's you I was a big fan of and liked. Thirdly, I didn't even think about dating her," I explained.

"Now you're thinking there was an option.' Asked Sabrina.

"No, no," I quickly answered.

"Listen, I am in the city for another week. Let's meet a few times."

"Okay, I will reply."

She walked off and sat in her car, and her driver drove off, taking her. I was still shocked and confused about just what happened. I looked up at the sky and saw the clouds changing colour and becoming greyer. I was back at the hotel, and the whole crew and cast were celebrating the completion in the restaurant. A bit crowded, but it's all good at the same time. I am standing by the bar, just glancing and taking in this new experience in my life. I was super happy that my dreams were coming together. The lighting, the music, and the excitement were overwhelming. George walked up to me, wearing blue jeans, a white T-shirt, and a black jacket. This was all he wore throughout the filming of the film. I think he could be an actor himself.

"You did a great job, Raj," Said George.

"Thanks, George," I replied. "What's the plan next?"

"Well, we will spend the next month editing, and luckily, we recorded all the dialogues on the set; we wouldn't need anyone to come and dub the dialogues," Said George.

"That's good," I replied.

"Raj, when this film releases, you will become a superstar overnight, so get ready for it," said George.

"I hope so," I replied. "I know Raj. You have what it takes. You have great acting skills, looks, and a great body. You will take Bollywood by storm." He continued to share and encourage me.

'Thanks,' I replied.

"Can I ask how Sabrina became part of all this?" I asked.

"Yes, of course," he replied.

Just then, someone grabs my arms. I turn around, and it's Kusum. "Hi guys,"

"Hi, Kusum," said George.

"I hope you like my work, George," asked Kusum.

"Of course, I did, and you two are going to be a big success. Well, Kusum, you already are," Said George.

"Thanks, George," she said.

"Listen, Kusum, you did a fabulous job, and you will be in the industry for a long time. I need to go and speak to the editor now," Said George and left.

'Thanks, George," said Kusum whilst George walked away.

"So, what's your plan?" asked Kusum

"My plan?" I asked.

"Yes, I think this film will be a huge success. We will get many other offers and a lot of TV ads and endorsement deals," She shared.

"Wow, I never thought of any of that," I said.

"You should get yourself an agent and get more work. I have a feeling you and I will get at least two or three more movies together paired up after this release."

"I hope so," I said.

"What are you doing for the next few days?" She asked.

"'Not a lot," I replied.

"I am stopping for another week, so why don't we meet up for coffee and meals?" she asked.

"That's a good idea," I replied.

"Plus, I can introduce you to my manager, and he might represent you," she said.

"That would be great, and I appreciate it," I said.

Just then, Sabrina walked into the room. She looked our way and gave that look, 'ok, you with her then.'

I watched her walk around the room, talking to George and other crew members but looking at me from the corner of her eye. This felt a bit freaky. I felt like she wanted to hit me. She finally made her way to me and Kusum.

"Well, you both did some outstanding work," said Sabrina.

"Thank you very much, and thank you for having me in your first film production. I would have thought you would have starred in it," said Kusum.

"I did think I should have, but then I thought you have become the recent hot news, so why not take a chance with you?" said Sabrina.

"I can't complain, but you are still a huge star, and I'm a fan too," said Kusum.

"Don't worry. I have a line of films coming in the next three years, and hopefully, I will be able to share screen space with Raj. What do you say, Raj?" Sabrina asked me.

"Of course, that would be a dream come true," I stutter to answer her question.

"OK, you two enjoy the evening, and I have to go. Oh, and Raj, tomorrow morning is our meeting, remember? My driver will collect you at 9 am sharp," said Sabrina.

"Ok, I'll be ready," I replied.

The next morning, I got ready and thought this was another historical moment in my movie career. Like many other Indian film actors, I could make history by being involved with a famous actress. I was looking in the mirror and remembered a time when I was about fifteen, looking in the mirror and combing my hair; my aunty walked in and said, "Look at him admiring himself. You're not going to marry any actress."

Back to the present, staring in the mirror. I was going on a date and doing exactly what they said I couldn't do. Sitting waiting, and my mobile bleeps. I looked, and it was a text from Sabrina saying, "Sorry, I won't be able to make our breakfast as something has come up. Let's meet for dinner in two days, xxx."

I replied, "It's ok, and see you then."

I came down to the hotel lobby, and it was quiet and boring.

"Raj," I heard someone calling me.

I looked behind and saw it was Kusum.

"Hi Kusum, how are you?" I asked.

"All good, and I'm just thinking about what to do. And you just answered my question," she said.

"What was that then?" I asked.

"You and I are spending the day together," She replied.

"We are?" I asked.

"Yes, we are," she replied.

"Come on, let's explore London."

We got into a black cab and were driven into the city. The weather was nice and warm. We visited most of London's tourist places. We went to Piccadilly Circus and took pictures outside the four horses, Leicester Square and took pictures outside the Empire Cinema and sitting on the bench, and we both asked for drawings of both of us together by the artists. Kusum and I spent the whole day around London. We went outside Buckingham Place and had lunch at Hyde Park. We visited the Millennium Dome and finished off on the tourist bus. We were on the bus and enjoyed how lit up London City was in the dark.

Kusum and I sat next to each other. She looked at me and kissed me on the lips. We began to kiss. We stopped, and we laughed. She said, "I like you."

"Thanks," I replied.

"Thanks?" she replied.

"Well, aren't you dating film director Sudesh Kumar?" I asked.

"I am, but I am not happy in our relationship," Kusum shared.

"I don't know if this is right. You are still in a relationship with him, and I think this would be wrong," I said.

"Wrong? This would be a good thing and help promote our film. This could be a good move, and maybe we get signed for more films," she said.

"Sudesh is a big director, and if he finds out, he will ruin our careers before they even start," I shared.

"Don't worry about that. I have too much on him in secrets; he wouldn't do anything," she said.

"I will have to think about it," I said.

"Think? Again, do you want to or not?" she asked.

"Not now," I replied.

She looked at me in disgust. We came back to the hotel and went our separate ways.

The next morning, I woke up to receiving a call from an Indian film magazine reporter.

"Hello, is this Raj?" they asked.

"Yes, this is he," I replied.

"We have received information and a picture of you kissing Kusum. Is this true?" they asked.

"What? No!" I replied.

I came downstairs for breakfast and found Kusum sitting there, too. She stood up from the table and walked over to me.

"Thank you for ruining my career and life," she said.

"What are you talking about?" I asked.

"You leaked the story of us having an affair." She accused me of.

"What are you talking about? Why would I do this?" I asked.

"So, you can get famous," she screamed at me.

"How would I get famous like this? I even said this would ruin our careers if you remember?" I asked.

She calmed down, and I don't know who did this then.

"Well, we were together, and you kissed me," I said.

"Kissed you? You kissed me back," she said.

"Listen, we are making this worse and in public more than it is," I said.

"It's ok, as I'm going to India this evening," she shared.

"It was nice knowing you," she said and walked off.

The next morning, I lay in bed, and the room phone rang, and I answered it.

"Hello," I said.

"Your driver is here," said the receptionist.

"Oh, sorry, I will be down in twenty minutes," I replied.

I rushed downstairs into the car park and found the driver outside a black limo. I walked towards the limo, and the driver opened the door. I went to step in and found Sabrina sitting in the car waiting.

She smiled, and I smiled back.

"You never keep a lady waiting," said Sabrina.

"I am sorry and didn't know you were waiting," I said.

"Because you didn't know I was in here, I forgive you." I sat in the car and said I was sorry.

The driver drove off. We began drinking champagne and making out before we got to have breakfast. The car pulled up, and the driver opened our door. I stepped outside, and I saw the Ritz Hotel. Sabrina stepped out and said, "Follow me."

We walked in, and it felt so British or English. We found the place so lit up, and I felt surrounded by gold. We sat at the table after I pulled out the chair for Sabrina to sit on. We ordered our breakfast, and the food arrived, but there wasn't that much communication. Sabrina was staring at me, and I could feel a connection.

228

"So, you're seeing Kusum, I hear?" Sabrina asked.

"No, no. No, of course not," I replied.

"So why is there a lot of noise in the Film Industry?" She asked.

"It's fake news," I replied.

"You told me you liked Kusum," she said.

"I know, I said this, and it seems like this is the only thing we talk about," I said.

"Listen, Raj, I like you a lot. I haven't met anyone like you ever. You are humble, honest, funny, good-looking, and someone I can trust. We don't get that in our world," Sabrina shared.

"I like you too, and I am who I am. I don't like to be fake," I said.

"That's all I want," she said.

We spent all morning together, finding out that we had so much in common.

We walked out of The Ritz hotel and found a couple of photographers taking pictures of us. An Indian female reporter walked up to us holding a microphone, with a man holding a camera.

"You are seeing this man who is also seeing Kusum?" She asked. We got into the limo and drove off.

In the car, Sabrina was upset.

"What have I done? I am stupid," she said.

"Stupid?" I asked.

"I thought you liked me?" I further asked.

"I don't know what to say at the moment," she said.

She told the driver to take her to her country home. While driving to her home, she made a couple of calls with people I thought I would never witness to be part of conversations with celebrities. We got on countryside roads, and the driver said, "Miss Kumari, we are being followed by a van and car holding camcorders."

"Try to lose them," said Sabrina. The chase went on for at least five minutes until we ended up in a car accident.

I was in pain, and everything was blurry. I could see the driver hurt and unconscious, and I looked at Sabrina, and she was unconscious.

I tried speaking but couldn't.

***

I woke up back in the hospital, and everything was blurry, and I was in pain. But I saw my cousins laughing. Then, the nurses came in and asked them to leave before she called security.

"It seems like they increased the morphine painkiller," the nurse said.

***

I was in the hospital after the accident. I saw nurses and doctors running around. I looked to my left, and I saw Sabrina. Sabrina had all the wires on her pads, and I could hear the doctor saying. "We are going to lose her."

I looked at the monitor, which was beating, and then it bleeped with just one sound. The doctor said she was no more. Tears fall down my face as I think why this had to happen. She was a great actress and a nice human being.

For the next two months, I was being questioned by the police and the press. I had Sabrina's family members visit me, asking what we were doing together. A text sent to her sister, Sareena, cleared me of any legal issues I was being accused of. The press wrote me off due to the accident and having an affair with Sabrina and Kusum at the same time.

We waited months for the premiere and release of the film. I got a call from Sabrina's India office telling me they have canned the film, which will not be released.

Chapter Forty

At home, I got frustrated with the pressure of getting married to Madhu. One night, I sat in the gym with all the lights off, thinking my movie career was over. The gym business wasn't doing too well due to new competitors opening larger fitness centres within a two-mile radius.

My mobile phone rang, and I answered.

"Hello," I said.

"Hi Raj, this is Julie. How are you?" she asked.

"I'm great, and how are you? So happy to hear your voice," I shared in excitement.

"I'm good, and I heard you were involved in an accident. Are you okay?" asked Julie.

"I have recovered, and thanks for asking," I replied.

"That's good," she said.

"Can we meet?" I asked.

"I am back home for a week; let's try and meet in a couple of days," she said, and then she hung up.

I danced around the gym in excitement.

I got home, walked through the shop, and found Shelly serving customers.

"How come you're in the shop at this time?" I asked.

It was close to ten o'clock, and my father usually served customers around this time.

"They're all in there waiting for you. Just be careful," Shelly warned me.

"Story of my life. I get some good news, and it follows with some bad news."

I walked in and found my grandad, dad, grandma, aunt, and uncle sitting, waiting for me.

"Come and sit down," said Grandad.

I sat down.

"What's wrong?" I asked.

"Son, we are proud of all the achievements."

"Thank you, I guess," I said.

"If you remember, you asked for time from us so you could live your dreams?" Grandad asked.

"Time?" I asked.

"See, he has forgotten," Grandad continued before being interrupted by my aunt.

"You are getting married to Madhu. You forgot!" she exclaimed. "You have embarrassed my father in India."

"How?" I asked.

"Everyone calm down as I'm in charge here," Grandad said.

"We are going to India next week, and your ticket has been bought, and you are going with us. Your Mum and Dad don't need to be there," my aunt said. "We are going."

"You guys just want free holidays. Why don't you two get jobs instead of eating off my dad all the time?" I said to my aunt and uncle.

"That's enough; I have made my decision," Grandad said.

"Decision?" I asked.

"I am a grown man now. I run my own business. I have appeared in films, and I could have married Sabrina," I said.

"You were bad luck for her, and that is why she died," my uncle said.

"Hey, it has nothing to do with you. You go home and advise your criminal sons," I said.

"How dare you talk to me and disrespect me," he got up to hit me, and I blocked his punch. I went to hit him back and ended up punching the glass cabinet.

My dad stopped me. My hand was bleeding.

"Go and wash your hands and come back in here," instructed my grandad.

When I came back into the room, my aunt and uncle were gone, and my dad's cousin Rupinderjit and his wife Sheela were sitting there.

"What happened here?" she walked over to me, trying to hug me.

"I'm fine, Aunty," I replied.

"I have bought some uncooked chicken. I've seasoned it for you guys to cook."

Later, we questioned her actions and found out it was a form of witchcraft. We were told she tried to put a spell over the family, killing each one by one so her husband would be the next in line to receive all the assets. It did work; many family members believed that, and many were ill over the years.

"You can't live under my roof until you agree to fly to India with us, my grandad says. You can stay with us for a couple of days until things calm down," said Rupinderjit.

I agreed. I never thought this guy was a crook and a sneaky character until later in our lives. He was charged by the law for breaking laws and had long-term court charges against him from the Inland Revenue. We left, and I followed the sneaky couple to their house.

I walked into their house, and it always had this smell and a very dark feeling. Even though the house had a very wooden interior, Rupinderjit and I sat down in the living room.

"So, Raj, what have you thought about this whole situation? Just before you answer, think about it all logically."

He always was great with words and knew how to convince people. Just then, Sheela came in with a cup of warm milk for me. She sat down and waited for Rupinderjit to speak.

"Raj, you have lifted weights and recently worked in films. You have done what most dream about doing, but you must think about this logically.

You will get married to this lady from India, you will need to get a job, and more importantly, you must think about the income to pay your bills. Do you want to live a life of people thinking you lived off your rich dad all your life?" stated and asked Rupinderjit.

I nodded, "No."

"We all have a dream of singing songs and working in films, but you have to face the real world and do what is right for your family. But my career just started, and I can get more work to pay for bills," I said.

"Raj, think about it. If you don't listen to your grandad, you will be cut off from any funds. How are you going to survive if you went to India to work in films? You have to pay rent there for even a house or an apartment," he added.

"I have income coming in from my gym and courses I run from the college," I said.

"Raj, listen, if you are not here to run the course, that income won't be there. Plus, I think the gym was a bad idea with new fitness centres opening up; you will be closed within a year, if not less."

This got me a little angry as I felt he was cursing my dreams and business.

"I will get you a blanket to sleep on the sofa there, Raj," Sheela said and then left.

"Raj, listen to my advice carefully. Go back tomorrow and say you will go to India with them. Get married," said Rupinderjit.

"But Uncle," I said.

"Let me finish, Raj," he continued. "You get married and bring your wife. She will begin her career as a lawyer, and when the money is coming in, do what you please. Until then, listen to your grandad. Plus, your in-laws are very wealthy in India. Use them for their wealth in the future."

I was uncomfortable with what he just shared. Sheela walks in with a blanket and pillow.

"What do you think, Raj?" asked Rupinderjit.

"Ok," I said, as I didn't have a choice.

Just out of the blue, Sheela said, "Raj, there is a bag here with a bottle of water and a bag of almonds."

I didn't think then, but that just appeared out of the blue. I would have been better with a bandage instead of a towel wrapped around my hand. They both left the room, and I lay on the sofa, thinking of my life being ruined by my family. All the past couple of years had been going through my head. Seeing Sabrina hurt in the car, dead, played on my mind. I was having nightmares all night. The bathroom was upstairs. I went upstairs to use the bathroom. Their children slept all in one room, and the spare room, I think, was probably storage. After using the bathroom, I was urged to go into the spare room.

I opened the door; I saw four video players, two small televisions, and many video tapes. Something was being recorded. I switched on the television and found it was hardcore pornography. I switched off the TV and

233

made my way back downstairs. This explained why this uncle was taken to court. He was charged with selling porn movies which were illegal at the time.

The next day, I woke up, and we all got ready and made our way back to my house. I found my mum's brother's car outside, which made me happy. I walked in and found my two uncles sitting with respect in front of my Grandad. They both were very wealthy individuals but were always humble with everyone. I greeted them both with hugs.

"What have you done here, Raj?" the eldest uncle asked.

"Nothing," I replied. "It's okay, and it's part of life. You keep persevering in life."

My mother walked in, holding a tray of cups of tea for my uncles. She saw me, put the tray on the table, and hugged me. "Come to the kitchen and let me put a bandage on your hand."

My mother and I went into the kitchen. My mother began to clean my wound with antiseptic liquid.

"Why do you get so angry?" she asked.

"Are you asking me? It runs in the family," I replied.

"But you should listen to your dad and grandad. They will make life hell for me, too," she said.

"Don't worry, Mum; I can earn my own money. I will get us a house for me, you and Shelly to live in," I said.

"Don't be stupid," she said.

"What is wrong with that girl in Punjab?" she asked.

"Nothing, but I'm not in love with her," I replied.

"Forget that nonsense. They are not going to let you marry anyone you love. You will have to fall in love with her when she arrives," Mom said.

"But mom," I said.

My mum's elder brother walked into the kitchen.

"Hey, what's going on? I heard what happened. Listen, Raj, you have my full support with your film career. It's not every day that people get opportunities to star in movies. You have this opportunity. I don't know about you getting married to this girl in India, and if you're not happy, you shouldn't. But that didn't come from me, as your grandad will verbally abuse my sister. I can give you ten thousand pounds to go to India and try your luck in movies," he said.

"But what if it doesn't work out?" I asked.

"So what? At least you tried. We all, including your dad and grandad, have dreamed of appearing on the big screens. Which Indian hasn't? You need to try, and I have spent twenty-plus thousand pounds on my other sisters' two sons, each sponsoring them to come to this country. You are my nephew, too," he shared.

"Okay," I said.

He shook my hand, which was still hurting.

***

Back at the hospital, the nurse gives me an injection, and it hurts. Just then, my mother's eldest uncle walks in.

"Hey Raj, how are you feeling?" he says in his Southern accent. He has always been full of energy.

"Listen, you better get well quickly, as you must appear in more movies. You don't want to enter movies when you reach my age. Stay strong; you will come through this," he says.

I smile and close my eyes.

***

Grandad, Grandma, Dad, Mom, and Rupinderjit were back in the living room.

"So, what have you decided?" my grandad asked.

I looked at my mum, who was looking down. "Okay, I will get married if I am allowed to carry on with my career in movies," Grandad looked at me and looked at Rupinderjit.

"Okay, I agree," he said.

We hugged it out to make up.

"Let the preparations begin," my grandad said.

They all shook my good hand. "You made the right decision, and as soon as you get married and your wife comes here, you will be too busy to think about anything else," said Rupinderjit,.

"Yeah, and my films, I say. We will see," he replied.

"Yes, as my uncle from Southampton said, he would give me ten thousand pounds to go and work in films," I shared with this evil man.

The jealousy on the face was a moment to capture.

"We don't need his ten thousand pounds; we have our own ten thousand pounds, which we could give you," he said with a jealous look.

In my room, I lay on my bed thinking about what I had agreed to. I had to prove I could make it in films.

"Should I agree to move to India to live with Madhu, or should I have her come here? It would make life easy if I moved there to work in films," I thought to myself.

My mobile phone bleeped, and it was a text from Julie. It read, "Are we still meeting tomorrow?"

"Of course we are, and where?" I replied.

She texted, "At the new Witherspoon on the high street at 9 pm."

"Okay," I replied.

I was so excited the next day, and I didn't even train. I sat in the sauna, showered, and got ready. I arrived at Witherspoon's thirty minutes early and sat at the bar with my usual Diet lemonade and lime. I looked at the doors every time they opened and when someone entered the bar. She finally walked in, and my heart began to beat very fast.

I got nervous, and I could see her cheeks were red too. She put this large art folder down first.

"Hi Raj," she kissed my cheeks and hugged me.

I hugged her tight and longer than usual, and she hugged me tight. We looked into each other's eyes and smiled.

"How have you been, you big movie star?" she asked.

"A big movie star?" I asked and laughed.

"What would you like to drink and eat?" I asked.

"Eat?" she asked.

"Come on, we haven't ever done this," I said.

"Well, if this is your type of date, I'm not happy."

"Not a date, but just a quick bite to eat. I will take you on a great date to one of the best restaurants in Wolverhampton, Birmingham, or wherever you want to go," I said.

"Calm down; you are getting nervous, Raj," she said.

"Here is as good as anywhere as long as I am with my best friend," and she hugged me again.

I got Julie her glass of wine and I, this time, ordered a half a pint of Guinness to help me with my nerves. We sat at the table and ordered our food.

"So, Julie, tell me what you have been up to?" I asked.

"I should? My life has been boring compared to what I have been reading about you," she said.

"No, you will never be boring to me. Please share."

"Well, I worked in Manchester in a Bank," she shared.

"Wow, that's great," I said.

"You look in great shape," I said.

"I do work out, too, so I can keep up with my best friend," she shared.

I laughed and said, "Well, you look fabulous."

"You always give me compliments," she said.

"What else do you do in your spare time?" I asked.

"You draw? Yes, here, look." She picked up her folder and took out artwork of my drawings.

"Did you draw me?" I asked. "Yes, who else?" she asked.

"Look, I have all the newspaper cuttings. My mum cut them out for me and posted them to me. Look, I watched your movie and took pictures of you in the movie."

"You did all this." I looked at her and fell more in love with her.

"You could have gotten fined," I said.

"I was willing to take a risk," she said.

"Julie, I love you." There was a pause.

She smiled and said, "Raj, I love you and always have."

"Really?" I asked.

"Yes, and calm down with the excitement. You don't want your wicked aunties to hear." We both laughed.

"How long are you here for?" I asked.

"I am here for only another two days but will return soon. I am trying to get a transfer to here in Wolverhampton," she said.

"That's great. Raj, I am so happy that you have achieved all your dreams and goals. You wanted to be the British Champion, and you achieved that; you wanted to work in movies and have achieved this, too. You are like your role models."

My eyes filled up with happiness that she remembered. So did hers. "Why are you making me cry?" she asked.

"This is a celebration. I am so proud of you," she said.

"I am proud of you that you moved away, got into a professional job, and you have an amazing talent, and you are using it. Even though it's doing artwork of me only."

"Not only draw you," she shared and laughed. "I sketch people, pets, and family portraits. A side business."

"Wow, you're a businesswoman too. This is amazing."

"I don't know about that," she said.

"You are a businesswoman. You provide a service doing your artwork and get paid for it. I am so proud of you," I said.

"Bet your aunties didn't think I would achieve this," she said.

"Who cares what they think? Both their kids are off the rails in or out of prison. It is a slap in their faces."

"What is next for you, Hollywood?" she asked.

"I wish, and I am still trying to break into Bollywood," I said.

"You have already; you just need to get more movies," she said.

"It's not as simple. My grandad doesn't want me to go," I shared.

"Really?" she asked. "I thought he would be very proud of you."

"He is and isn't," I replied. I didn't want to share about the wedding thing and ruin this great moment.

"Let's get out of here and go for a walk by our usual place."

We left the Witherspoon bar, and I drove us to Bilston Library. As it was late at night, the library was closed, and so were the side gates. We got onto the side wall, walked across, and jumped over. She walked over to the field and looked up at the sky.

"I have always gotten peace here," she said.

I watched and enjoyed the moment. The moon was shining so bright that we didn't need any street lighting in the park.

"Remember all our childhood moments here?" I asked.

Julie turned around and kissed me on the lips. We kissed passionately, then sat on the bench and kissed, then lay on the grass and kissed.

I looked into her eyes and said, "I love you, Julie, and I want you to be my wife."

She laughed and said, "Wife? And yes."

"Yes?" I asked.

"Yes, I will marry you."

"I haven't got a ring," I said.

"Don't worry about it," she said.

I took off a religious ring I was wearing and put it on her finger. We continued kissing passionately.

237

Raj and Julie

"We ended up in the local hotel on Green Lanes and walked into our hotel room feeling embarrassed. The room was a bit cold and had that stale, dusty smell. As soon as the door closed, I pulled her close to me and ran my fingers through her hair. We looked into each other's eyes, and I kissed her on the lips, and it was everything I'd hoped it would be. It was slow to start with, and it became more passionate. Julie tried to undress me, and I tried to undress her. We began to laugh in between. Julie lay on the bed naked in the Centre of the bed. I lay over her and looked into her beautiful blue eyes. I kissed her neck, which she enjoyed, and bit her slightly on her shoulder. She stopped me, and I looked back into her eyes, and she said, "I love you, Raj". I love you too, Julie, I replied. Oh, damn, I say. What's wrong? Asked Julie I haven't got any condoms. Julie looked at me and said It doesn't matter. We began to kiss, and as I entered her beautiful body, she gave the impression that it hurt. Do you want me to stop? I ask. No, please carry on. She replied. We began to make love, stopped, and made love again all night. Our bodies were hot and sweaty and breathless. Julie said touch my heart and feel my heartbeat for you. I touched her chest and could feel her heart beating strongly. This is a dream come true, Raj. I know, and mine, I reply. My heart beats for you, Raj. We continued to kiss and make love. At times we stopped and laughed about seeing each other naked. I looked into the blue eyes that I'd fallen in love with at the age of ten. And as I stared at her, I thought about all those moments I had dreamt of this happening. Her beautiful blonde hair, sparkling blue eyes, and her soft lips. The first time she kissed my cheek, the first time she had made my heart beat fast, and when I fell in love with her all those moments came back to me. This was a dream come true.

"What are you thinking?" She asked.

"I was thinking about the first time you kissed my cheek, and I fell in love with you while we were in junior school," I replied.

"I loved you too, Raj, from school times until now," she said, and this made me smile.

"You have the best smile, Raj," she said.

We kissed passionately, and made love until we became exhausted and fell asleep still smiling. I had the song 'Never gonna change my love for you playing in my head. Then, it was swapped by 'The power of love.' I woke up in the morning smiling and found Julie was not in bed. I got out of bed and looked in the bathroom, and she wasn't there. I shouted, "Julie."

I sat on the bed, thinking, "She's gone, breaking my heart." That tune started playing in my mind. Every time these clouds change direction, you break my heart. Tears fell down my face. My phone bleeped on the table. I looked at it, and I saw a note there. I walked over to the table and opened the note, and it read, "Raj, I love you a lot, but you hurt me by not telling me you are getting married next week. Your grandad's text came early this morning, and it wasn't the first time he texted through the night. He asked where are you? You are getting married next week. Hope you haven't let us down again. I don't want to come between you and your family. Hope you

238

will be happy being married to your wife. Don't bother contacting me ever again. Julie."

I screamed, "Why?"

I drove back home crying and hating my life at this present time. I pulled up outside the shop and house. I didn't bother going through the shop but knocked on the house door. Grandad opened it.

"Where have you been?" he asked while I walked in.

"We have been worried all night. We thought you ran off," he said.

"I went to see a friend, and I shared about my wedding, and he got me drunk," I replied.

"You could have at least called us and told us," he said.

"I was drunk," I said. One by one, family members came in, hugging me and telling me how worried they were. Rupinderjit gave me that evil look and said, "You know how to worry us."

Chapter Forty-One

The next six days had been the hardest of my life. Firstly, I had been thinking about Julie and her leaving me. She thought I had lied to her, but I had been willing to leave everyone for her. I had been willing to start a new life with her. I had just wanted to tell her all this. I went to the park behind Bilston Library every day, hoping to meet her there. I walked past her house and knocked on the door a couple of times, and there was no answer. I came home and typed her letter.

"Hi Julie, I am so sorry that I didn't tell you about my parents forcing me to get married to a lady in India. After meeting you, I knew it was you I wanted to be with for the rest of our lives. I had decided in my head that I was going to leave my family and everything to have a fresh start with you. When you said you would marry me, I was ready to make all the changes. I want you to know that I am still willing to do this, and I love you. Please contact me as soon as possible. I only have until Friday as I am flying to India on Saturday."

I tried for the last time and posted the letter after trying the doorbell.

The time had come. Even on Saturday morning, I had been hoping that Julie would turn up and I could leave my family. I got in the car, and we drove to the airport. We boarded, and even then, I had been hoping, like in movies, that Julie would turn up at the airport and stop me from going.

I boarded the plane, and my grandad bought me and himself business class seats. He thought this would make me happy, but it didn't. I stared at the TV screen most of the way, watching Hollywood movies like "Sleepless in Seattle," "Forever Young," and even mine and Julie's favourite, "Back to the Future."

I couldn't sleep through the whole flight. We landed in New Delhi, and the drivers collected us in new jeeps. That long drive to our city. It was déjà vu as nothing had changed. Just people had got older. The honking, a whole family on the motorcycle, traffic, congestions, and drivers driving like maniacs. We pulled over and had something to eat from the street restaurant. I just had the Indian tea, which still came in a small glass. A song was playing in my head from Bryan Adams's list, "When You Love Someone," to "How Am I Supposed to Live without You" by Michael Bolton.

We arrived at my grandad's house in the city, which was decorated with lights covering almost the whole house. I entered the house, and everything else was the same as last time, with just a lot of decorations, music playing very loud, and more smiling faces of people I didn't even know.

I went into my room and lay down. With the same songs playing in my head, a record scratched by Grandad comes into my room, "Raj, can you get freshened up? We're all going to a function," he said.

"But Grandad, I'm tired from all the travelling," I said.

"Don't worry; we'll be okay. Just get ready."

I got ready, and my grandma, my dad, and aunty travelled to a banqueting suite. Followed by a minibus full of relatives behind us. We got to this banqueting suite and found it all lit up with lights.

There was an Indian band playing tunes outside. We walked out onto a red carpet with dhol players playing the dhol. We made our way to the entrance of the suite and entered the lobby area, and we found all of Madhu's family waiting to greet us.

"Oh gosh," Madhu's mother came running to me and hugged me.

"What's going on, Grandad? I thought I was getting married next week," I asked.

"This is a welcome celebration just with close cousins and relatives," he replied.

We walked in, and I saw Madhu all dolled up and sitting on the stage.

I was guided to the stage. Madhu got up and hugged me. She whispered, "Thank you."

I didn't know what she meant. I was seated next to her. I looked around, and everyone in the room was smiling and freaking me out as they all looked like The Joker from the movie Batman. They were all dancing and hugging and enjoying the event.

"So, Raj, you finally came?" said Madhu.

"Well, I had no choice," I replied.

"So, you didn't want to come?" She asked.

I looked at her, telling her no.

"Can we speak privately?" I asked.

"Here now?" She asked.

"Yes, I just want to ask you something," I said.

"Ask me here."

"It's too loud, and everyone is looking like the character Joker from the movie Batman to me," I said.

"What is the Joker?" She asked.

I looked around and saw a room empty. I grabbed Madhu's hand and dragged her with me. I dragged her through the dance floor, pretending to dance. We got to this room, with Madhu out of breath.

"You know no one has ever done this?" She said.

"Done what?" I asked.

"Dragging the bride-to-be like the way you did," she replied.

"Does it matter?" I asked. "Plus, I don't care," I said.

"Madhu, if we go through with the wedding, I need to make a deal with you," I said.

"What's that?" She asked.

"I want to live here in Punjab, India," I said.

"Live here? But I want to live in England," she contested.

"Listen, Madhu, you know I have got into films, and if we get married, live here, and I can travel to Mumbai to work in movies from time to time," I said.

"How about my law career?" She asked.

"You can do that here," I said.

"But I want you and I to open a practice in England. Raj, I am not embarrassing my parents any longer. You are marrying me, and I am coming to England, and that's final," she said.

"Plus, your film career is over," she said, pointing at me.

Someone opened the door; I quickly grabbed Madhu and kissed her on the lips.

Her mother walked in and looked shocked.

"She wanted to see if I was any good at kissing and better than some guy named Jagga," I explained.

"He's lying," she screamed.

I walked out laughing and tutting.

Throughout the whole party, she hated me and gave me the evil eye. She pretended to enjoy herself. I pretended to enjoy myself, and this must be my best-acting performance. I went around hugging Madhu's relatives and showing how much I enjoyed being with Madhu. I could feel heat off Madhu at times, and I knew she wanted to hit me.

The party ended, and just before leaving Madhu and her family, Madhu's mother came up to me, hugged me, and whispered in my ear, "Don't worry, I won't tell anyone what happened, and please keep up the kissing after the wedding," and laughed. Madhu came and hugged me and whispered in my ear. "I will destroy you in England."

I looked at her and said, "Bring it on."

The next day, I was too tired to get up. Maybe jet-lagged, but I knew I had a busy four days ahead.

Day one, I woke up thinking I just had to go with the flow and somehow convince Madhu to stay in India. I looked at my phone, and there were no missed calls or texts.

I kept my UK line on just in case Julie would call or text. The moment she would tell me she wanted to be with me, I would get on the first plane back home.

I walked out of my room to the bathroom and brushed my teeth.

Later that morning, feeling depressed, I saw a car pulling up. I looked closer, and it was my mom. I immediately ran to greet her. I opened the door.

"Mom, you came," I exclaimed.

"Of course, I would. How could I miss my son's wedding?" she replied.

"I am so happy, Mom," I said and hugged her as soon she got out of the car. I also saw my uncle Ramdass and Aunty Manjit.

I just looked at them, and my face expressed, "Why are they here?"

I walked into our house with my mother. A lot of people visited the home, and food was made for all of them. It was a tiring and busy day.

Day two, and there was still no message from Julie. I texted her a few times and got no reply.

I tried to keep away from my uncle and aunt. Today was a traditional event with the cleansing and purifying event. I sat down in the middle rooftop area. All were women there. At least a hundred women were dressed up in different coloured clothing. Some in pink, some in yellow, some in green, some in orange, some in brown, some in blue, some in red, and some in purple. It was like seeing the rainbow colours around me. I sat in the centre on a plank of wood. Oil is poured over my head. Then, turmeric paste was applied to my face, and I am sure my mother applied the paste to my face first. I was wearing a pair of shorts and a vest and couldn't shower until the wedding day.

One after the other, almost all the hundred women covered me with this paste from face to toe. My whole body was covered with this stuff. The smell wasn't great. The women sang many traditional songs. Red strings were tied around my left wrist. So many knots and each knot had a verse sung to it. Then I saw my mother mixing the flour on the floor with some other paste and putting her handprints on the wall. It was all new to me. I probably grew up seeing this at other weddings but never questioned it.

The next couple of days were just music, many guests eating, and the men getting drunk. A karahi ceremony took place by making savoury and Indian sweets.

On the fourth day, more of the turmeric paste was applied to me. It was weird as I was only allowed to brush my teeth and not shower.

On the fifth day, henna was applied to my feet and hands, with all the ladies having different patterns painted on their hands. There had been a party every day of the week.

The day of the wedding came. I woke up, and an uncle had to shower me. Luckily, I could keep my boxers on. He was a cousin brother of my mother's, and I think I met him the last time I visited.

After pouring a bucket of water on me, he left and said, "You can wash yourself."

I said, "I'll take it from here."

So, he left. It was the best shower I had. I must have been in there for at least forty-five minutes, with many complaining that I was taking too long.

I came out with a towel wrapped around me, and the women screamed.

"Cover yourself, you naughty boy," they said.

I replied, "It's my last time to be naughty, and who's up for it?"

I laughed, and they looked at me in shock. My mother told them that I make jokes all the time.

I got ready in the traditional Sikh Punjabi groom's outfit. I looked in the mirror and found that the turmeric paste worked. I was glowing, and my skin looked super clear. My grandad walked into the room with my father.

"Can I tie the turban on you, son?" My grandson asked.

"Of course," I replied.

He tied a red turban on me and placed traditional pearls on it. My father put a gold necklace around me with four layers and a red scarf for me to carry. Then my grandad gave me a golden-coloured sword to carry. I put on the Indian shoes. If I had to describe them, they looked like Aladdin shoes called khussa. I looked in the mirror, and I was dressed very traditionally.

I walked out and found a queue of people ready to put these flower garlands over my head. I was sitting on a chair in the middle of the room with this young guy sitting next to me. If I had a younger brother, he would have been sitting there, and this guy was a cousin. I was told he was the best man. They were putting Indian sweets in my mouth and giving me money— Indian notes.

As soon as my mother, father, grandad, and grandma had done this, I told them, "No more sweets. It will upset my stomach."

So, they all just put these flower or money garlands around me. I couldn't breathe at one point. So I took them all off and kept one on. I must have made five hundred pounds, probably.

"What do I do with this money?" I asked my grandad.

He said, "That's your wedding gift from all these relatives and friends."

"I don't want this," I said.

I took the money and gave it to the guy sitting next to me. He couldn't stop smiling. All the people began to speak about me, saying I was so spoilt.

I replied, "Hot-headed and dangerous at the same time. Come on, and let's get this over and done with."

We walked out, and I got this young kid to get me my suit and shoes from the room to get changed into later for the reception – a suit my grandad picked out for me.

"I hope it fits me," I thought.

We all walked out, sat into these jeeps, and drove off towards the banqueting suite. We were supposed to go to the bride's house, but they decided to skip this part and do the ceremony at the banqueting suite.

On the way to the banqueting suite, I kept on thinking and asking myself while looking out of the window, "Do you want to live here full time?"

We all stopped about a quarter mile from the place. My father said, "Come out."

I got out, and there was a white horse all decorated for me to get on and travel on.

I got on the horse with a man guiding it.

Then a wedding band appears in the front and starts playing wedding songs, which I have only seen in movies.

My relatives and family members danced and walked in the front with my dad throwing coins on the floor.

The street was busy with honking traffic, and we had our band playing music while we all travelled to the banqueting suite.

We arrived outside this beautifully constructed and decorated banqueting suite.

We reached the entrance, and this place looked amazing. It was like a traditional temple with a bronze feel and look to the brickwork. All decorated and with flowers. It was something like what a famous Hollywood film director used for movies. It was open-spaced and had amazing brickwork leading up to each floor, which went off on the ground floor in four directions. It was nicely lit up, and a gold colour effect shone in some areas.

Raj and Julie

The seating was set for royalties from traditional times, which included beautiful cushions for armrests, gold-coloured posts holding parts of the building up, beautiful chandeliers, and a lot of open space. Beautiful curtains were hanging from the walls.

I got off the horse, and my family and I walked through the entrance, and the place only got better as we walked in. We were guided into one area of the suite. Madhu's family was all there and greeted by each family member. The men went to one side and the women to another side of the banqueting suite. We all could see each other. The introduction began with flower garlands on each other. Each side gave each other gold rings or necklaces. I had been given a gold Sikh bangle, a ring, and a necklace. We all moved over to the wedding ceremony part. I was hoping I would be getting married in a Sikh temple, but they had an area to keep the Sikh holy bible Guru Granth Sahib Ji in another room, which was kept very clean. All shoes were taken off and left in a waiting room. Everyone was expected to wash their hands. One by one, we all entered the room where the holy book was kept. The worship songs began. I was seated in front of the Guru Granth Sahib Ji; I bowed down to pay my respects. I looked back, and Madhu was being walked in by her father, her mother, and another lady I had never seen before. I have to say she looked very pretty. She bowed down, paid her respect, and sat next to me. The wedding ceremony began. We got up four times and walked around the holy bible clockwise, with me holding this dark pink material that Madhu was holding on to behind me. She pulled this material a couple of times to slow me down as I was walking faster than I should. We sat down after the fourth time, and everyone congratulated each other. Then again, the garlands started piling on, with guests giving each other money. Madhu and I were asked to get up and bow down to the holy book. We did and we walked out, and I gave all my money to Madhu. She asked, "Why are you giving me this money?"

I replied, "It's rupees; I can't spend that in England."

"Don't worry; I will be spending your money in England when I get there," she said.

I ignored her at this point.

We walked over to the changing rooms, where I got dressed, shaved, and got into my suit. That young kid who was sitting next to me playing my best man followed me everywhere and kept on smiling. I got ready and met Madhu, her sister-in-law, and her mother outside.

"You look very handsome," Madhu's mother said.

I was hoping to get that compliment off Madhu, I replied.

"Well, no one complimented me," said Madhu.

It started before we even moved in together. I didn't want to ruin anyone's day.

"You look beautiful," I said.

"Thank you, and you look very handsome too," she replied.

We walked through the carpeted walkway to the dance floor. A dhol (drum) player was playing, and the guests all clapped as we walked to the dance floor. We reached the dance floor, and the DJ instructed the guests and family members. We danced to our first Bollywood song, which I had not chosen and never heard before. The song complemented the bride throughout the song. I tried to lip-sync to the song but was told off by Madhu.

"Close your mouth," she would keep saying.

I was going with the flow for my grandparents. After the first song, we cut the wedding cake and then sat on the side with guests giving us more money and taking pictures. At one point, I got up and ran onto the dance floor and danced with guests I didn't even know. After a couple of songs, Madhu's uncle pulled me off to do a traditional eating session. I told him not to pull me. I had to share the same food they ate and drank from the same glass.

"How disgusting," I thought.

I looked at my grandad a couple of times, and he just gave me the look just to do it. Then, I was pulled to another traditional game, where I sat down next to Madhu. We had to play a game to find a couple of rings in this small bucket of milk and fight over who wins and finds them. I let her win; I felt there was someone behind me stroking my hair or even cutting it each time. The women made statements that Madhu would wear the trousers in the marriage and control me. Then one of her aunties is combing my hair, which I didn't get. I felt she was bagging pieces of my hair into a bag. Then they gave me a metal cup of milk to drink, and Madhu had to stop me. This went on and on for a bit, and at one point, I was too tired to care. I didn't feel good at this point. The room felt like it was spinning from time to time. I was looking around, and I saw Julie, all dressed in an Indian wedding outfit, walking up towards me and would vanish. I missed Julie at this point and hoped she would have rung me, and this could have been us.

Then, it was all over, and we drove to Madhu's parents' house in our wedding car. We were greeted and sat in their living room, where traditional activities were carried out. Then, all her female relatives, family members, and friends began to cry. We got home, and my mother had to carry out the family traditions before we entered the house. In the doorway, Madhu had to stop my mother from drinking a glass of milk.

Then Madhu stepped forward and entered the house with her right foot, pushing on a metal jar of rice. We all sat down in the living room and carried out a traditional ancestor prayer.

Madhu and I were in our bedroom, and she said, "I'm too tired to do anything; I'm going to sleep."

I thought great and replied, "I'm tired too."

The next day, we woke up very late, and Madhu woke up just before me, got dressed and went and sat in the living room with my mother, grandma, and other relatives. We spent the rest of the day eating food when guests arrived. A day before I had to leave for the UK, Madhu's parents came to collect her. That evening, we all had dinner, and in our bedroom, Madhu said, "You make sure you get me over to England. Then only you can sleep with me."

246

Raj and Julie

I thought and replied, "I wouldn't call you then. It is in the immigration department's hands now. You make sure you do your part right with your interview, etc."

"Don't worry; I'll handle all that. I'm educated enough to deal with the interviews," she said.

"All the best," I said sarcastically.

She left with her parents, and I was happy to wave goodbye to her and her mum. I remember waving to the back of her car. The next day, I was driven to the airport to make my way back to England. My grandparents and parents were going to stay another two weeks. Flying back on a flight, the only thing I could think about was, "I'm married now. What would happen between me and Julie?"

I looked around the place and saw many Indians and a couple of Caucasians. This Caucasian couple was dressed like hippies. They were talking to another couple about their trip and how they visited Karnataka, Kasol, Goa, and Varanasi to meditate. I looked on my other side and found others watching the TV screens and watching movies. They were laughing and looking serious. I put on a movie to watch to get my mind off things. I began to watch an eighties Indian movie that had been filmed in New York. Two couples hate being married and want out. They first began to have affairs and then ended up being divorced. I thought this film could be a sign and maybe eventually I could divorce Madhu, as her mission is only to live in England. I arrived back home and found that the evil Uncle Rupinderjit and his evil wife had put together a house party for me. I walked in, and they all shouted surprise! I found my dad's sister, Baljit, her children, and her son Narinder's girlfriend, Debbie, which was so ironic that Baljit's son was allowed to date English Caucasian women and Manjit's children. I couldn't see Shelly. Rupinderjit said, "Welcome back and congratulations."

I always thought Ramdass, Manjit's husband, was the sneaky one, but this guy, Rupinderjit, was on another level. He was very good with words and cover-ups. After we stopped talking to him and his wife over the years, we got to find out about all the criminal activities he committed and got away with. He lives in a multimillion-pound house and owns a large portfolio of properties. But he always showed he was struggling financially all the time. They all came up to me one by one, hugged me, and congratulated me. Rupinderjit's wife, Sheela, came running to hug me and said, "Congratulations, Raj. I have made you home-sweet rice pudding. We wish we had red flags come up about her sooner."

Shelly came and hugged me. "Congratulations, Raj, and I hope you're happy," she asked before I answered. "You will have to get married to someone from India, too," said Baljit.

"I don't think so," replied Shelly.

"You talk too much, said Baljit."

"Tell her off, Rupinderjit" said Manjit.

Rupinderjit said, "That's enough." To Shelly

"Listen, she can marry who she wants," I said.

247

"Look at what your son's done," looking at Debbie.

"Don't know why I bother coming to congratulate you," she said and stormed off into the dining room.

"There's no need to act like that, Raj," Said Rupinderjit. "You have just got married and have a lot to achieve yet. Your dad has built you a house to move into as soon as Madhu arrives. He shouldn't spoil you; I told your dad," Rupinderjit continued to say, "You need to get a job and pay your own way."

This guy had a way with words that challenged me to prove him wrong, and I said nothing at that moment. Unfortunately, I listened to Rupinderjit most of the time as I saw him as my father's younger brother. Later, we found out that Rupinderjit was only after properties in the will from my grandad, his uncle, which he did manage to get. I left everyone enjoying the party, food, and music downstairs and went to my room. I lay on my bed, looking at my posters and just dreaming and thinking about Julie.

Chapter Forty-Two

I didn't wake up until the next day. When I did, I walked into the shop and found Julie's mom, Mrs. White, talking to Shelly. "Hi, Raj, and congratulations," said Julie's mother. There was a little hurt in her voice I could hear.

"Thank you," I replied.

"Not the best part of my life," I said.

"You have a lot to face moving forward as a married man now," she said.

"How is Julie?" I asked.

"She is okay and back in Manchester," she replied.

"I thought she wanted to move back," I asked.

"She did, but things changed, didn't they, Raj?" she asked back.

"I tried to explain, and I would have moved out for Julie," I said.

"No, No, Raj, that wouldn't have happened," she said.

"I would have and still can, as I plan to divorce my wife as soon as she arrives here in the UK," I said.

"You can't do that to that poor girl coming over," she said.

"You haven't met her, and she is not a poor girl," I said.

"Listen, Raj, please try and forget about Julie," she said.

"I love her," I said.

"So did she, and now she is heartbroken, Raj," she said and left.

"Are you okay, Raj?" asked Shelly.

I looked at her and smiled. "I'll be okay, and thanks," I replied.

"Raj, you have left the gym in the hands of your customers, and Martin is running the whole thing. He has scared most of the morning gym members away," Shelly shared with me.

I drove to the gym. I turned up at the gym and found Martin there. Sometimes, you can give people too much control. Martin was a mixed-race African British person, very muscular, with dreadlocks, and he wore a lot of jewellery.

"Hi, must have worn fifteen gold chains around his neck, three hand bracelets on each wrist, and every finger covered with gold rings. He must have worn at least thirty thousand pounds of jewellery. He would come to the gym with three of his girlfriends."

"Martin, let's sit and speak," I said.

We sat in my reception area.

"Martin, what's going on?" I asked.

"It's all good, bro," he replied.

"Why have sales dropped? You were only supposed to open up for me until the afternoon when the staff came in. Heard you have driven customers away?" I asked.

"No, brother, I just tell people to put the weights away," he replied.

"It seems like we've lost sales and clients in the morning," I said.

"Not my fault, bro, you know me better than that," he said.

"OK, carry on training."

I looked through the books for the past three months; it has been quiet. I rang around to find out what was going on in the area. I called a guy within the council to find out if any other gyms had opened up in the area.

"Hi, Singh. Have any other gyms recently opened within the area? My sales are down," I asked.

"Where have you been? Two chain owners opened in the past two months. Two American Chains, Health Country, which can cater to nine thousand people, and the other side of the town, City Fitness Thirst, which can hold up to four thousand members. Sorry, Raj. They both may be state-of-the-art centres, and you won't be able to compete," he shared.

"Oh shit, what am I going to do? I was planning to build a larger fitness centre by buying an American franchise," I said.

"That would have been good if you had put the application in twelve months ago. It would have been okay, but the council will not allow another permission fitness centre too soon. Even the council is updating its three fitness centres," he shared.

"Also, Raj, I've been to see the Health Country Fitness centre only a mile up the road from you. They are charging one hundred pounds a year for the next five years. Five hundred pounds over five years is the best deal anyone has ever heard of," he continued to share.

"OK, thanks for the information."

I sat planning new strategies. I called my father in India.

"Hi, Dad," I said.

"How are you?" he asked.

"I am good, and how are you and mum?" I asked.

"All good, thanks," he replied.

"Dad, I need a favour. I will email you designs of marketing material and vouchers, etc. Could you get these printed in India and bring them with you next week?" I asked.

"Of course, son," he replied.

"Okay, take care of yourself," I said.

We hung up. I emailed over all the designs I needed to my dad in India.

My parents were back a week later, and my grandparents decided to stay an extra two weeks. My father gave me all the marketing material. Five thousand leaflets, a one-day free pass to use the gym vouchers. I spent the next two weeks posting these to every household within my area. Ironically, a local politician spoke to me when I was posting my leaflets and vouchers. He said I should help him with his campaigning.

We spoke for a while, and he even suggested that I consider joining politics and standing as a candidate in the next elections.

"It's not part of my plan," I said. "Yet, maybe when I'm in my fifties."

"We need young minds," he said.

He gave me his card and said, "Call me if you change your mind."

We got a few inquiries, and a couple of people joined. But this wasn't working. Sales weren't covering the bills. I could have asked my father to help me, but I remembered Rupinderjit's comments, so I decided to take a door-to-door sales job to pay the bills.

We had financial difficulty keeping the gym operating for the next six months. Everything I was earning went back into the gym. I remember my first day knocking on doors for a utility company. The utility market had just been deregulated, so companies were selling utility prices at competitive rates. The commission was great.

I remember the first day. I had to travel to Birmingham via bus as the company said I would be joining a team of five, and transport would be provided. I registered with the company and completed all the documents. My team leader walked into the room to greet me. I couldn't believe it at first; I thought it was Sabrina Kumari. She was the spitting image of Sabrina Kumari. Everything was the same: blue eyes, very fair-skinned, maybe slightly taller, and the voice was almost the same. Her smile was the same.

"Hi, I'm Saira," she said, shaking my hand.

"You'll be joining my team," she said.

"Hi, I'm Raj," I said.

"Come and follow me," she said.

I got up and followed her. We walked out and got into the lift as we were on the fourth floor.

"Have you done sales before?" She asked.

"I have by selling memberships at my gym."

"Oh wow, you own a gym?" She asked.

"I do, but unfortunately, it's not doing as well; hence, I have to work to keep it going," I said.

"Oh, ok," she said.

"Has anybody told you that you look like Sabrina Kumari?" I asked.

"Yes, many times," she replied.

"You should work in movies," I said.

She laughed and said, "My brothers will kill me."

We walk outside to a Suzuki, a people's carrier. When I looked inside the car, three other women were already sitting in the vehicle.

"This is Raj," said Saira.

"I'm Shabbo, I'm Konkona, and I'm Neeru," They said one by one.

I was the only male on the team. Shabbo and Saira were from a British Pakistani ethnic background, Konkona was from a British–Bangladeshi background and Neeru was from a British Punjabi family.

We drove out to our patch, and we began knocking on doors. I first watched Saira, then picked up the spiel and knocked on the doors myself. I managed to sign five deals on my first day, and the record was eight.

This journey of working and knocking on doors went on for months, but over time, I realised Saira had fallen in love with me. We knocked on doors, and when we all managed to sign six to eight deals, we went to the local park and played basketball.

251

One of the days, we went to play basketball, and the girls wanted to test my strength and asked me if I could push them down on a seesaw with them all sitting on one end and me pushing down on the other end. While I was pushing the seesaw down a few times, Shabbo fell off and whacked her head on the metal bar, causing her forehead to swell. At first, they all couldn't stop laughing, including Shabbo.

"Oh my gosh, your forehead is swollen," said Konkona.

"I think you should go to the Accident and Emergency," I suggested.

After so much convincing, we drove to the local hospital.

We all sat in the Coventry Accident and Emergency department while Shabbo was being checked. We cracked jokes and made a lot of noise. The security guard came and asked us to leave the A and E.

We came outside, and Konkona went for a cigarette.

"Saira likes you, Raj," said Neeru.

"No, Neeru likes you," said Saira.

I was a bit embarrassed. Konkona came skipping to us and said, "They both like you," and asked, "Which one would you date?"

"I don't know," I said.

I looked at Saira, giving her a hint because she looked like Sabrina Kumari. Shabbo came out of the hospital and said, "I'm fine. Let's go home."

Time passed, and a couple of months later, I got a call from a London friend telling me that Rajiv Singh was in the city and had asked us to meet.

On the weekend, I went to see Rajiv. We were at an Indian restaurant in central London. It was great catching up. When Rajiv was on his own, I showed him Saira's picture.

"Is that Sabrina?" Asked Rajiv.

"No, it's a lady I know named Saira." I shared.

"Get her into films," said Rajiv. "I'm doing a film with Sabrina's Sister, Sareena, and we need a second female lead. I can introduce her," he continued.

"I will ask her," I said.

Back at work, I shared with the girls at work that I was friends with Rajiv, the actor, and I appeared in a movie. They didn't believe me until I showed them my photographs. They couldn't believe the fact I was working with them knocking on doors, and why I wasn't in Bollywood.

I was on my own with Saira.

"Saira, I got some good news for you," I said.

"I love it when you say my name," she said.

"What's the good news?" she asked.

"I met Rajiv on the weekend, and I showed him your picture, and he said you should join films, and he is willing to give you an opportunity in his next film," I shared with her.

"I told you last time that my brothers will kill me. You don't know much about Pakistani families, do you?" She asked.

"I don't," I said.

Raj and Julie

"I like you, Raj and would like to date you," she said.
"My life is complicated," I said.
"I have saved eighty thousand pounds from this sales role within one year." she shared. Just then, Konkona came.
"Have you told him?"
"She has, and my life is complicated so that nothing can happen," I said.

We were back at Konkona's flat. They played music, and we all danced. Then Saira danced closer to me, and Shabbo stopped her.
"What are you doing? You fool, your brother will kill you," she said to Saira.
"He's a Sikh, and you're Muslim. Nothing can come of this," she said.
Saira cried.
"Listen, guys, just to help the situation, I'm going to get out of your lives, and I quit my job today. " I left the flat and caught a bus home.
I never saw that team again in my life. The business began to struggle with a lack of funds coming in, and so I had no choice but to close the business. I called all the clients and asked them to come to the gym on the final day. Having loyalty to me, they all turned up at different times of the day. They all understood and thanked me for all that I did for them. It was heart-aching as I had coached five of the best powerlifters in the country who were under twenty. I put a course together for the local college to educate others about sports and a program with the local police to help local vandals get away from crime and into sports. It was one of the worst days of my life.
I was sitting in the living room, thinking about how it all went wrong— no more gym, no more films, married to someone I don't love, and Julie in my life. Grandad, Dad, and Rupinderjit walked in.
"What's wrong, son?" asked Grandad.
"Nothing," I said.
"Listen, son, in life, you have ups and downs. It's part of life. You win a few and lose a few," said my grandad.
"A lot of money has been wasted. Now, find a job and get ready to run a home. You need to be paying bills," said Rupinderjit.
"You have wasted a lot of money," my dad said.
"It's ok. If you opened your letters from the immigration office, you would have known that Madhu did well on the interview months ago. It has been almost seven months, and she will be here next week. You just get the house decorated for next week," said my grandad.

253

Chapter Forty-Three

Another worst day of my life had arrived. Madhu had arrived in England. My grandad had hired a limousine to collect Madhu from the airport. My mother, grandma, Aunty Manjit, and grandad had travelled to collect Madhu from the airport. Luckily, the flight had landed in Birmingham, not London. My mother had ordered a boutique of flowers for Madhu.

We got to the airport, and the driver parked the car in the car park. We had walked into the arrivals area. Many passengers had come through arrivals. All were welcomed by their family members or friends. Some were happy, some sad. We had stood waiting until she came out. She had looked bothered and frustrated. She had walked over to my grandma and hugged her, then my mother, Aunty, my grandad, and then me.

"Did you enjoy your flight?" asked my grandad.

"Yes, Grandad, it was very good," replied Madhu.

"Well, it had to be, as I booked you, business class," said Grandad.

"Yes, Grandad, it was great, and thank you," said Madhu.

"Business class?" I asked, "Why?"

"Why not?" asked Madhu.

Before I answered, my grandma said, "It doesn't matter, and let's get you home."

We had walked to the car, and she had been impressed. She had soaked in the buildings, the British air, and the less pollution. She had looked at the limousine.

"You did this for me?" asked Madhu.

Before I answered," Grandad said, "of course he did."

Madhu hugged my arms and smiled at me. We all had gotten into the car, and she had been very impressed. Grandad had popped open a champagne bottle, and we all had a glass of champagne each.

"Congratulations and cheers to my grandchildren," said my grandad.

"Cheers, Grandad," said Madhu.

"And you say cheers also," said Aunty.

"I said cheers to Madhu."

We had pulled up outside the house and shop. My mother had gotten outside first to get the oil ready. Madhu and I had stood outside the house. A dhol player was playing the drum my dad had hired to play on our arrival.

"I thought you all would have lived in a mansion," stated Madhu.

I looked at her and said, "This is our mansion."

My mother and Aunty Sheela had been standing in the doorway. My other aunties had begun singing along with many other Indian ladies from the area, friends of my parents. These were the same families who had been there since my parents' wedding.

My mother had poured the oil on either side of the doorway for us to enter. I had never understood what the pouring of the oil meant. We had walked in and found all my cousins and local friends waiting to meet Madhu. Luckily, our living and dining rooms were very long and had enough sitting room.

"The rooms are big," Madhu commented to me. We had both been seated, and they all greeted Madhu one by one.

"How was the flight?" asked Rupinderjit.

"It was great, thank you," replied Madhu.

"This is my nephew but no different to my son," said my grandad.

"I am the real son," said Rupinderjit.

"So, you have travelled on business class and collected in a limousine. This has put a lot of further expectations on you now," continued Rupinderjit.

"I have grown up with drivers and servants, so this is nothing different, uncleji," replied Madhu.

"Raj, time to get ready to serve your wife as a servant," said Rupinderjit.

"I have come from all that and don't expect it here," said Madhu.

"I am sure you'll wrap Raj around your finger," said Rupinderjit's wife.

They all laughed. Towards the evening, the whole family walked us down to our new home. I had this house specially built for you two. We hadn't put in a kitchen as we want you to both eat at ours daily," said my grandma.

"Plus, we are scared that Raj might leave the gas on as he is that clumsy," said Aunty Sheela.

"I agree," said Rupinderjit.

"You have to keep an eye on him," continued Rupinderjit.

Madhu and I had walked into the house, and my family members had all returned home. I must thank my father and my grandfather for blessing us with this house. It had been a newly built three-bedroom house. I had painted the whole house in the colour peach, as it was Madhu's favourite colour. I had only one sofa in the living room, no dinner table in the dining room, and the kitchen was an open plan attached to the dining room. I had carpeted the whole house in a dark peach colour carpet. Madhu had walked through the house downstairs.

"With a family with a lot of money, properties in England, and very expensive houses in India, you all live in a shit house here," she said.

"I beg your pardon," I said.

"Come on, look at your parent's house; it's an embarrassment. The kitchen is basic, the bathroom is basic, and you have two long living rooms that are long for all your cousins to sit in. It's too obvious, and I am already embarrassed to show that house to any of my relatives in the UK," she said.

"Well, if you don't like it, you know what to do," I said.

"What is that?" she asked.

"An economy seat back to India," I replied.

"You wish. I had come here to become a successful lawyer and give my family back home a proud name. Show me the rest of the house," she said.

We had walked up the stairs, and she had looked at the bathroom. "Very basic," she commented. I had shown her the two spare rooms, one of which was a dressing room, kitted out with wardrobes. I had taken her into the master room, which had a nice wooden-frame bed.

"This is probably the best room in the house," said Madhu.

She had laid on the bed and made an 'ah' sound.

"I am so tired and had to meet all your relatives until late. Don't people think I have travelled almost eighteen hours and then I had come and smiled at all your relatives?"

"As I said, if you already don't like it here, you know what to do. Just tell me, and I'll buy the ticket myself for you," I said.

"Be quiet, and guess what? You're not sleeping here either," she said.

"It's ok. I wasn't going to anyway. I have a spare duvet and pillow to sleep on the sofa downstairs."

This had been the beginning of numerous arguments we had every day for months. After three months, it was the day of my graduation, and my entire family was ready to come with me. My grandad, Grandma, mother, Uncle Rupinderjit, and Aunty Sheela had all been ready to come with Madhu and me.

We had all been sitting in the theatre, and we had been asked to queue up and get called up one by one to walk across the stage when our names were called.

They announced, "Raj Singh has graduated from Business Studies with 2:1."

I walked onto the stage, shook the presenter's hand, and was given a rolled-up paper mimicking my degree certificate. I had looked at my family, and Grandad had been looking angry, and so had Madhu, who had been miming something. Rupinderjit and his wife had smirks on their faces, and the only person smiling was my mother, who was clapping. I smiled at Mum and mimed, "I did it, Mum."

She smiled back.

We had all sat in the people carrier.

"We sent you to study law; why have you graduated in business?" my grandad asked.

"This is so embarrassing, and what am I going to say to my parents?" said Madhu.

"Have you got anything to say?" asked my grandad.

"I didn't enjoy studying law, so I changed," I replied.

"You changed just like that? What am I going to tell your in-laws?" he had asked.

"He has a degree," my mum had said.

"You don't have a say in this," he told my mother.

"I don't think he had the capability to study law. He has always been slow," said Aunty Sheela.

"That's enough about calling my son slow. He has achieved a degree, the first in our family," said my mum.

"I said be quiet," my grandad had said to Mother.

"You don't say a thing, sister-in-law, as he just embarrassed us," added Rupinderjit.

"I have a degree; I am a catch with actresses, so I am not sorry about anything. Many wanted to marry me, and you know that, grandad. She is lucky to be married to me, so why all the fuss?" I asked.

"Oh, you could have married actresses, so why didn't you instead of ruining my life?" said Madhu, and she began to cry.

We had driven home all sad on one of the happiest days of my life. We had gotten home and walked into my parent's living room.

"You don't know what you have done, Raj. You have caused trouble in India now. It took me years to build relationships and respect in India, and they will be destroyed now," my grandad said.

"Isn't our son graduating a big thing? He has done well in sports, which everyone was against, he appeared in films, which everyone was against, and today he graduated as the only one in our family," my Mother said.

"Didn't I tell you not to say anything?" said Grandad.

He went to slap her, and I had stopped him.

"That's enough. You will not raise your hand on my mother," I said.

"You have verbally abused her all her married life and us as kids, but not anymore," I said.

"Who are you?" my grandad asked.

"I made all this and earned all this money. You are nothing. You are living in my house; I will kick you and your mum out," my grandad said.

"My mother has worked for thirty-plus years for all of you and in the shops. Actually, you owe her, and that is her house, not yours," I said angrily.

"Mum, you are coming with me to stay at our house," I said to my mum. "And you, Madhu, it's up to you if you want to follow us or stay here or go back to India. I was forced into the marriage. I didn't want to marry you," I had said.

I had walked out with my mum and gone to our house. The next day, Baljit came over to our house and sat in the living room.

"What are you doing, listening to your children?" she asked my mother. "We are a well-known family in the community, and what will people say?"

I sat down and said, "They insulted my mother."

"What do you know about life responsibility?" she asked.

"We cleaned your nappies, and you're trying to teach us?" she said.

"I'm the logical one in this family," I had said.

"I don't want to speak to you," she said.

"I don't want to speak to you," I said back.

"If you are good at educating anyone, why don't you educate your children?" I had said in anger.

She ignored me and continued convincing my mother to return home. She eventually convinced my mother and took her home. I had been defeated again by my controlling family.

For the next couple of weeks, there were continuous arguments between Madhu and me. We had all been sitting and having dinner on a weekend. My grandad had walked in with his solicitor friend James. He had introduced each of us, and when he came to me, he said, "This is my useless grandson who let me down. This is his wife, Madhu, who is a law graduate from India."

"Nice to meet you, Madhu. Your grandad has many nice things about you. You are very lucky. Without an interview, I am going to offer you a position in my firm. You can do LPC with us," said James.

Madhu had jumped up in joy.

"Thank you very much, Mr. James. See what I could have done for you," my grandad had said.

"I didn't want to become a lawyer," I had said.

"What are you going to do then? Your wife will be a qualified lawyer in two years, and you will wait for her to give you money to spend?" said my grandad.

"What sort of a man is that who lives off his wife?" said Sheela, who is always around when she is not needed.

"Something to think about and go back and study four modules in law subjects. Maybe you could focus on the business sector, for example, contracts, etc.," said James.

"That is a good idea, James, Raj, you can do this," said my grandad. I looked at him and smiled just to keep the peace.

I had shaken James's hand and my grandad's hand.

Madhu started her job on Monday and instructed me to enrol in the course James advised me to. I had sat in my living room, watching TV and trying to make myself laugh watching American sitcoms.

I had gone for a run to help me focus and bumped into Julie's mother.

"Hi, Mrs. White? How are you?" I asked.

"I am fine, Raj, and how are you, and married life treating you?"

"I am not good and not enjoying it," I replied.

"That's a shame," she said.

"How is Julie?" I asked.

"Tell you the truth, I don't know. She hasn't called or replied to my messages in months. She sent me a message three months ago saying she was too busy to come back and talk. It was best not to disturb me. So, the answer to your question is I don't know, Raj," she said.

"That's not good. Don't you have her address so you can surprise visit her?" I asked.

"We do, but she has asked to respect her space," she said.

"If you give me her address, I will visit," I said.

"Like I said, Raj, respect her space," she said.

"I hear you," I replied.

"You just look after yourself and try and make your marriage work," she said, rubbing my arm, comforting me, and walking off. I continued to run and think only if I knew Julie's address.

I came back and showered, and while showering, I thought my excuse would be that I needed to go to Manchester University to find out if I could do the course there.

Madhu returned home looking exhausted. I was sitting on the sofa watching TV and working on my laptop, typing a script. She threw herself on the sofa.

"Why haven't you made me any tea? You knew I was going to be back at this time."

"Firstly, you said you don't like English tea, and I thought you'd want me to pick you up on your first day," I asked.

"James, handsome son, John, dropped me off," she replied.

"We are working together; he also completed his degree at the same time as me," she said.

"Same time as us," I said.

"I'm talking about law, not business, which you guys already have," she said.

Another argument started.

"I don't want to argue with you," I said.

"I have been ringing around, speaking to universities regarding my completing my course and can join you and your handsome John," I said.

"He is handsome and has long wavy hair," she said.

"Anyway," I said, "I have found out that Manchester University will allow this, and admissions want to speak to me. I will have to go tomorrow."

"That's a good idea; tell your grandad, as I don't care what you do. I want my indefinite stay after three years, then you will go your way, and I will go my way," she said and got up and walked up the stairs.

Later that evening, we were having dinner with my parents. "Grandad, I have managed to find out where I can do my course, and it's in Manchester," I said.

"Manchester?" He asked. "Isn't that too far?"

"It is, but it's the only place I can study the modules," I said.

"I will have to talk to James to see if he knows anyone at Wolverhampton," said Grandad.

I quickly had to think, how do I get over this one?

"I am only finding out details from the admissions department, and you can find out from James," I said.

"What do you think Madhu?" Grandad asked.

"I don't mind where it is, Grandad," she replied.

I think she didn't care now that she had this John guy in her mind.

"Okay, I'll go tomorrow and find out, Grandad," I said.

The next day, I was on the early train to Manchester. On the way, I hoped to bump into Julie when I got there. I called her several times, but there was no answer or reply to my texts. I looked out the window and saw different buildings and landmarks and how areas have changed over the years. I saw people coming on the train and people leaving. I felt that sometimes this is like life; people come into our lives and leave, and we experience all the emotions. I just wanted to experience the happiness of meeting Julie.

I got off the train, walked out of the train station and saw a large city. I found it very different from Wolverhampton. I walked around the city and saw trams, nothing like I had seen before and added a tour of Manchester. I went to the bank Julie worked at and walked in, hoping to see her. The automatic doors opened, and I walked into a very lit-up bank. There was so much light from windows and indoor lighting. People were queued up to be served. I looked at the security guard and nodded, "What's up?"

Then I walked around, checking out each staff member working that day. There were ladies with brunettes, black hair, and red hair, and women working there, but no one with blonde hair.

I saw someone walking and talking to a guy in a grey suit who resembled Julie. But she looked pregnant, so that couldn't have been her. They walked through the doors before I got to them, and only staff were allowed behind that door. The security guard tapped me on the shoulder. "Can I help you, sir?" he asked.

I said, "I'm looking for a friend, Julie, who works here. Is she in today?"

"Sorry, sir, I can't share any information with you, and if she is your friend, you must have her number; it's best you call her," he said.

"Only if she answered," I whispered.

"I will have to ask you to leave if you have no business here, sir," he said.

"Okay," I said and walked out of the branch.

I waited outside for a bit, walked around for a bit, and sat in a café not too far from the bank, hoping to see Julie come out of the branch.

I waited until it was after six o'clock, and there was no sign of Julie. I had to return back to Wolverhampton on the seven o'clock train. I walked back and got to the train station in time, but as I felt rushing through the station to get to my train, I thought I saw Julie. I got on the train and just about got to my seat.

After thirty minutes on the train, I saw a blonde lady whose name was Kim. I remembered her working out at the gym and all the guys drooling over her. They all said she should be in an American beach TV show.

I approached her, "Hi Kim, is it?" I asked.

"Yes, and Raj, I remember working out at your gym. I'm sorry you had to close," she said.

"I know, and now I'm out of work myself," I said.

"You looking for work?" she asked.

"Yes," I answered.

"I know it's probably insulting, but Health World is looking for personal trainers, and you would be ideal for the role," she shared.

"They did put me out of business, and it's best to learn their secrets. Thanks," I said.

We chatted about her career and life all the way back home.

When I got home, I thought I better apply for this personal trainer role. As usual, I walked into the living room and found everyone sitting in the living room.

"How did it go, son?" asked my Grandad.

"It went very well, and they said I can't join until next year," I said.

"So, what are you going to do until then?" asked Grandad.

"If you could ask James if he can help?" I asked.

"I will tomorrow said my grandad. Maybe I can help around their office," I said. Madhu walked in and said, "Don't get me wrong, I would like to work on my own at the firm. If we both work there together, it will make it awkward. It will seem like husband and wife are trying to take over the firm."

"You might have a point," said Grandad.

I looked at Madhu, thinking, "She is only here for her gains."

She looked at me, giving me the look that she was winning this.

The next day, I got in touch with the fitness centre. I spoke to the centre's manager, Karen. She was excited to get me on board and get the clients interested in Powerlifting.

I came home and found Madhu sitting on the sofa and excitedly speaking to someone on the phone. I sat next to her, and she gave me that look, "What are you doing sitting next to me?"

I put on the TV to get her attention. I flicked through the channels and began to watch a TV series based on Housewives.

I think this episode was about all the wives in the street who are best friends hiding a secret about a murder in the street. "Secrets," I thought.

Madhu continued to laugh and speak, mainly about her day in court, shadowing her colleague.

"Oh, John, you are so funny," she said, speaking to someone on the phone.

It seemed like it was this John guy who she was always talking about and to on the phone.

"Okay, I look forward to seeing you tomorrow," she said to John on the phone while looking at me at the same time.

"Bye and sweet dreams," and laughed and hung up.

"New boyfriend?" I asked.

"Watch your mouth," she said.

"He is a friend and a very bright one at the same time. Any woman would be happy to be his girlfriend," she said.

"Okay, you enjoy being his girlfriend. I don't care," I said.

"I got a job offer today working at a fitness centre," I shared with Madhu.

"At a fitness centre?" she asked.

"How about your career in law?" She continued to ask.

"I will look into that next year. Meanwhile, I must get a job to bring in funds as my funds are running out," I said.

"Well, don't look at me. I will not give you a single penny from my income," said Madhu.

"I don't want your money," I said.

261

"We have your parents' money," she replied.

"I don't want to run to my parents. I want to be known for my own success," I said.

"You are so naive; you won't be able to earn enough for what's coming in the future."

"What's that supposed to mean?" I asked.

"You'll find out as time goes on, but you need to know that our life will not excel into a new home and new cars with the income you will bring in," she said.

"What? You want to move into a new house?" I asked.

"Yes," she said.

"But this is a brand new house."

"Yes, it is, but look at it. It's not very big, has no furniture, and does not even have a kitchen because your parent thinks you might leave the gas cooker on accidentally. Plus, this area is very downhill. I want to live in a posh area, the same as where James and John live," she said.

"How do you know where they live?" I asked.

"They showed me their house coming back from the courts the other day. They live in a mansion, which your parents should have with all the talk about the number of properties and money your grandad has he boasts about," she said.

"That's none of your business how my family lives. They have built their empire working hard and don't need to be told how they shall live," I said. "

"I can, as I'm married into the family and now a family member. They still have the mindset of villagers back home in India. I'm a city girl and far advanced even than your family," she said.

"How dare you judge us?" I asked loudly.

"Don't raise your voice against me; I'll slap you," she said. "You don't know who you have married. I'm from a wealthy family who had servants put on my shoes when I instructed. You are nothing."

I felt like a deflated balloon and sat down on the sofa while she continued insulting me, standing over me.

"I only have to call my uncle back home, and he will destroy your grandad in India," she said.

"How dare you try and threaten my grandad, who brought you here," I asked.

"My grandad is no pushover. He came over to this country and fought against racism and built his business," I said.

"I don't want a history lesson, thank you very much," she said and walked up the stairs.

On my first day on the job, I was nervous. I hadn't really done this in a long time. I walked in, and this was the state of the art. I could see why I could not compete with this place. I walked in, and the reception area was amazing. The two receptionists looked like the models on game shows. I turned to the left; there was a health bar, then a cardiovascular area; on one side, there were machines with a timer, a ten-station workout. I could see two swimming pools through the glass windows, and I looked up; there was an open space on the first floor with more machines. I took a tour upstairs, and there was a loose weights area, a dance studio, and a spin room. This was my dream gym business. I wanted to create a similar fitness centre in my city, but the founder from South Africa had done it before. This founder had two hundred of these worldwide, mainly in the United States. There were glass windows surrounding the whole building, which meant a lot of daylight was coming in.

I was given a further tour of the building. Downstairs on the right of the building was a large area of rooms for twelve salespeople; then, there was a childcare facility so their parents could work out, which I thought was an amazing idea. Both changing rooms had steam rooms and great locker facilities. This founder had got everything right. I wanted to shake his hand and congratulate him. I was taken into the boardroom and found a room full of personal fitness. I looked around the room. I had never thought or said this, but all these trainers were good-looking individuals. It was like they were all models.

"Well, come in, Raj, and let me introduce you to the team," she went around the room and said, "This is Deputy Manager Jemma, Carl, Samantha, Lorraine, Joel, Richard, Alison, and Sarah."

I spent the day understanding how they all ran the fitness centre. I was introduced to gym members, and at least eight women asked me out on my first day. It was a tiring day. When I got home on my first day, I found Madhu lying on the sofa again, talking on the phone. It did sound like her friend John again.

"It would be nice to come home and have my space back, the sofa I sleep on," I said. She looked at me and gave me that evil look. "Why don't you have your phone calls with your boyfriend upstairs in your bedroom?" I asked.

She got up and left the room. I stretched out over the sofa and took a long sigh. I was super tired. I went over the day and couldn't believe I was working for a company that put me out of business and had significant financial losses. I still have a debt I am paying back to the bank, which the family does not know about.

At the same time, this place was the best fitness centre I have ever seen. I was more happy working here than angry. I was so tired that I fell asleep in seconds.

I woke up in the morning with Madhu making all the noise, getting ready for work. I walked upstairs to the bathroom and asked Madhu, "You want a lift to work?"

"No, John is picking me up," she replied.

"Okay, have a good day," I said, trying to keep the peace.

"You too," she replied, which I was surprised about.

Back at the fitness centre, I enjoyed coaching members. I had female members asking me out again. This fitness centre was like a world you would find in futuristic movies. I connected with many members, and almost all the

263

Indian members recognized me in my film. Each one of them asked the same question – "What are you doing here? Why aren't you in Bollywood making films?"

At the end of the week, the personal trainers asked me if I wanted to join them to go out clubbing. I agreed. I would have been happier to be out than staying indoors and arguing with Madhu. I got to the first wine bar called Bright House. It was a very open-spaced bar with very high ceilings. Carl, Samantha, Lorraine, Joel, Richard, Alison, and Sarah were all out, along with the two receptionists, Gemma and Donna. The drinks came out, and I ordered an orange juice. They laughed and said, "Try Tequila first."

I tried, and it burnt my throat all the way down to my stomach. Before I knew it, I had five of them and was drunk. We were all drunk and dancing most of the night.

Then I found Gemma kissing me, and then after a while, she left, and Donna started kissing me. I didn't know what was going on. This was a different world. I saw the personal trainers laughing and saying, "Welcome to our team, Raj."

The next day, I had a super hangover. I found myself on the sofa, still in my clothes, and I did not have a clue how I had got home.

Madhu came into the living room.

"You decided to wake up drunk?" She asked.

"Yes, and I have a severe headache," I said.

"You would have a headache as you came home super drunk, singing and then crying about how you hate your life. I don't care if you hate your life, but I love mine, and I don't want to live a life of being the wife of a drunk," she said.

"I am not a drunk," I said.

For the next few days and weeks, I just got used to coaching fitness centre members until the bomb was dropped on me. Karen called me into her office and said, "Raj, you will have to take part in the spin class today."

I said, "Why? I'm a powerlifter, not a cyclist."

"No, you're a fitness instructor as part of this centre, and we can ask you to take part in any of the classes we want you to. We need you to learn and take the early morning spin classes from next week."

"But I have never taken spin classes," I said.

"It's ok, you'll learn and pick it up within two classes. Join Carl's class, and you'll learn quickly," she said, and I agreed to take part.

I walked into the spin studio and found members setting themselves on the bikes, getting ready for the session. Like a school kid, I went to the back of the studio. Carl saw me.

"Raj, sit near the front," he said.

"No, it's ok. I'm here to observe," I said, and he laughed.

The class began, and it got harder after every two minutes. This was one of the toughest sessions I had done. I was sweating buckets.

At the same time, I was trying to work out his routine and timing. That week, I took eight spin classes, and I must have lost four kilograms. Over the weekend, I put together my spin session plan.

The time came to hold my spin class at seven o'clock early in the morning. I played the music and started my class with Rocky soundtracks. I began instructing the group in the spin room. On the heavy uphill cycling, I had them all cycling with their hands on their heads, and I had them shouting, "Adrian, I love you."

The session got easier as the weeks went on, and I was asked to change my soundtracks, and I used garage soundtracks.

Six months later, four of us personal trainers travelled down to Milton Keynes one weekend at an event where close to two hundred personal trainers from across the United Kingdom from all their fitness centres. We all held classes to coach each other, and they put a name in a hat, ranking the top spin class instructors in the country and ranked second. I couldn't believe that I ranked as the second-best spin instructor in the country in a workout I disliked to coach and take part in.

On the way back, there was a tailback of traffic on the motorway for at least four hours. A high percentage of people came out of the cars and sat on the sides. As a group, we came out, sat on the side, and began to speak. We spoke about a lot of personal stuff, and a couple of secrets came out of two instructors. I wish these two never had shared these secrets with us.

Time went on working at the fitness centre, and Madhu continued with her career at the solicitor's firm. We also continued sleeping in separate bedrooms. From the time we got married to now, we never had any physical contact. I had a feeling that something was going on between Madhu and John. Gifts were appearing, which she said she bought herself, treating herself.

Arguments were on a daily basis, the first thing in the morning and the last thing at night. I walked into the fitness centre to start my shift and was told that the founder was walking around and to be on my best behaviour. I was excited, not scared. As an ex-gym owner, I saw myself at the same level as an entrepreneur, and I wanted to learn from this guy. I carried on my shift, hoping to bump into this guy.

Finally, I met him.

"Hi Raj, I have been told a lot about you by Karen," he said.

"Thank you," I replied. "Plus, I am so happy to meet you, the founder of this great worldwide establishment," I said while shaking his hand.

"Thank you, and it wasn't easy. It all began in the back of my garden shed in South Africa," he said, going on about how he grew his brand worldwide, owning over two hundred fitness centres. He also shared how his company went public and traded on the stock market. His plan was to open a centre in a new city every month.

That night, I got home from work and found Madhu sitting on the sofa, looking angry.

"Do you know what day it is today?" she asked while I was walking in shattered.

"What day is it?" I asked.

"It's our wedding anniversary, and you haven't even booked a table at any restaurant," she said.

"I am sorry, as I totally forgot, and I didn't think we were in a good place, as we are not even talking to each other. I will go over to the other house and put a meal together for us," I said.

"Why can't you take me out to a restaurant?" she asked.

"Because I can't afford it. I only earn so much as a personal trainer, and I'm still paying off debts from the gym," I replied.

"What have I married into? You can't even afford to take me out for a meal. You are a failure, like your family said. You're just a clumsy idiot," she said.

I was too tired to argue and left to make an effort. I came back making boiled chicken and boiled potatoes with vegetables. I lay on the table and lit a candle to make an effort. She came down and saw the food on the plates.

"That is a powerlifter meal. I don't want that," she said.

"Can't you make anything else, you clumsy idiot?" Her language was a bit filthier.

She grabbed the plate and threw it at me. My clothes got covered with the gravy.

"I just called John, and he said he is taking me out for a pub meal. You can enjoy your donkey food," she said and left.

The next day, I woke up, and it was a weekend. I wasn't working as one of the other fitness instructors changed shifts with me to have a weekday off. I walked into the living room and found Madhu, grandad, and grandma sitting in the living room. I looked at Madhu, and she was crying.

"What happened?" I asked.

Madhu cried even more.

"You can't even afford to take Madhu out for dinner. How embarrassing is that!" said my grandad. "You could have asked me for funds if you are struggling," he continued to tell me off.

This didn't help my relationship with Madhu from this day forward. I tried my level best to keep out of her way. Especially at weekends, I spent more time in nightclubs, and someone who was against drinking was drunk almost every weekend.

I was out every weekend and found myself kissing one lady after another. I probably made out with over a hundred women over the next twelve months. Even one lady wanted to marry me. She asked her father to let me live in their Goa holiday home so I could focus on my acting career from there. This lady had golden blonde hair, beautiful green eyes, and an amazing body. As well as being beautiful, she had this beautiful soul who wanted to help me. Her parents were wealthy and owned properties in Europe, the United States of America, and Goa. She didn't need to work but worked as a prison officer. She felt this was her calling to help inmates of the prison. She wanted to help them change their lives around.

When I first saw her library collection, it was biographies of prisoners and ex-prisoners. This concerned me for a bit, especially as she loved the biographies of famous gangsters. She lived in Cannock, an area which the English Caucasians moved to twenty-plus-years-ago to get away from the Asian and Black communities due to racism. So that was back in my head, thinking her parents might be racist and might not agree to let Katrina and me live together. Unfortunately, I destroyed this very relationship, and the other thing on my mind was that if Madhu and I divorced, I would like to marry Julie.

Time flew, and financially, I was struggling to pay off my last business debts and build up other expenses. One day, I got a call.

"Hey, is that Raj?" they asked.

"Yes, this is Raj; how can I help?" I replied.

"This is the casting director for a British-Indian television film we are planning to film in India and the United Kingdom, and we would like to cast you for a role. Could you come in for a discussion?"

"Of course I can," I said. Luckily, I was sitting in my car just before my shift at work. I write down all the details.

I went home that evening and walked into the living room. Madhu was on the phone again, but her conversation was a lot different from usual – when she was on the phone with John or other colleagues. She hung up.

"Who was that?" I asked.

"It was Aunty Sheela. We have become very good friends over the past few months, and when I need advice, she is always there for me," she said.

I was shocked but okay with it at the time. Then she said, "Uncle Rupinderjit thinks I'm going through depression because of you."

"Because of me?" I asked.

"Yes, you. You have a useless job that does not pay a lot. You can't afford to pay for dinners, holidays, gifts, the cooker I had to pay for, the cinema, and nothing. You're a worthless piece of a loser," she said.

"You earn your own money to do all that," I said.

"I am not spending any of my own money on anything. You have wasted money on trips to London on auditions and stupid business meetings. Enough is enough. Get a higher-paying job," she said.

"I just got offered a television acting role, and it's one of our four channels. I will earn a lot more," I shared.

"Is the filming in England?" she asked.

"Yes, and India," I replied.

"No, you're not doing these cheap films and not making anything from them," she said.

"What?" She ran upstairs in a rage and came back downstairs holding my passport and a pair of scissors.

"You are not leaving this country. Uncle Rupinderjit said you live in cloud cuckoo land, and you're a shit actor. You will never make it in films," she said while cutting up my passport. My eyes fill up.

"What are you doing?" I asked.

"This will stop you from running off into films. You get another job, and if you want any funds to help you from me, you have to give up your dream of acting," she said.

"You can't tell me to forget my dreams," I said.

"All your family are unhappy with you. First, you study the wrong degree; you lost a lot of money from your business, you start this low-paying job, and can't even pay for decorating this house," she said.

"What are you talking about? I bought all the paint which is under the dinner table," I said to defend myself.

She threw the passport pieces at me.

"You're just a useless shit," she walked up the stairs swearing and calling me names. I was super hurt to see my dreams shattered again. The room felt like it was spinning, and I felt I couldn't breathe.

The next day, I phoned in sick and went over to speak to my parents. I was sitting in the living room waiting for my dad to return from operating one of his other stores. Eventually, he walked in with my grandad, discussing something wrong in India.

"Dad and Grandad, I need to speak to you both," I said.

"We can't speak to you at the moment," said Dad.

"Your grandad made some promises to people in India, which have put us in a financial mess with our investments. We both must go to India," he said.

"It's all Raj's fault," said my grandad.

"My fault?" I asked.

"If you hadn't lied to me about your degree and upset Madhu, this wouldn't have happened. I bet your in-laws have something to do with this," he said.

"But you asked me to marry her," I said. "Now you're blaming me? I came to this country with no money and made an empire, and you can't even pay your bills."

I walked out of the room feeling lost and battered. I walk back and find the street spinning again. I got home and was feeling the same for at least an hour.

During the next couple of months, I spent a lot of time at work, walking around the park, thinking about Julie and all those moments with her that will be with me for a lifetime. Head spins began to happen on a regular basis. To forget about all the pain, I spent every weekend clubbing with the guys from work. I spent those clubbing nights with a different lady, sometimes two ladies.

My parents had turned their back on me and said they couldn't help me financially. Madhu and I had daily arguments, and I didn't know what to do for the first time in my life. One of the days, I went for a walk, and as I was walking, a Rolls Royce pulled up near me, and the window came down. It's a British Indian guy I recognize from British Asian Millionaire Magazine.

"Hi Raj, I'm Dhillon. You wrote to me a year ago regarding funding for a film idea you had," he said.

"I did, but not in the film business anymore," I said.

"You know I am the richest and the only powerful Indian businessman in Wolverhampton. I don't like anyone saying no to me, and I don't like any Indian getting ahead of me. Even though you're not involved in films anymore, people think you went further than me in fame. I give you a day to think about it. Come to my offices tomorrow with the right answer."

I turned up at Dhillon's office the next day. As his receptionist walked to Dhillon's office, I heard him say, "I knew you would come."

I looked in the boardroom, and there was a Chinese character, an Afro-Caribbean guy whom I recognized from a television show, and a blonde lady.

"Sit down, Raj," he said.

I sat down and listened.

"This is my team. I want you to work with the film director, casting director, and one of the actors. You and the director Joseph, who you might think is Chinese but is mixed-race Chinese and Caucasian, will come up with a storyline within a week and start filming soon. Jane, the casting director, will find the rest of the artists for us. Your job will also produce the film for me. So, you will handle locations, crew, actors, catering, hotels, and everything. Don't look worried; I am making your dreams come true. Spend time with Joseph."

We spent a day with Joseph with brainstorming ideas. We came up with a martial arts movie fighting against racism. With my character, whose mother moved into a racist area after she divorced her husband for two-timing her, the local council gave this house to her within this run-down area, with most of the residents who lived in the area disliking Asians and Blacks. The TV show actor, who was very muscular, would train my character on how to defend myself against physical attacks. After the meeting late in the evening, Dhillon walked in.

"Have you come up with a good idea?" he asked.

We explained the concept, and Joseph and I said we would both create the script, even though the story idea was mine.

On my days off and evenings, I worked on the script and travelled to London to meet up with Joseph to complete the script. Within four weeks, we managed to put a great script together. The cast and crew were put together by Joseph, and even though I sat through auditions, I felt like they were all Joseph's friends.

At home, Madhu was kicking off daily, saying I should be finding a higher-paid job, and was ringing home complaining to her parents to complain to my grandad and dad, who were in India. I did apply for a higher-paying job but wasn't getting any opportunities. I was having blood tests to find out what was happening with my health.

269

As I was also taking the tae box classes, I could not carry out the spin classes by this point. My tae box classes were eighty per cent of women, and my sessions had the highest number of members participating. I had to take this class just by instructing and not taking part with the help of one of the other instructors, Sarah.

She felt sorry for me and took my classes. Without her saying, it was obvious she liked me. We once sat in the instructor's canteen, and she said, "Remember that secret I told you."

I said, "Yes."

"So, with me sharing, I am also a stripper on the weekends; you wouldn't date someone like me, would you?" She asked.

"My life was very complicated to date anyone, regardless of what they or you did," I said.

"Anything I can help with?" She asked.

I held her hand, "Thank you, Sarah, but I'll be fine."

She got up and said, "I am only a call away, and you don't look too good; get yourself checked out," and left.

Two weeks later, we planned to start filming in a week's time. I was sitting in Dhillon's boardroom. "Well done, guys," Dhillon said to me and Joseph.

"Dhillon, before we move forward, I was thinking we have contracts in place. Plus, I should be getting paid for the parts I'm playing," I asked.

Dhillon began to laugh and said, "You don't trust me?"

He took out his chequebook and said, "Look, I just wrote a cheque for four hundred thousand pounds to purchase a building, and this film is only going to cost me two hundred and fifty thousand, according to Joseph's breakdown."

"But you have set this company up in my name, and only I'm the director," I said.

"As I told you before, I can't open too many companies in my name as I have a main brand. This is to make you famous, don't forget. If you don't trust me, I will get my solicitor to prepare a contract for you," Said Dhillon.

I think my love for making films took over at this point.

My father and grandfather were not around to get advice from them. I went ahead and booked the crew and locations, hotels, catering company, actors, and locations with Joseph's help. I booked a couple of weeks off for filming. I told Madhu, and she hit the roof.

"Film making again," she said.

"How about becoming a lawyer?" she asked.

"I never wanted to become a lawyer," I said.

"So, you guys lied to my family and me," she said.

She swore a lot and used abusive language to express how she felt. I felt faintish in this moment of argument. I sat down on the sofa.

"I'm not feeling good," I said.

"There's nothing wrong with you. You are just an idiot who keeps making mistakes and knows this is another mistake you are making. Have you seen you? You are no star material. Forget about filmmaking. I thought you would listen to Uncle Rupinderjit?" She said.

My heart began beating faster, and I asked her to call the ambulance. She looked at me and said, "Call them yourself," and stormed up the stairs.

I called 999 and had them come to check on me. The ambulance took me to the hospital, and they did an ECG and blood tests.

The doctor said, "We can't seem to understand what illness this is, but you are losing your blood. Haven't you noticed you have been losing weight?"

They put me on a blood drip and water.

After two days, I was released and sitting at my parents' home.

"Why are you hurting yourself?" my mother asked. "Why can't you look after your health?"

She continued, "I have been through a lot with your health issues since you were born."

"He just cares about his dream of becoming an actor," said uncle Rupinderjit.

"You must stop being stupid and care about Madhu." Said Aunty Sheela.

A couple of weeks passed, and Dhillon called me. After a couple of days of him trying to contact me, I answered the call.

"Raj, why haven't you answered my calls?" He asked.

"I have been in the hospital with an illness. They are trying to find out why I'm losing blood," I explained.

"I am ready to produce this film starring you. How can you mess me around like this?" He asked.

"I think you approached me, not the other way around." But I was too ill to argue my case.

"Listen, Raj, just start the film, and you can have much of a break to get yourself treated." I agreed just to get him off my back.

Plus, I was getting nonstop calls from Joseph. The week after, everything was all set up to roll the camera. We filmed for two days until the catering company asked for their payments. I called Dhillon and said, "Dhillon, the catering company needs their payment."

"How much is it?" He asked.

"For two days so far, it's two thousand pounds," I said.

"That's okay, just you pay them, and I'll pay you when I get back. I'm in Paris for a couple of days." He said.

I thought I didn't have this money. I remember applying for a credit card with a five-thousand-pound credit limit. I never wanted to use this, but I did this on this occasion. Four days of filming and I was paying the catering and actor travel expenses. And at this point, I had used up all my five thousand pounds of credit on the card. I called Dhillon and said I had spent all the money I had, and I needed him to start paying the actors, crew, and locations.

When he arrived at the hotel, we sat in the bar. Joseph, Dhillon, and I were sitting, and I was telling him about the costs. "I was not only acting in the film but overseeing everything else. I also went out twice after midnight to get other actors their snacks from the supermarket. I needed money to hire a runner and other staff to help me," I said.

Dhillon looked at me and Joseph. "I have changed my mind and don't want to invest in this film anymore."

My heart sank. I looked at Joseph and then back at Dhillon.

"What do you mean? All this time, you said you were going to invest." I said.

"If I have changed my mind, I have changed my mind. Just tell everyone that I have changed my mind and send them all home."

I felt like dying to be put in this position. I knew Madhu, Rupinderjit, and Sheela would tell me they were right. I walked away feeling destroyed and a big failure.

The next day, I called in all the crew, actors, and everyone involved in the project into the hotel's restaurant.

"I am sorry to say that the investor has pulled out of the project, and we have no money to continue. We have been all asked to pack up today and asked everyone to leave."

I had many of them swearing at me and telling me how I wasted their time. I came home and told Madhu what happened, and she swore and threw things at me. She said, "You have got us in a massive mess."

She tried cutting her wrists with a knife. She said she didn't want to live. At this point, I felt like taking that knife and ending my life.

Two days later, after being insulted by family members and Madhu, I felt it was time to end my life. I got a call from the television show actor.

"Hey Raj, you can't get away with having me work from five in the morning until five in the evening and not pay me," He said.

"But I didn't hire you; your friend Dhillon did. You should ask him for the money." I said.

"No, you are the producer, not him, and you will have to pay me."

"But he is the main producer, as you were there when it all started," I tried to explain.

"I don't know nothing, but you had me acting for you, and I want the money from you," He said.

Then I got angry and said, "Listen, films go bust all the time due to funds. That doesn't mean actors chase the producer for money when the investors pull out. Do what you must do."

"You don't want me to do that as I will come and beat you up and your family daily."

I put the phone down on him. At first, I thought these were extra issues I didn't need. Luckily, my dad and grandad flew back. I explained everything to them, and they said, "You didn't get anything in writing with Dhillon, so you are at fault."

I then told them about this television actor.

"We just have to pay him," they said.

"As we have too many problems going on in India," my grandad said.

"I can report this actor to the press," I thought.

Just then, I got a call from an England strongman contender who threatened me too and asked to meet him at a local pub. I went to this pub and saw him sitting there with that actor. I looked around, and there was no one else in this pub. I sat down.

"So, what decision have you made?" Asked the actor.

"Like I said, actors don't get paid if the film goes bust."

He grabbed me to hit me. This guy was muscularly huge, and at this point, I had lost a lot of size and strength to even take him on. I said, "Do what you have to do."

He roughed me up by punching me in the face a few times, in the stomach, and I was sure he cracked my ribs. I was finding it hard to breathe and in a lot of pain.

"Phone your family to bring me my five hundred pounds; I want a thousand pounds now," I called my grandad, and he turned up.

He looked at me, and he said, "You guys don't know who you have messed with, but because it's Raj's fault, I'm letting this go."

He gave them the envelope of a thousand pounds, and we left. Back home, the whole family told me of my actions. Madhu was crying her eyes out and saying.

"I want to go back home. See what you have done," said my grandma.

"You both should be family planning, not getting into debt. He needs to leave his fitness trainer job and get another job if you guys want any grandchildren." Said Madhu.

I walked into the fitness centre and held my final Tae Box session with Sarah's help. I thanked all my members; it was overwhelming when I saw many women crying and many hugs. I walked out of the studio, and the Sunday line dance teacher, Jane, was waiting to talk to me. She always reminded me of one of the American actresses from a television show about the six of them. She was very attractive.

"Hi Jane," I said.

"Hi, Raj, so this is your last day here?" She asked.

"It is," I replied.

"What are you doing next?" She asked.

"I am going into Sales, which pays double what I earned here," I replied.

"That's good for you, and I'm happy for you," she said. "Listen, Raj, I have liked you from the first time we met, and I have never had the opportunity to tell you as you were dating most of the women members in this place."

She continued to share.

"Jane, you are a beautiful woman with a great heart, and any guy would be happy to be with you. You need someone who would watch you watch movies, wake up in the middle of the night with you, and share topics you love and love your smile. Oh, I also hear you're a great teacher, too." She laughed, and tears fell from her eyes.

"Raj, that's the nicest way to say no, you don't like me." She said.

"Jane, no, I do like you, but I'm ill and living a complicated life with ties I can't get rid of. Plus, to be honest, I have been in love with someone else since the age of ten, and I am hoping that she and I will get together one day." I shared. "Oh, that's so sweet," she said. She went on to hug me, but I passed out.

The next time I woke up, I was in the hospital. I opened my eyes and found my mother crying, with Shelly hugging her and comforting her. I smile at her. "Mum, it's going to be ok," I said.

"You're losing blood again," the doctor said, walking up to the bed. "But don't worry, we have that covered with applying a drip on you."

I looked at Mum and said, "See."

I looked outside the room and found Madhu on the phone. After a couple of days, I was taken home, and I lay on the sofa watching television. Madhu walked in with food made by my mother to give me to eat. She put everything on a tray for me to eat. She looked at me and said, "You're just a loser."

This broke me. My eyes filled up, and I couldn't even swallow the food. Before she went up the stairs that night, she said, "You better hurry up and get better and start that new job because my mother is coming over from India to live with us."

Chapter Forty-Four

The journey of life was a rollercoaster. Some moments turned our lives upside down. We didn't know who we were and didn't know where we might end up. But I have to say that all my favourite moments had to be when I was with Julie. It was these moments that had been part of our history. These moments were like our favourite songs that we played in our minds as many times as we liked—moments of love I had in my life. The moments I thought were going to have ripple effects of different chapters in my life with Julie. Could I have all those adventurous moments in sports and films with Julie? Buying Bilston Library and turning it into our home. So, we could spend our time together in the park as our garden.

I lay in this bed thinking, "I don't know what happened. But if I could just see Julie again, I could take my last breath."

Time went by, and my health was getting worse.

I was losing hair and getting weaker and slimmer. I took another sales role, knocking on business doors one after another, and selling television advertisements.

This paid well and kept Madhu and everybody else happy. I tried to keep away from the family working, and when I got tired and weak, I slept in the car. I didn't want my family to worry about me, especially my mother and father. I began to shave my hair, saying I was keeping clean-shaven as I couldn't afford haircuts.

The moment was to come when I had to live with not one lady from India but two from the same family. The time came when my mother-in-law came from India. Her trip was delayed by three months as Madhu's father had a fall and broke his leg. Madhu had my grandad book a limousine to collect her mother from the airport. I couldn't go as I was feeling weak and decided to stay with my parents, waiting or dreading this moment. I knew I didn't have a voice in my family. I was too ill to fight back, and now Madhu's mother was going to live with us for six months.

I was standing in the shop looking at the movie DVD covers, thinking about how times had changed from video cases to these DVD cases. Julie's mother walked in and began talking to my father.

"Who's that?" She asked my father.

His eyes teared up, and he said, "It's Raj."

"Is he okay?" She asked and walked over to me. "Hi, Raj."

I just about turned around as I was trying to stand in one spot and trying not to give it away that I was in pain.

"Hi, Mrs. White," I said. "Are you okay?"

"I am fine, Mrs. White, just on a serious weight loss program," I replied.

"Really?" she asked. "Well, if it's a diet you are on, you might be happy to know that Julie teaches dance fitness classes part-time—something called Zumba," she shared.

I teared up in happiness and said, "That's amazing, and I am so happy. It's a shame we couldn't teach it together."

"That's right, and she would have loved that. Anyway, what's with the skinhead look?" She asked.

"Something I am fashioning," I replied.

"Raj," she said and stopped.

"What, Mrs. White?" I asked.

"Nothing," she replied. "I better be off."

"Mrs. White," I said, and I slowly moved toward her and hugged her.

"Oh, why the hug, Raj?" She asked.

I speak into her ear. "I think I am dying, Mrs. White, and I want you to tell Julie I love her and always will until I die."

She slowly pushed me off, looked into my eyes, and began to cry. "Oh, Raj, oh dear," she stroked my face and said, "Julie loves you too and always has done. I will be praying for God to heal you, Raj."

"Thank you, Mrs. White, and please don't tell Julie."

"Raj, I need to tell you something," she said, and just then, Grandad walked in with Madhu's Mother.

"I better go," and Julie's mother left crying.

"What's wrong with her?" She asked my father.

My father walked around the till area and hugged her.

"Welcome to England," he said. "Thank you, and thank you for the nice welcome at the airport and the beautiful car," she said. The shop's entrance was crowded by my family—my grandad, grandma, mother, Madhu, and Madhu's mother. The customers couldn't get in, so they left, saying we'd go to the other shop up the road. We were losing customers as soon as Madhu's mother arrived.

"Where's my son-in-law?" she asked.

"There he is," my grandad said, pointing in my direction.

"Him?" She asked. "That's not him."

"The idiot is on some diet to lose weight and shaved his hair following some footballer," Grandad explained my illness.

"Come over here and hug me," she said.

I walked over in pain and hugged her, and she squeezed me. I could have screamed. She looked at me and said, "You look old as well."

"Let's go in and speak inside," my grandad said. They walked in, and I noticed my mother crying. Madhu walked past me and did not even look at me.

We were all sitting in the living room, drinking tea.

"Please don't get me wrong, but I thought you would have lived in a bigger house," Madhu's mother said.

"This is big enough for us," My grandad said.

"But you have many houses in India, which are five to seven times bigger than this. Why do you live here?" She asked.

"I have been here in this town since the sixties. It's been hard to build respect and a strong relationship, which we have. We would have to move out of this town to live in those types of houses, and I'm too old to start over," Grandad explained.

"Plus, our daughters live nearby," My grandma said.

"This shop has been a gold mine for us," My grandad said.

"What is my Madhu's house like?" She asked. "That is brand new, and I had it developed for Madhu and Raj," Grandad said.

"Raj, you are very quiet," Madhu's mother said.

She looked up at my trophies displayed in the cabinet.

"You won't be achieving any of these anymore looking the way you look," she said.

"Let's go to my house and rest, Mom," said Madhu.

They left, and my grandpa got up from his chair and said, "All your problem now."

Two weeks went by, and I had to take time off work as I was in more pain and couldn't walk without being in pain. I was lying on the living room sofa, and Madhu and her mother were in the dining room. The doors were open, and I could hear their conversation.

"How are you going to cope with having an ill husband?" asked Madhu's mother.

"I don't know. He might die," replied Madhu.

"You don't want to be a widow," said her mother.

"I have spoken to my work colleague about divorcing Raj, and he said he will guide me," said Madhu.

"Don't leave it too long; make sure you get paid out well, too," said Madhu's mother.

"Don't worry, I will. All the perks of being a lawyer."

"Do you think that stuff I sent you to put in Raj's clothes and food affected his health? As that witchcraft was to have control over him, not kill him," said her mother.

"No, don't worry about it."

"Also, have you slept with him?"

"No, Mom, I told you I haven't slept with him at all. I don't think he even gets an erection," she said while laughing.

"That's okay, as your next husband needs to know you're still a virgin," said her mother.

I didn't have the energy, as I was in pain, to kick them out of my house. The only thing I was thinking was, what did they feed me? What was in my clothes? I spent the next two months on the sofa at my parent's house and watching comedies on the television.

My bathroom was upstairs in my house, which I don't think was my house anymore. Madhu and her mother lived there and took over.

One evening, while I was lying in pain, trying to sleep, Madhu walked in with an Indian Man.

"Sit here and keep Raj Company while I get my things," said Madhu.

I looked at him, and he sat down on the sofa next to me. "How's it going, bro?" he asked.

"You don't look too good." He said in broken English. It was obvious he was from India.

"You are wondering who I am? Well, I am Madhu's ex-boyfriend from India. She tracked me down here in England. Let's face it, bro, you haven't got what it takes to keep Madhu happy. I have," he said.

He got up and ran up the stairs. I heard them giggle and make out. Then, it was obvious they were having sex. After they were done, they both walked past me, laughing.

After a while, I did not see Madhu and her mother for weeks as they were touring the United Kingdom. The day I came over to my parents was the last time I saw Madhu. She had helped my sister put me in a wheelchair. My sister went upstairs to get my clothes as Madhu and I were not talking to each other. This was because Madhu punched me in the stomach just because she had helped me up the stairs to use the bathroom. This wasn't the first time. During the years when we were married, whenever she argued, she would punch me in the stomach, in my ribs, and even scratched my arms, which still have scars today.

When my sister left, Madhu said, "You're just a loser."

That was the last time I heard her voice. I moved to my parent's house and slept on the sofa. I crawled to go to the toilet and didn't want anyone's help. I got support from the walls, doors, radiators, and tables. My grandma burst out crying one day.

"Call his wife Madhu. She should be here helping him," she said to my mother.

"I don't know where she is," replied my mother.

Grandma walked into the living room to speak to my grandad.

"Can't you see your grandson is in pain? Why can't you say anything to Madhu? She should be here helping Raj," shouted out my grandma.

"What can I do? She is her own boss. She said she doesn't want anything to do with Raj," he explained.

"But you forced him to marry her and bought here," she said.

"Yes, I did, and maybe it was a mistake, but we can't do anything now." I heard this and fell on the floor with pain.

***

Back in the hospital, I am woken up by James, the solicitor.

"Raj, can you hear me?" I slowly open my eyes. "Sorry to disturb you, Raj, but I need you to sign these divorce papers."

I look at my dad and mother, and they nod their heads to sign the papers. I sign the paper, and James reads the following: "In your divorce, you will be signing over full ownership of your property. Even though Madhu does not want to live there, your father has offered to buy her a new house costing three hundred thousand pounds. She has claimed that you have been ill on and off since childhood, and she was lied to. She also asked for you to support her financially. But looking at your last few P60, that was not possible. So, your dad has also agreed to pay a total amount of two hundred

278

and fifty thousand pounds to complete the divorce, and your family do not want any contact with her and from her now and in the future."

I feel sorry for my parents that they have to pay that much out of their hard-earned money. Giving it to a gold-digging woman who only came to this country to find her boyfriend. I give James a thumbs up.

Chapter Forty-Five

Lying in bed, dealing with that illness and pain, I think when it's going to be over. Staring at the machines, wondering if I should switch them off and pull the drip. Just then, I feel this feeling of relief come over me. It's hard to explain. It's like I can breathe, and the pain doesn't matter. The doors open, and a three to five-year-old kid runs with Mrs. White holding the door. I look at her, and she smiles back and then enters Julie.

I couldn't believe it. My wish or prayer came true. She slowly walks towards me, tears falling down her face. She gets close to the bed, grabs my hand, pulls it up, and kisses it.

"Why, Raj?" she asks while crying. I want to say I wanted her here but didn't want to hurt her.

"I have missed you so much. I have followed your success in sports, entering movies, and starting your business. I wanted to be part of it all and support you. I am sorry I left you. You just needed me to be by your side, and we could have achieved everything we wanted together."

I look up and mouth and say, "Sorry."

In my head, I say, "I am sorry too. If I hadn't let family, culture, and fear of my aunties at the beginning, I would have married you earlier."

"Raj, we both made it difficult for each other. We just should have decided to be together and tried our best," says Julie.

I nod my head and agree.

"Raj, I came back many times to tell you I love you and was sorry. Thanks to my mother, I came to see you off for the tournament in Holland. I came and watched your play. I was in our park straight after. I kissed you as you lay on the bench, sleeping. I was at the Moss Side Leisure Centre and watched you win your dream British Powerlifting Championships. I was in the cinema when you were watching your film with your cousins."

"The night we spent together made me so happy. My dream came true."

"Raj, we are in love, and I know you will get better. Raj and Julie are meant to be together. Raj, life has been hard, and it can't get any more difficult than it is. Especially for young Raj."

"Young Raj?" I try to ask.

Tears of happiness fall on my face, and I try to get up but manage to sit up.

"So, Raj," Julie gets down on one knee. "Raj Singh, will you marry me?"

I laugh a bit. "I thought we were already engaged."

I look, and she still has the ring on. She takes the ring off. "Raj, I'm down on one knee here and will stay in this position until you say yes." She continues to protest.

My father and mother walk in.

Raj and Julie

"Mr Singh, I know you don't like me and never wanted me to be with Raj, but I love him and can't live without him. I am asking him to marry me," says Julie to my father.

"But he is ill?" says my father.

"He will get better, and even if anything happens, and I know it's not going to, I would rather live as his widow," says Julie, kneeling on the floor and talking to my parents and me simultaneously. Luckily, she is wearing jeans.

"My son, give her your answer and hope it is yes," says my mother.

"You have our blessing, Julie," says my father.

Julie and I tear up and laugh in joy.

"Well then, Raj, what is it?" asks Julie.

"I said yes," and I felt half of my pain lessen. She got up, kissed me on the lips, and hugged me.

"You're going to be ok, Raj. I feel it in my spirit."

Young Raj claps. Julie turns around, picks up Young Raj, and says, "Say hi to your dad, Young Raj."

"Did you name him after me?" I ask.

"Yes, I had to name him after his father," replies Julie.

"He's mine?" I ask.

"Yes, Raj, he's your son," says Julie, crying with joy.

"How is this possible?" asks my father.

"Mr Singh, Raj and I met up for a catch-up a week before he left for India," she replies.

"The night you never came home, and we were all worried?" asks my mom.

"Yes," I reply, and I nod.

"We had spent the night at the hotel on Green Lane," says Julie.

"That's great," my dad says.

"That's great? We slept in the hotel," asks Julie.

They all laugh.

"This is my grandson," my Dad holds Young Raj off Julie.

"I'm your grandad, son. This is your grandma," my parents both begin to cry with happiness.

"His ex-wife told us that Raj couldn't have children," says my mother.

"We never slept together, Mum," I reply.

"She made it all up that I couldn't get her pregnant. She just wanted to move to England."

I look at Julie, "We never slept together," I say.

"Who cares? She is out of your life now, and I'm in. I mean, we are in."

"We are so happy," says my mother.

She holds Young Raj and kisses him on the cheek.

"My grandson," she says.

"We will show you the whole world, Young Raj," says my dad. "You will be a champion and actor like your dad."

"So, we're engaged again, Raj; how do you feel?" asks Julie.

"Super happy," I reply.

"When do you want to get married?" asks my dad.

"Don't know," says Julie.

"How about today?" he says.

"Today?"

"Yes, what's wrong today?"

"Call everyone we want here today. And I will ask the hospital chapel to get a priest."

"You okay with this, Raj?" asks Julie.

"Of course," I reply. "I will need to go home and get ready."

"You can wear my dress," says Mrs White to Julie, and they both hug each other.

"I am so happy for you, Julie," says Mrs. White.

"Oh, I must get an outfit for Young Raj," says Julie.

"Leave that to me. Let me take my grandson and get the best outfit from Beattie's," says my dad.

"I also need to get changed," says my mom.

My father looked at me and said, "Son, I will get everything in place in hours. I will get a cameraman and photographer, a cake from Gordons, and you an outfit too, and my grandson the best suit."

"How will you, Dad?" I ask.

"I will make it happen; I need to make it up to you, son. I owe this to you and you, Julie," he says.

"Raj hasn't spoken a word since he's been in here, and he is speaking. He is in less pain since you have been here, Julie. I am sorry, Julie," says my dad.

"Nothing to apologize about, Mr. Singh. We got a lot to do," says Julie.

"Julie, call me Dad," says Dad.

Julie hugs Dad. "Thanks, Dad," she says.

Julie hugs my Mum.

"I can call you mum now," says Julie.

"Yes, you can," says Mum.

They all left.

I tear up with happiness. I do have a lot less pain, and I am able to move and speak. I couldn't believe how this was all happening. There was a cross on the wall, which Julie's mother put up. I prayed and said, "Thank you, God, for giving me this happiness. Please make me fully well so I can spend my life with Julie and young Raaj. Amen."

My eyes close.

I wake up and see my mother and father holding young Raj, who is dressed up in a suit and wearing a bow tie, my sister, her husband, a cameraman holding a video camera, a photographer, a priest, a nurse, and a doctor.

At first, I wondered if it was a dream that I had experienced earlier. But when I see all these people.

I smile and ask, "Is everything ok?"

"Of course it is, my son," says my mother.

I look at myself and find I have been dressed, wearing a white shirt, sky-blue bow tie, and sky-blue waistcoat. The nurse and doctor open the doors. Julie walks in, wearing a beautiful white wedding dress, holding a bouquet with her mother. Her mother is smiling, excited, and giving me the thumbs up.

The Doctor and nurse help me sit up, and I find I am wearing cream-coloured trousers with my shirt sticking out. I still have the drips on me. My body is so weak, and I find it hard to sit up again.

The priest walks closer, "Dear beloved, we are gathered here in the sight of God and in front of family, loved ones, doctors, and nurses to join this man and this woman in Holy matrimony."

Julie's mother looks at the priest to speed it up.

"I can do the long or short version. Which one?" he asks.

I say, "I will try whichever Julie chooses."

Julie walks forward to me. "Raj, I have loved you from our junior school times as my best friend; I fell in love with you along the way. I don't know why I waited so long for this moment. You have a kind and loving heart. I haven't known more than anyone with this pure heart, and I want to spend the rest of my life with you, being not just your friend but your wife and the mother to your son. I give you my life. Let's skip to I do now," she says in excitement, with her eyes filled with joy.

"I remember seeing those beautiful blue eyes for the first time when I was ten years old. I remember when you kissed me on my cheek in the Green Acres school classroom, and I fell in love with you then, and I have been in love with you since then. Julie, I loved you the moment I saw you; I loved your humour and your passion in life, and cause of this, I became the person who believed in my dreams. So today, I give you my heart, my soul, our future."

"Can I have the rings?" Asks the priest.

My father takes out the rings. Julie takes a ring, and I am given a ring for Julie.

"Do you, Raj, take Julie to be your lawfully wedded wife?" Asks the priest.

"I do," I say and place the ring on Julie's finger.

"Do you, Julie, take Raj to be your lawfully wedded husband?"

"Yes, I do," says Julie and places the ring on my finger.

"I pronounce this man and wife in the name of the Father, the Son, and the Holy Ghost. Amen."

We all say Amen together.

"Congratulations," says the priest, shaking our hands.

"You can kiss your bride now if this is allowed," asks the priest.

"Of course, it's allowed," says my dad.

Julie leans forward and kisses me on the lips, and I feel this electric shock through my body. It is like the same time I went to church, and the priest prayed for me.

Young Josh claps, and my father claps with him. They all clap and congratulate us.

Julie's mother congratulates us by kissing us both on our cheeks.

"Raj, it has been a long journey of you wanting this to happen. I pray you get well soon and will be able to be with Julie and young Raj," Julie's mother says.

"I will, and you will have more grandchildren," I say.

We all laugh.

I don't know whose prayers or the hospital treatment helped me survive, but I am able to tell you this story. I know it was Julie's love that kept me alive. We get married in the hospital. After I recovered and was well, we held one of the biggest wedding reception parties in the city.

Twenty years after this story, my son is now twenty-three years old and dating a young Indian lady. But her parents are cultural Indians even in today's time. They don't like the fact that my son Raaj is a mixed race.

Hopefully, I will share how that turns out. But the fascinating twist here is that we never got to learn about Julie's journey in Manchester.

Look out to read about this in Raj and Julie part 2.

Printed in Great Britain
by Amazon